Readers everywhere are signing on as Roxanne Henke fans.

Here's what they say about her first novel in the Coming Home to Brewster series, *After Anne...*

From California: "A dear dear friend gave me *After Anne* several weeks ago...Your book was awesome and should be sold with a box of Kleenex!"

From North Carolina: "I felt as though the characters were my best friends. The last time I cried this much was when I read James Patterson's *Suzanne's Diary for Nicholas.*"

From Oregon: "I could hardly put the book down. Oprah should know about this!"

From Christianbooks.com: "*After Anne* is probably my favorite [book of the year]. This moving story of an unlikely friendship between two women will have you laughing and crying and longing for a relationship like theirs."

From an Amazon.com reader: "I don't know how I got this copy of *After Anne* but however I got it, I am so glad I read it!...It is one of the must-reads for the coming year if not tomorrow."

And book number two, *Finding Ruth...*

From Virginia: "I read *Finding Ruth* after I finished *After Anne* and I thought this book couldn't be as good...but sure enough you did it again! You are my favorite author."

From California: "I just finished reading the last page of *Finding Ruth*....the tears went down my cheeks as I read it...But what kept me so on the edge....was your showing me Brewster town. I could see everyone, even their laugh lines."

From Kentucky: "Thank you for a touching story that fit quite nicely into my life. I was moved by it...If I had my way, your book would be topping all the best-seller lists."

From Indiana: "I chose your book from the new fiction section at our public library without realizing it was a Christian book...I could hardly bear to put it down."

Via e-mail: "I love your characters, all of them, even the broken ones...I can't remember the last time a book has made me feel such empathy for a fictitious person, first with Anne and Libby and now with Ruth's friends and family. I feel like I know them personally."

And book number three, *Becoming Olivia...*

From Indiana: "I've been burning up the e-mail lines telling anyone who will listen that your books are required reading. Please hurry with number 4!!!!"

From North Carolina: "Just finish⟨...⟩ ⟨...⟩ristian insight and faith shine through as realistic and ⟨...⟩

From South Dakota: "I could not ⟨...⟩ things Olivia went through, especially the struggle wit⟨...⟩ was the first of your books that I have read, and I look ⟨...⟩

From Ohio: I've just read *Becoming Olivia* and am so moved. There are many words to describe the book, but none seem adequate enough."

"I just finished *Becoming Olivia* and *had* to write and tell you how much I loved it. I have read all 3 of your books...but *Becoming Olivia* especially spoke to me...I know that this had to have been a difficult book for you to write, but you did a superb job, as always."

"[Becoming Olivia] is amazing for its healing powers...I'm going to use the book in my clinical practice to give to patients who know they don't feel right but don't think it's bad enough to be classified as depression."

And about book four, *Always, Jan...*

From "Dorothy"..."I just finished reading *Always Jan,* and, like your other books, I loved it...God has truly given you a beautiful talent...one which I pray you will continue to use so that we can share in His goodness and mercy through your stories."

From "Ellen"..."I just finished *Always Jan* and hated leaving Brewster as I read the last page...I absolutely loved this series...I want to go to Brewster and see these wonderful people. I want to go to Pumpkin Fest. I want to visit Aunt Ida. I wanted to buy her house. I want my life to be transformed like Jan's and Kenny's and I want to be a friend like Libby."

From "Nancy"..."I just finished your book, and Man! This is your best work yet!"

From "a housewife and mother in Indiana"..."I just finished reading the fourth book in the Brewster series. Wow! What a read...Life can sure be difficult at times and a good uplifting honest book is a treasure."

And the final volume in the Coming Home to Brewster series, *With Love, Libby...*

From "Brenda"...Roxy, " just had to drop you a note about *With Love Libby.* I just finished the book last night and I was sad when I was finished as it was so good that I wanted more. I have all 5 of your books and they are all such great reads. Whenever I purchase your new book, I think that it can't be as good as your last one but you prove me wrong. You do have a special gift!!"

From "Judy"..."It was a fabulous, tear-jerking, wonderful, "stellar" read. I really enjoy the way you write and how you weave the story.

From "Cecilia"...I finished "With Love, Libby" within a couple days...it was fantastic..."

From "Kathy"..."It was with great sadness that I finished *With Love, Libby.* I enjoyed it immensely, and felt like I could walk into the little town and know people. I will miss them."

After Anne

ROXANNE HENKE

College of the Ouachitas

Become the friend
you long to have!
Blessings —

Roxy
Henke

HARVEST HOUSE PUBLISHERS

EUGENE, OREGON

Cover by Koechel Peterson & Associates, Minneapolis, Minnesota

While some of the medical aspects of this book are based on fact, the story is fiction and was written as a tribute to the power of friendship. Any resemblance to persons living or dead was meant to honor the memory of all friendships that leave a permanent mark upon your heart.

AFTER ANNE
Copyright © 2002 Roxanne Sayler Henke
Published by Harvest House Publishers
Eugene, Oregon 97402
www.harvesthousepublishers.com

Library of Congress Cataloging-in-Publication Data

Henke, Roxanne, 1953–
    After Anne / Roxanne Henke.
        p. cm. — (Coming home to Brewster; 1)
     ISBN-13: 978-0-7369-0967-9
     ISBN-10: 0-7369-0967-2
     1. Female friendship—Fiction.   I. Title.
   PS3608.E55 A69 2002
   813'.6—dc21

                                    200105154

Printed in the United States of America

07 08 09 10 11 12 / BC-MS / 13 12 11 10 9

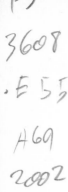
Proverbs 18:24
…there is a friend who sticks closer than a brother.

In memory of my best friend:
Lori Susan Duggan Abentroth
(October 19, 1957-July 9, 1987)

You told me to "put it in the book."
Here's the book.

Brewster, North Dakota. Middle America, USA. The kind of town where everybody knows your name. Where everybody knows what everyone else is doing...or thinking of doing. A place where neighbors run cookies over with the latest gossip. Where the waitress at the café is your next-door neighbor. Nine-man football. A twenty-bed hospital. A grocery store that offers home delivery on Thursdays. All these things can be found in Brewster.

What else can be found there? People with hopes and dreams. People in love and people with broken hearts. Friends and foes. Families and faith. When you get to know the people of Brewster, you'll find it isn't all that different from where you live.

Welcome to Brewster...it's a good place to call home.

Prologue

Libby

"*Anne is my best friend.*"

There. I said it.

"Anne is my best friend." I say that in the present tense because I don't like to think of her as gone. Instead, I think of her as...away. Off someplace where I can't talk to her everyday like I used to.

After Anne...left, I thought I had two options:

One. Go crazy.

Two. Die of loneliness.

It turned out there was a third option I hadn't imagined. But then, that's my story.

Our story.

The Beginning

Five years earlier

Olivia

If someone would have told me that first night I met Anne that we would end up being best friends, I would have told them they were nuts. Pure and simple crazy.

What didn't I like about Anne? It's easier to say what I did like. Her scarf. That was about it. Her canary yellow scarf. If it had been tied a little bit tighter I might have liked it even better. Something about Anne just rubbed me the wrong way.

It was late October at a high school football game. The Brewster Badgers were playing for the conference title, and it was freezing that night. A typical North Dakota evening that matched my mood. Chilly. Our son, Brian, was playing. Well really, he was standing on the sidelines. Freshmen don't often get to play in the varsity games. But even from the sidelines Brian seemed to have a talent for getting injured. Bob and I felt it was our duty to be there, doing the "parent thing," cheering him on, insurance card on standby. Little did I know that Brian's knack for minor injury would turn out to be one of the best things that ever happened to me.

Out of the corner of my eye I could see Dan Jordan, Brewster's self-appointed Welcome Wagon, making his way down the sidelines trailing a new couple in town. He was stopping every foot or so, introducing them as though they were royalty. I really wasn't interested.

Frankly, I'm not the most liked woman in Brewster, so the fact that I wasn't as enthralled with Anne as everyone else seemed to be came as no surprise to me. I have my opinions and I'm not afraid to share them. And Anne just seemed like the type of person who would naturally become everybody else's best friend.

But not mine.

I couldn't help but overhear the bits of conversation that drifted my way. In-between the thunking of football pads and the cheer-leaders' frantic yelling, I caught the basics. They had recently moved to Brewster. He was an insurance rep and on the road much of the time. Brewster was in the middle of his territory; that's why they'd moved here.

Looking back, I know Anne was overwhelmed trying to make a good impression on practically everyone in town that night. And she was doing a good job of it. I could already see Jan and Connie, the only two sort of good friends I had, following Anne down the side-line, chatting up a storm.

Anne bugged me before I even met her.

For instance, the way she said, "Hiiii-yiii!" to everyone she met irritated me.

She'd whip off her too-cute purple mitten and stick out her hand. Everyone else scrambled to get their hands out of their pockets, or from under their arms, then yanked off their own gloves just to shake her perky little hand, with its long, slender fingers. It wasn't until much later that I noticed Anne's crooked thumbs.

Then there was her hair. A jumble of auburn, corkscrew curls sticking out every which way from her purple stocking cap—with a tassel on top, no less. It was just too cute.

But the thing that bothered me the most was when Dan said to her, "I'd like you to meet Olivia Marsden, Brewster's resident bard." He was referring to my column for the *Brewster Banner*.

"Hiiii-yiii!" Anne said, whipping off her glove one more time. "Olivia—now there's a name I'll remember. I had a cat named Olivia. My sister and I called her Libby. We loved her soooo much. Glad to meet you, Libby."

Well, meow to you too. No one, and I mean *no one*, called me Libby.

Oh, and did I mention how, for reasons unknown to modern science, Anne took to me like cold macaroni and cheese to a kitchen counter top? That woman would not leave my side for love or rudeness. She stuck to me like glue through the whole game no matter how many people came by to say, "Hiiii-yiii!"

Anne

I knew the minute I met Libby she was someone I would like. It never occurred to me that night that we would become the friends we did. But right from the start I knew there was going to be a bond between us.

She was so cool. She didn't grab my hand and pump it like everyone else, all the while inviting me to coffee, lunch, dinner, PTA meetings, or making any of that insincere, first-meeting, I-just-know-we're-going-to-be-best-friends, kind of chit chat. Not Libby. She just stood there in her black wool coat, her breath forming measured puffs in the night air, and gave me a slight nod, a one-sided smile, and said, "Welcome to town." Then she turned to watch the game.

I envied her coolness. I just knew she was the kind of person who never said yes just to make someone feel good, or no, adding a million excuses, trying not to feel guilty. Libby was the kind of person who said yes, or no and left it at that. The kind of person who didn't play word games but told it like it was. The kind of person I'd prayed, with this move, to become.

There was an older woman in our last church who made a lasting impression on me. You could tell just by looking at her she was a woman of character. She stood so regally, and when she spoke, well, it practically sounded as though her words came straight from the Bible. Don't get me wrong—she wasn't one of those people who quote scripture verses at you in response to anything you say. No, it was just that her words were so wise and compassionate; the way she said them made me feel I'd been embraced with kindness. That's the kind of person I wanted to become.

The way Libby stood, and her simple but heartfelt words, reminded me a little bit of that woman. Oh, I liked Libby from the start. It made me feel calm just standing by her. So I did.

Olivia

Our ten-year-old daughter, Emily, had been begging to take piano lessons for the past five years. I'd been resisting just as long.

I have nothing but bad memories of my own years of taking lessons, including that infernal ticking of the metronome while my piano teacher tapped along to the beat with a twelve-inch ruler. Was I so bad that I needed two things keeping time for me? I know people only think these things happen in bad movies, but my teacher actually hit my hands with a ruler during one lesson when I wasn't keeping time to her liking. It was after that incident that I came home and told my mother in no uncertain terms that I was quitting lessons. To emphasize my point I took my piano theory book and tried to tear it in half. It rather ruined the drama of the moment when I realized it was too thick and I was too weak to tear it all at once. But I must admit, even all these years later I remember how good it felt to rip through that book page by page, my mother standing there in astonished quiet. When I was through, Mom walked to the phone and told my piano teacher, "It seems Olivia has a conflict that will make her unable to continue lessons this year." I guess she knew I meant it.

I have never had the urge to take up the piano again.

Mom, however, had the last word. Apparently, my mother never gave up hope that I would discover a love for the instrument. And even now I fondly remember the Christmas nights we stood around the piano, Mom playing, the rest of us trying our best to harmonize "Jingle Bells." Five years ago, when my mom died, my brother called and said, "Mom left you the piano."

Oh.

That old, mahogany-brown upright has sat in the far corner of our living room ever since. It's been a handy spot to display the kids' school photos and my one and only Waterford vase, a wedding gift from Bob's grandmother. On the few occasions we've needed extra seating, the bench has come in handy. Other than Emily, I don't think anyone in the family had given that piano a second thought in the last five years.

It must have been either a weak moment or that PMS time of the month when everything seems sad and emotional. Whatever the reason, this time when Emily asked in her all-things-are-possible voice to take piano lessons, I didn't give her the "lessons are expensive and you have to practice everyday" lecture. Instead I told her I would check into it. And I did.

Brewster's the size of town where no one is exactly a stranger, but you don't know everyone by name, either. I started asking around, and someone gave me the name of a Mrs. Abbot, who had just started teaching piano lessons. As luck would have it, when I was grocery shopping that day my eye was caught by a flyer featuring a black baby grand piano, the large words Piano Lessons, and those cutsey little tear-off-my-phone-number tags. "Mrs. Abbot," they said.

I knew the minute I heard her voice that it was Anne.

"Hiiii-yiii! You've reached the Abbots! We can't come to the phone right now, but if you leave a message..."

I almost hung up. But I was so surprised, and Emily was so set on lessons, that I found myself blurting out a message. "You probably don't remember me...we met a couple weeks ago at the football game...well, uh, my daughter...ummm, I heard that you were teaching piano lessons...uh, if this is the wrong Mrs. Abbot could you get back to me? Oh, this is Olivia Marsden...*Libby*...your cat, remember?"

Someday I'm going to invent an answering machine that enables callers to erase their failed attempts at coherent messages. Good grief! Could I have sounded any more unorganized and unsure of myself? I decided to make good use of my frustration and headed for my computer. My weekly column for the *Brewster Banner* was due, and a column about leaving messages on answering machines was certainly a good way for me to vent.

I barely had the first paragraph typed when the phone rang.

"Libby, hiiii-yiii!"

It was Anne. Mrs. Anne Abbot. Even her name was too cute. Why, she'd just run in from putting up the last of her tear-off phone number signs around town. She was the right Mrs. Abbot. Yes, she did teach piano lessons. She would be delighted to have Emily as a pupil.

Why didn't that surprise me?

⌒

Emily was totally infatuated with Anne as a piano teacher.

"Oh, Mom," she gushed when I picked her up from her first lesson. "Mrs. Abbot—Oh! I mean *Anne,* she asked me to call her, Anne, Mom, really she did—is *so* cool. I mean they don't have any kids yet or anything, but I can tell they are *so* in love. Her husband, *Kevin,* is an insurance salesman, and he's gone a whole lot, so Anne teaches lessons so she can keep in touch with people while he's gone, and she *loves* chocolate, and the color red, and she hates to talk on the phone—it makes her ear hurt—and did you know she had a cat named, Olivia? Just like you. But she died, well, not you, but the cat, and Anne was so sad, and…"

My goodness, what was I paying for? This woman's psychoanalysis? I thought she was going to teach Emily piano. But to give Mrs. Abbot—I mean, *Anne*—a little credit, Emily sat right down at our newly dusted piano and started practicing.

When Bob walked in from work that night, Emily was still at the piano. She was even playing a somewhat recognizable tune.

"Is that 'Chopsticks'?" Bob asked. "Haven't heard that since second grade, I believe. Hey, Em, I'm impressed." Bob stood by the piano and plunked out an octave-higher version of the tune, somehow managing to match Emily's uneven timing.

I hadn't seen Emily grin that big in ages. I also didn't know Bob could play piano, even if it was just "Chopsticks."

Anne was already teaching me things I didn't know.

Anne

I realize now that if it hadn't been for Emily, Libby and I probably would have never become friends. I didn't have a clue that Libby had taken an instant dislike to me. Each week, when she would drop Emily off for lessons, Libby always gave me what I thought was a friendly wave from the car. The fact that she never came inside to get Emily after lessons totally escaped me. I just assumed she was busy and in a hurry to get home.

Emily, however, had all the time in the world to chat. She was my first pupil, and Kevin was on the road almost constantly, so I guess I was lonely for company—even the company of a ten-year-old.

Emily was a fast learner, zipping through her scales and lessons, talking nonstop. I'd never seen a student who could talk in the meter of the music she was playing. In four-four time Emily would say, "I-had-a-fight…with-my-friend-Steph…I-got-a-B…in-ree-eea-ding." If it was a three-four tune she'd talk along with her fingers, "I-rea-lly…love-your-house…my-Mom-should…be-your-friend." She'd complete her final assigned piece and then look up at me with that Cheshire cat grin of hers. She knew she had me wrapped around her limber little finger.

I found myself hurrying through Emily's lessons so that we would have time for a cup of tea, which Emily stated, "makes me feel like Cinderella at the ball. But not when those mean old sisters were, like, mean to her." I always doctored her tea up with lots of sugar and usually had a plate of cookies waiting too. I started sending the extra cookies home with Emily. Kevin was never home to eat them, and eating cookies alone is no fun.

I'd been praying for a way to make new friends in Brewster. *Even just one friend would be fine, Lord.* And it seemed to me that Libby was crossing my path for a reason. Cookies seemed like a pretty non-threatening way to let her know I was available for friendship.

I had no idea that Emily jumped into her mother's car, offered Libby cookies, then repeated practically everything I said, word for word all the way home. Now that I know Libby practically inside and out, I can see why she saw me as a threat to the friendships she had so carefully cultivated. For a time, she probably saw me as a threat to her relationship with Emily too. Libby was not the kind of person who made friends easily I found out. But when she was your friend, well, that's my point—she was your friend. There is a Bible verse in Proverbs that states, "There is a friend who sticks closer than a brother." For me that friend turned out to be Libby. Period.

Olivia

"Okay, so what's with the cookies? Does this woman think I can't bake or something?" I'd finally confessed my unreasonable and unfounded dislike for Anne to my friend Jan.

"Oh hey, don't sweat it." Jan took a long swallow of coffee. "Look at it as one less thing you have to do. Say, Joey's supposed to bring treats to his class next week. You don't suppose you could get her to bake a batch for me, do you?" As usual, Jan had turned my confession into a joke, and then changed the subject. "I'm thinking of adding eggplant-colored highlights to my hair, but Jacob says…"

I was sorry I'd told her about Anne. I knew Jan would be on the phone within the hour telling Connie everything I'd said, even though Jan acted as if she wasn't really listening to what I'd told her.

At that time, Connie and Jan were the two people in my life I could count as friends. I know now the friendship we had was so shallow a fish would have had a hard time staying afloat. But like a bullhead, I kept trying to swim in my old familiar pond.

Connie used to work at the bank with my husband, Bob. I met her at an office Christmas party about ten years ago. When we started talking about the upcoming school bond issue, she asked me to pass out campaign flyers in our neighborhood. Since she worked with Bob, I felt I needed to keep quiet for once and just do the job. After that she'd call me now and then for lunch. Three years ago Connie quit her job to start a freelance design firm out of her home. She is very committed to her business. There's isn't much she lets interfere once she sets her mind to a task. Needless to say, her business is flourishing, our friendship is not.

With Jan, on the other hand, what you see is what you get. Appropriately, I first met her at the hairdresser's. She accused me of trying to steal Jacob from her. He's our stylist. I was in the salon for my usual six-week, shoulder length, blunt cut when Jan pranced in fifteen minutes early (the only thing she's ever early for), and announced, "You're in my chair."

"Okay Goldilocks," I replied, swinging my head toward Jacob. "As soon as the wolf here gets done I'll get out of it."

It was supposed to be a joke, but I realized the moment I spoke that I sounded catty. As I started to apologize, Jan laughed. It was a high-pitched, tinkling, little girl laugh. I couldn't help but laugh, too.

By the time Jacob finished evening out the chunk he'd removed when I swung my head, Jan had grabbed a cup of coffee, plopped into the next chair, and started telling Jacob and me her latest dilemma. As I remember now, it had something to do with her "lousy first husband and his candy-apple-red Camaro." Whatever it was, she wouldn't let me leave in the middle of her sad and sordid tale. Eventually, we traded chairs and I listened, and listened…and listened. Jan could talk. Jacob had another appointment waiting and Jan still wasn't done. I found myself in a nearby cafe, drinking coffee and still listening. The only thing that made it bearable was that Jan was funny too. It was the next best thing to a junior high slumber party—the parties I never got invited to—talking about men and laughing. I interrupted Jan two hours later and told her I had to go pick up Emily from the sitter's. That was eight years ago. Jan and I have had back-to-back appointments with Jacob ever since. We always make a day of it, and we always laugh a lot. That's my point—she talks, I laugh. As Jan says, "I don't do listening very well."

She's right.

⌒

"Hey, earth to Olivia." Jan was waving her hand in front of my face.

"Oh, sorry." I glanced at my watch. "Guess I zoned out for a moment there." Actually, I was feeling guilty for the unfounded things I'd said about Anne. "Sorry Jan, I've got to cut things short today." I put on my coat and grabbed my car keys.

"But I just started telling you about the date I had last week." Jan got that pouty, little girl look on her face that signifies, "you're hurting my feelings."

Well, too bad. She was hurting mine too by never listening, never really hearing what I said. "I've really got to run, Jan." It was a feeble excuse, so I tried to appease her. "Give me a call later and I promise I'll listen."

I drove around town until it was time to pick up Emily, hearing the mean things I'd said about Anne to Jan echoing in my head. I cranked the radio up trying to drown out my words. It didn't work.

Emily hopped in the car from her piano lessons, foaming at the mouth with a new batch of Anne Announcements, and balancing another plate of cookies.

"Anne was wearing a beau-ti-ful, long blue skirt today." Emily had a dreamy, fairy-tale expression on her face. "She looked so pretty, Mom. Mmm, these cookies are sooo good. Anne showed me a picture of her twin sister and they don't look *anything* alike. Mom, do you want a cookie? Anne said they are very different. Not the cookies, I mean her sister. Did you know that Anne has, like, *pretend* apples on her table? She said every home should have a touch of red in it. I told her they looked nice."

Oh, great. Now my daughter is going to have a fondness for fake fruit, all because of little-Miss-perfect-pretty-skirt-cookie-baker-piano-teacher.

My guilt over complaining to Jan sure hadn't lasted long. I made myself feel even worse by taking out my frustration at home. I yelled at Brian for leaving his tennis shoes in front of the door for me to trip over. Later, I screamed at Emily to stop playing those infernal scales. They reminded me of Anne. And then, just to make sure no one felt left out, I berated Bob for not carrying his hammer back downstairs after he fixed the loose table leg I'd been harping about. Too bad we didn't have a dog—I could have kicked that too.

All because of a plate of cookies.

Anne

Looking back, I realize those first months in Brewster were awful. Although back then, awful had a whole different meaning for me than it does now. But at the time, I was excited about the move—our fifth in eight years of marriage, and supposedly our last. I was especially excited about buying our first house and about Kevin's promise that he would be home every night.

We moved into our little "bung-gallow," as Dan Jordan called it, as he handed me his business card. "Real Estate Magnet," it read. He went on to explain, "The house needs a tish of fixing up. Nothing that a well-stocked tool chest won't handle…and some elbow grease." He winked at Kevin.

Unfortunately, the only elbow around was mine.

Kevin had promised me this move would be different. By moving to Brewster we'd be in the very heart of his territory. Why, he'd be home every night! Why, we would have dinner together all the time! Why I believed him, I don't know.

So there I was, using my excited little elbows to paint, wallpaper, and scrub every corner of our new home. Kevin kept his promise to be home for dinner. For three weeks. After that it was the same excuses as before. "I have a bunch of calls to make and it's so much easier if I spend the night." "I'm going to piggyback these meetings together, so I'll be home later." He was a salesman, all right. But this time I wasn't buying.

In the last two towns we'd lived in I had spent my time in a sort of limbo. Always waiting for Kevin to come home and announce, "We're moving." I didn't join any clubs—it was too hard to make friends and then leave. I'd learned that during our first three "stations," as I came to call these towns. Places we passed through like a slow-moving freight train. Sometimes I wondered if anyone there remembered me. Did anyone ever say, "Remember Anne? She always wore those purple mittens"? or "What would I have done if Anne hadn't been here then?" I doubted it. I isolated myself from the pain of saying goodbye.

This time, things were going to be different. Kevin promised, and I wanted to believe him. But even if he wasn't going to make our life any different, I was.

For the last few years I'd been praying that Kevin would feel a desire to be home more. The things he felt he needed to provide for us just weren't as important to me as they were to him. I'd tried to explain that I'd rather have time with him than have things, and he had always responded, "Just a couple more years, Anne. Then you can have both—things and me."

For years my twin sister, Andrea, had asked me why I stay married to Kevin. "He's a jerk, Anne," she had barked. "Dump him."

It's not that easy. I loved Kevin, faults and all. He wasn't mean to me, he was certainly a hard worker, a quality my dad always touted, and I married him. When I said those vows I meant them. For better or for worse. If this was the worse, well, I guess I could take it. I kept hoping Kevin would decide that being home with me was more important than being out on the road, climbing some ladder of his own invention. Until that day comes, well, let's just say I'm still here. Lonely. Waiting. Praying.

I have to admit I was scouting for friends at that first Brewster football game. We'd been in Brewster a month, and between working on the house and realizing Kevin wasn't going to be around any more here than the last town, I was lonely. I gladly accepted Dan's offer to take Kevin and me to the game and "show us what Brewster hospitality is like." Kevin was glad to go, too. Any social event was a potential marketplace for business in his eyes.

The number of people I met that night was mind-boggling. Besides Libby, the only people I really remembered after the football game were Jan and Connie. I only remembered Jan because she had attached herself to me, asking me question after question as though

I was a game show contestant or something. And Connie handed me her business card with the comment, "In case you need a little help with your fixer-upper."

Everyone was really nice, and that was the problem—they were too nice. I got the feeling Brewster was so small that people were tired of their old friends and were desperately looking for new ones. Namely, me. Libby was the only person who didn't gush, who didn't hand me a business card and make me feel as if she wanted me for something besides a friend. She was the only one who looked at me, said hello, then seemed to accept me for who I was.

As I said, I believe what people say, and when Libby said, "Welcome to Brewster," I believed she meant it.

Little did I know she hated me.

Olivia

Emily had been taking piano lessons for about a month. You'd be surprised what a piano teacher can tell a student in four weeks of lessons. I'd learned that Anne loved candles and books, a point I have to admit that was in her favor. She also hated gladiolas. I questioned Emily on that one. Who ever heard of anyone hating gladiolas? But Emily, totally enamored with Anne, agreed that gladiolas were "tall, lanky flowers that looked gaudy in any arrangement." I'm sure that was a direct quote. Anne had missed being an honor student in high school because she practically flunked driver's education—a fact I was to find out for myself soon enough. And her husband was gone practically all the time.

In four weeks I knew Anne better than I knew Jan or Connie. Oh, and one more little thing—Anne had had coffee with Jan, twice, and Connie was coming over to give Anne some tips on decorating her house. My, weren't we the little social-butterfly-friend-stealer?

I knew the minute I saw Anne at the football game that she was going to march right in and take the only two friends I had. Why was I surprised to hear she'd already heard Jan's life story and would soon hear Connie's? Was I angry that she hadn't sought out mine?

Of course, now I know how foolish those thoughts were. But at the time, all I felt was left out as usual.

Anne

I'd met Jan for coffee twice. Once would have been enough. But I was lonely, and any company was better than none. In the first two hours I'd heard about Jan's "lousy first husband and his candy-apple-red Camaro," about her second marriage and her son, Joey, who "was the only good thing to come out of that," and about how she'd been trying for years to get her hairdresser, Jacob, to ask her out. She thought he was afraid he'd lose her as a customer if things didn't work out. Not that she'd be that petty or anything. The second time we had coffee I heard it all over again. I also learned that Connie would do anything to make her business succeed, so I should "watch out" if she offered to do any decorating for me. And Olivia, well, she was a good listener; didn't talk much, but you could count on her "in a pinch."

No kidding. If Jan only knew.

Lord, I questioned on the drive home, *is this the friend you're sending me? She's not what I had in mind, so if Jan is the one, you're going to have to help me see her through your eyes.* I was really hoping God had some other plan in mind for me. For Libby, too.

Actually, Emily was my best source of information about Libby. At times I felt like a stalker, asking questions about this woman I wanted so badly for a friend. "So," I'd casually ask between scales and theory, "what did your mom say about the C-minus on your history test?" Then I would microanalyze her answer while Emily counted out loud in three-four time.

Something about Libby intrigued me. I certainly couldn't explain it, because she gave me no encouragement at all. It had to be God, prodding me to keep on making an effort, because the plates I sent home with Emily, piled high with cookies, came back washed with no note of thanks. The times I turned my friendly Emily's-piano-teacher waves into arm movements that beckoned Libby to come in and visit, were politely dismissed with a quick wave and a finger pointed at her watch. So whatever possessed Libby to call on me that day for help I can only say was a gift. From God to me. He knew how desperately I was going to need a friend.

Olivia

When I think about it now, it's incredible how fast my unfounded animosity toward Anne melted. All it took was a week and a very bad day. Which actually turned out to be a good day. A very good day. The day I became friends with Anne.

I was waiting outside Anne's house to pick up Emily from her lessons, as usual, when Anne stepped out and waved, then motioned for me to come on in. Emily didn't help matters. She stood beside Anne, hopping up and down in that I'm-so-excited-I-could-squeal way that ten-year-olds have. I was still mad about Anne trying to make inroads with Jan and Connie. I'd also heard that Anne had put an ad in the *Brewster Banner* about starting a book club—something I'd been meaning to do for ten years. It seemed this woman was trying to take over not only my daughter and my friends, but also my life. No way was I going into her house; she'd probably siphon my mind right out of my head as she had Emily's, Jan's, and Connie's. I pointed to my watch and mouthed through the window, "Sorry, not today," acting as though I were in a hurry to get somewhere. Somewhere besides out of there.

I thought I'd done a good job of looking sincere, but when Emily hopped in the car she cried, "Mo-om, that was sooo lame!" She sat in sullen silence for a while, then launched into her usual Anne Announcements. "Did you know that Anne painted every room in her house by *herself*? I could never do that by myself. And she's going to play piano at her church on Sunday. Anne is, like, an *awesome* piano player. Oh and Mom, Anne, like *totally* wants to be your friend." Emily paused for a breath, then added, "I mean, she asks questions about you *all* the time."

And then, for the first time in months of Anne Announcements, Emily quit talking.

I was finally forced to ask my first post-piano lesson question. "What kind of questions?" I said in my "I'm really not curious" voice.

"Oh Mom—" Emily became animated. "Anne thinks you're some kind of celebrity or something. She asked if you were *the* Olivia Marsden. You know, cuz of your newspaper column. Anne said she'd never met anyone who was a writer before, and she even has your column hanging on her fridge door. And, did you know that Anne..."

She called me a writer. Anne had called me a writer. After seven years of writing my column, "The Wry Eye," for the *Brewster Banner*, even I couldn't call myself a real writer. To me that column was just a way to make me write. My true dream (which I'd never admitted to a single soul) was to write a novel. A real novel. Not a boy-meets-girl-they-fall-in-love-break-up-get-back-together novel. But a novel. A serious novel. About? About?

That was the problem. I'd always wanted to write, but I could never figure out what to write about.

A writer wanna-be—that's me.

My daydream was interrupted when something in Emily's tone of voice led me to believe I'd missed something important in her ramblings about Anne. "Say that again, Emily."

"I *sa-id*—" Emily was always very impatient when she realized I wasn't giving her my full attention. "Anne and Kevin are going to have a baby. Don't you think Kevin should be home more if he's going to be a dad? I'd hate it if my dad was never home. Kevin is never home. But Anne says that when the baby comes, Kevin will want to be such a good dad that he will for sure find a way to be home more. Next week after I do my scales Anne's going to..."

Okay, now I really felt like a heel. Even though I'd hardly had a thing to do with this woman since the day she'd moved to town, I actually felt as if I knew Anne better than Jan and Connie combined, thanks to Emily's weekly Anne Announcements. I wasn't often very good about putting myself into other people's shoes, but I remembered vividly how I felt when I found out I was pregnant with Brian.

I'd wanted to tell the whole world, not just a ten-year-old piano student. Even if Emily was my daughter, charming and precocious, she was still ten. There was no way a ten-year-old could share the excitement of a pregnancy the way a girlfriend could.

Therein was the problem. I may have been a girl, but I was no friend to Anne.

Anne.

The first person to ever call me a writer.

That was when the first crack in my armor against Anne appeared.

~

As luck so often has a way of doing, it intervened. Or maybe I should say bad luck. In any case it was something. I didn't find out until much later that it was an answer to a prayer I hadn't known to pray.

The next week after I dropped Emily off at her piano lesson, I dashed home to pick up a letter that I'd planned to mail but had left lying on the counter. I was headed out the door when the phone rang.

"Mrs. Marsden?"

"Yes?" The male voice had a familiar ring, but I couldn't place it.

"This is Coach Rollins."

Small wonder that I didn't recognize his voice. He was usually screaming semi-cuss words from the sidelines of a ball game whenever I'd heard him speak. "Brian had a small mishap at basketball practice a few minutes ago. One of the assistant coaches took him over to the hospital and I think you should get over there right away. I don't want you to panic, but there was a lot of blood, and—"

That's when I hung up and ran out the door. I was halfway to the hospital when I remembered I needed to pick up Emily from Anne's in half an hour. There was no way I'd get to the hospital, check things out, and get back to pick up Emily in time—if I would be able to leave the hospital at all. Well, this was one week that maybe Anne would finally run out of things to tell Emily.

It turned out that Brian had a rather nasty cut on his chin. He'd come down from grabbing a rebound, his chin pounding into the top of Dave Meier's head on the way down. Before the doctor would clear Brian to go home, he wanted to "run a few tests—concussion, jaw fracture, those sorts of things."

I left my insurance card with the nurse and went to find a pay phone. I called Bob at work to see if he could swing by and pick up Emily, but his secretary said he was out for the afternoon. I remembered then that Bob had an afternoon meeting in a nearby town and would be late for supper.

I dialed Jan to see if she could pick up Emily. "I'd love to, Olivia, I really would, but I have an appointment to get my nails done in five minutes. I'm already running late and you know how hard it is to get an appoint—"

I was getting really good at hanging up on people.

My last option was to call Connie. As I half-expected she told me, "I won't be able to fit that into my afternoon schedule." Connie was like that. No explanation, no guilt.

As it turned out, Connie wasn't my last option. Anne was.

Anne's number wasn't in the phone book yet, so I had to call information. Thanks to Emily's frequent Anne Announcements, I had no trouble remembering it would be listed under Kevin Abbot. I was hoping Anne would answer the phone, instead of letting it go to the answering machine during Emily's lesson.

"Hiiii-yiii! This is Anne."

I paused a moment, thinking it was the machine. Then I heard again, "Hiiii-yiii, this is Anne. Is anyone there?"

For once that "Hiiii-yiii!" of hers was music to my ears. "Mrs. Abbot, uh, Anne? This is Olivia Marsden, Emily's mom."

"Libby?" Immediately Anne sounded concerned. "Is something wrong? We were looking out the window, thinking you'd be pulling up any second."

"Actually yes, something is wrong. No, it's nothing serious. It's just that Brian got hurt at basketball practice and will need a few stitches. I'm over at the hospital right now. My husband, Bob, is out of town for the afternoon. And, well, I can't find anyone to pick up Emily from her lesson."

Anne went into what I now call her Super Friend mode. Even though you could have hardly called us acquaintances, much less friends, Anne announced that Emily would be staying at her house for supper. Better yet, why didn't I call Anne when I got Brian home from the hospital, and she would run supper over for all of us? Was there anyone she should call for me? Or, if I wanted, she could come to the hospital and sit with me.

All of a sudden I felt like crying. It was then that the second crack in my armor against Anne began to show.

Never did I imagine that by the end of the day I wouldn't be wearing any armor against Anne at all.

Anne

The day started out ordinary enough. Kevin was up early, packing. He said he'd be gone three days this time. He insisted he really was excited about the baby. And once again, he vowed to make more time for us after the baby came. He even agreed to attend birthing classes with me. Of course, that was an easy promise to make since the classes were months down the road. Kevin gave me a quick kiss on the cheek and was out the door.

I walked to the kitchen, ready to mix up my weekly batch of cookies. Emily had a lesson that day. I pulled my recipe box from the cupboard, flipping through the cards until I spotted the gingersnap recipe I was looking for. Reaching into the cupboard, I grabbed my large mixing bowl from its familiar spot. This house and this town already felt like home. I'd had three calls about the book club I was trying to start. I had mentioned the club to Jan, thinking she'd feel bad if I didn't ask her. Her response was typical. "Listen, Anne honey, I'd love to be in this little club of yours, you know I would, but you have to promise me that the books aren't going to be too long, and I'm just assuming they'll be romances, right? I mean what fun would it be? What else would we talk about?"

Connie's response was typical, too. "I'll have to check my planner and get back to you. Leave me a message when you decide on a date. Oh, and did you decide on a carpet for the upstairs yet?"

I had really hoped Libby would call. I'd asked Emily to tell her about the club, because according to Emily her mother loved books. But the phone was silent.

Emily came bouncing in for her lesson which, as usual, seemed to fly by. Afterward, I offered Emily a cookie, then glanced out the

31

window. No Libby. I offered Emily a second cookie, then a third. I didn't want Emily to worry. Finally, I allowed Emily to eat a fourth cookie. By now Emily and I were standing in front of the window, watching. Neither one of us said a word, but we both knew Libby was late. Really late.

When the phone rang, Emily and I jumped. I could tell right away something was wrong. Libby sounded distracted and on the verge of tears. She said Brian just needed a few stitches but I knew that sometimes the relief of knowing nothing serious is wrong can cause you to cry just as much as if you'd found out you had cancer or something.

Olivia

If I could have eaten every bad word I'd ever said about Anne, I would've. Twice.

I don't know why I reacted so badly to Brian's injury. It really was nothing. Five stitches under his chin that made him look like a "tough dude," as Bob had been teasing him. I found Brian secretly examining his chin in the mirror on several occasions, trying to hide a small grin. He even gained a small measure of celebrity on the basketball team. The first guy with stitches that year. His tough-guy attitude didn't put me at ease, however. I had a lingering uneasiness about that day.

Maybe it was because I realized how quickly our lives could be changed.

Brian could have really been hurt—even paralyzed.

When I mentioned this to Jan, she said, "Good grief, Libby, get a grip. The kid had five stitches. Quit watching the news; it's putting goofy ideas in your head." I didn't even tell Connie what happened, and she never asked.

Maybe that's what bothered me. The only people in my life who were supposed to be concerned, who were supposed to care, didn't. And the one person I didn't expect a thing from, did. Anne.

There I was, sitting in the waiting room with Brian, waiting for the nurse to come back and give us some ointment and cleansing instructions. I was shaking like a leaf, wondering if a person could drive with one foot tapping like a jackhammer, when in walked Emily and Anne. At that moment any bad feeling or thought I'd ever had about Anne vanished like mist in the sun.

Emily ran to look at Brian's chin, which she pronounced "Gross!" and "Cool!" in the same breath.

Anne ran to me. Wrapping me in a tight hug she whispered, "It's okay. Sometimes these little things can be so hard." I thought she said something about "my thumbs," but just then the nurse walked in and I forgot all about what Anne had said. Until much later.

Having someone there calmed me down immensely. Enough to drive home, anyway. Anne followed with Emily and supper, as she had promised. It's amazing the appetite a person can work up just by worrying. The four of us polished off Anne's hot dish so fast that Anne kept apologizing, saying she should have grabbed two casseroles from the freezer instead of one. Emily, Brian, and I, with our mouths full of the last bites, said in unison, "Yeah, you should have!"

We all laughed. Anne, too.

Just like old friends.

By the end of the evening, Anne sat at the piano improvising versions of almost every childhood song I'd ever heard. Emily sat on the bench beside her, plunking along on the higher-octave keys that Anne pointed out before each song. Even Brian had shed his usual too-cool attitude and had moseyed to Anne's other side. I stood behind her, listening as Anne's voice and my children's combined in joyful harmony. Anne's fingers rolled across the keys, the opening bars of "Row, Row, Row Your Boat" sounding through my living room.

"Listen up, everyone," Anne said, "we're going to sing this as a round. Emily, you and your mom start; Brian and I will join in after the first phrase. Here we go—" She trilled the keys like a drum roll.

"Just a minute," I announced loudly, "I don't sing."

Anne's hands continued moving, replaying the introduction. "Of course you do, Libby. Everybody sings." She trilled the keys again.

"I don't," I declared.

"She doesn't." Brian and Emily backed me up.

Anne stopped playing. She turned her head, looking over her shoulder at me, her brows furrowed. "I've never heard of anybody who doesn't sing."

"Well, now you have," I responded. "I don't."

"She doesn't," Emily said again, sounding like a perfectly trained parrot.

Anne placed her hands on her knees, as if to brace herself from this awful news. "I don't believe you. Everybody can sing."

"Let's put it this way," I explained, "I can sing. In fact, I can sing three notes at the same time; it's just that none of them are on the piano."

"That's just nonsense," Anne declared.

"Show her." Emily stared up at me with sad, puppy dog eyes. "Pleeeeaassee, Mom?" She was really laying it on.

"You'll see," I declared, clearing my throat like a maestro warming up his orchestra.

Anne played the introduction again, trilling the keys, nodding her head in an exaggerated down beat at Emily and me.

"Ro-ooow, ro-ooow…" the sound coming from my throat sounded like a sick animal. "Ro-ooow your bo-aaat…"

Like a valiant soldier, Emily kept singing. But when it came time for Brian and Anne to start their part, Anne was laughing so hard she couldn't get any words out of her mouth. Without Anne to back him up, Brian wasn't about to sing. He started laughing along with Anne. Emily sang her little solo, while the three of us dissolved in laughter.

Finally, Anne pounded on the piano keys three times, as if in a huge, Ha! Ha! Ha! "You're right," she cried, "you really can't sing!"

"She can't!" Brian and Emily chorused.

We laughed until we were clutching our stomachs in a sort of delighted agony.

Just like old friends.

But it was only the beginning.

The Middle

Olivia

Those first two months of our friendship were like a junior high dream-come-true for me. At last I had the best friend I'd always dreamed about. It's not that I never wanted a friend, or even that I never had a close friend. It's just that I never had one like Anne.

Growing up had been hard for me, although I wouldn't dare say that to too many people. Most people in Brewster think I was born with a silver spoon in my mouth, and to a certain extent, I was. But I've learned that every person has a story—a scene or scenario that defines their life and explains it in a unique way. I have my story, too.

I grew up in Brewster and was known as "the Banker's Daughter." People assumed I had it made. I didn't realize this until junior high when I heard Wayne Hughes call after me as I walked down the school hall, "Hey, Money Bags, why don't you throw some our way?" He elbowed his friend David, and they laughed, "Mon-ey Bags! Mon-ey Bags! Ha-ha-ha!"

I remember looking around, smiling, wanting to be in on the joke. Up until that moment I'd thought I was one of the group. When I looked around, there was no one else there, and suddenly it hit—they were laughing at me.

That day became a moment that defined my life. I'd never thought of myself as different from the other kids in my class. We grew up together, skinned our knees on the same playground, and swiped tomatoes from old Mrs. Hanner's garden. But just like that, I saw myself through another kind of mirror. One with a new reflection—someone else's prejudices. My classmates had decided they didn't like me because they thought I was rich. Even though I received a small weekly allowance and an occasional new outfit that my mother had sewn, according to Wayne and David, "She thinks she's better than the rest of us." Almost overnight I was ostracized from the group.

Who knows? Maybe I started acting differently, too. When my mother asked, "Why don't Missy or Paula ever stop over anymore?" I'd shrugged my shoulders as junior high kids have been shrugging them for ages, and I mumbled, "I dunno." But one thing I did know was that their laughter hurt, and ignoring them was the only way I knew to protect myself.

That was when I started insisting that everyone call me Olivia. Not Libby, as I'd been called until then. Libby had been one of the group. Olivia wasn't. Somehow the name Olivia set me apart from the others. Made me seem sophisticated and distant. Set up a barrier between me and the people I used to think of as my friends.

Of course there were other defining moments in my life, but that was a big one. It made a deep impression. I built up a barrier between myself and others that was almost impossible to break down.

But Anne did it.

With pure and simple kindness, she did it.

I was a bit uneasy the first time Anne invited me over. I was sure her house would be filled with those cutesy wooden country cut-out figurines that I'd never been able to stomach. If it was, what would I say?

But I was wrong. Her house was lovely. Of course, the black baby grand piano was the first thing I noticed.

"It was a gift from my parents," Anne explained. "I think they still felt guilty." Before I could ask what she meant, Anne sat down, running her fingers expertly up and down the keyboard, producing a sound I'd only heard coming from speakers in my living room. When she was done playing I pushed my jaw closed with my hand as a joke. But it wasn't funny; she was *good*.

Anne got up from the piano bench and apologized, "Sorry, I can't keep my hands off piano keys when I see them."

"Wow." I was speechless. I cleared my throat and tried not to sound dumbstruck, "Where? How? When did you learn to play like that?"

"Well, for one, it takes lots of practice, but I can't take all the credit. It's a gift."

"What do you mean? A gift from who?"

"From God." Anne tilted her face upward, smiling.

I'd never heard anyone talk like that before, and it made me nervous. I tried to make light of her comment. "If He's handing out gifts, I wish He'd give some to me."

"Oh Libby," Anne laughed, "you've got gifts, too. You've got the gift of words."

"Yeah, right." My words came out sounding sarcastic. "If that's my gift, how come I'm always putting my foot in my mouth?"

"I was referring to your ability to write. Your column." Anne pointed to her fridge where, sure enough, there hung my latest column.

"Oh, those words." I couldn't help but smile, a feeling of pride rising in my chest. Right away I stuffed it down. "My gift isn't amounting to much. Seven dollars a week for a couple hours of work. I bet even God's laughing about good old Olivia's gift."

"Libby, did you hear me earlier? God gives you the gift, but you've got to put it to use." Anne ran her fingers lightly over the piano keys. "I practice a couple hours every day, I play in church whenever I'm needed, and until I started teaching piano lessons, I didn't get paid a penny to share my gift. It's just…" Anne struggled to find the right words. "…just…well, a gift. A present from God to me. I have to work really hard to be good at it, but when I play it's pure joy. Using my gift for others is my way of giving it back to God."

Okay, I was squirming now. If I'd have wanted to hear a sermon I'd have gone to church. Anne must have sensed my uneasiness. She pulled the piano cover over the keyboard and asked if I wanted to see the rest of the house.

Ah yes, like fifteen minutes ago. Before this conversation.

I thought I had pushed Anne's words out of my mind, but they kept floating through my thoughts as she took me through the house. I didn't know then how often in the coming days they would reappear to haunt me like an old ghost.

The house wasn't very big. The piano definitely dominated the living room, but Anne had done wonders with paint and a little creative furniture placement. Two denim-covered, overstuffed arm chairs were backed up to the baby grand piano, a rustic-looking chest displayed between them.

"Kevin's grandpa made that." Anne pointed with pride at the chest; a framed picture of Grandpa sat on top. Anne had thrown a blanket over a worn-looking sofa that faced the chairs. "I've been looking for a red couch to replace this old college thing." Anne straightened the blanket a bit. "But I'm not buying one until I find a couch I love."

"You're going to get a red couch?" I'd never heard of a red couch, and it certainly would never have occurred to me to actually buy one.

"I love red," Anne explained. "I think every house needs a touch of red in it. Of course, a red couch would be more than a touch, but what can I say? I love red."

Oh yes, I'd heard that decorating tip from Emily.

It didn't take long for Anne to show me the rest of the house. Except for the living room it was small, but oh, so comfortable-feeling. And Emily was right; Anne's pretend apples in a blue bowl on her kitchen table were pretty.

I started accompanying Emily to her piano lessons just so Anne and I could work in a few more minutes of visiting. As badly as Emily had wanted us to become friends, even she grew tired of our constant chatter.

"Mo-om, An-ne," she would whine, banging the piano keys harder than necessary. "Stop talking and listen to me play."

Once, with beyond ten-year-old wisdom, she stopped playing and announced, "Remember Mom, you're paying for me to be taking this lesson."

Anne and I clapped our hands over our mouths, but before Emily had played five measures we were talking again. Emily gave up trying to get us to be quiet. She just played a little louder each week.

I felt extremely guilty about the way I'd treated Anne those first months she was in Brewster. I confessed to her that I had decided I wouldn't like her. I told Anne how I was afraid she would steal Jan and Connie away from me. Anne laughed hard at that and told me, "You should be so lucky." In an effort to be totally honest and to let her know just how petty I could truly be, I also told Anne how much it had bugged me the way she'd said, "Hiiii-yiii!"

That greeting became our private joke.

"Hiiii-iii-yiii-iii!" She'd exaggerate when I'd answer the phone.

I'd squeal back, "Hiiii-yiii to you, too." Then we'd giggle like ten-year-olds. My own resident ten-year-old would roll her eyes.

The one thing I could do to make up for the time we'd lost was to share the joy of Anne's pregnancy with her. Anne bubbled over every time she spoke of her "baby to be," as she called it. Sometimes she'd say, "baby for me," or "baby for we," meaning her and Kevin.

I hadn't had a chance to get to know Kevin very well. He seemed to be gone an awful lot. When I asked, Anne seemed resigned. "It's always been this way, Libby. I've accepted the fact that Kevin is a workaholic, and all the nagging in the world isn't going to change that fact. I'm hoping when our baby is born he'll naturally want to stay home more. But I've also decided that I'm not going to live my life waiting for him to come home, either."

Anne went on to explain how in the last couple of towns they'd lived in, she'd created a barrier, not unlike the one I'd created for myself, to keep from getting too close to people and then having to leave. But unlike me, Anne had had many best friends over the years. Just none lately. I could see by the cards perched on her shelves and windowsills that the friends she did have had not forgotten her. There were "Congratulations, you're having a baby!" cards everywhere I looked. I too added my congratulations to her treasure trove by sending Anne cards, even though I saw her nearly every day. I brought her small presents—a rattle, a bib, and a tape of lullabies played on the piano. I almost felt as if this was my pregnancy, too.

How uncomplicated and carefree those early days of our friend-ship seem now. Anne was filled with joy, and so was I. I'd never known how wondrous it could be to have a best friend.

I'd never imagined how hard it could be, either.

Anne

It was April, four months into my pregnancy, and it was so exciting to have a girlfriend who cared about this baby as much as I did. Libby seemed to hang on my every word as I described the changes in my formerly trim body. I'd never been obsessed with my figure, but I have to admit, the day I couldn't, absolutely *couldn't* zip up my favorite jeans, I learned that a sleek physique was more important to me than I'd thought.

During those first months of my pregnancy, Kevin was attentive. Well, let's put it this way—Kevin was as attentive as he was ever going to be. I know he tried to listen to my glowing descriptions of what was happening inside my body. And I know it was truly wonderment I saw cross his face the first time he felt the baby kick. But Kevin remained Kevin. There, but preoccupied. And not even there all that much. When he was home, the next big customer was always on tomorrow's schedule. Always on his mind. Sometimes I envied those people because of the attention he gave them. But I was not going to let those feelings take away any of my joy. Besides, I had Libby.

Shopping for maternity clothes with her was a hoot. Maybe not for the salesclerk, but it was for us.

"Hey Anne, check this out." Libby walked out of the dressing room draped in a tent the size of a small country.

"No way. I am not getting that big."

"Wanna bet?" Libby turned full circle, the dress billowing around her in great folds.

Just then the formerly aloof salesclerk approached, a tight smile on her lips. "And just when is *your* baby due?"

Libby didn't miss a beat. "Ten years ago."

She bounced back into the dressing room. I crowded in behind her. Hugging our stomachs, we laughed until we were red in the face.

When the saleswoman called through the door in an unap-proving voice, "I think you girls would be more comfortable in sep-arate rooms," we mouthed to each other, "girls?" and had another laughing fit.

At four months I really didn't need maternity clothes; a big safety pin did the trick expanding my slacks. Actually it was a huge, old diaper pin that Libby had dug out of her collection of "ancient baby things," as she called them. Libby was constantly telling me how things were during her years of having babies. There were only five years between us, Libby being older, but she'd had Brian in her first year of marriage—almost fifteen years ago—and it was amazing how things had changed.

She told me about using cloth diapers, rinsing them out in toilet water, soaking them in bleach, and washing them in hot water, twice. That chore alone made me glad we'd waited to have our baby. She also told me how I could heat up a bottle on the stove in a kettle, "just in case your microwave ever blows up." And how she'd love to lend me a car seat, but they weren't invented back then. "Okay," Libby admitted when I questioned her, "maybe they did exist, but they weren't the law."

The only unchanging thing she could remember was how to pre-pare my breasts for nursing. And oh, how I wanted to nurse this baby. Libby talked to me in a woman-to-woman way, on a level I'd never experienced before. She was like the sister I'd always hoped to have.

People always assume that having a twin sister means we've been joined at the brain since birth. Maybe some twins are like that, but Andrea and I were never close. Andrea had viewed me as competition since she was old enough to grab my bottle away. I spent most of my growing-up years trying to appease her for whatever I had done to make her angry. And it seemed like most everything I did made her mad—including my pregnancy.

I hadn't given up trying to understand Andrea, but at times it had been hard to have her for a sister. Andrea had two children ages six and two. She had a hysterectomy right after Cari was born, and she's been mad at anyone who's been pregnant since—including me.

I'd been trying to keep baby talk to a minimum during our rare phone calls. That was why Libby's womanly baby advice had been so welcome.

I'd always been a modest person, so when Libby started talking to me about preparing my breasts for nursing, well, I could feel myself turning beet-red simply listening to her. But leave it to Libby to tell it like it is.

"Anne, you have to look at me." Libby grabbed my chin and turned my face to her chest. "Believe me, you'll thank me some day."

She then took a washcloth and showed me how to brush it back and forth across my breast to condition my nipples for nursing. All I could see was the design on her blouse moving back and forth as she demonstrated. It was making me dizzy.

But what she said made sense, and I promised her I would do this embarrassing exercise twice a day. And, I did.

It hurt.

Libby was like a prison warden following up on a parole violator when it came to doing that exercise. I didn't dare skip a day. I was into my second week of conditioning when I noticed the lump.

At first I thought it was just one of those body changes that came with any pregnancy and that had been occurring for me with almost daily regularity. Something so insignificant I ignored it for a week. But the next week, the lump felt a little bigger, and I mentioned it to Libby.

"Oh yeah, I had that too," she assured me in that matter-of-fact way of hers. "It's probably a swollen milk duct."

But it wasn't.

Olivia

I really did think it was nothing. The day Anne told me about the lump on her right breast I pooh-poohed it as if it was just another "welcome to motherhood" rite of passage. I'd had swollen milk ducts during both my pregnancies. It looked and felt exactly like what I'd had. Even the doctor agreed.

Anne waited for her regular monthly checkup, her five-month check, to ask the doctor about it. She told me Dr. Barry examined the lump thoroughly and said, given her age, in his opinion it was nothing to worry about. Probably just a swollen milk duct.

"Let's keep a watch on it," he said. "In the meantime, your blood pressure is a little high. Why don't you swing by next week and have the nurse check it?"

Anne and I examined that lump daily. It was under her arm, and it was starting to hurt when she put her arm down close to her body. Both of us thought maybe it was getting infected—if a milk duct could get infected. We didn't know.

The next week when Anne stopped in for her blood pressure check, she mentioned the pain she was starting to feel to the nurse. The nurse too said, "Oh, it's probably a swollen milk duct. I'll mention it to Dr. Barry and see if he wants to do anything about it."

Dr. Barry did step in to take a look, but wasn't too concerned. "Listen Anne, I've got a five-day conference out of town next week. I don't think this is anything for you to worry about, so let's give it another week to subside. If it doesn't then we might want to consider sending you on for a few tests." He gave her a reassuring pat on the shoulder. "In the meantime, you go home and take good care of that baby."

And that's what she did.

Anne

It was time for my five-month check anyway, so when I saw Dr. Barry I was surprised when the first thing he said was, "Let's take a look at that swelling under your arm."

I thought for sure he would have forgotten about it.

It hadn't gotten any better; in fact, the lump seemed bigger. Dr. Barry thought so, too.

"Mmmm, Anne," he said as he gently prodded the side of my breast, "I don't think you need to get alarmed about this, but I do want to send you over to Carlton. The hospital there is better equipped to biopsy something of this nature."

"Bi-op-sy?" My voice cracked as I repeated the word. I probably sounded as though I didn't even know what a biopsy was, because Dr. Barry jumped right in.

"Anne, as I said, this is nothing for you to get alarmed about. They'll go in and take a small tissue sample from this area." He gently rubbed his fingers over the lump. "I'm trying to play it cautious. A lot of doctors would say let's just watch this for a couple months. But if it turns out to be something, well, then we've lost a couple months. If you know what I mean."

I really didn't know what he meant. "What are you trying to tell me?"

Dr. Barry seemed uncomfortable, but he looked me straight in the eye and said directly, "Anne, there is an outside possibility that this could be cancerous."

Okay. He'd said it. The word that had been floating around in the back of my mind for a month. Cancer. My hands went immediately to my stomach and my first thought was a prayer: *Dear Lord, protect my baby.*

Dr. Barry noticed my nervousness and assured me, "Anne, I don't want you to panic. Let's find out what we're dealing with before we jump to conclusions.

"Honestly, in all my practice, I have never seen anyone at your age have a positive biopsy. It does happen, but it's so rare I don't want you to give it a moment's worry until we know exactly what's going on in there. Okay?"

My mind had gone into a limbo-like state. Dr. Barry's words seemed to come from far away, a muffled echo.

"Anne, are you all right?"

"Yeah. I guess."

"Do you have any questions?" Dr. Barry's voice was clearer now.

"Ummm, no." I sounded dumb. I was. Dumbfounded, anyway.

Of course, the minute Dr. Barry told me to get dressed and closed the door I thought of a million questions. When was I supposed to go to Carlton? What if this was cancer? Would they put me under for the biopsy? What about the baby? How, what do I tell Kevin? What do I do now?

What I did was pray.

All the way to Libby's house.

Olivia

The minute I saw Anne's car pull into the driveway, I knew something was wrong. Not that her stopping over in the middle of the day was unusual—it was just a feeling I had. I'd known she had a doctor appointment that afternoon, and I'd even helped her think of baby questions she should ask Dr. Barry. And of course, I knew she was going to ask him about the lump under her arm again, too. We had decided that if he didn't do anything about it, then she would ask for another doctor's opinion. Anne had told me she would probably stop by after her appointment, so I had the coffee pot on—decaf, in deference to the baby. Call it woman's intuition, but I'd had an uneasy feeling all day.

I walked outside to meet Anne. One look at her face confirmed my fear had foundation.

"What happened?" It was chilly for mid-May, and I wrapped my arms around myself for warmth.

Anne got out of the car and stretched her back the way only pregnant women can, as if she needed to realign her body as well as her thoughts. She straightened, then looked at me, tears welling in her eyes. "It might be cancer, Libby."

I felt as if I'd been hit with a brick in the pit of my stomach. Only old people got cancer. People I didn't know. Not pregnant people. Not people full of life like Anne.

All of a sudden I was freezing. I hurried Anne into the house, poured us each a steaming cup of coffee, stalling for time while I tried to absorb what Anne had told me.

"Tell me exactly what Dr. Barry said." I sat across the table from Anne, ready to analyze every word of her appointment. When Anne finished telling me what the doctor had said, I tried to think of something to say. My mind was blank. I knew I was supposed to give her some sort of encouragement, but I couldn't think of a thing to say. Me, the woman with the gift of words, the person Anne had called a writer not so long ago—I was speechless.

I took a deep breath and drew both hands through my hair. "Let's think of something worse." Oh, good grief, that was brilliant.

Anne laughed, tension falling from her body. "Oh, goodness, I suppose there's all kinds of worse things. For starters, Dr. Barry could have told me he *knew* it was cancer. That would have been worse."

And it would have been then.

Anne

By the time I got home from Libby's, there was already a message on my answering machine. "Dr. Barry asked me to set up an appointment for Mrs. Abbot with a surgeon at the hospital in Carlton. Dr. Lebalm can see you Monday at ten. Please stop by the clinic and pick up your file before you go. Dr. Lebalm will need this information when he sees you."

"What's that about?"

I hadn't heard Kevin come in the house. I glanced at my watch; he was home much earlier than usual. I hadn't had a chance to think about how I was going to tell him the outcome of my appointment. We'd never really had any tests in our marriage, except for moving a zillion times. The stress of moving suddenly seemed like minutia compared to the possibility of having cancer. My grandparents had died when I was too young to know them or even remember. Kevin's had, too. My parents were still living, as healthy as could be. So was Kevin's dad. His mother had died a year before I met Kevin. Over the years I certainly thought about all the "what ifs," if something should happen to one of our parents. I never dreamed the "what if" might be about me.

"Anne," Kevin asked again, "who was that on the machine?"

Kevin had felt the lump under my arm a few times, but claimed, "I don't know anything about this pregnancy stuff. You're going to have to ask the doctor about it. If I knew anything about medicine I would have gone to med school."

"What was that about a surgeon?" Kevin was getting right down to business, as usual. "Who needs a surgeon?"

"I do."

I told Kevin about my appointment with Dr. Barry. As I should have expected, Kevin picked up on all of the facts and missed picking up on any of my fears.

50

"You don't know a thing at this point, other than you have a swelling under your arm. Anne, let's keep this in perspective. You'll go to the surgeon, he'll do a biopsy, and then we'll see what we're dealing with. Don't get all bent out of shape about this now. It's probably nothing."

As it turned out, Libby went to my appointment in Carlton with me. Kevin had a full schedule of meetings. After all, as he told me before he left for work, "It's probably nothing."

One thing I'd learned about Kevin was that he often made blanket statements, describing things the way he wanted them to be, instead of the way they often really were. So when he said, "It's probably nothing," I knew that's what he wanted this lump to be. Nothing.

So did I.

Olivia

That's the last time I ever let Anne drive us anywhere. She was telling the truth when she told Emily she practically flunked her driver's test. She should have. We almost ran two red lights, and she practically threw me through the windshield by stomping on the brakes in the parking lot. When we were finally stopped, I told her, "We're never going to find out if this is cancer if we don't live until your appointment!"

I held out my hand and made her turn over the keys, then and there. I was the self-appointed designated driver from then on.

The clinic was the usual visitor's nightmare—register and wait, and wait, and wait. Little did I know what good preparation it was for the months ahead.

I watched as Anne filled out the first of many registration forms. A-n-n-e F. J-e-n-s-e-n A-b-b-o-t. She sped through the section of the form that asked for previous illnesses or family history of cancer. No, no, no, no. As she checked no to each question, we seemed to take it as a sign that she was going to be fine. Anne turned the form in and the clerk told her, "Just have a seat; the doctor will see you in a minute."

"In a minute" must have been the clerk's idea of a joke. An hour later we were still sitting there, paging through year-old magazines. Anne seemed as if she didn't have a care in the world. In fact, that morning she started what I came to call our "What If..." game.

"What if..." Anne slowly turned to face me, a curious grin on her face, "...what if your old high school boyfriend showed up on your doorstep? Would you invite him to stay for dinner with you and Bob?"

"That's easy. I didn't have a high school boyfriend."

"No fair." Anne poked me in the ribs with her elbow. "It's just a game, Libby; use your imagination. Okay, how about this? What if

Bob was offered a promotion, but you had to move to New York City to take it?"

"No brainer. In a heartbeat."

"You would?" Anne sounded incredulous. "I thought you loved Brewster. I mean, you grew up there."

"Precisely."

Anne looked at me strangely.

I explained, "That's exactly why I'd like to move. Brewster was a good fit for me when I was young, but I outgrew it years ago. The people here have never let me grow up. I've always been Olivia, the banker's daughter, and then the banker's wife. I've never had an identity of my own. I'm so tired of everyone thinking of me as little-Miss-got-it-made. I've had problems in my life, too. But just because we have a good income, well, that's supposed to make up for anything else in life that has ever bothered me. Sorry, but sometimes the anonymity of a big city seems like nirvana to me."

Anne looked surprised. "That was an answer I didn't expect. I'm glad you told me." Anne flipped through the pages of her magazine. "Libby…" Anne pointed to a model in the magazine she was holding. "What if someone gave you a million dollars? Would you spend it on a dress like that?"

I didn't have to think for a second. "No, that dress wouldn't pack well for my move to New York. If I had a million dollars, I'd be off on a three-month European cruise, after I returned I'd start apartment hunting in some exciting city while I had my travel agent checking out African safari adventures, and then I'd—"

Anne interrupted my litany, asking softly, "What are you running from, Libby?"

The question hung in the air between us. The nurse saved me from answering by calling out, "Anne Abbot."

Anne handed me the open magazine as she rose to follow the nurse down the hall. I sat there staring at the exotic dress, Anne's question tumbling about in my mind. What did she mean, "what was I running from?" I wasn't running from anything. I just wanted to travel. I wanted to live somewhere exciting. I wanted a…a…a different life.

Oh.

Sometimes I wasn't sure I liked this friendship with Anne. She seemed so lighthearted and fun, and then out of the blue she'd say something that would stop me cold. Anne made me think about things I wasn't sure I wanted to think about.

I tossed Anne's magazine aside and forced myself to read an article on "Preparing Your Thanksgiving Turkey." Riveting reading. After I was positive my brain had turned completely to mush, I closed the magazine and eavesdropped on other people's conversations. Now *that* was riveting.

I shouldn't have allowed my expectations for the biopsy appointment to get so high. I had thought that by the end of the day I'd at least have an answer to the looming question—is it cancer? I'd walked around for a week feeling as if I had a surgical scalpel hanging over my head. I was going to have to walk around with it a few days more.

Dr. Lebalm was thorough. He went through my history chart meticulously, questioning me further on several of the questions—especially the one about a history of breast cancer in my family. I wracked my brain, trying to dredge up any long-lost relative I could think of who'd had it, but I came up empty.

"That's good," Dr. Lebalm said.

He explained that the biopsy would be relatively easy to do since the lump appeared to be close to the surface. His nurse cleansed the area, Dr. Lebalm made forgettable conversation as he waited for the local anesthetic to take effect, and then before I knew it, he was done. He walked out of the room before I had a chance to ask any questions.

The nurse told me to get dressed, and when I was, she came back and told me they would be sending the tissue sample to the lab. It would be a few days before I could expect to know the results.

"We'll call you," she said and walked out.

Out in the waiting area I grabbed my coat and made a "let's go" motion to Libby.

I guess if I had thought about the appointment at any length, I probably could have figured out that I wouldn't know much more a few minutes after it than I did a few minutes before. As it was, the appointment felt anticlimactic. I thought we'd have some big test results to analyze. Instead, I had nothing. I had prayed and prayed for courage to hear the results. But it wasn't courage I needed; it was patience.

Libby and I sat in the car. I knew she was waiting for me to tell her the news. But I had nothing to tell. Unreasonably, I started crying.

I should have known Libby would interpret my tears to mean it was cancer. She grabbed my hand and squeezed. Hard. The minute I looked at her face I knew she was thinking *cancer*. For some reason, that struck me funny. At this point, it was *nothing*. I burst out laughing.

Libby looked at me as if I'd lost it.

I couldn't quit laughing. The tension of the day rolled from my body. The harder I laughed, the better I felt and the more concerned Libby looked, which made me laugh all the harder. Finally, I gulped in a great breath of air and, still laughing, shook my head, "No."

Libby slugged me.

Eventually, my laughter did turn to tears, of a sort. I told Libby about the letdown I felt, and about still not knowing. "It's like living with a secret, but I don't know what it is, and it's about me."

"I know," Libby stated, pausing as if she was going to say something terribly important. As if whatever she said next would solve the problem.

I waited.

Finally she spoke. "Let's think of something worse."

Of course we laughed. Libby went on to describe in detail the horrible constipation story she'd been forced to overhear in the waiting room.

She was right. Just then, that would have been worse.

Olivia

When we got to the car after Anne's biopsy, I thought for sure she was going to tell me it was cancer. I mean, she didn't say a word when she came out of the doctor's office, and she was silent the whole time in the elevator. And then, when she sat in the car and started crying, I knew it had to be bad news.

I've never been any good at comforting people. Every time Bob's had the flu or a cold he's told me, "Libby, don't ever become a nurse. You'd get fired your first day on the job." And he's right. I don't have that comforting gene most women seem to have. Unless the kids are actually bleeding, I don't even think about the fact they might be hurting.

So when Anne starting laughing and I finally figured out it wasn't the C word, I hit her. She had me scared.

I was totally unprepared when Anne called a couple days later.

"Libby?" Anne's voice was soft and shaky. "The doctor called."

I was working on my column for the week, something about the inefficiency of doctor's waiting rooms. "Yeah, what'd he say? Everything fine?" I hit the save icon on my computer and sat back to listen.

"No, not exactly."

My heart started beating faster, and I sat up straight, pressing the phone to my ear. "What do you mean, not exactly?"

"He wants me to come in so he can go over the test results with me. I don't think that's a good sign."

"Did you ask him if it was…" I was going to say cancer, but the word stuck in my throat. "…uh…if there was anything wrong?"

Anne took a deep breath. "I tried, but the words wouldn't come out."

I knew that feeling.

Anne went on, "I think maybe tomorrow will be soon enough to find out. The reason I'm calling, Libby, is…well, I was wondering if you could come with me. Dr. Lebalm said if my husband was available he might want to come. But Kevin's out of town until tomorrow night, and I'm sort of afraid to go alone."

Oh great—she wanted Nurse Ratchet to go with her. I stood up and did my best, dredging up my confident, everything-is-going-to-be-all-right voice and said, "Sure. I'll drive."

It was another hour's worth of material for my column. We waited, again. Anne started in on her "What If…" game right away. I had my guard up; I wasn't going to be tricked into giving any revealing answers this time.

"What if…what if your sister asked you to have a baby for her. Would you?"

"I don't have a sister."

Anne nudged me with her elbow. "Libby, you're a writer, you're the one who's supposed to have an imagination. You're supposed to pretend you have a sister."

"Okay…yeah, if I could have a pretend baby."

Anne rolled her eyes. "Try this one, what if you were going to write a book. What would you write about?"

My head whipped her way. I'm sure I looked like a deer caught in headlights. How did she know about that? No one, not even Bob, knew about my dreams of writing a novel.

Anne didn't look surprised at all. "Libby, what would you write about?" She was looking at me as if she fully expected me to have a full-blown plot and chapter outlines ready to spout out.

"Well…" I shifted uncomfortably in my chair. I knew she wasn't going to let me off the hook a second time. She'd intentionally asked a question right up my alley. "You really want to hear this?"

Anne glanced around the crowded waiting room. "I think we have time."

"A book, huh? You want to hear about my book." Oh, big mistake. I'd already called it *my* book.

Anne picked up on it right away. "Oh, *my* book—so you have thought about it. Good! Finally, a question you can answer." She crossed her legs, rested an elbow on her knee and put her chin on her hand, all ears.

"What would I write about? Well, I have thought of combining my columns into a book. You know, *Wry Eye Observes*, or something like that." I knew I was trying to squirm out of this, and so did Anne.

"Okay," Anne played along, "let's pretend I already have a copy of *Wry Eye Observes* on my shelf; what's the title of your second book?"

"*Just Friends.*" The words fell out of my mouth before I could stop them. I started to explain. "I've always been fascinated by women who have these bosom buddy friendships. I've never had anything even close to that, and well, I've always thought it would be an interesting avenue to explore in a book. You know, sometimes when I write about other people, it's almost as if I'm living their lives for that moment. It seems if I wrote about two close friends, it would sort of be a way of experiencing that kind of friendship myself." I could feel my heart start to pound. I felt as if I was digging a hole deep enough to hide in. I'd never talked about this to anyone before. Heck, I'd hardly dared to think about it. How could I explain it? I kept trying. "I mean, I've always dreamed of writing a book; it's just that I never knew what to write about. And lately, I've started wondering what it would be like to—" Abruptly I stopped. I was foaming at the mouth, a condition I absolutely detest.

"Like to what?" Anne prodded.

What in the world was that doctor doing? Brain surgery?

"Like to what?" Anne asked, again.

Oh, good grief, I might as well spit it all out. "I've been wondering what it would be like to have a close friendship with...uh, well..." I blurted the last few words out as one: "have-a-close-friend."

"Aahhh." Anne leaned back looking like the cat that swallowed the canary.

I was beginning to hate that stupid game, but I found myself grinning at Anne all the same. *Just Friends* did have a ring to it.

We waited over an hour before the nurse called Anne. Anne and the nurse had started down the hallway when Anne stopped, turned, and called, "Libby, come on."

When Anne had asked me to come with, I didn't think she literally meant come *with*. I found myself tossing the old magazine aside and trotting down the hallway after them, acting as if going to doctor appointments with other people was something I did every day. I don't even go into the doctor's room when Emily gets her booster shots anymore. I felt as though I were some weird, alter ego person traipsing to my doom.

I didn't know why my heart had started pounding so hard again, but it had.

Anne

I don't know what I would have done if Libby hadn't been with me during my appointment with Dr. Lebalm. I knew the minute he walked into the room that it was bad news.

Dr. Lebalm was shaking his head as he walked in.

"I don't like the looks of this at all, Mrs. Abbot." He tossed the chart on his desk and then noticed Libby. "Oh, I'm sorry." He stuck out his hand.

"Olivia Marsden." Libby matched his firm handshake and didn't even try to explain her presence.

Dr. Lebalm raised an eyebrow at me as if to ask, *are you sure you want to discuss your medical situation with her here?*

"It's okay," I answered. "Just tell me what you found." My palms were sweating, and his words sounded as if they were coming from a million miles away, and in slow-motion to boot.

His words sounded as if he was talking under water. "Iiii-tttt'ssss cccc-aaa-nn-cc-ee-rrr, Aaaa-nnnnn-eee."

I must have given him a stupefied look, because he cleared his throat and repeated, "It's cancer, Anne."

Dr. Lebalm rubbed his face with both hands and looked at the wall. "This doesn't get any easier."

I felt like crying, but instead my body turned numb. I stared at a diploma on the wall, but couldn't read a word.

"So what do we do now?" Libby's voice was surprisingly clear.

Dr. Lebalm shook his head as if to chase away cobwebs, and picked up my chart. Now he was all business. "The first thing I want you to do is see a surgeon. I've already talked to Dr. Cleary about your case. She can see you first thing tomorrow."

Tomorrow? That had to mean things were really bad.

Dr. Lebalm went on. "After you see Dr. Cleary, I want you to meet with Dr. Barrows. He's an oncologist. Cancer doctor."

I knew what an oncologist was, but at that moment I was glad Dr. Lebalm wasn't assuming anything. My mind felt like Jell-O.

"Dr. Barrows will go over some treatment options with you. He's the best we've got, Anne. He knows his stuff."

"Dr. Lebalm," Libby began asking the question I should have, "what do we know about this cancer? Is it in the early stages? What about the baby?"

Oh my goodness! I hadn't even thought about my baby! It was as though a lightening bolt hit me. I woke up.

"How is this going to affect my baby?" I actually sounded coherent.

"Let's see…" Dr. Lebalm checked my chart, "you're not quite six months along. Studies show that as long as you're past the critical first three months, you should be able to take chemotherapy without harming the fetus."

"Chemotherapy?" I felt the blood drain from my face. I must have looked as if I was going to faint, because Libby and Dr. Lebalm grabbed my arms for a moment. I shrugged my shoulders and they let go.

"Listen, Anne," Dr. Lebalm looked me in the eye. "Let's take this one step at a time. I want you to talk with Dr. Cleary tomorrow. She'll be able to tell you what your options are as far as surgery goes. I do feel I need to warn you, though—I'm sure she will recommend a full mastectomy."

Libby interrupted with the questions I couldn't ask. "A full mastectomy? What about a lumpectomy? Just what are we talking about here?"

Dr. Lebalm looked uncomfortable. "I was hoping Dr. Cleary could explain things better tomorrow. The biopsy showed we are most likely dealing with an advanced stage cancer. Of course, that will have to be confirmed at the time of surgery. But if it is, I'm sure Dr. Cleary will not want to take any chances leaving any stray cells in there. I've already talked with her, and I think it would be best to let her tell you about the surgery she has planned."

Libby helped me put my jacket on. I think she may have started the zipper for me, too. I really can't remember much about the rest of that day. I do remember getting in the car and saying to Libby, "Okay, tell me something worse." This time it wasn't a joke, I really wanted to know.

Libby was quiet all the way to my house. When she parked the car she turned to me and said, "This may not seem like much, but at least the cancer is just in one breast."

For some reason, right then, her words did make me feel better.

I spent the rest of the afternoon on my knees in prayer.

Olivia

If someone had told me that within three months I would be cross-stitching a sampler for Dr. Cleary's office, I would have called that person a liar. But then, the past two days seemed like a lie. I kept thinking that someone was going to call and say there had been some tabloid-television-like mix-up at the hospital. That Anne's perfect lab results had been accidentally switched with some other poor soul's. That Anne and I would wake up and find that we'd both had the same nightmare.

We did. We just didn't have to go to sleep to have it.

Anne finally tracked Kevin down in some small town hotel, but he was too far away to make it back for her early morning appointment. His response when she told him that Dr. Lebalm said it was cancer was, "Let's not jump to conclusions. We have to wait and see what the lab results are after surgery. You hear about labs screwing up test results all the time." He did promise to get back to Brewster as soon as he could the next day.

I was underwhelmed by his empathy.

Once again, I found myself sitting in a doctor's office with Anne, hearing more bad news.

I didn't know if it was because Dr. Cleary was a woman, but I felt more comfortable with her on Anne's case. The first thing Dr. Cleary did after introductions was to tell us about herself. Her training. Her family. It made her seem more human and made me feel she understood what Anne must be feeling.

Dr. Cleary went on to say this was an unusual case given Anne's age, her pregnancy, and the nature of her cancer, but she also reassured Anne that her situation was certainly not unheard of.

When I questioned the doctor about the possibility of a lumpectomy instead of a full mastectomy, Dr. Cleary said it certainly was a possibility, but that she wanted to make that decision in the operating room. Given what appeared to be the advanced stage of the cancer, the placement, and the palpable size of the lump, she suspected there may be some lymph node involvement. They would remove some of the nodes and send them to the lab during surgery; those results would help her determine what procedure to do.

"Anne," Dr. Cleary spoke gently, "I want you to be prepared to wake up from surgery and face either option—the lumpectomy or the mastectomy."

Anne nodded solemnly.

"I know this is happening awfully fast. It's not often someone your age has to face something of this nature, especially while she's pregnant. But I want you to know that you've got a whole hospital on your side. We're going to do the best we can to see that you have a good outcome." Dr. Cleary smiled and put her hand on Anne's knee. "Your baby, too."

If I would have been a hugging kind of person, I might have hugged Dr. Cleary right then and there. As it was, Anne put her hand over Dr. Cleary's, squeezed it and murmured, "Thanks."

Dr. Cleary picked up her pen. "Now let's get that surgery scheduled. Uh…" she looked at me, "is there a husband involved?"

As we walked out to the car Anne called out, "Okay, I've already got it: Something worse…there could *not* be a husband involved."

We laughed as if it was the funniest joke we'd heard in ages.

Turns out it wasn't funny. But we didn't know then that Kevin's way of coping was to work harder—and be home even less.

⌒

The week leading up to Anne's surgery couldn't have been worse. Anne tried to keep her piano lesson schedule, but Emily came home and told me Anne cried when Emily played her long song, as she called her two-page piece.

"I thought I was doing, like, *really* bad, but Anne told me it was beautiful. So I must have been doing really good." Emily ran off to her room.

I knew what Anne's tears were really about. She'd been putting on a brave face for me.

Then, the next day I got a call from Coach Rollins. He didn't sound pleased.

"Mrs. Marsden, Coach Rollins here."

I didn't like the tone of his voice. Turns out I didn't like what he said, either.

"One of the teachers in the junior high building reported that he observed your son, Brian, smoking behind the storage garage on school property this afternoon with two other boys. I'm sure you know this means Brian will be automatically benched for three games or more."

Since school was almost out for the year, that meant Brian would be sitting out three football games next fall. And sitting in his room the rest of his life. I could feel my blood pressure rising.

It seemed I'd barely hung up the phone when Bob came home from work in a foul mood. Unannounced, auditors had shown up at the bank. Someone was suspected of embezzling, and they were there to find it. Everyone was under suspicion, including Bob.

My husband is the most honest person I have ever met. He will re-add restaurant bills and show the waiter he forgot to charge us for a soda, even when the kids and I remind him, "Refills are free." Bob always says, "I want to be sure." I've witnessed him driving five miles to return fifty-cents to a gas station attendant. Once I actually saw him look for the owner of a stray penny on the street.

Not only Bob was mad; so was I.

To top things off, my weekly column was due, and I didn't have a clue what to write about. I was emotionally tapped.

Leave it to Anne to come to the rescue. Anne, who had every reason in the world to be curled up in a fetal position lamenting her fate, was the one who reminded me, "Libby, look at the tulips on the south side of my house. They look like a rainbow peeking through the ground. And guess what I saw yesterday? A robin building a nest in the tree out my kitchen window. I threw some yellow yarn in the yard a few days ago and now I can see it woven into the nest. Aren't God's creatures amazing?"

If she was referring to herself, then I would have to agree. If I believed in God, that is.

I wrote a column about spring and the beauty of God's creatures. I just left out the God part.

Anne

Kevin was able to change his schedule and spend the week at home with me. That meant he was worried, and that made me feel even more anxious.

When I told him about the surgery Dr. Cleary had described, Kevin was matter-of-fact. "Whatever needs doing, we'll do." He turned on the sports channel and spent the rest of the week engrossed in one sort of game or another—when he wasn't on the phone with clients, that is. At least he was with me.

The person whose reaction really surprised me was my mother's. She acted as if she didn't even hear what I'd said.

"Mom, I have some bad news to tell you."

Before I could say anything more she moaned, "Oh, don't tell me you lost the baby."

"No, Mom," I assured her, "the baby's fine, for now. It's me, Mom. I have cancer." I was having a hard time getting the words out, "Breast cancer."

I heard a small gasp and then, "Well, thank heavens the baby is fine. Is Kevin there? You know, I've always thought he traveled way too much. I hope when this baby is born he plans on staying home more—"

I interrupted her, "Mom, my surgery is scheduled for Monday. I may need a mastectomy."

"Anne, Honey, you know I can't come visit right now; things are real busy at work and I can't get any time off right now. Dad and I will try to come sometime, okay? Did I tell you that Andrea is redecorating the kids' bedrooms? I don't know how they can afford that, but you know Jim has such a good job, and…"

I held the phone away from my ear and looked into the receiver. I couldn't believe what I was, or wasn't, hearing.

"Mom, is Dad there? Let me talk to him for a minute."

I thought I heard Dad's voice crack when he promised they'd be here on Monday.

As it was, I had quite the send-off crew. I checked into the hospital Sunday night. Monday, before they wheeled me down for surgery, the nurse said there were a few people who wanted to wish me well. She wasn't kidding. Three women from church and our pastor held hands around my bed and said a prayer. Jan poked her head in and toasted me with a cup of take-out coffee. I think that was supposed to mean good luck. Kevin was there along with my dad and mom, who still hadn't stopped talking about everything except my cancer.

And there was Libby. She brought a card for me that Emily had made.

As they wheeled me down the hall, Libby stood right in the middle of the hallway, so that doctors and nurses and everyone else had to walk around her. She stood there with a "just make me move" look on her face, one hand clutching her breast, the other held high above her head, fingers crossed.

I teased her about that later—my own personal Statue of Good Luck.

Olivia

I probably looked like a fool, standing in the hospital hallway when they took Anne down for surgery, but I didn't care. I had this overwhelming urge to *do* something. To help Anne in some way. Not that imitating the Statue of Liberty in a hospital hallway ever healed anybody, but it probably never hurt anybody, either. Besides, it made Anne laugh. I figured that was good.

I thought Evelyn, Anne's mom, would drive me batty with her nonstop jabbering. I should have checked my tongue for puncture marks. I bit it all morning to keep from screaming at her, "Be quiet!" She talked continuously. "Andrea, this," and "Andrea, that." Not once, not even for one millisecond, did she so much as breathe Anne's name.

I've seen the scene a million times on television shows. The doctor comes out to talk to the family after they've spent hours pacing the waiting room. The family stares at the doctor as though they are dreading the words that will come out of her mouth. Well, the only thing I thought when I saw Dr. Cleary was, "Thank goodness, now Evelyn will have to stop talking."

And she did.

We all did.

For a long time.

The news wasn't good. Dr. Cleary had removed eleven lymph nodes. It looked to her as if the cancer had spread into the lymph system. "But," she told us, "we won't know for sure until we get the lab results back."

I'm sure she was trying to offer us some hope, but it felt like a dog getting tossed a pre-chewed bone. It didn't seem like much.

Dr. Cleary looked straight at Kevin. "I felt it was in your wife's best interest to do a full mastectomy. The tumor seemed to reach quite deeply into the lymph nodes as well as the chest wall. I'm afraid there may be some slight muscle impairment. Anne will probably need some physical therapy to regain good use of her right arm. But I think she'll be pleased—the cut was nice and smooth, and things sewed up quite nicely. She won't have much of a scar. It's the shape of a smile."

I think that was supposed to be another bone.

Dr. Cleary left the room, and we all sat down as if we were waiting for a different doctor—one with a better report. No one came.

Of course, it was Evelyn who broke the silence. "You know I really think Andrea should think about putting her kids in private—"

Anne's dad, Ed, looked at her as if she'd lost her mind. "Evelyn," he said in a listen-to-me-or-else tone, "be quiet."

And she was.

It seemed almost forever until a nurse came into the waiting room and said, "Mr. Abbot, you can go in and see your wife now." Kevin stood up and looked at me as if I was supposed to tell him what to say, or something. I shrugged my shoulders. This time, he was on his own.

He sat back down and rubbed his face. "I don't think I can go in there right now. I've never been good with hospitals and things…" his voice trailed off.

Evelyn looked as though she might faint, and Ed was trying to comfort her.

"I'll go." I was standing by the nurse before I realized I had stood up.

"She's pretty groggy," the nurse said as she led me down the hall, "but I think she'll be glad to see her sister."

I didn't correct her, but suddenly found myself blinking back tears. Did I feel sorry for Anne because none of her family would even walk down a hallway to see her? Or were the tears for me, the woman who had never had a friend—much less, a sister?

Anne

"Aa-nn-nn-ee." I kept dreaming that I was hearing Libby calling to me from a far-off place. But no matter how many times I called out in my dream, "What, Libby? What do you want?" She never answered me; she just kept calling my name.

I don't remember much from that first day in the hospital. Between the anesthetic and the confusion and shock of surgery, my memory is rather patchy about that time. Libby sitting by my bed, just looking at me, smiling when she thought I was awake. Kevin walking back and forth past the foot of my bed, pacing between the window and the door, never looking my way. My mother standing by the bed, talking to Andrea on the phone. "Would you run over to the mall and pick up some laundry detergent that's on sale?" And my dad reading Ann Landers aloud to me from the daily paper.

It didn't take long to figure out Dr. Cleary had done a full mastectomy. I had tubes coming out from under my arm, and it felt as though a whole set of throw pillows had been either taped to, or stuffed under my right shoulder. And everyone looked at me with a sad-eyed, sympathetic expression every time I happened to open my eyes. Everyone except Libby, that is. She looked at me just like normal.

Dr. Cleary came in first thing the next morning, about the same time Libby showed up with a cup of steaming coffee in her hand.

"How are you feeling, Anne?" Dr. Cleary held my chart in front of her as if it contained dynamite. Which, in a sense, it did.

The smell of Libby's coffee reminded me I hadn't eaten in a day. I struggled to sit up a bit but failed. "Actually Doctor, I'm starving." My voice was hoarse.

"That's good." Dr. Cleary sounded pleased. "As soon as we go over these test results, I'll ask the nurse to get you breakfast." Dr. Cleary looked around my room, "Is your husband here? He might like to hear these lab results too."

Frankly, I didn't have a clue if Kevin planned to stop by. I had been pretty much out of it until I woke up this morning. Dr. Cleary kept looking around as if she expected Kevin to pop out of my minuscule closet or out from under the bed.

Libby answered. "Kevin said he'd stop in a little later. He had some phone calls he needed to make first." I could hear Libby's voice, trying to make it sound perfectly normal that Kevin couldn't come here first.

"Well, then..." Dr. Cleary turned some pages on the clipboard. "The surgery went well, Anne. You may or may not remember me telling you that we did perform a full mastectomy. Your tumor was deeply embedded in the chest wall, and I wanted to make certain we got it all. We removed a number of lymph nodes—eleven, to be exact. It seemed to me, visually, that there was some migration into the lymph system, so I removed a few extra beyond what the involvement appeared, just to be on the safe side. I think we got it all. You responded very well to the surgery, Anne. The baby, too. We kept a close monitor on both of you."

"Thank you." I felt as if Dr. Cleary was giving me a compliment for just lying there.

"The nurse will be changing the dressing on the surgical area soon." Dr. Cleary's voice softened. "I know it may be hard for you to look at this, Anne, but after the initial shock, I think you will be pleased with how smooth the surgical site is. Now then..." Dr. Cleary's voice took on a new edge. She cleared her throat and continued, "I stopped by the lab before I came here this morning..." her voice trailed off. She cleared her throat again and continued, "We're dealing with a Stage Four cancer, Anne."

I felt as if I'd been turned into a statue; a freezing feeling swept through my body. I must have looked confused, because Dr. Cleary explained, "That's an advanced stage cancer. Not exactly what we were hoping to find, but now that we know what we're dealing with...well, we'll deal with it. Dr. Barrows, the oncologist, will be stopping by to see you sometime today. With this kind of cancer we're going to want to treat it somewhat aggressively. But with the baby, there are other factors we're going to have to work around."

Dr. Cleary glanced at Libby then back at me. "You may want to see that your husband is here when you talk with Dr. Barrows. You may need to make some decisions at that time."

I closed my eyes and tried to pray, but all I heard was Dr. Cleary's voice saying, "Stage Four. Stage Four. Advanced cancer. Stage Four."

I felt Dr. Cleary's hand touch my left shoulder and opened my eyes. "You're going to do fine, Anne." She squeezed my shoulder lightly and turned to leave. "I'll ask the nurse to get you breakfast."

I didn't fail to catch the deliberate phrasing of Dr. Cleary's words, "You're going to *do* fine, Anne." There's a big difference between *doing* fine and *being* fine.

Suddenly, I wasn't hungry anymore.

Libby carefully placed her no-longer-steaming coffee on the windowsill and turned to me. She took a deep breath and said, "Okay, let's think of something worse."

For a long time we were silent. Time hung heavy in the air while we replayed Dr. Cleary's words in our minds, trying to find even a grain of good news in her report. It took a while, but finally Libby declared in her usual confident tone, as though she really believed it, "Dr. Cleary said she got it all. She could have said she didn't."

And that's exactly what she had said. I chose to believe it, too.

By the time Kevin arrived, I was ever-so-slowly trying to eat breakfast with my left hand. Libby and I were laughing as she half-fed me and half-tried to guide my unsteady, unpracticed hand.

"Hey, Kevin," Libby called out as he entered my room, "look at Anne. She's doing just fine."

And it seemed I was just then.

Olivia

I spent the entire day in Anne's room. Just once it occurred to me that maybe I should be home doing something else, but at that moment I couldn't think what that might be.

The day didn't seem long at all, what with nurses in and out almost constantly, monitoring tubes and temperature, checking Anne's heart and the baby's. Kevin stopped by mid-morning as he said he would, and seemed relieved when I said I'd be staying through lunch. I honestly think he would have left immediately if Dr. Barrows hadn't interrupted his exit.

Dr. Barrows must have missed the bedside manner class in med school. Good grief—the man had no tact at all, but to his credit, he did seem to know his stuff.

"Mr. Abbot. Mrs. Abbot." He nodded at Kevin and Anne, ignoring me entirely. "I'm afraid I don't have very good news for you." He took up a spot as far away from Anne's bed as he could possibly get and still be in the same room. "The lab reports show the cancer has spread into the lymph system; all eleven nodes showed some involvement. I'm going to want to hit this cancer with all I've got at my disposal. Of course, this baby complicates things. It would be much easier if you weren't pregnant."

He paused as if he expected Anne to apologize for having a baby. When she stared back at him, he continued, "Yes, well, since we're dealing with a pregnancy, too, I've been doing some consultation with the doctors down at Mayo. We don't see this situation much here. Studies have shown that it is safe for you to undergo a chemotherapy regimen once you are past the six-month point. Looking at your chart, by the time you've healed up from the surgery, we'll be well past that point and can commence with the chemo. Any questions?" He turned as though he really expected to leave.

"Dr. Barrows?" I spoke up from my invisible spot right in his line of vision. "What will this chemo regimen involve? Is it daily? Weekly? Anne's never dealt with this before and I think we need to know what to expect."

He looked at me as if I had appeared out of nowhere, and he wasn't happy about my showing up. Too bad.

"Since you asked, Miss...?"

"Olivia Marsden." I stuck out my hand. Dr. Barrows had a surprisingly firm handshake for the cold fish he appeared to be, but he didn't look me in the eye.

He addressed his remarks to Anne, his voice warming, but only slightly. "Chemotherapy can be a bit unpredictable. We'll want to schedule you to start on a weekly basis; however, subsequent sessions will depend entirely on your blood count levels. We'll monitor those closely. It's not uncommon to miss a week of treatment, even two, while we wait for your levels to rise."

Again, he turned to go.

Did he really think he had answered all our questions? "Dr. Barrows?"

I got that *you again* look.

"You mentioned waiting until Anne heals from surgery before she can begin chemotherapy. Wouldn't it be better to start chemo as soon as possible?"

Maybe it was a gender thing, but I really think if Kevin hadn't chimed in with his manly, "Yeah?" Dr. Barrows would have left. As it was, he gave an exasperated sigh and explained slowly, as if to three-year-olds, "We must wait for Mrs. Abbot's surgical incision to heal before we begin the chemotherapy drugs. The drugs are quite toxic and would interfere with the healing process should we begin too soon. Anything else?"

Actually, there was. But by now, even I was intimidated by the man and kept my mouth shut until he was almost out the door. "Doctor?"

Dr. Barrows stopped, barely turning to glance over his shoulder.

"What's the prognosis for this kind of cancer?"

He turned to face me, looking at me fully for the first time. "That's a question I don't have an answer for."

Okay, so I should have kept my mouth shut.

Anne

I don't know what I would have done without Libby those days in the hospital. Kevin was busy trying to catch up on work he'd missed the week before. He figured that since I wasn't home anyway, there wasn't much he could do sitting around keeping me company in the hospital. Truthfully, there wasn't.

It was Libby who helped me sit up and get my pillows arranged just so. Libby who helped me actually get meals into my mouth with my left hand. It was also Libby who walked up and down the halls with me, dragging beside us my wobbly IV pole with wheels like a bad shopping cart. We named my pole Ethel and talked to it like an old friend coming along for a walk. At first, the nurses looked at us as if we were patients who'd taken a wrong turn out of the psych ward. They'd possibly never seen anyone having fun after a mastectomy before. But before long they were talking to Ethel, too.

"Hey Ethel, tell Anne she should get you some nicer clothes," they'd call out as we shuffled past the nurses' station.

For a joke on our next round, Libby grabbed an extra hospital gown and tied it around the pole. The next day she brought in a blond wig and plopped it on Ethel's spindly head. Even Dr. Barrows couldn't help but crack a tiny smile when he stopped to review my chemo treatment schedule.

"I think they'd make a nice couple," Libby whispered as Dr. Barrows paused by the door to write on my chart.

"Who?" I asked.

"You *know*..." Libby tilted her head towards Ethel and then in Dr. Barrows' direction.

"She's too skinny for me." Dr. Barrows closed my chart and walked out.

Libby and I looked at each other, our mouths open wide. Then, we laughed hysterically. I laughed so hard my IV pole shook. It looked as if Ethel was shaking her blond head, laughing along with us, making us laugh even harder.

Actually, it hurt my chest to laugh so hard, but I didn't mention it to Libby. The laughter felt good, too. I was reminded of one of my favorite verses in Proverbs, "Laughter does good like medicine." I'll take that kind of medicine any day.

⁓

I don't want to make light of my time in the hospital. I had dark moments too, especially at night, when everyone had gone home, the lights were lowered, and I was supposed to be sleeping. That was the time when fear seemed likely to overwhelm me. It came in great waves. Feelings of panic engulfed me like a rising tide, wave after wave coming so fast that at times I felt I wouldn't be able to breathe. It was during those times when I tried so hard to pray. But my fear was so great, my thoughts so fractured, all I could do was repeat words from a favorite hymn, *Be still my soul, Be still my soul,* over and over and over again.

Those were the only words I could find that would calm me...*Be still my soul...Be still my soul...the Lord is on your side.*

And finally, I would fall asleep, tucked safely in His arms.

Olivia

When I got home after three days of keeping Anne company at the hospital, I felt as if I'd been run over by a truck. Not only was I physically beat, I was emotionally drained, as well. I'd found I could do a great imitation of a person not affected by what was happening around her. That's what I'd done during my time with Anne, pretended the news the doctor was giving her wasn't all that bad. No matter what Dr. Barrows threw at her, my response was, "We'll deal with it." Inside, I was shaking like a cornered rabbit. I didn't have a clue what to do.

I had planned on visiting Anne once a day while she was in the hospital, but my visit ended up stretching into three solid days. Kevin had "so much work to catch up on," and the 40 miles from Brewster to Carlton "ate up so much time." Toward the evening of the day of Anne's surgery, Evelyn announced she had to get home. She never did say what was more important than her daughter recovering from cancer surgery, but I'm sure her ficus must have needed watering or something.

That left me.

Even though the nurses were in and out of Anne's room like a trail of ants, they weren't there to help her with little things, such as reaching her water glass, which they somehow always managed to push just out of Anne's reach. Or helping her eat. It's not every day a person has to become left-handed overnight. Anne really did need help just getting food into her mouth. And then there were the breathing and blowing exercises Anne was supposed to do every couple of hours to keep her lungs expanded or something. Anne needed help holding the contraption, getting her mouth on it just so, and then recording how far she managed to blow the little ball up the tube. Laughing every time Anne started blowing wasn't part of her recovery plan, but we figured laughter was good for her lungs, too.

One of Anne's nurses took pity on me, sneaking me a hospital-issue toothbrush and paste. I told Anne some poor soul probably got billed $49.50 for it on their Medicare bill, but by the second day it was worth that much to me. I managed to snag a blanket off an empty bed and spent my nights on a couch in an out-of-the-way waiting area. By five-thirty I was awake, doing my best to freshen up with a washcloth and the lipstick and powder compact from my purse. Then I tiptoed into Anne's room, ready to take up my daily post.

I called Bob at work to let him know what was going on. He promised they'd be fine at home. "You take care of Anne; I'll take care of things around here."

One step inside my house made me wonder where it was Bob meant by "here." Obviously, "here" didn't mean our house. The kitchen looked as if the same truck I'd felt had run over me had also driven right through the middle of my house. It was a disaster.

Before tackling anything, I stripped out of my three-day-looking (and smelling) clothes and jumped in the shower. As the hot, silky water washed over my body I mentally awarded a Nobel prize to whomever it was who invented hot showers. It felt fabulous. I was ready to tackle the mess.

The physical work of trying to put my house in order was good for me.

Gathering clothes from the kids' rooms, sorting the lights from the darks, throwing them into the washer and then the dryer, and even folding them (a job I normally approach with distaste) felt good. It was as if I was accomplishing something.

Cleaning my house turned out to be the easy part of getting life back to normal. Catching up on what had happened in Bob, Brian, and Emily's lives was another matter entirely. I hadn't realized how much I'd counted on our limited daily contact to stay in touch. What had worked during our life the past umpteen years had fallen apart in three days.

Bob still had auditors breathing down his neck. He'd been leaving the house early and coming home late. I wondered if he'd even noticed I'd been gone. The kids, however, were another story. Both seemed to resent every minute I'd been away, and they were cutting me no slack.

Other than telling Brian he was grounded after the phone call from Coach Rollins, I hadn't sat down and talked with him about the incident. It showed. Brian walked around the house slamming doors, yelling at his sister, and acting defiant in general. I was afraid to imagine what life had been like for Emily the past three days. I'd assumed Brian would fill in during the time Bob wasn't around. Turned out I was wrong. From the looks of the kitchen and the empty peanut butter jar, it seemed everyone had been pretty much on their own for three days.

I decided to start with Brian. Bad idea.

"Brian, can I talk to you for a minute?"

He'd just come home from school, kicked off his shoes, and sent his books careening across the kitchen table. "What do you care, anyway?" His voice was as cold as his words, and they stung.

"Hey," I admonished, "I don't deserve that. I know I've been gone a bit, but it was an emergency. We all have to pitch in and help out sometimes."

"Yeah, well who was pitching in around here?" Brian swung the fridge door open and slammed it shut, hard. "There's never nothing to eat in this house."

I thought I heard him swear under his breath and called him on it, "What did you just say?"

He acted as if he hadn't cursed and repeated his words very slowly and sarcastically, spitting out, "There's. Never. Nothing. To. Eat. Around. Here."

As if I was deaf, I ignored his poor grammar and tried a different tactic.

"Listen Brian, I know things have been unsettled the past few days. I've been very concerned about Anne, but everything should calm down now. I know we never had a chance to talk about what happened at school—"

"Like you care." Brian flung the words at my face.

"Of course I care. What makes you think I don't?" I could feel myself getting angry.

"All I heard for three days was—" The words burst from Brian's mouth, his voice rising and cracking in a poor imitation of me. " 'Make sure Emily wears a sweater to school. Make sure Emily practices her piano. What did you give Emily for supper?' Emily. Emily. Emily. I'm sick of her and I'm sick of you, too!" He turned to leave.

"Brian, I'm sorry; it's just that you're fourteen, Emily is only ten, and I was counting on you to—"

"What?" Brian's voice had an edge I'd never heard before. "Be the *man* around the house? No one's ever around here anyway."

I took a deep breath and blew it out in frustration. "No, that's not what I meant." I turned back to the sink of dishes, starting a stream of hot water into the basin. "Let's talk about this later when you've had a chance to cool off. Why don't you take your tennis shoes upstairs and think about things. I'll come up as soon as I finish."

"Why don't you just go live at that stupid hospital?" Brian shouted at me. "We were just fine without you." He stomped up the steps, muttering.

I turned off the water and followed him up the stairs into his room. Brian had thrown himself across the bed and had turned his face to the wall. Sitting on the edge of the bed I tried to explain, "Listen Brian, I know I've been gone a lot lately. Too much. I should have known your dad was going to be busy. I didn't realize—"

Brian turned and screamed at me. "There's a lot you don't realize!"

A cold feeling went through me. "What's that supposed to mean?"

In typical teenage fashion, he clammed up, shrugged his shoulders and mumbled, "Nothing."

No matter what I said, he wouldn't talk anymore. Not even when I dryly asked, "I suppose you don't want peanut butter sandwiches for supper?"

Brian didn't crack a hint of a smile. I decided to leave him with his crabby self.

Compared to Brian, Emily was a pushover, but I tried to let her think she was holding her own.

"Hey, Em," I called as she walked up the sidewalk from the bus, "how was school?"

For a moment Emily forgot she was mad and gave me a quick smile. She almost started running toward me, but then remembered and wiped the smile from her face, slowly shuffling to the door.

"F-iii-nnn-ee." Emily tried her hardest to sound really bored.

"I missed you these past few days. We haven't seen much of each other, have we?" I rubbed my hand across her stiff shoulder and felt it soften.

Emily shook her head, then remembering, shrugged my hand away. "I'm hungry." She looked unhopefully around the messy kitchen. "Are there any snacks?"

"No," I confessed, then had an idea. "How about you and me mixing up a batch of chocolate chip cookies?"

Chocolate chip cookies—magic words to a ten-year-old's ears. Emily threw her back pack into the corner and flung her arms around me. "Oh Mom, I missed you so much." The dam broke, and as we measured and mixed, Emily caught me up on the past few days. "Brian has been so crabby. When I'd ask what we should make for supper he'd always say, 'Make your own sandwich.'"

The kid could do a mean imitation of her brother.

"…and then he would stand outside on the corner and talk to Pete, even though you said he was grounded, and then when I told him, he would yell at me and come in and talk on the phone for *hours*. And then, when I tried to practice my piano, Brian would holler at me to be quiet, and that made me sad because I was trying to play really good so I could surprise Anne. So then I had to cry for a while."

I should be strung up for as often as I have degraded motherhood into a thankless, mindless task. Apparently my presence had been missed. What a way to find out.

Anne

Kevin came to take me home from the hospital. He talked non-stop the whole forty miles, telling me about a new client he was working with who could be our "ticket to the big stuff." He said one of my piano students had forgotten I'd canceled lessons for the week; her mom had dropped her off at the house and driven off before they realized the mistake. Kevin had to entertain her for thirty-five minutes. "After ten minutes I had asked every little kid question I could think of, so I had her play through her lesson while I did some paperwork." He looked at me hopefully. "I hope that was all right?"

"It was good for her to practice," I answered. I smiled to myself, imagining Kevin trying to wrack his brain thinking up conversation for an eight-year-old. "You're going to have to get good at little kid talk pretty soon, anyway." I rubbed my pregnant belly with my left hand. "It was good practice for you, too."

Kevin smiled, reached out, and squeezed my hand. "I missed you, Anne."

And then we were home.

Home. It felt as if I was walking into a different world. Kevin hadn't done a thing to the house—not even messed it up. But it seemed my world had changed with this operation. As if I were looking at life through a new pair of eyes. It didn't seem the same anymore.

Oh, my couch still looked old, the overstuffed chair still needed reupholstering, and Kevin's college end table could still use a paint job. I couldn't explain it—it was just different. I felt odd. It was as if maybe I didn't belong in this place, in this world anymore. As if there were a huge clock ticking over my head, counting down minutes, letting me know that my time was short, and I'd better appreciate every minute of it.

It was hard getting back into a routine, too. For one thing, I'd canceled my piano students for two weeks, so those half-hour segments of my day were free leaving me with blocks of time I hardly knew how to fill. In the past, when a student canceled I would spend the time practicing my own piano skills. But it got monotonous playing scales over and over with my left hand. Every now and then I'd play a bit with my right hand, but my arm tired easily, and would swell if I overdid it.

The one thing that did help was Libby stopping by, acting like a drill sergeant, making sure I did my exercises. She would sit comfortably on the living room couch, feet curled under her, and force me to stand in the door frame, marching the fingers of my right hand up and down the woodwork. "To get back my musculature," was how the doctor had phrased it. Libby claimed she'd have me looking like Arnold Schwarzenegger before she was through. I didn't doubt her.

"Oh come on, Anne," she would coax, "you can get them up a little higher than that. Go…go…oooohhh, just a little bit more." And then without missing a beat she'd add, "When was the last time you shaved under your arms?"

Of course, I'd crack up laughing, and she'd make me start all over again.

While I exercised and Libby lounged, we talked. If the circumstances hadn't been so grim I'd say it was one of the best times of my life. We covered just about every minute from our births. Libby was a breach baby who kept her mother in labor for two days, which explains, as Libby stated, "Why everything I've ever done since has been backwards."

Libby was the only person I could talk to about my fear. She didn't dismiss it with an exasperated sigh, "Oh, don't talk so foolish!" like my mother had. Or try to ignore the possibility, like Dr. Barrows, "We'll cross that bridge another time. Hopefully, we won't have to."

Libby just listened.

"Have you ever thought about dying?" I asked, my fingers walking the edges of the door frame.

"No, but I have thought about murdering Bob on occasion. Just kidding." Libby laughed. "Of course I've thought about dying.

Actually, maybe I didn't think about it until after Brian was born. Then for a while I was obsessed with the thought. What if I died? Who would take care of him?" She stopped abruptly, covering her mouth. "Ooops. Do you want to hear this?"

I nodded. "It's exactly what I want to hear, because I can't stop thinking that either. What if I die? Who will take care of my baby?" I dropped my arm to my side and sank to the floor, leaning against the door jam. "I know Kevin will be here and he will be a good dad; I know he will. But there's something about having a mom around that's different.

"My mother hasn't always been the way you've seen her. Oh, she's always favored Andrea, probably because there were the two of us at once. It was just easier for Mom and Dad to split us. Dad would carry me; Mom would tend to Andrea. So in a way, it's natural that Mom is closer to her. I'm closer to my dad. But ever since I told Mom I had cancer, she can hardly even look at me, much less talk about it.

"I was raised to go to church and believe in God, but I never knew what it was to truly love God until a few years ago. In college I rebelled against a lot of what I'd been raised to believe. I was into the party crowd. That's when I met Kevin. He was Big Man on Campus, and I was flattered to have him even notice me, much less ask me out. He was a senior, and I was floating through college, majoring in nothing but a good time. Looking back, it seems just a blink of an eye between the time I set eyes on Kevin and the day I walked down the aisle.

"Kevin started with the insurance company right after graduation, and by some fluke I got a job as a church secretary. Even when I wasn't following God, He had a plan for me. One of the older ladies' groups met at the church on Tuesday afternoons, and they started inviting me to sit in on their Bible study. I was pretty lonely with Kevin being on the road all the time and with most of my friends still into the party scene. It didn't seem like the sort of thing a married person should be doing—partying, I mean. Besides, we couldn't afford it. So those church ladies became my best friends. Surrogate mothers in a sense.

"It was something one of those ladies said. She'd spent almost her whole life trying to figure out what her purpose was, and it wasn't until she was almost eighty that she figured it out. It was to *serve.* Just that—to serve. She wished she would have known her purpose a lot sooner, as it would have saved her from a couple lousy jobs and one husband.

"Her words got me to thinking about what the purpose of my life was. I figured the sooner I found out, the better off I'd be. If my purpose was to serve, I sure wasn't doing a very good job of it. Oh, I was living to serve, all right. To serve me. But it wasn't making me very happy. It was shortly after that when I decided to rededicate my life to God.

"Ever since then the thought of dying has never really bothered me. I always thought, what's so bad about dying if I get to live with God? Don't make me out to be some saint, though; I'm all too human. I've always said I don't care *when* I die, but I do care *how* I die. I mean, I don't want to die in a car accident, or suffer, or…well, you know what I mean. But now that I'm going to have this baby, I feel so selfish. I don't want anyone else to raise my baby; I want to be here to do it myself."

Libby had sat quietly listening to my faith journey. I didn't know how she would react to hearing it. I didn't even know if she was a Christian. I'd said much more than I ever intended to say, but something about Libby always made me talk more than I normally did. She seemed to hear things I didn't say, as well.

Now she nodded. "I hear you, Anne. I really do." There was a softness to her voice I'd never noticed before. "We all have a story to tell, don't we?"

Libby was thoughtful as she unfolded her legs and stretched. Suddenly, she was back in her drill sergeant mode. "So let's do everything we can to keep you here." The usual take-charge tone was back in her voice. "The attitude you need is that this cancer's not going to get you. You're going to beat it. So get up and give me five more of those Arnold-makers."

She was back to the old matter-of-fact Libby, and I was back to walking my fingers up and down the door frame.

Olivia

*To serve…to serve…*I couldn't stop those two words from running through my mind. You'd think listening to Anne talk about dying would have me obsessing about death. Instead, all I could think was, what was the purpose of *my* life? I doubted it was to serve, but heck if I knew what else it could be. That woman—I don't know what it was about her, but with just a couple words she could get my mind tangled up in itself for a whole day. Sometimes Anne still bugged me.

I felt as if I were two different people. The Olivia that Anne knew—the take charge, deal with things head on, Olivia. And then, Olivia, the wife and mother. The Olivia who was trying to keep up a normal routine of grocery shopping, cooking, cleaning, and writing a long-overdue column, all the while trying to act as though everything was peachy keen on the home front. The Olivia whose life seemed to be falling apart.

Bob and I had barely seen each other the past few weeks, not to mention the fact that we'd hardly spoken. Our love life was nonexistent. I wasn't sure what had happened, but it was more like living with a brother than a husband.

Brian continued to give me the cold shoulder. I was thinking of un-grounding him to clear the air, but I was too mad to give in. He'd push me to the point of explosion, then retreat into his bedroom, slamming his door in a don't-you-dare-knock way. Well, I could be just as stubborn. Until he was ready to talk to me about what had really happened at school, he wasn't going anywhere. Meanwhile, I was convinced new gray hairs were sprouting on my head nightly.

Emily was the only person in the house who was communicating with me. The problem there was that Emily was preoccupied with Anne's cancer.

"Mom," she'd ask at breakfast, "will Anne still have cancer when her baby is born?" Or coming in the house after school, the first thing out of her mouth would be, "Could someone catch Anne's cancer, like if you played the same piano, or something?" Then, as I'd tuck her into bed at night she'd ask, "Are you going to get cancer, too?"

How is a mother supposed to answer questions like that?

I was having a hard enough time dealing with my own obsessive thoughts. I examined my breasts at least twice a day, certain that every tiny, slightly uneven bump of tissue was my own personal tumor. I called my gynecologist more than once, positive that I was overdue for my yearly Pap and breast exams. The receptionist assured me it had only been eight months since my annual checkup, and that I was on the list for an appointment reminder card in six weeks. But if I thought there was a problem, she would be glad to work me in to see the doctor. Finally, I was convinced that I felt a lump, confident it had grown over the three days since I'd noticed it. I scheduled an appointment.

"Olivia," Dr. West gave me her usual nodded greeting and smile, "aren't you in early this year?" She checked my chart. "Usually when you come in September, you and I are kicking up our heels because the kids are finally back in school. They're not even out of school yet. What's up?"

I'd been seeing Dr. West for at least twelve years. She'd delivered Emily and had a son Brian's age, Pete. I'd often thought if I were the type to have a close friend, Dr. West would be someone I'd pick. As it was, she always seemed to make extra time for me. We spent as much time catching up on our past year as she did examining me. She was the closest thing to a confidante I had. And right now, I needed her in more ways than one. I needed her to listen to my fears, to check out my lump, and to give me her professional opinion about Anne.

While Dr. West was doing a manual exam of my breasts, I found myself telling her about Anne and all she'd been through the past weeks. Dr. West listened intently as I summed up Anne's diagnosis, then asked, "So, it's been since you've been through this ordeal with your friend Anne that you've discovered this lump in your own breast?"

Right away I knew what she was insinuating, and I felt like a fool. I am not the kind of person who sits around and imagines herself sick. But what she'd said was true. Red-faced, I found myself nodding.

"You can sit up now, Olivia." Dr. West leaned back against the wall near me, ready to talk. "Olivia, I'm sure your friend's situation has put you under a great deal of stress."

Again, I nodded.

She went on, "It's not unusual in these circumstances to find yourself exhibiting the same sorts of physical symptoms your friend is going through."

I nodded. I was beginning to feel like one of those goofy dogs with springs in its neck. The kind old people like to put in the back window of their cars. I was totally speechless but unable to quit nodding.

"I have to tell you, Olivia, I don't feel a thing in either one of your breasts. But what you have experienced is not uncommon." Dr. West chuckled. "Why, in medical school I'd say half my class was ill with whatever disease we happened to be studying that particular week. It's a common phenomenon."

"I really feel stupid." I was still nodding like a dumbfounded pup.

"Tell you what we're going to do, Olivia, I'm going to order a baseline mammogram for you. You're about the age when you should have one anyway, and your breasts do show some signs of being fibrocystic, so this will be a good way to monitor any further changes. And don't feel weird about coming in today. I'd question your judgment more if you had thought you'd felt a lump and didn't do anything about it." Dr. West closed my chart. "So, how's Brian? I'm about ready to give Pete estrogen patches. If I live through his adolescence and all these hormone changes, I'll consider it a major victory."

Hormones? Puberty had never occurred to me as the cause of Brian's bad temper, but it made sense. Brian had always lagged behind his classmates, being a little shorter than most. Recently he'd been eating like a horse, demanding that I buy him longer jeans in a voice that sounded like an unreliable instrument. Of course it was hormones. Dr. West's offhand diagnosis of Brian's problem was worth the price of my unneeded exam.

I found myself nodding again like a mechanical dog with a big grin on its face. This time, I didn't care.

Anne

I'd been dreading the day. I'd read, or heard, every chemotherapy horror story that existed: extreme tiredness, constant vomiting, a metallic taste in the mouth, and of course, the ever-popular hair loss.

I'd always had a love-hate relationship with my hair with its natural curl going the wrong way, refusing to form whatever style was the latest. If flips were in style, my hair turned under; if a pageboy was in, my hair flipped up. So, I figured, if I lost my hair, maybe it would grow back sleek and straight. I was trying to look on the bright side.

I was scared to death.

Although several women from church had offered to help "in any way we can" the minute they'd heard I'd been diagnosed with cancer, and my pastor's wife called every couple days to say she was praying for me, it was Libby who said, "I'll drive you to your appointment." She told me she wasn't sure I'd make it there alive the way I drove. Maybe I should have been offended, but I was glad for her concrete offer to do something, and unsure how I'd feel after my first treatment, so I took her up on the offer. She arrived in my driveway with a thermos of coffee and two mugs, ready to drive the forty miles to Carlton. As Libby shifted into drive, I poured two cups of fragrant, steaming coffee. My hands were icy from nerves, and the coffee helped warm them.

I was still trying to figure Libby out. Almost always she had this I'm-in-charge manner about her that made her appear tough, in a way. Then, every so often, she'd say or do something so right that it would bring tears to my eyes. Like bringing coffee. Her gesture made riding to this dreaded appointment seem not so bad. It was as if we were just two girlfriends on our way to a fun day in the city.

Libby timed our drive perfectly. By the time I'd registered at the desk and we found our way to the treatment area, a technician named Heather was calling my name. "Follow me, Mrs. Abbot."

I'm glad I didn't have to sit and wait; the brief look I got of other people waiting for treatments wasn't encouraging. There were a couple ladies wearing turbans, someone who looked way too young to be there without a mother, and a couple of grandpa-looking types who had an unhealthy paleness about them. I was glad to bypass the waiting room.

Libby hesitated until I gave her my *we're in this together* look, then followed along with a *just make me leave* attitude she can pull off so well. I was glad she was there. The things Heather was telling me as she snapped rubber gloves onto her hands weren't exactly comforting.

"Okay, we're going to get you hooked up here. These drugs are pretty toxic, so we want to be careful not to get any on your skin."

I swallowed hard. "But it's okay for them to be inside me?"

"Uh-huh," she answered routinely. "Let's see which arm has the better vein." She looked at my inner arms and frowned, snapped at a vein on my left arm, then grabbed for a needle. "Has anyone explained what you can expect from your treatments?" She slid the needle into my arm.

"We-ll," I winced as the needle pricked my skin, "Dr. Barrows gave me some literature to read, but I guess I focused more on the side effects." I blurted the rest of the words out, "I'm really scared."

"There," Heather loosened the tourniquet from my arm. "Yeah, I don't blame you, chemo isn't too fun. But you never know," she forced a cheerful sound into her voice, "everyone reacts in a different way. I'm going to let this go now. It might burn a little as it flows into your arm. I'll stop by and check on you now and then."

I leaned back, watching as the pink liquid flowed down the tube and into my body. I don't know what I expected—maybe to go into convulsions or shock—but something more dramatic than the slight burning sensation I felt as the drug worked its way into my system.

I put my head back and closed my eyes. I felt funny, but I knew it wasn't from the chemotherapy. It was a kind of letdown I'd had before, anticipating the worst, then feeling weird when nothing actually happened.

I hoped God wasn't as disgusted with me as I was. I'd been praying for my first chemotherapy session to be uneventful, and now that it was, I felt a feeling similar to disappointment.

Would I ever learn to trust God?

Olivia

It didn't take me long to learn that most hospitals were designed by people who build mazes for laboratory rats. By the time Anne and I took "the first elevator to the right, take a left, go down the long corridor and follow the signs to the lab waiting room," we were practically late. As much as I hate being late, there are advantages—at least we didn't have time to play that infernal "What If...?" game. We ran into the waiting room just as this Heather-person was calling Anne's name.

I couldn't believe they let someone like her handle a responsibility as serious as administering chemotherapy drugs. Heather didn't look old enough to have graduated from high school, much less responsible enough to give Anne chemotherapy. With her double-pierced ears and a butterfly tattoo on the underside of her wrist, not to mention her over-processed, purple-tinged hair, she looked more like a member of a heavy metal band than a medical technician. If Anne had even looked sideways at me I would have demanded to speak to a supervisor. As it was, I was biting my tongue, waiting for Anne to say something. I couldn't believe Anne. She seemed to accept what was happening to her, without asking a question, just sticking her arm out as if to say, "Whatever it is, give it to me. I trust you."

I'm sorry, but I wanted to know if Heather knew what she was doing.

"Heather?" I wasn't about to let her waltz out without some more information. "If Anne has a reaction to the chemotherapy, when will it happen?"

"Oh, well," Heather glanced at her watch. I'm sure we were making her late for her soap opera break. "A lot of people don't react much at all."

She wasn't getting off the hook that easy. "But what if Anne does? What do we do? I mean, you read all this stuff about hair falling out and—"

"Oh! I almost forgot the head thing." Heather started rummaging through a nearby cupboard, pulling out what looked like a cap my hairdresser would use to frost someone's hair. "Here we go."

As Heather prepared the cap and put it on Anne's head she explained, "With some patients we've noticed if we put a cold cap on their heads while they get their chemo it seems to stop the hair loss—for the most part." Heather tied the cap neatly under Anne's chin.

This was getting weirder by the minute.

Heather grabbed a stack of magazines and handed them to me. "Here, this might take a while, so…"

It was a surreal moment—Anne lying in her chair, eyes closed, arms out by her sides as if she were suntanning on the beach. With that little cap on her head all Anne needed was a hair dryer and we could pretend we were at a spa instead of the hospital.

I chanced a question. "I don't suppose you have any coffee?"

"Oh, sure." Heather pointed down the hall. "Regular, or decaf?"

Good grief! Take the most serious situation you can imagine, such as getting chemotherapy, add a punk rock type technician, beauty shop style head gear, magazines, and coffee—it was like a scene out of Candid Camera. I expected Suzanne Somers to show up any minute, dressed as a French maid, to offer us *hors d'oeuvres*.

When in Rome, do as the Romans. I couldn't beat 'em, so I decided to join 'em. I sat back, opened a year-old magazine, and pretended to read, all the while keeping close watch on Anne.

Anne

Waiting was the hard part. Waiting to see if I'd get sick, waiting for my next doctor's appointment, waiting to hear what my blood counts were. Waiting, waiting, waiting. My prayers were for patience.

In a way I felt as if I'd breezed through that first treatment. I did feel a bit more tired than usual, but not enough to make me cancel a piano lesson. My blood counts were right where they were supposed to be for my second round of chemo, and I went into that appointment feeling as if I were stopping by to visit new friends. So Libby was as surprised as I was when on the way home I shouted, "Pull over. Now!" I whipped open the car door and vomited. It happened twice more. By the time I got home I felt like an overcooked noodle. Libby had to help me walk into the house.

The phone was ringing as we entered. I mumbled to Libby, "Could you get it?" then collapsed on the couch.

"Hi, Jan," Libby answered. I could hear Jan's high-pitched voice, talking nonstop, from where I was sitting.

Libby mouthed to me, pointing at the mouthpiece, "Do you want to talk to her?"

I shook my head.

"Jan? Jan!" Libby interrupted her monologue. "We just walked in from Anne's chemo treatment, and she's kind of tired from—"

Jan hardly paused for air. "I just wanted to tell her that Jacob is having a special down at the salon! Perms are half-price, and..."

As sick as I felt, I had to laugh. Why would I want to pay even half-price for a perm on hair that may be falling out of my head any day? As Jan continued to talk, a wave of self-pity swept over me.

Having this baby was supposed to be the highlight of my life. I was consumed by thoughts of life, all right, but it wasn't my baby's life—it was mine.

I rubbed my stomach. *Oh, you poor thing. I should be reading you bedtime stories, filling out pages in your baby book, and telling you how much you're loved.* Instead, I was reading books on cancer treatments and praying for sleep without nightmares.

I blinked back tears. *Why me, Lord? Why now?*

Olivia

Anne scared the living daylights out of me on the way home from her chemo treatment. Of course, I didn't let her know that; I acted as if it was every day someone yelled at me on the highway to pull over so they could puke. "Oh, hey, no big deal. Don't worry about it. I'm not grossed out. Promise."

Anne was embarrassed.

I was scared.

It's surprising what a person can get used to when you have to. I remember when the kids were little and seemed to have the flu every other week. I thought I would collapse from having to get up in the middle of the night to change bedding and give a kid a bath at three A.M. But I didn't.

If I'd have been told that someday I'd be sitting by the roadside in a car, watching someone throw up and viewing it as routine, I would have said, "Yeah, right." But by the time Anne's fifth treatment rolled around, that's how it was. We almost had knowing where to pull over down to a science. Twice each trip. Then I'd drive Anne home, help her to the couch, get something started for her and Kevin's supper, put a cold cloth on Anne's forehead, and head home to get something started for my own family.

My real life was on hold. At first I found myself thinking, "As soon as Anne has surgery everything will get back to normal." Then it was, "After she starts chemo…" Now, I was thinking, "As soon as she's done with chemo, life will be the way it used to be."

In the meantime, I found myself arranging my days around Anne. I'd call first thing each morning. First thing for her was around eleven for me. I knew she was having trouble sleeping, so I'd wait until late morning to check in. I spent the early morning quickly

making beds, washing dishes, and doing whatever else needed immediate attention, just in case Anne needed me to come over. Even on
the days when she sounded tired, Anne had a lightness in her voice
that made me feel everything was going to be fine.

"How'd your night go?" I tried not to have that oh-I'm-so-sorry-
for-you tone in my voice so many people had when they asked about
Anne.

"Pretty good," she'd answer. I could usually tell by the way she
said "good" if she meant it or not.

"How's your day looking?" That was my way of asking if she
needed any help.

"Oh, I have a couple piano lessons later this afternoon." That let
me know she was feeling fairly well that day. She had to cancel lessons
on several occasions, but lately, she seemed to be bouncing back
easier after treatments.

"Want me to swing by after lunch? I'll be out running errands
anyway. Need anything?"

"Would you mind stopping by the cleaners' and picking up
Kevin's shirts?" Anne apologized as she added, "Sorry to ask, but if it's
not too much trouble and you're going by the grocery store anyway,
could you get me two cartons of milk? Skim? If you're not, that's
okay. We have a little left and I can get Kevin to pick some up later."

I knew how hard it was for Anne to ask for help. Never in a million years would she ask someone to do tasks for her if she was able
to do them herself. But she wasn't.

Helping Anne was so routine that sometimes I forgot how life
used to be. I didn't forget how it was before I met Anne—I remembered that much all too well. Lonely. Only then, I didn't know what
that empty feeling was. I thought I was fine all by my lonesome self.

But it did seem that those early days of our friendship were part
of another life, another time. Each of us running in our own little
circle, never really thinking about each other, unless it was to get
together for a casual gab session. Could the time I remembered possibly be only months ago? A time when I would've never asked Anne
to run a simple errand for me, much less have thought to offer to

run any for her. Now, what seemed a lifetime later, it made me feel good to be able to help. Why did it have to take this cancer-thing for me to find out?

~

Meanwhile, life on the home front wasn't much improved. For one thing, my weekly column for the *Brewster Banner* was getting harder and harder to write. I'd started out writing the column as a way to force myself to write; now I was forcing myself in a whole different way. It was getting harder and harder to be entertaining when my life consisted of driving to chemotherapy appointments and arguing with my family.

Bob was being very closemouthed about what was happening at work. When I'd ask, "What's going on?" I'd get a cryptic answer along the lines of, "Auditors left. They'll be back." When I probed for more information, Bob would shake his head and say, "I can't talk about it, Olivia. Not right now." Then he'd head out the door for another long night at the bank.

If I didn't know better, I'd have suspected him of having an affair. I asked Bob about it late one night when we were tossing and turning, each pretending to sleep.

"Is there someone else?" My voice came out soft and weak, not at all like me.

"What?" Bob sounded as if I'd interrupted from another world. "Did you say something, Olivia?"

"I asked you, is there someone el-se?" My voice cracked.

"Good grief, Olivia, don't start on that." Bob sounded disgusted. "I have enough on my plate as it is."

"Well, then talk to me. You walk around here in your own private world. That is, when you're here." My voice turned the words into an accusation.

"Oh, and you're here so much more than me?" He accused me right back.

"Hey, I can't help it if Anne has cancer." My voice rose a notch. "I'm just trying to help her. I didn't think it would go on this long. I...I...I just...," my words trailed off. I realized I didn't have anything more to say to this man right now. We were occupying the same bed, but two different worlds. "Good night." I pulled the covers up to my chin and slid way over to my edge of the bed.

"Olivia," Bob spoke from his side, his voice sounding tired and discouraged. "Believe me, I'll explain things to you soon. I need to find some things out first—things I can't talk about right now."

As if that explained anything.

"As I said, good night." I rolled over for another night of crummy sleep.

Brian was no different. Maybe even worse. But I didn't have the energy to try to analyze a teenager's psyche right now. I noticed Dr. West's son, Pete, seemed to be hanging around more than usual. I didn't know Pete well, but I had the greatest respect for Dr. West. Pete seemed like a polite enough kid, so I didn't question this new friendship. Brian always seemed anxious to see him, ushering Pete quickly into his room and out of my way. We kept our conversation to a minimum, and as long as Brian kept his size ten sneakers away from the front door, and the door to his messy room closed, we seemed to have achieved an uneasy peace.

Things were peaceful with Emily, too. Too peaceful. Emily had started talking at eight months of age and had never stopped—until now. She was strangely quiet. When I'd ask her if anything was wrong, she'd shrug her shoulders. When I tried another tactic, asking if she'd like her back lightly tickled (something she used to beg me to do), she'd pull up her shirt and turn her back to me. But instead of the usual stream of words that would echo my soft touch, I'd hear nothing. Just a huge sigh now and then. Nothing more. Since she wouldn't answer my questions, I had to chalk up this change to hormones, too.

All we needed was for me to start menopause. We could keep the hormone industry in business permanently.

Being with Anne was easier than being with my temperamental family. Putting my family concerns on the back burner worked wonders. I acted like Scarlet O'Hara. "I'll think about that tomorrow," I'd say, then flounce off to Anne's. Actually, I'd never flounced in my life, but I did drive there rather defiantly, thinking, "I'll deal with them tomorrow." The only trouble was that I said the same thing every day. Tomorrow never came, because I never let it. I kept pushing it off until some future day.

Most days it was a relief to watch preoccupied Bob walk out of the house, listen to perpetually-scowling Brian slam the door on his way to school, and hope that whatever was troubling Emily would be over soon. I watched as Emily shuffled her way to the school bus to complete her last week of school, my hands closing around my car keys. "Helping Anne have cancer," as Anne put it one day, was easier. It made me feel good to be doing something that someone appreciated.

I was dreading summer.

Libby showed up unannounced on my doorstep. "It's time to go wig shopping."

As my chemotherapy went on, the doctor, the nurses, and the chemotherapy technicians had all mentioned I might notice some hair loss. I certainly did notice it, but thankfully, not from *my* head. Sitting in the laboratory waiting room, you'd have had to be blind not to notice the bald heads and the feeble attempts people made to hide them. Turbans, hats, hats with fake-looking hair sticking out from under them, crooked wigs, bad toupees, and one brave woman who had apparently said, "Heck with it." She sat there bald. She seemed defiant and cold.

I made Libby promise that if the day came I needed a wig, she'd be brutally honest and help me pick out something that at least looked close to my real hair.

But when she showed up and declared, "It's time to go wig shopping," I was totally surprised. Right away my hands flew to my head and felt around as though they were expecting to suddenly find a bald head. They didn't. My hair seemed to be in its usual thick and curly disarray. I turned and walked into my bedroom, Libby on my heels. I stood in front of my mirror, tilting my head this way and that, looking for bald spots I had apparently missed in my nightly examination.

Libby interrupted my search. "Quit looking—you're not going bald, yet. I just thought it would be easier to buy a wig when you didn't really need one. And if you never need it, well, so much the better. We'll have something to laugh about in our old age."

She was right. I could've kicked myself for not thinking of the idea. It would be much easier to shop for a wig now, while my hair was thick and full. We could remember what color it really was, see the texture, and try to find something that matched. We would be two friends out for a fun day at the mall. "*We stopped in to try on wigs for laughs.*" We could pretend I didn't have cancer.

It wasn't your typical trip to the mall. For one thing, we found a parking spot right in front of the main entrance—an impossibility most days. For another, it reminded me of the last time I'd been here, to shop for a prosthesis after my mastectomy. I used to think shopping for a new bra was not only a hassle, it was embarrassing, too. Try being pregnant, not knowing what your normal size is any more, and then needing a prosthesis for the other side. I was embarrassed and scared. I'd hardly been able to look at the surgery spot myself without quickly moving my eyes, not sure if I wanted a good look; now I was going to let a total stranger look, not only at my remaining breast, but at an empty area I was trying to ignore as much as possible. I was convinced that by the time I was through with this ordeal I wouldn't have a shred of modesty left. What choice did I have but to act as if it was every day that I went shopping for a prosthesis?

Luckily, God sent an angel to Herberger's that day.

"Can I help you?" A middle-aged woman with straight dark hair and cool black glasses approached Libby and me.

I took a deep breath, gathering my courage. "Yes, uh, we'd…uh, I'd…ummm." So much for courage.

Libby took over. "We'd like to see your, uh, prothes…prosthesises…or however you say it."

The clerk laughed. "Yeah, it's a hard one to say. Is this for one of you?" She acted as though it was normal for a pregnant, twenty-nine-year-old woman to be out shopping for a breast.

Foolishly, I held up my hand as if I was being asked a question in school. "Ummm, yes, it's for me."

"Okay, why don't you come over to the desk and I'll show you the types available. There's a variety out there. You may even want to get a couple different types, depending on the kinds of clothes you wear." She flipped open a ring binder as if it were just another day at her interesting job. "You see, this type is a bit lighter. It's the one you need if you're going to be wearing a clingy-type knit—possibly a bathing suit. Then, there's this brand that tends to be…"

I could have hugged her. She acted as if there were actually life after having a mastectomy. It had never even dawned on me that I would ever think about going swimming again. This woman made me feel as if I would need a whole *wardrobe* of prostheses to keep up with my busy, active life.

"I'll need your prescription to place an order, and then you can file it with your insurance company. Let's go in the dressing room and check what size you're going to need."

With my back to the door I unbuttoned my blouse and unfastened the old bra I'd been wearing, making sure my eyes avoided the mirrors on both sides of me.

"Are you ready?" Her voice sounded matter-of-fact. It didn't have that "oh you poor thing" tone so many people took on when they found out I had cancer.

She squeezed in the door and I turned to face her. "Oh," she said, "your surgeon did a marvelous job. It looks like a smile."

I glanced full-on into the mirror for the first time. She was right—it did look like a smile. I wasn't ugly or disfigured. My skin was smooth and healthy looking, interrupted only by a smile. A warm feeling rushed through me. One of relief and gratitude.

Now I was feeling embarrassed again, but this time I felt embarrassed for not trusting God. Surely He had been here with me today in the shape of this woman who made me feel accepted and whole.

"Can I help you two ladies?" The gum-cracking clerk in the wig shop seemed a far cry from the angel who'd helped me the last time I'd been shopping. If she was wearing one of her products, then it was a bad advertisement. Her platinum-blonde wig sat kind of cockeyed on her head, the bangs hanging over the top of her wire-rimmed glasses. I shot Libby an are-we-really-going-to-do-this look.

She shot back a look that said, "Yes-we-really-are." Then she said to the clerk, "We'd like to look at some wigs."

It seemed an obvious answer, considering wigs were the only thing in the store, lining the walls from the ceiling to nearly the floor.

"That so?" The clerk snapped her gum, sliding off a stool behind the counter. "You two got some big dates coming up?"

Apparently, she didn't notice my pregnant belly. Or, maybe that was normal for her clientele. Scary thought. I wanted to say, "Well, I usually don't consider my chemotherapy appointment a 'big date,' but maybe it wouldn't seem so bad if I thought of it that way." But the remark seemed rude, and I didn't want her sympathy, just a decent wig.

Libby answered for me. "We want to try out some new styles. You know, to see what we look like in, say…" she pointed to a blonde number that resembled the clerk's wig. "That."

The clerk put her hands on her hips and scolded, "Now I don't like gals tryin' on my wigs just to find a new hairstyle—they got books you can look at for that. These wigs is made of fine material. Some is even made of human hair. That don't come cheap. This isn't a shop just for fun and games—"

Libby interrupted her. If we weren't careful, we were going to get kicked out of the wig shop. "No, ma'am, we aren't here just for fun; we really are looking for wigs."

Libby couldn't help but chuckle as she finished her apology. It was funny. Who'd have ever guessed we'd have to be begging to try on this woman's wigs?

"We-llll…" The woman looked us up and down. I tried to wipe even the hint of a smile off my face and still appear friendly. We must have passed muster, because she walked over and took down the blonde wig Libby had pointed at, shaking it as if it was a mop instead of the fine human hair she claimed it was. "Now, which one of you wants to try this on?"

"I do." Libby grabbed it. "I've always wondered what I'd look like as a blonde." She posed in front of the mirror, adjusting the wig ever so slightly so it was crooked, like the clerk's. I didn't dare laugh.

"Looks good!" the clerk declared, climbing back on the stool behind the cash register. "You gals just try on what you want. If you need me to reach something, let me know." She rummaged in her purse and popped another stick of gum into her mouth, settling back into what seemed her usual pose, watching people walk past her store.

"How do I look?" Libby now had an almost black wig perched on her head. The dark brown hair hung straight almost brushing her shoulders, with long bangs grazing her eyebrows. It made her look like a cross between Cleopatra and that lady from the Addams family.

"Very dramatic." I was turning a curly, ash brown wig on my hand, trying to decide if it looked anything like my current hairdo. So far, every wig I'd tried on that looked close to my hair style on the mannequin's head made me look like an old lady with a bad perm.

Libby was gazing at herself in the mirror. "I kind of like it." Libby turned her head to get a side view. "It's a look I've always wished I could pull off. You know, that sophisticated New York attitude." She stuck her nose in the air.

"I'm sure Bob would be surprised. Brian and Emily, too. Everyone else in Brewster, for that matter."

"I don't think surprised is the right word." Libby yanked the wig off her head, her hair standing up on end, full of static. "Try flabbergasted. Here—you try it on." She pulled the wig I was twirling off my hand and replaced it with the dark brown one.

"Oh, yeah, right. This is really me." I held the wig out at arm's length.

"Go ahead, try it. Nothing else has looked right so far. It can't hurt. We've been trying to find something close to your style, and obviously that's not working. Maybe what we need to do is try the opposite. Instead of curly, we'll try straight."

I plopped the wig on my head and looked at Libby cross-eyed. I expected her to laugh, but instead, she reached out and turned my head towards the mirror. There I sat, looking at someone who looked just like me with a sleek, sophisticated hairdo. All those years of whining to my girlfriends about my naturally curly hair were apparently over. All it took was one look in the mirror to know without a doubt that this was the wig for me. My hair had always been dark with an auburn sheen; now the wig that had looked almost black on Libby made me look like a model. Okay, maybe not a model, but like one of those people who has a naturally pale complexion and naturally dark hair. Someone who is into arty movies and high fashion. Someone cool and sophisticated. Maybe I was getting carried away, but there was something about that wig and how it looked on me that made me feel as though I were a different person. Maybe someone who didn't look as if she could ever die of cancer.

Libby was grinning. "Anne, you look totally hip."

Even the store clerk stopped snapping her gum and announced, "Honey, that one's you."

Libby and I stopped for coffee and a cinnamon pretzel to celebrate. While we relaxed over a second cup of coffee (decaf for me), Libby started talking about the troubles she'd been having at home— Bob's preoccupation with something at work, Brian's leave-me-alone attitude, and Emily's unusual silence. I hadn't realized how wrapped up I'd been in my doctor appointments, blood count levels, and treatments. There was a world of things going on around me, and I hadn't noticed. Listening to Libby talk, even if it was about problems, made me forget for a moment that I had cancer, that I'd had a mastectomy, and that I had another chemotherapy appointment the next day.

I apologized to Libby. "I'm so sorry."

Libby blew on her coffee and took a small sip, looking puzzled. "For what?"

"For being so caught up in what time my next doctor appointment is, for instance. I've totally forgotten you might have worries in your life, too."

"Anne," Libby's voice was matter-of-fact. "My worries are nothing compared to yours. Bob will tell me what's going on at work. Emily will start talking again; I have no fear of that. And Brian will grow up. My worries will solve themselves in time; we don't know if yours will."

"Promise me you'll keep telling me about your life, too. Even when I forget to ask. It's good for me to realize I'm not the only person in the world with challenges in their life right now. We all have them, don't we?"

Libby nodded and stood up, tossing her cup in a nearby trash can. "Yeah, and my challenge right now is to think of a topic for my column. Help me brainstorm on the way home."

By the time Libby pulled up in front of my house we'd actually started joking about what life had been like at her house the past few months, living with three uncommunicative people. We'd also come up with a name for her next column: "Husbands, Teenagers, and Tweenagers: A Survival Guide."

"It's perfect. I think I can take it from here. Thanks." Libby put her hand up to give me a high-five, but I grabbed her hand and squeezed it instead. "I'll pray for you."

When I got in the house, I tried the wig on one more time, just to see what totally hip might look like. Then I carefully boxed it up and tucked the wig in a far corner of my closet, hoping I'd never need to wear it.

Then I sat down to pray for Libby.

I'll pray for you. I'll pray for you. What was it with Anne? One minute we could be having the most fun, and the next she'd say something weird like, "I'll pray for you." What was I supposed to say to that?

I mean there we were, having a fun time talking about all the different wigs we had tried on, and the next thing I knew I was pouring out my worries about Bob, Brian, and Emily. I couldn't understand how Anne did it, but she had a way of getting me to spill my guts practically every time I opened my mouth. It was cheap therapy, without the couch. Only I didn't feel better afterward.

Well actually, I did. It's just that I'd never been a person to broadcast my troubles to the world. It made me feel uncomfortable to talk about myself, although you'd never guess from the way I foamed at the mouth in front of Anne. I'd always figured it was best to keep your thoughts to yourself. Why would anyone be interested in my worries, anyway? But then, there was Anne, listening to me as if she had nothing better to do the entire day and no worries of her own. No one had ever listened to me like Anne did.

I had been feeling weird already because I told her about the junk going on at home. And then she got out of the car and said, "I'll pray for you." No one had ever said that to me before. It made me feel strange—in a good way, I guess.

I mean if anybody was going to pray for someone, it should have been me doing the praying for Anne, not the other way around. Somehow, "Now I lay me down to sleep," the only prayer I could conjure up, didn't seem appropriate. Besides, in order to do some praying, I figured you should have someone doing some listening, and I wasn't quite sure who that would be in my case. I decided good thoughts would have to do. *Bring healing to Anne. Bring healing to Anne.*

Funny—it sounded like a prayer. I hoped someone was listening.

Anne

By midsummer, my chemotherapy was through. Dr. Barrows had given me an "all clear" at my last appointment. At least as clear as he could. Cancer can be a tricky disease. What may seem to be a cure now, may not be in the long run—that much I'd learned. He'd told me to "go home and enjoy being pregnant; your tests look good," which was about as positive as I'd ever heard Dr. Barrows sound. Libby and I stopped at the Dairy Queen to celebrate. My baby seemed to like hot fudge Blizzards.

I'd felt pretty good through most of the treatments, other than the initial bouts of nausea and some tiredness. I never did need my wig. So there. And I'd discovered something after that day of wig shopping with Libby: when I focused my thoughts and prayers on other people's problems instead of my own, I felt a lot better. The huge surgical knife that had hung over my head like an imaginary guillotine had vanished, and the tick-tick-ticking of the shadowy clock that had started the day I was diagnosed had finally quieted down. In fact, there were whole hours when I forgot I had cancer.

I was doing my best to follow Dr. Barrows' orders, trying to enjoy being pregnant, acting as though I was a regular woman having her first child. Maybe *enjoy* would be overstating it, considering the July heat, my greatly enlarged state, and the fact that we didn't have air-conditioning, but I really was enjoying being pregnant. I liked feeling the baby kick inside my body and imagining how it would feel to hold him or her. I appreciated the way people seemed to treat me differently, as if I were special, offering to reach things at the grocery store or holding doors open for me even when I was coming from a long way off. They'd stand there waiting and smiling as though they were doing some great, noble deed. It felt as if they were. Even Kevin was getting into the dad-thing. He'd brought home a teddy bear from one of his trips, along with a book—*Baby's First Year*. After supper we'd go for a short walk, then sit outside in lawn chairs, swatting mosquitos while Kevin read parts of the book aloud as if we were attending some sort of parent school.

"Listen to this, Anne." Kevin held up a finger, as if what he had to say next was super-important. " 'Research shows all babies should be placed upon their backs when being put down to sleep.' Did you know that?" Before I could reply he'd mumble, "We'll have to be sure and remember that." Then before I could even nod, he'd read some more. " 'Breast fed babies tend to have less infectious—' Whoops. Guess we won't be needing that one, huh?" He grimaced and then quit reading out loud.

I don't think he meant to hurt my feelings; sometimes we both seemed to forget this pregnancy wasn't like everyone else's. Even I had forgotten I wasn't going to be breast feeding. Not that I couldn't try with my remaining breast, but with all the chemicals that had been put into my body over the past weeks, I felt maybe formula would be better for our baby. Sometimes Kevin seemed to forget I'd had a mastectomy or had taken chemotherapy. He was gone so much of the time, and Libby had driven me to all my appointments. I suppose it would be easy to forget when you were never there. I'd asked Kevin if he wanted to see my surgery spot. He'd always been squeamish—I'd known that ever since he fainted having his cholesterol checked during a health fair at college. Anyway, he'd said no, and I didn't insist. I'd had trouble looking myself at first.

Kevin talked about our baby a lot. He told me life was going to be different after our baby was born. He was going to cut down his time on the road and try to do more from home. After all, he'd spent these last years working hard so we could afford to have a child. He wanted his kid to have the best. Kevin insisted we go shopping for a stroller one Saturday. As often as I'd fantasized about Kevin when we were dating, one thing I'd never imagined was Kevin in the baby department at the mall. He looked good standing there, a diaper bag slung over one shoulder, wheeling a stroller to the counter. Mr.

Macho-New-Baby-Dad. It was a new kind of sexy. He was getting into his new role. However, he drew the line at the baby shower.

"Anne, I cannot go to a baby shower. I can't. I'm sorry." He didn't sound that sorry.

"But Kevin," I pleaded, "it's supposed to be a couple's shower. There'll be other men there. Jan has worked so hard to plan this...I can't tell her you won't be there."

"Yes you can, because I won't. Be there, that is." Kevin turned his hands palms up and begged. "Please Anne, it's one thing I just can't do. I can't sit there and listen to all that girlish baby talk, and we'd probably have to play games, too. No way. Besides, there's a golf tournament I was planning to play in that day. Anne, pleeaassee. You know I'm not a baby shower kind of guy."

He wasn't. Even I couldn't imagine him there.

I called Jan and gave her the news. Luckily, she hadn't sent out the invitations yet; she'd wanted to clear the date with me first. So, the shower was as Kevin had predicted, a bunch of women, talking girl talk and baby talk, playing games and, I might add, having fun.

Olivia

I thought I would lose my mind sitting at Jan's for four hours, listening to ten women talk about how many messy diapers they'd changed. I'd had Brian and Emily early in my marriage, and that stage of life was gladly behind me. I felt I was reliving those years in real time as I listened to those women tell their endless stories of late-night feedings, emergency calls to the doctor in the middle of the night, and labor horror stories. As if Anne needed to hear all that.

When Connie, of all people, started telling about her emergency C-section, I made one of those "let's-get-out-of-here" head motions to Anne and moseyed out to the kitchen. I could hear Anne saying, "I'm parched; I think I'll go get a glass of water. No Jan, really, you stay and listen. I can get it myself." She burst into the kitchen, panic on her face, looking ready to burst into tears.

"Is it really that bad?" Anne sounded as though she were having second thoughts, seven months too late.

"I can't believe those women." I was practically sputtering, in frustration. "They should know better! You don't tell those kinds of stories at a baby shower."

"I could understand if it was just one of them telling a story about a bad experience they had." Anne sounded close to tears. "But they all have some big, dramatic, baby story to tell. It scares me. What am I in for?"

"Listen to me, Anne." I grabbed her shoulders and looked her in the eye. "You know that old saying, 'Believe half of what you hear?' Well, in this case you can cut even that in half. I'm going to tell this to you true—to each woman their own labor story is the most exciting tale there is. Yours will be, too. To hear some of those ladies tell it, they would be in the *Guiness Book of World Records* if we were to believe every word they said. But there is one old wives' tale that's right on. It's the one that says, 'Once your baby is born, you forget all the pain.' Okay, maybe you don't forget completely, but it's like having a big fight with your husband—a couple months later you can remember you had a fight, but be darned if you can remember what it was about.

"I've never been much of a baby person myself, the older my kids have gotten, the better I've liked them. I had never even changed a diaper until I had Brian. But look at him. He's fourteen—actually fifteen next week—and he's just fine, barring this temporary glitch in his personality right now. Childbirth couldn't be that bad, or Brenda out there," I nodded toward the door, "wouldn't have four kids, right?"

Anne nodded.

"You're going to do fine. More than fine, you're going to do *great.* Okay?"

"Okay." Anne sounded as if she believed me. Maybe I did have a career in motivational speaking.

I must have been listening to my own pep talk, because I couldn't believe the next words out of my mouth. "Let's go out there and play some baby shower games. They're always so much fun." I didn't even sound sarcastic.

So there I sat in the grave I'd dug, trying to unscramble words like a-b-y-b and i-p-n. *Duh*, as Brian would say. I didn't feel a need to win any pacifiers or baby wipes. I zoned out.

That happens often to me when I'm in a situation I don't want to be in—I start thinking about what I'd be doing if I weren't there. For some reason I always imagine myself at home working on my nonexistent novel. I'd read somewhere we humans tend to fill our lives with distractions in order to avoid doing what lies deep in our hearts, what we instinctively know is our life's work. We also know it will be the hardest thing we've ever done. Maybe I heard it watching *Oprah*, another thing I'd do to avoid writing my novel.

That moment, however, writing a novel seemed like cutting through soft butter compared to playing stupid baby games. I flipped my game sheet over, ready to write. Okay, if I were home now and actually writing a book, what would I write about?

I started scribbling. *A thirty-something woman, with two kids who are going through a strange stage and a husband who's having problems at work (but he won't tell his wife what's going on…)*

As if that was a plot. Sounded more like the makings of a bad B movie to me. I made a little doodle on the page and started again. *There's this woman, still thirty-something.* They say to write what you know. And let's say, *she's never had a good friend her whole life, and then this new woman moves to town and starts changing everything about her—*"

"Hey, Olivia, how many did you get?" Jan was playing the game as if there were an actual prize involved. "I'll bet you got the most— you were writing like crazy."

I looked down at my game sheet, scribbled with words. *Thirty-something. No friends. New woman in town. Changes everything.*

I glared at Anne, seeing her in a new way. It wasn't exactly good. *Changes everything.*

"Earth to Olivia." Jan was calling my name. "How many?"

I carefully folded the sheet containing the scrambled words and slipped it into my pocket. "Sorry, Jan, I blanked out."

"But you were writing like mad. I thought for sure you were going for the win." Jan wasn't going to let me off the hook.

I pulled the paper out of my pocket and waved it at her. "Grocery list. Sorry." Maybe a diversion would work. "Aren't you supposed to serve lunch at these things?"

"Only after we find out who wins this bottle of baby lotion!" Jan squealed as though she were on a game show.

Anne was looking like Dr. Jekyll and Mr. Hyde, smiling at Jan, then turning my way, puzzling her eyebrows and giving me a *what's up?* look. I shook my head as if it were nothing. Nothing to her, anyway. Maybe everything to me. I didn't realize what everything was until much later.

Finally, Jan brought out Better than Dinosaur dessert, whispering she'd changed the name from Better than Sex cake for the sake of the kids, who were playing in the other room. In an attempt to be politically correct, Jan had placed a pink napkin under each cup and a blue napkin beside each plate on our trays, which we balanced precariously on our knees while making small talk. At least I had a topic for next week's column—"Baby, Oh, Baby!" It was about hating baby showers.

"I've got to get going." I started to get up. All I wanted was to get home and think. *Had Anne changed me that much? Who said I needed changing?*

"Just a minute," Jan announced, "one more game."

I groaned out loud.

Before Jan would let me leave, she forced us to go around the circle, each saying a name for a girl baby, or a boy. Everyone was trying to outdo the person before them. "Chantell, with two l's." "Phillipe, with an e on the end." Was this day never going to end? I was last and I'd had it. "Dick and Jane," I said bluntly.

Jan called me a party pooper.

Anne smiled and said, "I like Jane."

Anne

For a week after the baby shower, Libby acted kind of funny around me. She still drove me to my doctor appointment; this time it was just a baby check. The fun kind of appointment. But it wasn't that fun. Libby seemed to be preoccupied, wishing she were somewhere else. Usually I could tease her into playing, "What If..." But she would have nothing to do with the game that day. When Libby dropped me off at my house, rather than turn off the car and come in for a quick visit, she never even shifted out of drive.

"Thanks for driving." My thanks was answered with a polite nod. I felt weird. "Let me pay you for the gas."

Instead of her usual, "Absolutely not." Libby said, "That's okay. See you."

It didn't take a rocket scientist to know it was time to get out of the car, but I couldn't leave without trying to clear the air. "Is something wrong, Libby?"

She shook her head, hands on the wheel. "I have some thinking to do." She didn't look at me.

"Is Brian acting up again?"

"No."

"What about Bob? Has he told you anything about work?"

"No."

"Emily?"

"Uh-uh."

"Well, what?"

Libby stared out the side window and sighed, "It's about you, Anne." Her voice sounded low and hard.

"Me?" My voice came out a high pitched squeal. I actually pointed at myself. I had no idea why she would have to think about me. I was the least of her worries. My cancer was gone; my baby was fine. What was there to think about?

"Yes, you." Libby shifted into park, but didn't turn toward me. "I'm not so sure I like what you've been doing to me."

"What I've been doing to you." I repeated the words, not making a question out of them. I sounded clueless. I was.

"You know, all those religious things you say all the time. Sometimes I feel as if you don't think I measure up to your standards, as if you're trying to change me. I'm not sure I need to change, or want to."

"I haven't been trying to change you." I sounded defensive, but it was true. I had never tried to change Libby.

Libby looked at me now, eyebrow raised, a self-righteous glint in her eye. "It may surprise you to know I had a fine life even before we started spending so much time together—"

"Libby," I interrupted her, "you don't have to spend this much time with me. I thought you wanted to. I mean, I thought we were having fun. I can certainly go to my appointments by myself, I—"

She cut me off mid-sentence in her no-nonsense way. "Anne, I really didn't want to get into this now. As I said, I need to think about things."

I felt I should apologize, but I had no idea for what. "Libby, I'm sorry if I gave you the impression you weren't good enough, or something. That is the exact opposite of what I think of you. You've got all these goals you want to accomplish, like your writing. I admire you so much—I thought you knew that. I mean, I pray all the time that you'll write a…ooops, I wasn't supposed to say pray, I suppose."

Libby gave me a see-what-I-mean smile and said, "I'll call you."

But she didn't. When I called her she seemed pleasant enough, casually answering my questions, but even then she sounded remote, as though she wanted to get off the phone and do something else. She didn't bring up any conversation of her own, and when I'd ask her, "What's up?" I'd get a cool sounding, "Nothing new here" back.

During Emily's piano lesson at the end of the week I nonchalantly tried to ask if there was something more going on with her mother. I didn't dare ask too many questions—I didn't want to worry

Emily, and I knew she repeated practically everything we talked about right back to Libby. At least she used to. But then, even Emily had been acting differently lately.

"How's your mom?" I thought I sounded casual enough.

"Fine."

I gave her a strange look, but this was certainly different than the whole-paragraph-in-one-breath answers she used to give me.

"Has she been writing her column today?"

"Yeah." Silence.

"Okaaaay, how's your dad?"

"At work." More silence.

"And Brian?"

She shot me a worried glance, then quickly looked down at the piano keys. "Crabby."

"What about you?"

She shrugged her shoulders. "Okay, I guess."

"Is there something wrong, Emily?" I rubbed her back with my hand.

Again, she shrugged her shoulders, blinking her eyes rapidly.

"Do you want to talk about anything?"

A tear dropped from her eye onto the piano key. We stared at it. She shook her head.

I couldn't force the words from her, and this was supposed to be a piano lesson, so I asked her to play her next piece. It was an upbeat little number and seemed to change Emily's mood. When she finished, Emily took a big, shaky breath and said, "It's my mom's birthday tomorrow."

Well, this news floored me. Libby hadn't breathed a word, not even back when she had been voluntarily speaking to me. Birthdays have always been a big deal to me. Maybe it's because I'd shared a birthday with Andrea. We always had two cakes and were allowed to choose whatever we wanted to eat for dinner. Even if we each picked different things, Mom made sure we got our wish. We were also allowed to invite friends over, one friend for each year of our age. Luckily for my folks, Andrea and I tended to have the same friends, so even though the potential was there for us to have twenty kids at our tenth birthday, there were only eleven, counting us. Birthdays were special. I couldn't believe Libby hadn't hinted hers was coming up.

"Are you sure?" I questioned Emily, "I know Brian has a birthday soon."

"It was yesterday."

"Oh!" Libby hadn't said a word when I'd called her. "Did you do anything special?"

"No." Emily's mood had changed again. "Mom baked him a cake, but he got mad when we were eating supper. He wouldn't eat any." She sighed. "It wasn't very good, anyway."

That didn't surprise me, nothing tastes good when you're having a fight.

"Just because Brian's birthday was no fun doesn't mean we can't do something to make your mom's birthday special, does it?"

Emily brightened. "No-oo." Then added hesitantly, "We never do anything for Mom's birthday. She doesn't like it."

"Doesn't like a birthday? I've never heard of that."

"She says it's just like any other day after you turn, like, twenty, or something."

"That's too bad. But she can't stop us if she doesn't know about it, can she?"

Emily grinned. "Nope."

"What should we do?"

"Well-ll," Emily thought for a moment, then the words fairly burst from her, "We could play games, and have a cake, and maybe some presents!" She paused for a breath. "Except I don't have much money, and I don't know how to bake a cake, and I really don't think we should invite a bunch of people because I don't think Mom has that many friends, except for you. And I don't know what kind of games grown-ups like to play..." Her voice trailed off, it sounded as if she was talking herself out of a party. "Maybe Mom won't like this."

"We'll just make her like it." I was beginning to think this wasn't such a good idea, considering how cool Libby had been. But Emily was sounding more like her normal self, and I didn't want to disappoint her. I'd come to the conclusion Libby was preoccupied with her family problems and didn't want to talk about them, so I was trying not to take her coolness personally.

I should have.

Emily and I concocted a plan. When Libby came to pick Emily up, we would tell Libby that Emily needed a special lesson tomorrow to prepare for…prepare for what? We ran into a mental block. Emily came up with the idea—an end-of-summer recital.

"It's a great idea, Anne!" she sounded like the old Emily. "We could tell Mom it's only for your very best students, and that would mean me. We could tell her it'll be very fancy." She waved her hand in the air with a *la-ti-da* flair. "And we could tell her, like, you're going to serve tea, and stuff, and—"

"Just a minute, Miss Carrying-This-A-Bit-Too-Far. Remember, there really isn't going to be a recital—this is just a way to surprise your mom."

"Oh yeah," Emily giggled, "I guess I kinda forgot. But we could tell her that stuff anyway, couldn't we?"

I'd never heard of an end-of-summer recital, but it seemed a good enough ruse. "Sure," I agreed as Libby pulled up in front of the house.

Emily started playing scales, trying to make it look as though this was just a regular old lesson, while we waited for Libby to come in.

Emily played, and played, and played. She looked over her shoulder, glancing nervously out the window, missing a couple notes in the effort. "Whoops." She smiled my way.

I motioned for her to keep playing, then looked over my shoulder, too.

Libby was sitting in the car. Staring straight ahead.

Emily played some more, finally quitting in the middle of a scale. "Isn't Mom coming in to get me?"

I could feel the icy brush-off from my piano bench in my July-heated house. "I think your mom is really busy today," I explained.

"You'd better run on out there so she can get back to writing her column." I tried hard to sound convincing.

"Okay," her voice held a note of question. "We're still going to have the surprise for my mom, right?"

"Oh, yes!" I could hear the false enthusiasm in my voice. "Be sure and tell her about the end-of-summer recital." I tried to wink, but both my eyes blinked instead.

"See you tomorrow." Even Emily was losing enthusiasm for our impromptu party.

I watched from a corner of my window as Libby drove off without a backward glance.

Oh Lord, I silently prayed, *bring healing to Libby's hurting heart...and mine.*

I didn't know what else to do.

Olivia

I sat in the car outside Anne's house, wishing I knew what was the matter with me. For the past months I'd looked forward to picking up Emily from piano, viewing it not as a duty, but as more time to visit Anne. Now, I felt there was a thick wall between my car and Anne's front door. The steering wheel was like a magnet, holding my hands tightly in its circle as if by an invisible force. I couldn't, I wouldn't go into Anne's house. Ever since that stupid baby shower, I felt everything had changed between Anne and me. I hadn't even realized my life had been different since I'd met Anne, until I looked down at that dumb game sheet and saw the words "changes everything." My life didn't need changing. I'd never had a close friend before and I'd been just fine.

Sitting at the shower, I'd suddenly realized how much I'd been depending on Anne for listening, advice, whatever. I didn't need Anne to help me live my life. When I reviewed the past months, I realized just how much time she'd been taking out of my life. It was no wonder I never had time to work on my writing. Or that I hardly spoke to my husband anymore. Or that my family was falling apart. Now that Anne's cancer was gone, I decided I was going to have to pull away from her. I was going to find time to start my novel, once and for all. If my life was going to change, it was going to be me who changed it, not Anne. Not that it ever really needed changing.

I knew what I'd decided might be hard. Anne depended on me, too. Good grief, the woman couldn't even drive herself to the doctor without my help. She was going to have to grow up. I had a life of my own to live.

Emily swung open the car door and hopped in. I knew something was up the minute I heard her voice.

"Mom, guess what?" Her voice held a high note that sounded false to my ears. "Anne is having an end-of-summer recital for her very best students, and she said I'm, like, one of them."

Emily looked at me as if she expected me to correct her. I knew Emily had improved her piano skills dramatically, but one of Anne's best? I doubted it. "Just when is this recital?"

"Oh, ummm, it's, uhhh…" Emily bit her bottom lip, then said with a question in her voice, "it's, uhhh, the end of summer, I guess?"

"Oh?" I raised an eyebrow at her. I could see the wheels turning in her head.

"Mo-om, she didn't tell me the exact date. I'm sure she's going to send out, like, invitations or something."

"Or something?"

"Mom, she didn't tell me everything. Anne just asked if I could come over for a special practice tomorrow." Emily was starting to sound annoyed.

I didn't know what they had going on, but whatever it was seemed harmless enough. If Anne wanted to have Emily for company tomorrow, she could have her. Emily certainly hadn't been company material around our house for a long time. Let Anne put up with her for the day. Besides, I could use the time. I had a novel to start writing.

I'd been waiting for a call from Emily to let me know what time to pick her up from Anne's, so I was surprised when the doorbell rang around four o'clock. I wasn't expecting anyone. I'd been staring at a blank computer screen for most of the afternoon, unable to conjure up any words other than "she changed everything." The sound of the doorbell was a welcome relief. I opened the door to find Emily and Anne standing on my doorstep, grinning.

"Happy birthday, Mom!" Emily was bouncing up and down on her toes, practically juggling a small, beautifully wrapped, rectangular box from hand to hand.

"Happy birthday, Libby." Anne held out a chocolate cake.

"What's this?" I forced myself to sound excited for Emily's sake; inside I was steaming. Who did Anne think she was to *lie* in order to get my daughter over to her house? Was Anne trying to change my daughter, too? Emily knew I didn't care for birthday celebrations, especially my own. My birthday was an event I'd tried to ignore since the year I turned twelve. That was the year my mother baked me a birthday cake, telling me I could cut it as soon as my dad got home. He never did come home that night. At least not while I was awake. That was the night I learned I couldn't depend on anyone except myself. It was made clear to me that birthdays, especially my birthday, weren't all that special.

"...Happy birthday dear Mom...Libby...Happy birthday to you-oooo!" Emily and Anne burst out laughing. I'm sure they thought I was surprised instead of mad. I tried to play along.

"For a music teacher, I think you could use some lessons." I'd meant to sound funny, but instead my words came out sounding mean. Emily didn't seem to notice. Anne did. She gave me an apologetic smile. I didn't need Anne to try to make this day seem special. I knew better.

"Emily told me it was your birthday. We thought it would be a nice surprise to bake you a cake." There was an apologetic tone in Anne's voice that Emily picked up on.

"Mom? Aren't you surprised?" Emily was looking at me, a worried expression on her face.

"Oh yes, I'm surprised all right." I seemed to have no control over the tone of my voice. It came out sounding icy.

"Mom, you're not being very polite." Emily pushed her way past me and walked into the kitchen. Anne and I followed like wooden puppets.

I was beginning to feel sick. I imagined their afternoon, spilling flour, licking frosting, laughing over how happy they were going to make me. I thought of Anne wrapping that gift, probably having Emily put her finger on the silver ribbon while she tied the elaborate bow. I'd ruined their surprise, and I couldn't think of a way to salvage it. I wasn't even sure I wanted to, and that thought made me feel worse. What kind of person was I?

Emily opened the cupboard door and removed three plates, but already the excitement had faded from her voice. "We'll just use the everyday plates, okay, Mom?"

"Just get two out—I'm not very hungry." I couldn't believe what I was saying. It was as though some evil twin had taken over my body, determined to make this the worst day possible.

Emily froze, then pushed the plates back into the cupboard. "I guess I'm not hungry, either." I could hear tears in her throat. "Anne, could we just save the cake for when my dad and Brian get home?"

My ten-year-old daughter was acting more mature than I was.

"Sure." Anne sat the cake in the center of the table. "I'd better get home." She walked over and rubbed Emily's back. "You were a good baker today."

Emily nodded. I could see her biting the insides of her cheeks, chin quivering.

"Happy birthday, Libby." Anne closed the door behind her.

The minute the door closed Emily screamed, "You spoiled everything!" She ran toward the stairs, tears streaming down her cheeks. At the top of the steps she turned, flinging the present to the floor. "Here's your stupid present. I *hate* you." The door to her room slammed hard, shutting me out.

I hated me, too.

Anne

For the life of me, I could not figure out what I'd done to make Libby so upset with me. I'd sat down and tried to analyze every event and conversation I could remember, but nothing made sense. There had to be more to Libby's cool mood than the few religious things, as she'd called them, I'd said to her.

It bothered me so much that I explained it all to Kevin. How Libby had come to my rescue at the baby shower horror story session. How, even though Libby didn't like to play games, she had convinced Jan to start the games instead of listening to everyone's terrible stories. And how we had been laughing and having fun. Toward the end of the shower, I could tell Libby wanted to get going, but so did I, and it was my shower. Four hours is a long time to sit even when you're not pregnant. But on the way home, Libby seemed cool and distracted, and she had been that way ever since. I couldn't figure out what had happened.

Kevin, in his typical deal-with-it style, said, "Ask her."

"I did! What she said didn't make any sense."

"Then ask her again."

"Kevin, there is no way I can ask her; she's hardly speaking to me."

"Well then, give her some space. It'll blow over."

Arrrggghhh! Men! Kevin thought these things were so simple. I couldn't just ask her, and waiting was going to drive me crazy. How could anything change if we couldn't talk about it?

I played the birthday scene over and over in my mind. I couldn't believe how what was supposed to be a gloriously fun surprise had turned so bad. For now, there was nothing I could do but wait and pray.

In the meantime, I went about my normal routine as much as possible without Libby. She had become part of my days. A quick call in the morning to see what was on my schedule. A longer gab session in the afternoon, or a visit at one of our houses. And the doctor appointments she'd volunteered to drive me to were a good excuse to spend more time talking.

The dog days of summer dragged by. My days were full, tending my garden and teaching piano lessons, but they seemed empty. I missed Libby.

But, chauffeur or not, I still needed to see the doctor. My baby was to be born in a month, and I needed a checkup. I drove myself, carefully, quietly.

As usual the clinic was crowded. I knew it would be a long wait. I used to bring a book along to help pass the time, but ever since Libby had started accompanying me to my appointments, I hadn't brought one along. Between our nonstop gabbing, or playing "What If…," I hadn't needed one. Now I was stuck without Libby or a book. The magazines were old and so thumbed-through that they looked dirty. A rack of brochures stood on the table near me. "Dealing with Eating Disorders." "Drug Use: Signs and Symptoms." "Depression in Women." "Prostate Cancer." I closed my eyes and picked one. The minute I'd read the last word, my name was called. Heart pounding, I stuffed the brochure into my pocket and followed the nurse.

I should have grabbed all the brochures. I undressed in the small room and waited, and waited, and waited. I reread the brochure, a feeling of uneasiness filling me. Finally I heard rustling as my chart was removed from outside the door.

"Good morning, Anne." Dr. Lebalm greeted me. "Where's your friend this morning?"

I wasn't prepared for him to ask about Libby and felt my palms turn sweaty. He'd always sort of ignored her before. It seemed he didn't even notice she was with me most of the time. I felt nervous. I didn't want to lie, but blurting out, "*We had a fight, but I don't know what it was about,*" seemed more like something I should say to a psychiatrist, not a baby doctor. "I think she was busy today."

He nodded and looked at my chart. "Okay then, why don't we have you lay back so I can examine you."

I lay down, my mind grasping at Dr. Lebalm's question about Libby. He didn't care where Libby was, he was just making conversation. Why was I making a federal case about this? Maybe it was Libby who should be agonizing, not me. As far as I knew, I had done nothing wrong. But the couple of glimpses I'd had of Libby in the past few weeks had made it seem as if I'd turned into someone she used to know, someone she barely recalled now. She had been cordial, but remote. It didn't seem to me that she was doing much agonizing.

Dr. Lebalm's nurse stepped into the room while he checked me. She attempted the usual "I bet you're really excited about the baby" conversation, but my mind was preoccupied with the falling out between Libby and me, and I didn't sound very excited. Eventually she quit talking.

"Okay, Anne," Dr. Lebalm took off his gloves, "I want to do a quick breast exam, considering..." Everyone, even my doctor, had trouble saying the word cancer. He opened the front of my gown and ran his hand gently along my surgical scar, giving a satisfied nod. He murmured, almost to himself, "She did a nice job." Then he covered up my right side and uncovered the left. His hands were warm as he gently examined my remaining breast. He kept his eyes focused somewhere far off and asked me, "When did you finish your last chemo treatment?"

"About two months ago." I glanced over at the nurse, who seemed to be busy studying my chart.

"Hmmmm." Dr. Lebalm's fingers probed deeper under my arm, then went back to the inside edge of my breast. "I don't like what I'm feeling here." He walked over and flipped through my chart, then came back and examined the spot once again. "If you just completed your chemo, then I shouldn't feel anything. But I definitely feel a small density right here."

Instinctively, my hand reached toward the spot, and Dr. Lebalm took my fingers and guided them over my skin. A freezing tingling sensation swept through my body as I felt the small but definite lump.

It felt just like the other lump I'd had. My eyes must have frozen wide-eyed on Dr. Lebalm's face, because he gave me a gentle look and remarked, "Let's get Dr. Barrows in here and get his opinion right away. Nurse, could you page Dr. Barrows?"

Wouldn't you know it…the one time I'd rather wait an eternity for the doctor to see me, he shows up like a magician's rabbit? Out of nowhere.

Dr. Barrows, with his typical lack of bedside manner, examined me and then stated, "That's got to come out."

The one time when I could have really used a driver, I didn't have one. I thought of calling Kevin, but he was somewhere down the road by now. I thought of calling Libby, but couldn't bring myself to dial the numbers. I knew what people meant when they said, "You can only count on yourself." I took a deep, steadying breath, climbed behind the wheel, and prayed my way home.

Olivia

It was as if some writing curse had fallen on me. I'd heard of writer's block, but this was more like writer's Alzheimer's. I couldn't think of a thing to write about—not even for my weekly column. For the first time ever, I missed a deadline. The *Brewster Banner* editor called and told me he'd fill in with some wire service copy, but he didn't sound too happy about it. I sat and stared at the computer screen. It was blank, just like my mind.

The beautifully wrapped present Anne had given me sat on a shelf above my computer, mocking me every time I glanced up. I didn't have any desire to open it. I didn't deserve a present for the way I'd acted.

All of my life, whenever I had a problem to think about or an important decision to make, the only way for me to focus, to make sense of things, was to write. Sometimes I wrote in my journal. Sometimes I wrote a never-to-be-sent letter. Sometimes I made lists. Pro. Con. This time none of those methods worked. It was as if words had abandoned me.

Most days I sat and simply stared at the computer screen. The words, which had always been there for me, wouldn't come. I didn't know where to start, what to write about, what the problem was I was trying to solve, or if there even was one. As for trying to plot a novel—forget it.

I was spending another wordless afternoon at my computer when Emily poked her head into the room. "Mom, Anne's here."

I hadn't heard the doorbell ring, but Emily's words, "Anne's here," made my heart start beating as though a gong had sounded. What could she want? It had been at least a couple of weeks since we'd talked.

I walked out and met Anne by the door. In the weeks since I'd seen her, the baby had grown; Anne looked ready to burst. Memories of Anne's surgery and chemotherapy flashed through my mind, and I felt a wave of compassion for her. I quickly stifled it—I wasn't going to let her play on my sympathy. She was fine now, and she would soon be having her baby. I'd had two and handled it by myself. Anne could, too. I was going to be busy writing a novel and getting my family back on track. I didn't have the time being friends with Anne took.

Emily must have sensed the tension between us, because she quickly announced, "I'm going to go ride my bike for a while."

The door slammed and we stood there in silence.

"Could we sit down? Standing's not my best position these days." Anne smiled and looked toward the kitchen.

Without answering, I turned and walked to the table, pulling out my usual chair. Anne sat across from me the way she had when we shared afternoons of coffee and visiting. This afternoon felt different. The friendly camaraderie that had peppered our time together had vanished. We were left with silence.

"Libby," Anne cleared her throat, "I feel as though I should apologize, except I don't know what I've done. Could you tell me?"

I felt something like a shield fall into place, creating a distance between Anne and any emotion I might feel toward her. "You haven't done anything." My voice was flat and unconvincing.

"Well then, why do I feel such a...such a...oh, I don't know," Anne waved her hands, palms out, like an invisible wall. "...a *barrier* between us?"

"There isn't a barrier between us." I sounded like a parrot repeating what she'd said. Words were failing me still.

"Okay, let me start again." Anne took a deep breath, "Ever since Jan's baby shower, I've felt as if there's something wrong. I've tried to figure out if I did anything that could've possibly hurt you, and I just don't know what it could be. I know you said you wanted to do some thinking about things...about me. I've been thinking, too, and I can't figure out what I did wrong." Anne gave a little laugh, as though this problem would evaporate and be gone in a minute. "It's driving me crazy."

"You're not crazy, Anne." There was that parrot thing again.

"Well, then what is going on?" It was the loudest I'd ever heard Anne speak, and it startled me.

"Nothing." It was a cop-out and I knew it.

Anne's voice softened. She held both hands palms up on the table as if she was cradling something special. "Okay, let me just say what I came here for. I came here today to tell you two things, Libby. One is that I've missed y—"

"It's *Olivia*. Haven't you figured that out by now?" I was the Ice Queen.

"Olivia?"

"Yes, my name. It's Olivia. Not Libby, like your dead cat." It was as though I was taking out all my frustration about not being able to write and all the pain I'd been feeling over the way my family was falling apart on Anne, the only person I knew who truly cared. Yet, I couldn't stop myself.

"Oh." Anne pushed out her chair and stood, awkwardly. She looked near tears. "I thought you liked being called Libby—you know, a name *special* friends call you— oh." She turned slowly and started for the door.

"Listen, Anne," I was talking to her back, "here's the deal." I took a deep breath, not sure what I was going to say as she turned to face me. "I know you've been through a rough time these past couple months, but I've got problems in my life too, of which you're all too aware. I've spent the past few months driving you to the doctor and neglecting my family." It looked like Anne winced, and it made me defensive. "Hey, I know my family isn't in the greatest shape, you don't have to make faces at me—"

"I wasn't making—"

"I saw you, Anne. You gave me this poor-thing-her-family-is-falling-apart look."

"Lib—Olivia, I didn't…I was just…"

"Listen to me, Anne, I am so sick and tired of your do-good, righteous attitude. You've taken me on as your little project, trying to get me to change to be more like you. What if I tell you I don't want to be like you?" My voice was rising in anger. "You've been pushing me to be different since the day we met. You even changed my name, as if Olivia wasn't good enough. You've been pushing me to write—"

"Pushing you to *write?*" Anne sounded incredulous.

"With that stupid "What If…" game of yours." My voice took on a singsong tone. "What-if-you-wrote-a-book-what-would-you-call-it?"

"Libby—Olivia, it was just a game. I thought you wanted to write."

"And then…" words weren't failing me anymore—they poured out of my mouth as if Anne hadn't spoken. "You used a lie to get Emily over to your house. What? You thought birthday plans I made for myself wouldn't be good enough?"

"You have things so wrong."

I didn't even stop for a breath, talking right over Anne's words. "You got me to tell you everything, every worry, every problem, then you gave me your pat, churchy answers. 'I'll pray for you.' I don't need your prayers, Anne. I don't need your God, either. I don't need anybody. I'm happy just the way I am." I sure didn't sound happy.

"I'll be going home now, Libby. I'm sorry for whatever's making you feel like this."

That made me mad too, but I didn't have the energy to argue, or to correct my name. Anne walked out the door.

"Hey Anne," I called after her, "as long as we're getting it all out, you said you were going to tell me two things. What's the other one?"

Anne turned, reached into her pocket and pulled out a crumpled-looking brochure. She held it out, looking straight at me, a pained expression on her face. "I think Brian is using drugs."

Anne

On the drive home, Libby's parting words rang in my ears, "Leave. Now." She'd said them in a breath so low I could barely hear her. I'd tried to give Libby the brochure on drugs I'd picked up while waiting for the doctor, but she wouldn't extend her hand to take it. I finally laid it at her feet on the porch steps and left, as she'd asked.

I wished Libby had given me a chance to explain. Reading that brochure had been like reading a list of all the behaviors Libby had been complaining about in Brian for the past months: moodiness, dropping grades, different friends. It all added up. It's not as if I'm Nancy Drew, but when all the clues are placed in front of you, a light bulb goes on, and you can't help but notice the truth.

I was hoping I was wrong, but if I was right, then it would explain a lot of things about Brian's behavior. Libby and Bob could get Brian some help. Just maybe it would help their whole family situation, once they realized what they were dealing with.

I didn't breathe a word of what I'd discovered at the doctor's office about Brian to Kevin. After all, it was just a suspicion at that point. But I did tell Kevin about my appointment with Dr. Lebalm, that he had called in Dr. Barrows, and that they now thought the cancer was in my right breast. Kevin took the news matter-of-factly, nodding as though he were listening to an important business discussion. I explained that they wanted to do another biopsy next week.

"So we're looking at what?" Kevin asked. "An outpatient procedure early next week? And if it is…uh, like the last time, then what?"

"Dr. Barrows didn't say, but I suppose it would be kind of like the other one. Surgery and chemotherapy." My words sounded more like a question. It seemed unreal to be sitting in my living room on my worn-out couch (a hand-me-down from Kevin's college years), talking about another round of chemotherapy. When were we going to be able to enjoy the fact that we were going to have a baby? For a fleeting moment, I wondered what other couples talked about when they were eight-months pregnant. Certainly not an upcoming chemotherapy regimen. I reminded myself not to jump to conclusions; the doctors didn't know for a fact this new lump was cancer.

After our discussion, Kevin was unusually quiet. He didn't turn on the television to watch his nightly sports programs. I was so unused to the quiet, I finally got up and turned it on. As I walked back to my spot, Kevin patted the couch, motioning me to sit close beside him. I snuggled in and we sat together for a couple hours. I don't think either of us could say what we watched. We were each lost in our own thoughts.

I don't know what Kevin was thinking about—my cancer, I'd guess. But I remember clearly what I was thinking—Libby. Olivia. I was having a hard time remembering to call her that. You'd think, after the conversation we'd had, I would have been glad to wash my hands of her for good. But for some reason, I couldn't get her out of my mind. There was something I was missing. No, actually, it was something she was missing, and for some unknown reason God had decided I was the one to show her what it was—even if neither Olivia, nor I, knew what "it" was. I truly was asking, *Why me, Lord?*

What I did know, however, was that I needed to stay away from Libby—Olivia, for now. I knew she probably had her hands full at home. I hoped that she was at least dealing with the problem. I, however, was going to have to wait. For what, I wasn't quite sure.

Olivia

For a long time after Anne walked down the sidewalk that day, I'd stood frozen to my spot on the porch, gazing down at the crumpled brochure as if it were a ticking bomb. Finally, I bent down and picked it up, crushing it in my hands as if it were a hard-packed snowball, but there was no one to throw it at. I was stunned by Anne's accusation. I was also mad. How dare she accuse my son of using drugs? So what if Brian was moody, had made some new friends, and didn't especially care for school these days? Half the fifteen-year-olds I knew were exactly like him. It didn't mean they were on drugs.

I went back to my computer, spiking the brochure into the garbage, determined to channel my anger into something productive. Forty-five minutes later, I was staring at a blank screen, pictures of Anne, Brian, and that crumpled brochure swimming in my mind's eye. I pulled the pamphlet from the garbage, smoothing it as best I could. I knew there was absolutely no foundation to Anne's belief, but I found myself reading the information anyway. Good grief! It described just about every teenager I knew. I tossed it back into the garbage and turned to write my column. As usual, I sat and stared, my mind as blank as the screen.

Without meaning to, I found myself monitoring Brian's behavior, matching it to the symptoms the brochure had mentioned. Each time I found myself mentally saying, *maybe,* I'd quickly explain away his behavior as normal teenage obnoxiousness.

"Hey, Brian," I casually called when he sauntered in a few minutes before supper one night. "What've you been up to?" I added a can of tomatoes to the hamburger I had browning on the stove.

Brian flashed me an irritated look, as if he was mad I was making his favorite casserole. "Nothing," he mumbled.

I tried to hide my irritation at his vagueness; maybe I could humor it out of him. "Who were you doing nothing with?"

"Nobody." He kicked off his tennis shoes and headed for his room.

So okay, that conversation meant Brian was using drugs, huh? I remembered having the exact conversation with my parents twenty years ago. I turned to the stove, knowing Anne was wrong.

Just then the phone rang. "Hello, Lib—Olivia, it's Anne."

She'd never identified herself before, but just said, "Hiiii-yiii!" and kept on talking. Now she sounded tentative. "I'm sorry to bother you at suppertime."

What was it about her voice? Just hearing her made my heart pound as if I were nervous. "That's okay, we're not eating yet." I tried to keep my voice even, but if she said one word about Brian, I was going to let her know how I felt about her accusation.

"Uh, I'm calling about Emily's piano lesson. I'm going to have to cancel it next week." She paused and I could hear her taking a deep breath. "Something's come up."

It was on the tip of my tongue to ask, "What?" Only weeks ago, I wouldn't have had to ask—Anne would have told me, unprompted. There was an unnatural silence as she waited for my response.

I drained boiling water from the pasta and added it to the hot dish. "Okay."

It was as if an iceberg had taken up residence inside me. I knew my attitude toward Anne was out of proportion to anything she'd ever said to me, but there was a stubborn block of ice that had frozen my tongue, frozen my mind, refusing to let her into my life. Ever since my outburst at Anne, I felt a heaviness inside me, an unsettled feeling that had left me anxious and angry. I found myself blaming Anne for my inability to write, for my recent distrust of Brian, and even for the lack of communication I'd had with Bob these past months. If Anne was out of the picture, then maybe my problems would be as well.

"I'll tell Emily." I placed a cover over the casserole and turned down the heat.

"Sorry for having to cancel."

There was something in Anne's tone that made me want to ask if she was okay, if the baby was fine…but my words were stuck beneath the ice, and stayed there, unspoken.

As I hung up the phone a quick shudder passed through me. Pushing the feeling aside, I called the kids to eat. Bob would have to microwave his dinner later.

The casserole tasted lousy, and Brian didn't hesitate to tell me.

Anne

How could such a simple phone call bring on such a flood of tears? I'd called to cancel Emily's piano lesson because my biopsy was scheduled to be the same day as her lesson. I'd never expected the call to turn into an emotional minefield. I'd hung up the phone, sunk onto the couch, and cried as if I'd just lost my best friend.

Oh.

I'd cried harder.

What had I done to Libby that would make her act this way toward me? Had I asked too much of her? I knew the past months had taken a toll on both of us. Libby had invested a huge amount of time driving to and from the doctor's office, not to mention all of the time spent simply waiting for my appointments. Maybe that was it—I had been too much of a burden on Libby, demanding too much of her time, her attention. Time she could've spent at home, tending her family, writing. Maybe it was me, after all. Libby had been afraid to tell me, and it came out as resentment.

When I thought of the situation that way, it made sense. I didn't like it, but sometimes the truth hurts. I'd been a demanding friend and hadn't realized it. The more I thought about the past months, the more I understood there was a part of myself I hadn't known existed. There I sat, face-to-face with a person who could be self-absorbed, a person who could take advantage of someone without knowing it.

Kevin was right when he said I needed to give Libby some time and space. I could see now that I'd been smothering her with my needs. Taking away time she needed for herself and her family. How could I have been so blind? I laughed as I saw myself as a parody of *The Brady Bunch.* Sister Jan, whining, "It's always Marcia, Marcia, Marcia." I'd been acting as though it were "Anne, Anne, Anne."

143

I felt a great weight lift from my heart. I now knew why Libby had been acting as she had toward me. And that I could change. I was determined to learn from this situation. I was going to become more independent. I was going to be more sensitive to the needs of others. Maybe I did owe Libby an apology. Of course I did. It was all my fault.

Olivia

It was not Anne's fault, that much I knew. But for some reason, I was taking my jumbled emotions out on her. I had acted like a heel, and I felt like one, too. But I seemed helpless to change. I spent my days in front of the computer, brooding in silence.

I'd never been an introspective person. My way of dealing with emotions had been to ignore them, just like I did the time my dad forgot my birthday, or the day Mom told me Dad was sick. I didn't think about my feelings then, and I certainly wasn't going to think about them now. That was all in the past; what good could possibly come from rehashing it? Better to not think at all. Ignoring my emotions had always worked before.

But as I tried to blame Anne for the anger I was feeling, my harsh words washed over me as if I were a defenseless shell on a beach at high tide, pounding me again and again with feelings of guilt and shame. I knew the words I'd hurled at her had been heartless and uncalled for, but I thought it would be easier to forget them than to think about them. To act as though it had never happened, as if I'd never said those things. To pretend we'd never been friends. To act as if I didn't care. It didn't matter.

I tried.

Hard.

It didn't work.

I was left feeling agitated and out of sorts. My reaction to stress was to move. Do something. I was going through cleaning polish as if it were water. I realized my house was too clean when, for the second time in two weeks, I ran to the store for more dusting polish. I couldn't write—the column I'd put together last week was pathetic and I knew it. I prowled through the house as if I were a nervous cat looking for a place to hide. As a distraction, I turned on the television. A game show blared. I punched the remote and listened to the *Oprah* theme song, *Keep on workin', find out what waits for me.* Except for the occasional *Oprah* show, I'd quit watching talk shows years ago, disgusted by the parade of weird problems and people who felt the need to discuss theirs on national television. I flipped past, but somewhere within me the words of the song resonated, *Keep on workin', find out what waits for me.* Workin' at what? What could be waiting? I scrolled back. It was an intriguing concept, and I decided to see what Oprah had to talk about.

It was so unlike me, sitting down to watch a talk show in the middle of the day. I glanced around guiltily as if the talk show police were going to burst in at any moment. I felt like a lazy, brainless housewife. All I needed were bonbons to snack on.

Oprah appeared in a light blue, knit dress. She paused, waiting for the applause to die down before introducing her guest for the day, John Gray. The audience clapped wildly after Oprah explained that he was going to rid them of their emotional blocks.

Sure. In one hour.

Another guru with a book to sell. I ran the gamut, flipping through channels with the remote as if I were a testosterone-hyped sports fanatic. I ended up back at *Oprah*, the lesser of the evils. I crossed my arms across my chest and settled back with an "entertain-me" attitude.

Apparently, some of the people had been on the show before. There were short clips of previous appearances, of people telling their sad tales, tears streaming down their faces. Oprah was handing out tissues like candy. I flipped back to the game show, but the false enthusiasm was more than I could bear. I flipped back as a large chart of emotions filled the screen. Two words caught my eye. Blame. Anger.

John Gray's tenor voice spoke behind the graphic, asking questions I wasn't sure I wanted to answer. Was I someone who said, "It's not my fault! I didn't do that!" Did I always blame others for what happened to me?

I looked around my living room, wondering if this was my own, personal therapy session. Did he know he was describing me to a T?

Mr. Gray went on, telling me that if I was caught up in these emotions I needed to look deeper. Telling me there was always another, deeper emotion behind the blame and anger. Telling me to take time to *feel* the deeper emotion. It might be hurt. It might be abandonment. His voice continued, but I didn't hear it. I had been zapped back in time to my father's bedside.

"*Olivia*," my father's voice was weak, "*you're the oldest and you have to be strong for your mother.*"

I nodded, a stubborn sixteen-year-old who refused to cry at her dying father's bedside.

"You be sure the furnace has enough fuel in it."

Typical. My father was dying, and he was talking about the fuel gauge. Did this man ever have an actual emotion? He was going to be strong until the end. Mr. Stoicism. Mr. Keep Your Chin Up. Mr. Pull Yourself Up by Your Own Bootstraps.

All he needed me for was to be sure the house stayed warm.

Mom motioned that I should give my father a hug. It was time for me to go home and watch my brother while Mom kept vigil.

I leaned down and touched my cheek to his. I felt his arm try to move around me, not quite managing to get past my elbow. "Goodbye," he whispered in my ear.

Goodbye? Every time I'd left before he'd said, "Goodnight." This was new. I walked out of his room, tears clogging my throat. I wanted to run back, to throw myself over him and say, "I love you." Then tell him again and again. But I was a stubborn sixteen-year-old who would never let that sort of emotion get the better of her. I was just like my father. My dying father.

As I stumbled down the hall, I glanced into an empty room. All I wanted at that moment was to slip in, sink to the floor, and sob. But I was strong. I wouldn't cry. I took a deep breath, then another. I wouldn't cry. I wouldn't cry. I was a Willet, and Willets don't cry. I walked down the hall and out the door, my eyes dry. By the time I reached home, any tears I'd wanted to shed were safely stuffed in a tight corner of my heart. They stayed there later that night when Mom came home to tell my brother and me that our father had died.

The credits were rolling for the *Oprah* show. I jumped from the couch, stabbing the off button on the remote. I had to get supper started, or I was going to have an even crabbier family than normal.

Turning the burner on high, I dripped some oil into the pan and tossed in five pork chops. What had possessed me to think about my dad? I hadn't thought about that day in almost twenty years. Dad was dead, and that was that. I didn't think about it then, and I certainly didn't need to think about it now.

"Andrew, blow your nose." My brother was sniffling through the whole funeral and it bugged me. Didn't he know he looked weak wiping his nose like that? We were right up front and everyone was staring at us. There was no way I was going to let anyone see me cry. I was strong. I was a rock. I was—

What was wrong with me? I was burning pork chops.

Anne

I've always thought of fall as being more of a "new year" than January first.

There's something about the school year schedule that's imprinted on my mind, making September seem more the time for new beginnings than the actual new year. This year it was especially true. I was going to be a mom. I tried to ignore the fact that I was probably also going to be starting a new round of chemotherapy. I was forcing myself to wait until my biopsy to even think about that possibility. I also tried to forget that this was sort of the start of a new life, too—my life without Libby. Even after all she had said to me, I missed her, but I knew the time for us to renew any kind of friendship was in God's hands, not mine.

I couldn't help but think of Libby during my biopsy. It was scheduled for the same time as Emily's piano lesson, a time I always looked forward to. Emily had worked her way into my heart as firmly as Libby. It was hard to let go.

Kevin accompanied me to my biopsy appointment. I wasn't sure how much the doctor would sedate me for the procedure, and I knew they wouldn't let me drive home if I was at all groggy. Since I had no one else to rely on, Kevin was "it."

"How long is this going to take?" Kevin glanced at his watch as we drove around the parking lot, trying to find an empty space.

"I don't know; it depends on whether or not they're running on schedule. If they're on time, not too long, I suppose."

I was wrong. They were backed up, and each old magazine Kevin thumbed through seemed to make him more agitated.

"You'd think they'd know how to manage their time better." Kevin tossed a *Money* magazine onto the table and grabbed a two-month-old issue of *Time.* "Is it always like this?" Before I could answer he sputtered, "What time was your appointment, again?" He looked at his watch for the umpteenth time. Exasperated, I told him to drive back to Brewster and I would call him when I was done. Kevin realized the 40-mile drive would end up being just as much a waste of time as waiting, so he resigned himself to bad coffee and old magazines. It occurred to me to ask Kevin, "What If…?" but I knew he'd be harder to get an answer out of than Libby, and he wouldn't end up laughing as Libby and I always had.

I thought back to the many times Libby and I had sat here, passing time as if we were at a spa, waiting to be called for our manicures. What could have been a time of fear and dread had actually been kind of fun, if you could see past the cancer-thing. Today, I couldn't. A slow-rising panic rested behind my breastbone, threatening to press my very breath from me. I took a deep breath, then another, just to prove I could. Sometimes it seemed as if some other force was in control of my body instead of me. *Breathe Anne,* I could hear Libby encouraging me from some far off place. *Just breathe. Slowly, now…*I imagined she was here with me, breathing slowly, in, then out. I was surprisingly calm when the nurse finally called my name.

As usual the surgeon, Dr. Cleary, was noncommittal about what she suspected. "We'll have the lab results back sometime tomorrow. Try to relax, Anne." She touched my arm. "Worrying isn't going to change anything except your attitude. I'll call you as soon as I get the reports."

And she did.

They weren't good.

Olivia

I'd always looked forward to school starting. After a summer of having the kids underfoot, the prospect of having whole days to myself had always been marvelously appealing. This year, however, I found myself dreading the start of the school year. Even though Brian was still going through his "stage"—I refused to believe Anne's accusation—and battling a late summer cold to boot—complete with red, watery eyes and a runny nose, he didn't stop making it clear that his father and I weren't his favorite people in the world. You'd think I would have been glad to have him out of the house. But I wasn't. And, even though Emily had moped around the house like a sad sack half the summer, she'd occupied much of my days. Now, I was facing stretches of five days in a row when it would be just me and my roiling emotions alone for hours at a time. It was not a pretty picture.

My days developed a routine, of sorts. The morning was spent doing the usual chaotic rush to get the kids out the door, followed by an hour of cleaning up after them. After spending at least another hour downing a pot of coffee and reading every word of the newspaper, I forced myself to sit at my computer. I'd vowed to write my novel, and I was going to sit in that chair until I did it. I came to view that time as a new form of torture. Not a word entered my mind that was worth writing. My fingers seemed to be taken over by some weird sort of finger-numbing paralysis, and the coffee I drank ran through me like a sieve, sending me running to the bathroom with wear-a-path-in-the-carpet regularity. The only thing I could count on was my *Oprah* reprieve.

I was getting hooked on afternoon television. *Oprah*, anyway. It was the only time I allowed myself a break from my self-induced computer prison. I rationalized that my voyeurism was a way of nudging my brain into thinking. Maybe the people on her show would provide the nugget of a story idea—over-spending college students, sports stars with women problems, women with sports star problems, celebrities complaining about lack of privacy...all had a story.

But it wasn't my story to tell.

I found myself thinking about Anne, wondering what she was doing. Quickly, I forced those thoughts from my mind with a mental reprimand: "Stop it!" And just when I thought I'd exorcised any remaining thoughts about Anne from my mind, I'd glance up and see that stupid birthday gift sitting on the shelf above my computer. I had no desire to open it, but was helpless to move it. Refocusing on Gwynth Paltrow telling Oprah her life story, I shoved any curiosity I had about Anne, any lonely feelings that might have been creeping around, back where they belonged—in that tight corner of my over-stuffed heart.

Anne

Apparently, a team of doctors consulted with Dr. Cleary about my case before she called me with my biopsy results. It seemed strange that these people—Dr. Lebalm, Dr. Barrows, Dr. Cleary, and some unnamed physicians from the Mayo Clinic—all knew my fate before I did. It didn't seem like a good sign to me.

"Anne?" Dr. Cleary's always-calm voice comforted me even before I knew what she had to say.

I should've figured the news wasn't good. By now I'd learned that if the reports were fine, then a nurse called with the results (not that I'd had many of those calls). But a call from the doctor meant bad news. For sure. I held my breath.

"I'm afraid the cancer is back," Dr. Cleary explained softly.

"Ohhh." I'd been preparing for this report, but it made me feel breathless just the same.

"Anne, I went ahead and talked to your other doctors, and Dr. Barrows contacted some colleagues down at Mayo. I'm sure you know your case is quite unusual. 'Highly aggressive' is the what the Mayo Clinic people called it. We're going to be sending your reports to a doctor…" She paused, and I could hear her going through papers, "…Doctor Adams. He's an oncologist, specializing in breast cancer research. At this point we need to get on top of things, and he agreed to see you next week."

"Next week?" My mind raced, thinking of all I'd have to do to get ready for the long trip to Rochester, of all Kevin would have to do to rearrange his schedule.

"I have a baby checkup appointment next week, and my husband has clients to see, and my piano lessons…I don't know if I can—"

"Anne," Dr. Cleary interrupted my rambling, "you need to do this. Part of the reason we want you to go to Rochester is the fact that you're going to have your baby soon. Frankly, we don't feel we have the experience here to give you the best advice on your next course of treatment. The doctors in Rochester have dealt with this situation before and will be better equipped to give you sound advice. Our staff is working on setting up your appointment. They'll call you with the details later today." Dr. Cleary paused; I could hear her take a deep breath and blow it out slowly, as though she was meditating. "Good luck to you, Anne."

I know she meant them in a good way, but her words, "Good luck to you, Anne," filled me with fear. It felt as if I was going to need a lot more than luck.

"Oh, Lord," I prayed, "I need a friend."

Wonders never cease. The start of the school year seemed to bring a welcome change in Brian. Maybe being a sophomore made him feel more mature. I didn't know what it was, but I wasn't about to question him. All of a sudden he cleaned up his act, so to speak, actually speaking in civil tones to all of us. He spent, according to Emily, "hours" in the bathroom "getting pretty." That comment usually resulted in a quick punch to her arm from Brian and a loud wail from Emily, but it seemed she enjoyed the attention, even when Brian threatened to kill her. I was glad I hadn't confronted Brian with Anne's accusation; it was just as I'd thought all along—a phase.

"Mom!" Emily ran wailing into the kitchen minutes before it was time to leave for school, her hair full of static. "Brian used up all the hair spray! Look at me! What am I going to do? I can't go to school like this!" She waved her arms dramatically about her head.

Yes, surely she would die if she went to school with static-filled hair.

"Settle down, Emily," I urged. Yelling in the morning has never been high on my list of good ways to start the day. "Go in my bathroom and use my hair spray." Emily bounced off, the usually forbidden use of my beauty products a tantalizing treat.

Minutes later she was back, shaking an empty can in my face. "Yours is gone, too!" The tragedy was back in full force.

I grabbed the can and shook it. It was only a week ago I'd bought it, splurging when Jacob insisted this new spray would "revolutionize" my hair. Yeah, right. It was as empty as Emily had said. No wonder all those big-name beauticians could afford all that advertising—they gave you half the product for twice the money.

Emily was bouncing at my feet. "I'm going to die. Sarah is going to laugh at me all day. I look like a science experiment!"

Her words, "science experiment," jogged my memory. It was an old trick my mother used to use when my dress would cling to my nylons. She'd wet her hands, shake off any excess water, then rub them lightly over my legs. Voilà! No static cling. I quickly wet my hands and applied damp fingers to Emily's electric-looking hair. As though by magic, Emily's hair smoothed down just as the school bus rounded the corner.

"Thanks, Mom!" Emily screamed as she raced for the bus. My daughter would live through the day after all.

Brian came sauntering into the kitchen, hair sprayed into place. He tossed me an empty can. "Hey Mom, can you pick up more spray? Emily's having a fit."

"I know, I heard all about it." It amused me to think of my son and daughter fighting over a can of hair spray. Go figure.

"Why don't you just get her her own? Then she wouldn't be yelling at me all the time." He jammed two pieces of bread into the toaster and pulled the peanut butter from the cupboard. "If you go to the store, could you pick up some markers? I need them for my science project." Brian sniffed, swiping a wad of peanut butter over his toast with one hand, back-handing his nose with the other. His summer cold lingered. I was beginning to wonder if I should have him tested for allergies. A horn honked outside. "Gotta run, Pete's here." And off he went, two slices of peanut butter toast jammed between his teeth.

Pete? He didn't have his license, did he? I glanced out the window in time to see the back of four heads driving away from our house. Must be one of the older football players driving.

Bob walked into the kitchen. It was as if they had timed their morning so each could spend a few moments alone with me. Yeah, right—call us the Waltons. He walked over and nuzzled my neck. Oh. This hadn't happened in a while. It felt good.

"How about tonight?" I could hear the hope in his voice. I hadn't heard that tone in a while and it sent a shiver down my spine. I turned into his arms and laid my head on his shoulder, nodding. Yes.

After Bob left, I found myself humming through the morning, congratulating myself for not jumping to conclusions about Brian, letting Emily and Bob deal with problems in their own time. Today was going to be a good day. Maybe I'd finally be able to get a start on my novel.

Maybe today would be the day I stopped thinking about Anne.

Anne

They certainly didn't waste any time setting up my appointment in Rochester. Before I even had a chance to call Kevin, the clinic nurse called with my appointment date. Next week on Tuesday. The day of Emily's piano lesson. I was going to have to cancel again.

I didn't know who to call first, Libby or Kevin. I knew both calls were going to be hard, each in their own way. I called Kevin first. I could tell he wasn't pleased about having to cancel almost a week's worth of appointments, but it wasn't as if we had a bunch of options. I apologized. Kevin grunted, "I'll manage."

Libby was next. I dialed her number but hung up when it started ringing. How dumb. My hands were sweating. What did I think was going to happen? Libby would refuse to let me cancel? She would holler at me? She'd already done that once, and I'd lived through it. I feared her indifference most of all. And that's what I got.

"Lib—Olivia," I kicked myself. I just couldn't get used to calling her that.

I knew she recognized my voice because her own took on an aloof tone. "Yes?" Libby said the word as if I were a telemarketer she was going to cut off as soon as possible.

"Uh, it's Anne, ummm, I'm going to have to cancel Emily's lesson again next week." I waited for her to ask why. She had to know something was wrong; I'd never canceled two weeks in a row. Silence. I found myself filling it with a stream of words, "Kevin and I are going out of town for a few days next week. It's kind of unexpected, but we just thought…" I sounded as though we were going off on a midweek vacation, as if we were jet-setters with frequent flyer points that needed to be used. I wanted so badly to tell her the truth. *Libby, my cancer is back. Libby, I need to talk to you. Libby, help me get through this like you did last time.* But my cry for help stayed in my heart.

"Oh, Lord," I prayed after I'd hung up, Libby's cool "Okay," echoing in my ears, "I know You said You'd always be with me, but right now I need a friend with 'skin' on."

The phone rang and I grabbed it, convinced it was Libby somehow hearing my prayer.

It was a telemarketer.

That was the first time a telemarketer ever hung up on me. Of course, I suppose it was hard for him to understand me through my sobs.

Olivia

It didn't take long for my good day bubble to burst. Anne's phone call did it as quicky as a sharp pin. Something was up with Anne. I knew it deep in my bones. It didn't take a rocket scientist to figure out that Anne would never cancel piano lessons two weeks in a row if it weren't some sort of emergency.

I'd heard her babbling over my silence at the other end of the line. Words pushed at my throat, *Anne, what's wrong? Anne, can I help? Anne, let's talk.* But it was as if a thick rag had been pushed over my tongue, and the only word I could force out was, "Okay." I'd heard the tears in her voice as she said goodbye. I felt like a heel. It was getting to be a familiar feeling.

It wasn't that I didn't care about Anne; I did. I thought about her often. But lately I'd felt she'd come into my life and taken it over. Steamrolled my old life right into the ground. Before I'd become friends with Anne, my life seemed to run like a well-oiled machine. Bob went to work, came home for supper, and sometimes went back to work in the evening, but most times he was home, sitting on the couch watching television. We actually talked now and then. Brian was all boy—you name the sport, he wanted to play it or watch it. I never knew who would be out in our driveway on any given summer evening playing Horse, or Lightning, or One on One. When the game was over, no matter who won, they would troop in and devour whatever snacks happened to be in the cupboard. And Emily—she'd always been my "talker." I could count on Emily to keep me posted on what was happening at school, on our block, and especially with Brian. She was my own private Nancy Drew, and I loved her for it. It was as if I had a miniature girlfriend living right under my roof.

I had my routine, too. Coffee twice a month with Jan (any more would have driven me batty). Lunch every couple of months with Connie. I'd get the occasional invitation to a Tupperware or Pampered Chef party, which I'd weasel out of, saying I had a column to write. I had brilliant ideas for my column back then, too. My days were spent doing ordinary household tasks which managed to expand, filling any extra time I might have used to write. But as I worked, so did my mind, sifting through ideas for columns, outlining essays, always searching for possible ideas for the book I would write one day. On the whole I thought I was content.

That was before.

Since I'd met Anne, it seemed as if everything had changed, and not for the better. I no longer met Jan for coffee; she seemed to have latched onto Brenda, leaving me out of the loop. Connie had never been one to initiate our lunch dates, and after hardly talking to her in months, I felt awkward calling her now. I felt as though I were an outsider looking in on a group where I was no longer welcome.

And my home life? Where to even start on that? Bob no longer watched television; he was either at work or sleeping, and we rarely talked. He seemed to be existing in this house, but living somewhere else. Brian was living the life of a fifteen-year-old, not wanting anything to do with his parents, except borrow money, of course. And Emily, my dear, sweet, nonstop-talking Emily, had turned into a clam. I felt cut off from everyone. And it had all started with Anne.

Of course I thought of Anne. I blamed her for everything. I knew her baby was due any day, that was probably why she'd called—she was more than likely trying to line up someone to drive her to the hospital when the time came. If Kevin would ever decide to join Workaholics Anonymous then he might actually be able to drive his wife to the hospital himself.

I found myself cleaning my way around the house, something I do when I'm upset. There's nothing like a floor that needs scrubbing to help me stew over my problems. I rubbed the sponge hard against the floor. What had happened to the good mood I'd been in two hours ago? The thought made me even more upset. I bumped the bucket with my foot and water splashed onto my leg. If it weren't for Anne none of this would be happening. I'd thought today would be the day I'd finally start on my novel. Oooohhhh, Anne wasn't even part of my life anymore, and she was still interfering.

Thank goodness it was almost time for *Oprah.*

Anne

Looking back, that first trip to Rochester seems like a blur and a waste of time.

I don't know what I was expecting the Mayo Clinic to look like. I'd heard so much about it over the years, I guess I'd come to imagine an almost castle-like structure where nurses stood at alert like armed footmen, ready to rush to your defense at the first sign of trouble. Instead, it was a regular clinic. Bigger, but a clinic nonetheless.

Kevin stood aside while I registered at the desk, and then, as at clinics everywhere, we were told to wait…and wait. Even the magazines there were outdated. Kevin had gotten smart—he'd brought his briefcase along. He didn't waste any time pulling out files and a calculator, content to wait as long as he could work.

I sat quietly, trying to reconcile the reality of the place with what I'd built up in my mind. During the drive down, I'd imagined that the moment I arrived I'd be whisked into an examining room where a team of specialists would pour over my case and have a magic shot waiting that would make my cancer go away. I knew it was a fantasy even as I was thinking it, but I secretly hoped there would be a sort of miracle cure waiting for me. Instead, it was me, waiting…and waiting.

After what seemed like half the afternoon, but was probably under an hour, we were ushered into a small room and told the doctor would be in shortly. Kevin was antsy, wondering why the nurse hadn't checked my temperature or blood pressure, convinced that she was incompetent and that we'd waste more time waiting for her to do it later.

"Kevin," I patiently explained, even though I felt unnerved, too, "I'm not here because of a temperature—I'm here to get a consultation

163

about my…my…situation." Even I didn't know exactly what to call my case.

"Come on, Anne," Kevin rolled his eyes, "you make it sound like you're here for a job interview."

Just then Dr. Adams walked in. "Ah, Mrs. Abbot." He shook my hand. "I've been anxious to talk to you about your situation."

Aha. I smiled smugly at Kevin and saw an apologetic smirk.

"Somewhat unusual," Dr. Adams said as he looked at my records. He closed them and folded his hands, placing them on the cover of the file. "I have your previous charts here, Anne, but why don't you go ahead and tell me what procedures you've had done and your previous course of treatment." He leaned back in his chair as though he had all the time in the world, encouraging me with a motion of his fingers. "Tell me what's happened, Anne."

All of a sudden I felt like crying. This was the first time a doctor had ever asked me what had happened. At all my other appointments I'd been told, "This is what we're going to do." "Here's what's going to happen next."

I was speechless. It had never occurred to me to make an accounting of all I'd been through. I must have looked like a fish out of water, gasping for air, or for words, anyway.

"Why don't you start with how you found the first lump?" Dr. Adams guided my racing thoughts back to when it all started.

"I suppose that would be a good place to start." I took a deep breath, trying to remember back to what seemed another person's life. "Well, my friend, Libby—" I paused. There she was. Even if Libby didn't want to be with me, she was there all the same, part of my story whether she wanted to be or not.

I took a steadying breath. "My friend, Libby, told me that I had to get my breasts ready for nursing. You see, she showed me some sort of exercise I was supposed to do to…" Sitting in that small room, explaining to Dr. Adams how it all began, it was as if I was reliving those days. I heard my voice telling about finding the lump under my arm and being so sure it was just an infected milk gland, about my first biopsy and my mastectomy, about Libby helping me eat with my left hand those first days after surgery and the start of my chemo-therapy. My story sounded pitiful. I felt as though I were some decrepit old person who had a cornered audience and wouldn't let them go until they'd heard all my woes.

Dr. Adams listened, nodding thoughtfully, occasionally tugging his ear.

I didn't like the picture I was painting of myself, it made me sound wan and sick. So I told Dr. Adams about the day Libby and I went wig shopping, the fun we'd had, and how I'd never needed the wig. It was on a shelf in my closet and the hair on my head was mine.

"I like that story." Dr. Adams smiled along with me.

I told him about the checkup I'd had for my baby, and how Dr. Lebalm had discovered a new lump, and then called in Dr. Barrows who'd bluntly declared, "I want that out of there." When I was done recounting all the events that led up to me sitting in Rochester, I sat back, feeling as if I'd lived the past months all over again. I felt drained. I looked at Kevin. He looked grim and pale, like a person you see on the news who's been through a traumatic event. I realized it was the first time he'd ever heard the whole story at once. He must have suddenly realized all I'd been through these past months. Kevin looked at me with a shell-shocked expression on his face, then reached up and pressed the ridge between his eyes with his forefinger as if he had a terrible headache.

Dr. Adams sat forward in his chair and said gently, "You've been through a lot, haven't you?"

My eyes welled with tears, I nodded, swallowing the lump in my throat. "Uh-huh." It came out sounding like a croak.

"Anne, I'm going to make a deal with you." Dr. Adams leaned back. "For now, I don't want to do anything." He put his pen into his white coat pocket as if that was that. "I want you to have this baby before we do anything else. How does that sound?"

How did that sound? How did that *sound?* It sounded wonderful! My heart soared for a moment. But I knew there was more to it than that. It didn't take long for reality to intrude. "Then what?" I asked.

Dr. Adams quickly rubbed his hands together and put them on his knees. "Okay, here's what I see. We're going to want you to have this baby here, in Rochester. I suspect your baby will be just fine, but with the drug therapy you've had, well, one never knows. Don't worry," he rushed to explain, "we'll have people standing by who can handle any problems that might come up, although I don't anticipate any. Then," he took a slow, deep breath, contemplating my future, "Dr. Barrows was right—we need to get at that other lump. Barring any complications, I'd say we'll do surgery the day after you have your baby. I don't know how extensive the surgery will be. I'll have you consult with the surgeon before you leave, but I don't suppose they'll know until they get in there. Then, depending on the lab results, I'm guessing you're looking at another round of chemotherapy, possibly some radiation treatments."

"Oh-hhh." The word came out as if someone had pushed my stomach.

Chemotherapy and radiation? That didn't sound good.

Dr. Adams heard my unspoken fear. "Listen, Anne, let's not put the cart before the horse. First and foremost we want you to have a healthy baby; then we'll work on getting you healthy, too. Okay?"

I nodded, adding what felt like a feeble smile.

"Do you have any questions?"

I shook my head.

Kevin spoke for the first time. "Uh, do you have any idea when this is all going to happen? I mean, how soon, uh, with the baby and all?" He sounded so unsure. "Umm, how long we'll be here? She'll, Anne, be in the hospital?" This was a Kevin I hadn't seen before, stammering over his words, speaking in half-sentences. My straight-forward, deal-with-it husband suddenly sounded hesitant and scared. It made me feel scared, too.

Dr. Adams took the question in stride. "I'm going to let the obstetrician, Dr. Blaine, take over from here." Dr. Adams consulted a schedule clipped to my file. "Let's see, you're set to talk with him tomorrow at nine-thirty. He'll map out what to expect in the next week or two." Dr. Adams stood, leaning to shake our hands. "I'll be talking to you soon, Anne. For now, you go and have a healthy baby."

Dr. Adams breezed out of the room. Kevin and I sat there looking at each other, waiting for someone to tell us what to do next. After reliving the past months during my appointment, it seemed there should be some dramatic conclusion to the day. Instead, Dr. Adams had said, "Have your baby." I'd planned to do that all along. After expecting a miracle cure, being told to "have your baby" felt anticlimactic.

I placed my hands over my stomach and caressed the firm muscles. *Poor baby.* I imagined my little one floating helplessly in my abdomen. *You're always getting put behind your mother's problems.*

Kevin glanced nervously at my moving hands and worried face. "Are you feeling okay? You're not having contractions now, are you?"

I smiled. "Unfortunately, no. This could be a long week or two."

"You got that right." Kevin stood, grabbed my hands and pulled me to my feet. He leaned forward and gave me a quick kiss on the cheek, squeezing my hands before he released them. "Let's go back to the hotel," he said, slipping one arm protectively around my shoulder.

That night in our hotel room bed, Kevin reached for me, pulled me into his arms, and held me tight, not talking, just slowly stroking my hair. It was as if, for the first time, he was feeling what I'd been through these past months, and maybe, just maybe, thinking he could lose me.

After a time, his hands drifted down, running over my shoulders, around my back, pulling me closer to him. Awkwardly, we shifted our bodies to accommodate my bulging abdomen. For a moment it almost seemed like before, the way Kevin stroked his hand over my hip, whispering in my ear. Almost. Only this time, he didn't slip my nightgown over my head and gently push it off the bed. This time, he slid it up only to my waist, leaving the top half discreetly in place as if it were some sort of camouflage.

Olivia

I was starting to feel as if Oprah was my best friend. I really didn't talk to anybody anymore. Not Jan, not Connie, and certainly not Anne. The kids were uncommunicative, and although Bob made an effort to ask me about my day each night before we went to sleep, I usually heard his snores before he heard my answer. Not that I had much to tell him. "Oh, let's see. I cleaned, sat and stared at the computer, and then watched *Oprah*." My daily hour of television had become so routine that I finally admitted watching it. I was turning into a cliché, a boring housewife. In truth, *Oprah* was my only intellectual stimulation of the day, unless you counted the way my mind tumbled and turned over the days and the words and the resentment I felt toward Anne.

But, thank goodness, my daily staring session at the computer was over, I didn't have to think about Anne anymore, *Oprah* was on.

The familiar theme music played as I settled into the couch and listened to Oprah introduce her guest. It was obvious she was excited, the way she practically bounced in her shoes as a Dr. Phil McGraw joined her onstage.

Another one of Oprah's experts. Another one of those people who blame everything that's ever happened to anyone on their poor, deprived childhoods. I almost flipped the channel, but I knew there was nothing better on. I rolled my eyes but stayed tuned.

Oprah waved Dr. McGraw's new book in front of the camera, repeating the title at least three times.

Great. Another book I wouldn't have to read—they'd tell me all about it.

She repeated the title again.

"I got that, Oprah. Do you think I'm deaf?" Oh good grief—I was talking to the television. She must know this guy really well. She was calling him "tell-it-like-it-is-Phil." A person only says something like that if she knows them on more than just a guest level. Wonderful, now I was analyzing Oprah.

"Okay, tell me how it is, Phil," I dared him. I sat on my couch, a smug know-it-all, until I realized I'd spoken to the television again. "Hurry, Phil, tell me something I don't know, before they lock me up in the loony bin." I sat back and waited for Dr. Phil to pussyfoot around, the way people promoting a book usually did, never getting to the point, trying to get you to buy their book so you could find out what it was actually about.

Dr. Phil fired out his words with an authority that surprised me.

He was different. Someone who talked direct. I punched at the volume button as he listed his points. Get real, he said. Solve your own problems. Don't feel sorry for yourself. No blaming others. As if in answer to my unspoken question, "How am I supposed to do these things?" Dr. Phil said he'd tell me after the commercial.

I liked this guy. He *was* "telling it like it is." I was sitting on the edge of the couch waiting to hear his next words—

"Mommmm!" Emily came screaming into the house. Quickly, I punched the record button, Dr. Phil was going to have to tell it to me later. "Mom! Mom! Where are you, Mom? There was an ambulance at school when the bus was leaving and Brian was standing by it!"

Anne

Am I going to be fine, Lord? Am I? I felt groggy when I woke the next morning. Kevin had quickly fallen into a deep sleep in our strange bed, but I'd tossed and turned, trying to find a comfortable position for my taut stomach. Each time I found a relaxing spot, it would be only a matter of minutes until I began to feel restless and need to move again. My mind replayed the previous day. I was glad Dr. Adams wanted me to have my baby before doing anything about my new lump, but it also made me nervous to think of the lump having more time to get bigger, to grow deeper. A wave of fear swept over me as the darkness of the hotel room cast weird shadows over the walls. It was spooky. I slid closer to Kevin, but his light snoring near my ear was annoying, so I slid back to where I'd been. I pushed the pillow into a ball near the headboard and flopped onto my back, half-sitting in the bed. In the dim light I could see my coat hanging over the back of the hotel room chair. I wanted to put it on and go home.

I wanted to be home expecting my first baby. I wanted a whole body with two breasts and no scars. I wanted a life where the biggest problems in my day were going to the grocery store and deciding what to make for supper, not trying to remember which doctor I was supposed to be seeing, on what day, for which problem. I wanted a friend to sit across the table from me and tell me a new way to wear my hair. Suddenly, all I wanted was for Libby to be here. To sit in the waiting room and play "What If…" So what if she played like Scrooge; we always laughed. I wanted Libby to listen to every word the doctor said and then say, "Okay, let's think of something worse."

Even with Kevin right beside me, I felt as though I were all alone in the world. The dark, stuffy hotel room closed in on me. A new wave of fear and sadness engulfed me, along with a flood of tears. My body shook with sobs, tears flowing fast, over my cheeks and down my neck.

Kevin stirred in his sleep, mumbling, "Anne?"

A small whimper escaped my clogged throat. I sounded like a lonesome puppy crying for it's mother.

Kevin put his arm heavily across my thigh and fell back to sleep.

"Oh Lord, help me," I sobbed into the darkness, "I feel so alone." I took in a great gulp of air, a hiccup. "I'm scared." The words of an old hymn came drifting through my sad vigil—*What a friend we have in Jesus*...The tears flowed freely as I gave myself over to the comforting words....*all our sins and griefs to bear*...I swiped at a tear trickling into my ear. *We should never be discouraged*...I took a deep, shaky, breath. "Oh, Lord," I whispered, "I am. I'm so discouraged, and scared, and lonely. Help me. Please?"

I cried myself to sleep. Or maybe I prayed myself there. Either way, I woke with swollen eyes and a brain that felt as if it were partly-congealed gelatin. Kevin was whistling in the shower. Two hours before my doctor appointment, and I felt as though I could sleep for eight hours. If this was supposed to be a joke, I wasn't laughing. Thoughts of the night flitted through my mind; a low and rising panic threatened to engulf me.

Why now? There was no dreaded cancer appointment today. No surgery scheduled. This baby wasn't going to be born today—that I knew. And yet, a feeling of doom hung over me. Maybe, I reasoned, trying to make sense of my emotions, it was because nothing was imminent. I'd had time to react to all that had happened, and my emotions had finally caught up with me.

Or maybe something else was wrong.

Olivia

"Emily, calm down. I can't understand a word you're saying." I turned from the television as Emily came bounding into the living room.

"Mom!" She stopped and took a huge breath, her whole body seeming to fill with it. "It was an *ambulance*! With the lights going! And the sirens! And *everything*! The principal was standing there, and these doctor-kind-of guys, and they had a kid on that bed-thing, and—" She took in another gulp of air, the words practically exploding from her mouth, "Brian was there, too!"

"Okay. Okay." I knew I was supposed to do something. After all, I was the mom, but I didn't have a clue what to do. Should I call the school? Should I go to school? If Brian wasn't involved, then they wouldn't tell me anything, anyway. If I went to school, I'd more than likely miss him, since school had been dismissed. Waiting seemed my only option. I sat down.

"Mom!" Emily screamed at me. "What are you doing? *Do* something! Brian was there!"

"Emily!" I snapped. "Give me a minute to think." My head was spinning. One minute I'd been lazing on the couch watching *Oprah*, and the next I was being screamed into emergency mode.

"*Mo-om*!" Emily strung out the word as she doubled in half, her arms spread wide. "Brian was standing right there!"

"Okay, listen to me." I had to start from the beginning. "Was he actually getting in the ambulance?"

"Well-ll, no, I don't think so." Emily almost sounded sad, then barked at me, "But he *could* have been."

"But it wouldn't be quite the emergency if Brian wasn't the one in the ambulance, would it?" I was trying to reason this out.

Emily's shoulders sagged. "Guess not," she mumbled.

I made a decision. "I'm going to call the school and see if they'll tell me what happened. I think it's best if we wait here for Brian. If we go to the school we might miss him." I picked up the phone and dialed, giving Emily a get-back look as she tried to get her ear as close to the receiver as possible.

"Hello." The familiar, unruffled voice of the school secretary already assured me.

"This is Olivia Marsden. Uh, I'm calling about…well, you see my daughter, Emily, came home a few minutes ago…" Suddenly, I felt foolish. I didn't know what I was asking, or how to word my unknown question. I took a breath. "Okay, let me start over." I was quickly trying to make some sense to my train of thought. "My daughter, Emily, came running in the house a few minutes ago and said there was an ambulance in front of the school, and I was wondering—"

"Who is this, again?"

"Mrs. Marsden. Olivia Marsden." I felt a prickle down my spine.

There was silence on the other end of the line, then whispering. "Mrs. Marsden? Yes, sorry about that. You were wondering?"

"Yes, well, Brian isn't home yet, and Emily said she saw an ambulance in front of the school, and she thought she saw Brian standing near it. I was wondering if anything happened that I need to be concerned about."

"Yes, Mrs. Marsden," the secretary had a guarded quality to her voice, "there was an incident at the school this afternoon."

My blood ran cold. Emily must have noticed my pale face, as suddenly she became very still.

"The principal is talking to some of the boys right now. I believe Brian is one of them."

"Is he hurt?"

"No, no," she quickly reassured, "he's not hurt."

"But the ambulance?"

"Yes, one of our students was taken by ambulance to the hospital to be checked. Mrs. Marsden, I really can't give you any more information right now. The principal is talking to the boys and I'm sure, if he needs to, he will be in touch with you. Just know that your son is fine."

"But what happened?"

"I'm sure you realize," the secretary went on, "we can't give out that sort of information until *we* find out what happened, Mrs. Marsden."

I was beginning to hate the way she kept saying my name over and over, as if repeating it was giving me information.

"Don't worry, Brian is fine. I'm sure he'll be home shortly."

There was a tone in her voice that led me to believe things weren't as fine as she made them sound. But what could I do until I had more facts?

"Well, okay. Thank you, I guess…" My voice fell off in that questioning way so many young women have, making me sound unsure of myself.

Emily was trying to drag words out of me with her eyes. If her eyes could have opened any wider, I'm sure they would have. She glared as I hung up the phone. "Mom?" She was almost crying.

"Brian's fine. I guess." My own words didn't sound very reassuring.

"Tell me what happened!" Emily was pleading.

"I don't know. The secretary wouldn't tell me." I sounded stunned—not the way a good mom probably should in a situation like this.

Emily and I spent the next hour between the couch, the picture window, and the front door. If one of us was sitting, the other one was making rounds, gazing out the window, going to the door to glance down the sidewalk, and retreating back to the couch where we pretended to be patiently waiting. At the end of one of her many circles, Emily looked out the window and gasped, "He's coming!" Quickly, she scrambled to sit beside me on the couch.

There we sat, as if we were playing Monkey See, Monkey Do, when Brian walked in. Two innocent women, a mother and a daughter, passing the afternoon away, sitting and staring at the door.

For some reason I felt as though I were the one who had explaining to do. I decided to wait and let Brian tell things his way.

"Hullo," he mumbled, kicking off his tennis shoes. "What's for supper?"

Emily looked at me, her brows furrowed in puzzlement.

I had an inappropriate urge to laugh. All this excitement, all this worry, and he asks, "What's for supper?"

I decided to pretend I didn't hear him. "So, anything happen at school today?"

"Usual," he grunted.

If Emily hadn't been potty trained at two and a half, I think she might have wet her pants.

"Oh, really?" I casually remarked. "Emily said—" *oooffff!* Emily jabbed a sharp elbow to my ribs. "I mean, I heard there was an ambulance at school this afternoon." I couldn't believe how level my voice sounded.

Brian glared at Emily. "Snitch." He marched into the kitchen.

"It's not snitching! I saw it!" Emily jumped up, hollering and following after him. "And you were standing right there!"

"So? Big deal." Brian popped open a soda and took a big gulp.

I couldn't believe this was my son. Standing in my kitchen, drinking my soda, acting as if ambulance-watching was something he did every day. He wasn't volunteering a thing. I lost it.

"Listen here, young man," I sounded like my dad. "You will put down that soda, you will march into the living room, and you will tell me exactly what happened at school this afternoon. Do you hear me?"

"Geez, what's the big hairy deal?" Brian shuffled off toward the living room, still carrying the soda can. Emily was hot on his trail. So was I.

He settled on the couch, flopping his size-ten feet on the coffee table. I was going to have to pry information from him.

"I want you to tell me what happened at school this afternoon. I want to know *why* the ambulance came, *who* was in it, and why *you* were standing by it." My voice sounded hoarse; I was either really mad or really scared, and even I didn't know which it was.

Brian glared at Emily. "Tattletale." It was an old taunt.

"I am not a tattletale!" Emily defended herself.

"Are too."

"Am not!"

"Are too." Brian was buying all the time he could.

I stopped the fight. "Talk. Now."

"Chill, Mom." My little boy was trying to sound so cool. "Some of us guys were getting ready for football practice, you know, horsing around in the locker room and stuff, and Pete was holding his breath and he passed out. Hit his head." Brian took a swig of soda, acting as though this happened every day. "One of the other guys got scared."

Not Brian, of course.

"He ran to the office and told them to call 911. Hence, the ambulance."

Hence? Now he was Shakespeare. I wasn't buying it. Ever since Brian had been caught smoking last spring, he'd been on athletic suspension, which meant he could practice with the team, but not participate in games until six weeks into the season. He knew he was on shaky ground. Any wrong moves—more smoking, bad grades, high jinks in general—and he'd be off the team. I felt he was hiding something. "And just why was Pete holding his breath?"

Brian shot Emily a look, then shrugged my way. "Trying to see how long he could, I guess."

It sounded like a sophomore thing to do. Brian certainly made it sound innocent enough. I decided to give him the benefit of the doubt. I started laughing. "You sure had me worried." I reached over and ruffled his hair. "When I heard there was an ambulance at school, and you were near it…well, you should try being a mom sometimes." I leaned over and rubbed the back of my hand against his cheek. "It ain't an easy job." I tried to make light of my worry.

"Am I excused now?" Brian was smiling.

"Sure."

As if in punctuation to our conversation, the front door opened. The three of us turned to see Bob walking in, a good two hours earlier than usual, a worried expression on his face. His eyes searched out Brian, his face lighting when he saw him.

"Oh, thank goodness." I could hear relief in his voice.

Bob looked at the three of us staring back at him. "I was worried," he explained. "I heard at work that a sophomore boy was taken by ambulance to the hospital. Drug overdose."

Anne

The odd feeling I'd awakened with accompanied me through the day. Even though Dr. Blaine, the obstetrician assigned to my case, was completely upbeat about the baby's health, I still felt a queer nudging all day that something was wrong. I even mentioned it to the doctor.

"Do you have any questions?" Dr. Blaine adjusted the stethoscope around his neck.

I didn't beat around the bush. "I know you told me the baby sounded very healthy, but I've had this odd, nagging sensation all day. Do you think it has anything to do with the baby?"

Dr. Blaine looked thoughtful. "Anne, I'd say, with all you've been through the past months, it's more than likely a low-key anxiety you're feeling. It's natural for any first-time mother to have some concerns about her pregnancy and some trepidation about going through labor. Add to that the additional worries you've faced during your pregnancy, and I'd say you're justified in feeling a bit apprehensive." He went on, "Why don't you go ahead and get dressed. I'll have your husband come in, and then I'll talk to you about what you can expect in the next week. I see you're scheduled to talk to your surgeon shortly, so let's get crackin.'" He snapped his fingers and stepped out.

Within minutes he was back. "Okay, Anne, Kevin," Dr. Blaine looked between the two of us, "this is what I have planned. I'm going to want you here next week on Tuesday. Anne, you should be able to have a vaginal delivery—I see no problem there—so we'll induce labor that morning. I'm guessing we'll have a baby by early afternoon." He sat back, pleased with himself, as if we'd already delivered the goods, so to speak.

"I'll be talking to your surgeon. I'm guessing he'll want to get at you as soon as possible." He made me sound as though I were a tough piece of meat. Dr. Blaine seemed to realize his poor choice of words and tried to fix them, "I mean at the breast." Apparently this didn't sound much better, and he stammered, "Uh, I mean the lump."

I was beginning to realize that no one was familiar with a case like mine, which didn't make hearing the doctors stumble over their words any easier. Their hesitation seemed to emphasize that we were all treading in unknown territory. I was scared. Maybe that's why the persistent sense of trouble hung with me.

For once we didn't have to wait. By the time Kevin and I maneuvered the corridors trying to find Dr. Payne's office (a bad pun for a surgeon's name, as Kevin pointed out), we were ushered immediately into his office.

He was waiting for us. "Mr. and Mrs. Abbot, hello." Dr. Payne stood to shake our hands. "Sit down, please."

Dr. Payne looked to be about twelve. I found myself glancing over his shoulder trying to get a glimpse at his diplomas hanging on the wall behind him. I suddenly thought it might be a good idea to see if he'd graduated from high school, not to mention medical school. He noticed and chuckled.

"Don't worry," he reassured, "I get this all the time. Just so you know, I'm thirty four. I did my surgical residency with one of the top cancer specialists in the nation. You're in good hands." He spread his out, as if seeing them would calm me.

I noticed a wedding ring on his finger and felt sheepish for questioning his youthful appearance. "Sorry."

"No sweat. My wife and I are expecting our first baby, too. We're hoping the baby won't think I'm his brother." He laughed, and so did Kevin and I.

Dr. Payne's lighthearted manner finally made the troubled feelings I'd been having lift for a moment. That is, until he said, "I'd like to take a look at the suspect area now, if you don't mind." Suddenly he was all business, reminding me once again why I was here.

As I put on the thin gown, I wondered if it would ever feel normal to have a new doctor examine me. I felt self-conscious all over again. As I slid the gown over my scar, I gave my remaining breast a quick glance. Who knew if I'd have that one much longer, either? I gave a resigned sigh. What choice did I have but to let the doctor do his best for me? There was something about Dr. Payne that made me feel I was in good hands, and I told myself to relax.

As Dr. Payne examined my breast, taking special time, feeling carefully around the new lump, he explained, "Anne, I've read through your chart, and looked at your films, and I have to tell you, I don't like what I'm seeing. It's not often we get a cancer this aggressive in someone your age. Unfortunately, in your case the tumor was not estrogen-receptive. Sometimes, especially in pregnant women, we see a type of cancer that's made worse by the extra estrogen being produced by your body. In those cases, once the source of extra estrogen is removed—the ovaries or the conclusion of the pregnancy—the tumor responds well to treatment. That's not the situation here." He gently put my gown in place over my breast. He lifted the other side of my gown, running his smooth hand lightly over my smiling scar. "Nicely healed," he declared, putting my gown back in place. "Go ahead and get dressed, and I'll tell you what I'm thinking."

Kevin sat beside me, gripping the arm of his chair as though it were a lifesaving device. Looking at his clenched hand and white knuckles made me nervous. I worked my hand under his, but his sweaty palm didn't do much to calm my nerves.

"Anne, Kevin," Dr. Payne sat across from us. "I'm going to be frank with you. This new tumor, appearing so soon after your treatment, has me worried. I'm going to schedule you for surgery the day after your baby is born, barring any problems, of course. I want to get at this as soon as possible. Once we have you sedated, Anne, we'll take a section and send it to the lab. If it's cancerous, as I'm suspecting it is, I plan to go in there and get as much of it as humanly possible. I'm anticipating another full mastectomy." All of a sudden Dr. Payne didn't seem twelve anymore.

My face must have registered some emotion, even though I felt I'd turned to stone, because Dr. Payne added, "I'm sure that's not what you wanted to hear. I'm sorry, Anne. I know you've probably read all kinds of things about lumpectomys, breast reconstruction, and that sort of thing. Frankly, it's a good option for many women, but unfortunately, not for you. Right now we need to get at this cancer, and the only way we're going to be able to give you the best odds is to get it out of there." He jabbed my chart with his pen as if he were already cutting. "Do you have any questions?"

Kevin had been gripping my hand tighter and tighter as Dr. Payne spoke. Now he loosened his grip and asked, "What about a second opinion?" His voice held a challenge.

I gave Kevin a sidelong look. He'd hardly been involved with any of my previous treatments, never questioning what the doctors had said. Now that we'd been referred to the experts in the field, he was questioning. I winced, embarrassed.

"Of course. I understand your question, Mr. Abbot." Dr. Payne didn't seem one bit offended. "You're free to consult with whomever you choose. I do want you to know we have a panel of doctors who consult on the more problematic cases, as we've done with your wife's. We're in full agreement on this course of treatment. But as I stated, you're free to get another opinion."

"No, that's okay." Kevin seemed tentative and unsure as he mumbled, "Just wondering."

"Well then," Dr. Payne rose and shook our hands. "I'll be seeing you next week. Take care."

Once again, Kevin and I were left alone. Our immediate future was mapped out; our real future unknown.

The troubled feeling that had dogged me all day was back tenfold. It was a scary place to be sitting. I heard myself whisper softly, "Think of something worse."

"What did you say?" Kevin had heard my whisper. "Think of something worse? What could be worse than *this*?"

He was right.

I wracked my brain. I couldn't think of anything worse. My cancer was back. I was going to have another mastectomy. Chemotherapy. Radiation. Fear spread through my body. What could possibly be worse?

Just then I wished Libby were sitting beside me; she'd think of something worse. I just knew it.

Olivia

If Brian thought I was mad before I knew what really happened at school, well, now I was furious.

"Go to your room!" I screamed, pointing to the stairs. But when he got up to go, I shouted, "Just where do you think you're going? Sit down! You've got some explaining to do." I pointed to the spot on the couch he had just vacated. I was out of control and yelled at Bob, too, "How could this happen?" As if it was his fault Brian had been evasive.

Bob ended up telling Brian to go to his room until I calmed down. Poor Emily sat quiet as a mouse on a corner of the couch, afraid to even squeak.

"Emily, why don't you go to your room, too. Your Mom and I need to talk," Bob quietly suggested.

Emily jumped off the couch, glad for a reason to leave the situation in our hands. I wished I could go with her. Anywhere seemed better than here.

I took a deep breath, trying to calm myself. Sinking into the couch, I asked Bob to explain. "Tell me absolutely everything—every word you heard at work." My mind was reeling with the idea that one of Brian's teammates could be involved with drugs. They were all good kids. I thought back to Pete playing basketball in our driveway just the other day; how could he possibly be in the hospital with a drug overdose? It didn't register. I wanted to believe Brian's explanation that Pete was holding his breath. Goofing off. That explanation sure seemed naive in light of this news. Was I that out of touch?

Bob sat across from me, leaning forward, elbows on his knees, an intense expression on his face. "You know how news travels around here?"

I nodded. I knew all too well how people in this small town talked. Sometimes it was pure rumor and speculation, but more often than not, there was truth in what was said. Brewster was too small for much to go unnoticed.

Bob went on, "Dan Jordan called shortly after we heard the ambulance go down Main Street, past the bank. He'd been showing a house near the school, and when he heard the siren he drove over, being on the school board, and all…" Bob trailed off, remembering the imagined scenario. "Anyway, Dan talked to the principal, and he told Dan what they suspected had happened. Apparently the kids were fooling around, sniffing some stuff?" His words sounded as if he'd asked a question.

It didn't make sense to me, either. What could you smell that would cause a drug overdose? I remembered my own school days. We all stuck our noses in the glue jars, smelling the slightly sweet, medicinal smell. Nothing had ever happened to any of us. There had always been rumors that smelling our markers was dangerous, but all I'd ever gotten was a headache from coloring in letters on posters now and then. No one *ever* passed out. It was puzzling, trying to understand this new information.

"Then apparently," Bob continued, the same unbelief in his voice that clouded my thoughts, "one of the kids ran into the office and said Pete had passed out in the locker room. After the ambulance left, the principal and Coach Rollins talked to the other guys who were around when it happened. Guess no one wanted to say much, but one of the boys finally blurted out the story. Turns out Pete had been fooling around with this sniffing-thing for a while…before practice, other times, too. No one else was admitting to anything, but they're suspecting it involves more than just Pete."

Pete. Abruptly, the facts sunk in. It was Dr. West's son, *my* Dr. West's son this had happened to. Surely, the town gossips were wrong. Pete would never do anything like that. Would he? Would Brian? Anne's words echoed in my mind, *I think Brian is using drugs.* What had she seen that I'd been blind to?

Rage swept through me. If Pete had gotten Brian involved in this...I'd been mad at Anne for her seemingly unfounded accusation; now I was furious at Dr. West. Where had she been while Pete had been doing this? What kind of mother was she? There had to have been signs. Obviously, she hadn't seen them. Now her son was lying in the hospital. If Pete was responsible for getting Brian and who knows who else into this, well, that was the last Brian was ever going to see of Pete.

"What should we do, Olivia?" Bob's words cut through my racing thoughts.

"Do? What should we do?" I was indignant and took my frustration out on Bob. "I'd say the first thing we do is see that Brian has nothing to do with Pete, ever again. There's no way I'll have my son near anyone like that."

"Olivia," Bob's voice had a placating tone. "We don't know that Brian wasn't doing this, too."

"Of course he wasn't," I snapped back.

Just then Brian slowly shuffled his way into the living room, dropping onto the overstuffed chair, slouching as if to disappear into its cushions. He looked ready to cry. "I have to talk to you." His voice was soft and shaky.

I'd never seen Brian look so discouraged, and it frightened me. I'd been ready to send him back to his room, my anger still roiling, but hearing his shaking voice replaced my anger with a feeling of dread.

Bob spoke first. "We're listening."

Brian shifted forward, head hanging, elbows on his knees as if holding himself up. He didn't look at either one of us. "What Dad said—it's true."

"What's true?" My words sounded sarcastic, as if I would have a hard time believing anything he said. But in reality, so many conflicting thoughts and emotions raced through my brain that I was having a hard time sorting out speculation from fact. I repeated, softer this time, "Tell us, what's true, Brian?"

A sob burst from Brian's throat. "Pete was using drugs. We all were." Brian crossed his arms over his knees and hung his head lower, his body shaking with emotion.

Bob and I sat there, stunned. A minute ago I blamed Anne, Pete, and even Dr. West for things I didn't want to believe. Now here was my son, my precious, adolescent son, telling us that he was using drugs, too.

I looked around, a surreal feeling engulfing me. I saw our living room—the couch, the chair, the bookshelves and the fireplace all in place where they'd always been. I saw Bob, Brian, even myself sitting in spots we'd occupied hundreds of times, and yet everything had changed.

My instinct was to go to Brian, wrap my arms around him, and tell him everything would be okay. But I had the feeling that things might not be okay, not for a long, long time. Instead, I stayed sitting, frozen in my spot. I stared at my sobbing young son, a mixture of anger, sadness, and love tumbling through my heart.

If there was anything worse than hearing your child admit he was using drugs, I didn't know what it would be. I found myself wishing for Anne. She would help me think of something worse.

Anne

Kevin and I hadn't been home ten minutes when the phone rang. I knew it was Jan right away by the breathless quality of her voice.

"Have you heard?" she asked, a juicy gossip tone to the question. Not waiting for my reply, she told me the news, "Pete West is in the hospital for a drug overdose. They're suspecting the whole football team might be involved. That means Brian, too. Has Olivia said anything to you?"

Here was the reason for my feeling of dread all weekend! My whole life I've been blessed, and sometimes cursed, with an extraordinary amount of empathy and intuition. My mother used to brush me off when I'd ask if something was bothering her. She called it "Anne's overactive imagination." But more often than not, I'd find out something had been troubling her—an argument with Dad, or a falling out with a friend. My probing questions drove my sister, Andrea, crazy.

"I *know* you like Mike Connely," I'd declare.

She'd vehemently deny it, but late at night in our shared bedroom she'd confess, "I do like him. How'd you know?"

I'd shrug my shoulders in the dark because, in reality, I didn't know how I knew. I just did.

The past days had been no different. I had known something was wrong, but I'd assumed it had to do with my health. The minute I heard Jan's announcement, I knew this had been the reason for my uneasiness.

My thoughts bounced. How involved was Brian? Did Emily know about her brother? How was usually mild mannered Bob reacting to the news? I could hardly imagine how a parent would feel knowing this about their child. It would be heartbreaking. Even though I didn't know Pete, my heart went out to him, too. And Dr. West—she'd been something akin to a friend to Libby. Would they reach out to each other now? But mostly, my thoughts centered on Libby. Would she face up to the situation? Would she get past her denial and reach out to Brian? Did she need me to help her through this? I felt a physical pain, a longing to help my friend, but also a knowledge that I needed to wait. There was nothing for me to do now but pray. *Be with Libby, Lord. Give her courage and strength. Honesty, too.* It seemed inadequate, but it was all I had.

"Anne," Jan's voice cut through my prayer, "did Olivia ever say anything to you about Brian? You know, about his maybe using drugs, and stuff?"

It was obvious Libby hadn't been talking to Jan any more than she'd been communicating with me; otherwise Jan would have known that Libby and I hadn't spoken in weeks. I felt sad for Libby. There she was, going through a parent's nightmare without anyone to confide in. Jan was just interested in the juicy details, not in helping Libby. I didn't want to add to Jan's treasure trove of news by revealing Libby and I had argued, so I stalled.

"Are you sure about this?"

"Oh, yes!" Jan answered confidently. "Jacob was cutting Dani Phillips' hair—she works up at the school, you know. Well, my appointment just happened to be after hers, and she'd told him all about it. She said a lot of the guys are involved. It might even mean suspending the whole football season…you know, if they don't have enough players to make a team." Jan sounded almost satisfied to be relaying this bad news.

"What did you hear about Brian?" I felt crummy for asking, but I was concerned too, and I had no other way of finding out if Brian was in trouble.

"Well," Jan hesitated, "Jacob didn't say anything specifically about Brian. But he's on the team and he does hang out with Pete, so I'm just assuming he was involved. So did Olivia ever say anything to you about it?" Jan wasn't going to give up until she had more tales to tell.

I took a deep breath, knowing what I was about to say would more than likely put a wedge between Jan and myself, testing our tentative friendship.

"Jan…" I was nervous. Confronting people is not my specialty. "I don't feel comfortable discussing Libby's personal confidences with other people, even other friends. If someone tells me something private, I think it should stay that way."

"Well, of course." I could hear the assumption in Jan's voice. She was inferring, from my unwillingness to talk, that Libby had confided her fears about Brian to me.

I didn't want her to spread the story any further, so I went on, "I can honestly say Libby has never suspected Brian of using drugs." That was the truth. Jan had never asked if I suspected it. So there. Jan could take my noninformation and do with it what she would. I wasn't about to fuel her gossipy speculation with my private concerns. Those concerns I'd shared only with Libby, and only because I cared about her and her family so deeply. Again, a feeling of physical pain shot through me. I knew Libby was hurting, and there was nothing for me to do. I hoped trying to stem the gossip would count for something.

⌒

Once again, I learned that concentrating on others is a good way to take your mind off yourself. Even though I had another mastectomy almost positively lurking in the near future, my concerns about Brian and Libby overshadowed even that diagnosis. Every now and then that feeling of physical hurt swept through me, reminding me how connected we are to those we love, even when they don't always love us back. Whenever I found myself deeply worried about Brian, I forced myself to turn my worries into prayer. It helped. Being reassured that God was in charge of the problem was a good reminder to me that He was in charge of my problems as well.

I needed that reassurance when I called my mother to update her on my situation.

"Hel-lo-oh!"

"Mom?" I hadn't talked to her in a couple weeks; she sounded excited.

"Oh, it's Anne." I could hear her cover the receiver to tell whoever was with her about my call.

"Who's there, Mom? Dad?" I was hoping my father would be home for lunch.

"Oh no, your dad had a lunch appointment today. Andrea stopped by. I'm going to watch Cari while she runs to the mall. Go ahead, go on."

"I have some good news and some not so good news…" I started explaining why I'd called, until I realized she was talking to Andrea, telling her it was okay to leave. I stopped talking and waited for Mom to return her attention to the phone.

"What was that you were saying, Anne? Go on."

"Umm, I have some good news and some not so good—"

"Oh, you should just see Andrea and Cari today, they have on the cutest matching outfits. Jeans with matching denim vests, and they both have bright pink T-shirts under them. Cari has the most darling denim bow in her hair. Don't you, now don't you?" Mom's voice rose as people's often do when they're talking to small children.

"Mom, is Andrea still there?" If I couldn't get Mom to listen, maybe Andrea would.

"She's just ready to go out the door, why?"

"Could I talk to her for a minute before she leaves?"

Andrea picked up the phone. "What's up?" I could hear Mom cooing to Cari in the background.

The past few years Andrea and I hadn't talked much. Whenever I spoke with Mom, she had so much to tell me about Andrea, Jim, and the kids, I rarely felt the need to call Andrea for her news. And Andrea was so busy with her own life, she rarely called me. It actually felt strange to be on the other end of this phone connection with her.

"Andrea," I started, "it's Anne," even though I knew she knew it was me. "How are you?"

"Busy, as usual. Mom's going to watch Cari while I run some errands, then I have to pick Jimmy Jr. up from school and run him to soccer. Thank goodness Mom invited us for supper—that's one less worry on my list today."

Oh, to have such simple worries. Trying to cram in a few errands before I picked my child up from school. Wondering if my mother could babysit for the afternoon. Worrying about what to feed my family for supper. Were my problems really, in the whole scheme of things, any greater than Andrea's? To her they were what powered her days. She was dealing with her problems as I dealt with mine—a day and a problem at a time. For a moment I felt connected to her again.

"Hey Anne, I really gotta run. I have to get to the mall before one o'clock or I won't have time to shop before I have to get Jimmy Jr. from school. We'll talk soon, okay?"

The connection I'd felt seconds earlier slammed shut as Andrea handed the phone back to Mom. Through the phone line I could hear Andrea throwing exaggerated kisses to Cari as she left the house. Mom returned. "Oh, those two are so much alike. You should see them, Anne. Cari looks like a miniature version of Andrea when she was three. Well, you too, I guess." I could almost hear her making funny faces, entertaining her grandchild.

I was tempted to end the call without telling my mother about my upcoming schedule, but I knew it was something I had to do sooner or later, and waiting wasn't going to make it any easier.

"Mom, they think my cancer is back." I just said it so she'd have to hear.

"But you said you had good news!" So, she *had* heard the first two times I'd tried to tell her.

"Yes, I do, but I told you the bad news first."

"Tell me the good news."

"Well," I hesitated. I'd really been hoping to tell her the details of my upcoming surgery and possible treatment plan, and get the unpleasant description out of the way, then tell her about the baby. But Mom didn't want to hear about that, so I told her what she wanted to hear. "The good news is I'm going to have my baby next week, for sure."

"Oh Anne," I heard genuine warmth in her voice. Mom has always loved babies. "That *is* good news. Do you have names picked out yet? Did you get those bumper pads that were on sale at Penney's? Andrea said they were half…" Mom talked on while I blinked back tears. I suddenly felt sorry for myself. I so badly needed someone to confide my fears to, someone who'd really listen, who would stand by me through this. I'd mistakenly thought my Mother would do that, and then pinned my hopes on Andrea. But I could see now that neither one of them would be there for me. I was going to have to go through this alone.

Tears were streaming down my cheeks as I said goodbye to my mother in a false-sounding farewell. She didn't notice.

Oh, Libby, I sat and cried, *what could be worse than this?*

Olivia

For a moment after Brian made his confession, I wondered how I'd go on. That first night Bob and I let Brian cry himself out. At that point we were all too shaken with his revelation, and thoughts of what might have happened, to talk anymore. We told Brian to get some sleep, and we tried to do the same. Fat chance.

I woke up (if you can call the daze I'd been in all night, sleep) with a hollow feeling and an aching head. It felt as if I was just going through the motions of living. I got dressed and made Emily and Brian breakfast in a zombie-like state. Emily was silent, the pall over our house almost palpable. Brian actually mumbled, "Thanks," when I set his plate of eggs and toast in front of him. I took this as a small sign of hope. But after the kids left for school, the cold hollow feeling returned. I perked a pot of coffee, hoping the familiar smell and hot liquid would comfort. It was warm, but tasteless. My hands cupped the steaming mug in an effort to absorb any small solace. How could life continue?

I needn't have worried. The world seemed to take on a life of its own within the hour. The school secretary called to set up an appointment for Bob and me to meet with the principal. We'd have a private meeting with him, and then Coach Rollins wanted to hold a meeting for the parents of the football team members. In addition, the school counselor called.

"Mrs. Marsden?" Her airy voice made her sound younger than Emily. "This is Chrissy Kraft, the school counselor?" She said it as a question. Was she hoping I'd tell her it was true, that she really was the school counselor? I was in no mood to shore her up, so I waited.

"Uh, I suppose you already heard about the football guys?" When I didn't respond she filled the silence, "Well, uh…I guess I'm supposed to have a meeting, or something. I mean, sometimes people want to talk to someone who knows about this kind of stuff. Well, really, this is my first time for something like this, since it's my first year and all, but we talked about it in my classes, and I have some information on drugs."

There, she'd said it. My blood ran cold. It wasn't some nasty rumor Bob had heard at work or some cockeyed dream I'd lived through last night. It really was about drugs, and the whole town knew it. Like it or not, I was going to have to deal with it. But bet your bottom dollar it wasn't going to be with Chrissy.

"So, if you think it would be okay, we could talk?"

I had a sudden urge to laugh. If I hadn't been feeling so desperate it would have been funny. Here was this kid—well, actually, a young adult, barely out of college, trying to give me counsel over the phone and in the same breath asking me if I thought it would be okay.

"Chrissy?"

"Yes?" She sounded scared. Of course she was. The kids were only a few years younger than she was, and suddenly she was in charge of offering counsel to them and their parents. I decided to let her off the hook.

"I think we're going to be able to deal with this ourselves."

"Oh-hh." She sounded surprised and relieved. "Well, don't forget, if you want to talk?"

"I know," I tried not to sound amused, "we'll call you."

I hung up the phone. "Ha!" An unexplainable gurgle of laughter burst from my throat. It seemed hilarious that a twenty-two-year-old was calling to offer me information and guidance, as if I needed her to comfort me.

"Ha! Ha!" I bent at the waist, holding my stomach, it was so funny. I could imagine ditsy Chrissy trying to hug me or something. "Ha!" I gulped for air.

But with that gulp, something changed. Before I knew what had happened I'd sunk to the floor, the laughter gone. I was still holding my stomach, but now it was in a vain attempt to control my sobs.

I looked like death warmed over when Bob and I met with the principal, John Harris, later that day. I'd showered and even lay on the couch for fifteen minutes with ice cubes over my eyes, trying to assume some semblance of normalcy. Bob did a double take when I met him at the school, made-up as though we were invited to a gala presentation at the White House. I'd resharpened and applied an old brown eyeliner pencil I'd dug from the back of my makeup drawer, piled on a layer of plum eye shadow, (figuring it would blend with my red-rimmed eyes), and topped my efforts off with three layers of mascara. All I needed were high heels and a sequined gown to look appropriate. As it was I looked as if I'd been crying and was trying to cover it up.

The principal noticed. "I can see you've been understandably upset by what happened here yesterday."

I felt like a fourth grader who's been caught with her fingers in her mother's makeup drawer. All I wanted was a wet wash cloth and a hole to crawl into.

Bob spoke for us. "Yes, we have been, John. Actually, we haven't said much to Brian at this point. He was pretty shaken last night, and we thought it best to wait and see what approach the school was going to take before we sat down and talked with him."

"Bob. Olivia." John addressed us, all business. He was in the local Lions Club with Bob and we'd attended several social functions with him and his wife. Never before had I seen him this serious. "Frankly, our school system has never had a problem such as this. Not this widespread, anyway. We're talking, I'd say, at least five to eight young men. Unfortunately, not all of them are being as up front about things as your son, Brian." The principal leaned back in his chair. "I hate to have to tell you this, but we were compelled to call in the police on the matter. It is a crime, you know, to engage in this sort of activity."

My mind went reeling, immediately imagining Brian sitting alone in a lonely jail cell with some big, faceless brute standing nearby, waiting to accost him. I think I gasped.

"Don't jump ahead of me now." John held out his hand as if to settle me down. "I don't think there are going to be any charges filed. Unless a person is actually in possession of the drug, it seems there isn't much the police will do without physical evidence."

I could breath again, until he added, "We've found out the boys were huffing. It can be hard to pin down the evidence in these kinds of incidents."

"Huffing?" The word burst from my swollen throat like a frog's croak. "What's huffing?"

Bob was looking as confused as I was.

John sat up, assuming his teacher mode. "Oh, this is something we've been aware of for some time. Fortunately, we haven't had to deal with it until now." He paused, clearing his throat. "Let's just say we haven't known we've had a problem until now." He sounded more contrite.

"But what is it?" The only thing I could think of was the three little pigs cowering in their rooms, the big, bad wolf right outside their doors, huffing and puffing trying to blow their houses down. It was a silly thought in such a serious situation, and only reminded me of reading the story to Brian when he was small. Tears threatened to ruin my overdone eye job.

"What's huffing?" I repeated.

"It's when the kids sniff the chemicals in certain products," the principal explained. "It makes them high, so to speak."

Where had I been these past few years? This was news to me. I'd been worried about Brian smoking, maybe even drinking. Even the possibility of him being exposed to marijuana had crossed my mind, but sniffing something? What did I have to worry about next?

John went on, "It's been quite popular, especially among the junior high crowd, for several years. Not here, though," he quickly added. "Well, at least not that we've been aware of. But you'd be surprised. These kids try sniffing all kinds of things—correction fluid, glue, paint, even marking pens and hair spray. Who'd ever have believed it?" He looked to us for agreement.

Bob nodded his head, while I shook mine in disbelief. I recalled the sudden shortage of hair spray around our house and Brian's request for new markers "for school." Right.

John kept talking. "What we're planning now is to have a drug counselor come in from the State and talk with the kids involved and with the entire student body. We want to get to the bottom of this. See how many kids are involved, get them some help if they need it. The bad news is that the boys are going to have to sit out the rest of the football season. It's an automatic suspension by the State High School Activities Association. The good news is that maybe we can get them turned around and off this stuff for good."

Bob was nodding in agreement, eager to do something to get this problem over. My mind tumbled with images—Brian decked out in his football uniform, his bulky shoulder pads making him look years older than his actual age, bouncing from foot to foot on the sidelines, waiting for a word from Coach Rollins, ready to run out and take his position. If he got to play even a minute in a game, Brian came home pumped with excitement. "Did you see that block I made? I flattened him!" He was a little boy, saying, "Did you see me, Mom? Did you see me?"

I felt ashamed. Maybe I hadn't been looking at him very closely lately.

⁓

Our ride home was silent, except for the occasional murmur, "What do we do now?" "I can't believe this is happening." It didn't matter which one of us said it. We were thinking the same thoughts.

We were waiting for Brian when he came home from school. He kicked off his tennis shoes as if it was a normal day, but instead of heading for the fridge as he usually did, he stood in the doorway, his glance moving from my face to Bob's, then back again. I'd expected him to look defiant. Instead he looked scared.

"Sit down, Son." I shot Bob a look—he sounded as though he were imitating some television dad from the fifties.

Brian didn't laugh. He slid into a kitchen chair, and for once he didn't slouch into it, lifting the front legs from the floor. This time he sat as straight and still as if he were in church.

Bob and I slid into chairs across from him. Oh, how I wished I could plan a different day. I'd have a plate of warm chocolate chip cookies heaped in the middle of the table, glasses of milk filled to the brim for each of us. We'd laugh about our day, tell jokes, recall fun times. Instead, my half-filled cup of cold, tasteless coffee sat at the end of the table, left from this morning. The dirty dishes from the kids' breakfast were piled at the other end. It seemed fitting, considering the mess our lives seemed to be in.

Just as Bob opened his mouth to begin our talk, the door flew open and in burst Emily. "I'm ho-ome!" she called as if she didn't have a care in the world. Then seeing our faces, stopped in her tracks and declared, soberly, "Uh-oh."

"Emily," Bob addressed her like a grownup, "why don't you take a seat beside your brother. We have a family problem here, and I think you should be in on the discussion."

Emily dropped her book bag and scooted into the chair beside Brian. I couldn't help but notice the smug look she cast Brian's way. Brian hung his head.

"Brian, we know you've had a rough couple days here."

Brian's head seemed to dip even lower.

"Mr. Harris told your mother and me that you'll be sitting out the rest of the football season. Did he meet with you boys?"

Brian barely nodded.

"Your mother and I feel you owe us an explanation."

Brian looked up quickly. "I already told you what happened."

"I know you did, Son, and we appreciate the fact that you owned up to your behavior. We understand some of the boys are trying to deny being involved."

Brian shrugged his shoulders.

"What we want to know is how involved were you…uh, are you? Is this something you've been doing for a long time? I think your mother and I deserve the truth."

Brian shot a quick look at Emily. "Does she have to be here?"

I spoke up. "I think Emily already has a good idea of what's been going on. You know how talk flies around at school. I'd rather she know the truth from you than hear a bunch of rumors on the school ground. Okay?" I wasn't asking his opinion.

Brian took a deep, shaky breath, as if gathering courage. "Coach talked to us today. I knew about being off the team. Mr. Harris said we have to talk to a drug counselor person next week. But Coach said we can still go to practice to keep in shape. We can't play in any games, but we'll still be ready for basketball season."

"Brian," Bob sounded stern, "you know this isn't what we're asking you. We know all about that part of it. We want to hear how involved you've been with this huffing stuff." The word sounded odd coming out of Bob's mouth. It felt as if we were all in some sort of stage play and I was watching someone else play the parts of the mother and the father. They'd never practiced this act before, and their behavior looked new and strange.

"Huffing?" Emily asked eagerly. "What's huffing?" I could imagine Emily waving her hand wildly above her head in class the next day, volunteering a new word for the day. Maybe we shouldn't have let her sit in on this conversation.

"Maybe Brian would like to explain it to all of us." Bob's voice had taken on an irritated edge.

"Dad, I feel so stupid!" Brian was flushed, looking embarrassed. "It's not like I'm proud of this or anything."

Bob's voice was even-toned. "Just explain to us what you did."

Brian cleared his throat. Twice. "Well, uh, sometimes I'd take like...do I have to do this?" He looked at Bob, then me, begging us to give him a reprieve.

"Go on." Bob stood firm.

Brian cleared his throat again. "Sometimes I'd take Mom's hair spray and spray a bunch of it on some clothes and then, you know, like, smell it."

"That's what huffing is?" Emily sounded incredulous, then added, "I saw him do that lots of times. But he said he'd kill me if I told you."

My jaw dropped. No wonder Emily had been so silent lately.

"Ouch! Brian kicked me!" Emily yelled, holding her shin. She looked at me wide-eyed. "I didn't know it was dangerous or I would've told you anyway." Then she added meekly, "I thought you'd be mad 'cause he was using your hair spray."

I felt inadequate as a mother. My son had been getting high right in our house—with my beauty products, no less. And my daughter had watched him do it, the threat of being *killed* hanging over her head if she told. Where had I been while all this was happening under my own roof? If there was a worse mother than me, I'd like to meet her.

Suddenly a mental picture of Evelyn, Anne's mother, appeared in my mind. I recalled how she jabbered on and on, not facing up to what was happening to her daughter. I'd been so judgmental of her at the time. Now I was forced to look at myself.

Was I any better?

Anne

The pain I'd been feeling over the difficulties Libby and her family were going through continued each time I thought of them. I wanted so badly to call Libby, to ask if she'd please talk to me.

My motives weren't entirely unselfish. I thought Libby needed me, but I needed her just as much. After my phone call to my mother, I realized the next few weeks would be a test of my stamina—physically, emotionally, and spiritually. I knew Kevin would be with me, but it wasn't the same as having Libby or some other woman who loved me there to talk me through my fears. And fears I had.

It seemed as if each night was eighteen hours long. I went to bed at my normal time, but Kevin's light snoring roused me out of the lightest sleep. I'd toss and turn, my mind tumbling too, repeating the doctor's words as if they were a mantra. *More chemotherapy. Radiation. Full mastectomy. Aggressive tumor.* They replayed in my head, a CD stuck on repeat. Kevin and I had decided not to tell anyone about the reoccurence of my cancer until after the baby was born, trying to bring some sense of normalcy to these last couple weeks. But in the dark of this night I wished for someone to share my fears. I roamed the house as though I were an alley cat searching for a comfortable spot—any place that would distract me for a few moments.

It was in the middle of one of these nights that I felt a new pain, different from the ones I'd come to associate with thoughts of Libby. I woke Kevin.

"I think I might be in labor."

Kevin turned over, rubbing his eyes. "That's impossible." His voice was filled with sleep. "We're not going back to Rochester until Monday."

"I don't think babies know about the calendar," was all I could think to reply. I grasped my stomach and breathed through the pain.

Kevin leapt out of bed as if he'd been shot. "I'll call the doctor!"

Dr. Lebalm was calm as he examined me.

What a job, I thought as he calmly waited for a contraction to pass before checking again to see how far I was dilated. It had been a case of hurry-up and wait. We'd rushed to the hospital in Carlton, and rushed into this room, but now we were waiting, timing contractions, and then waiting some more.

Kevin paced back and forth between contractions, mumbling, "We've got to get her to Rochester. What about Rochester?"

"Oh, well now," I heard Dr. Lebalm's surprised voice from somewhere below, "I'm afraid you're not going anywhere. You're going to have this baby right here."

I glanced nervously at Kevin. His nerves didn't seem any better than mine.

"But what about going to Rochester?" Kevin asked once again. It was as if he thought our going there to have the baby was a talisman of sorts.

"Nope," Dr. Lebalm said firmly, cutting off any idea Kevin might have had of speeding me off in the dark of night. "This baby is coming tonight."

"But the doctors in Rochester said—"

"At this point," Dr. Lebalm interrupted, "it doesn't matter what they said. Nature doesn't wait for doctor's orders." He looked at Kevin. "You'd better get ready to be a dad."

Kevin didn't faint, but he did sit down on the floor. Hard.

It turned out we had almost a whole day to wait until we became Mom and Dad. Kevin wouldn't admit to being nervous or woozy, but announced that since things didn't seem to be happening any too fast he was going to try to "get some shut-eye."

His pale face made me think that was probably a good idea. The nurse directed him to a nearby chair where he slouched weakly.

I didn't have the luxury of resting. I tried to concentrate on the Home Shopping Network, playing loudly on the television hanging from the wall. Apparently my nurse thought this would be a good distraction, as if buying jewelry over the phone was something I might like to do between contractions.

The night dragged on, the nurse by my side trying at times to make conversation but mostly keeping one eye on me and another on "*The Jewelry Showcase,*" playing overhead. After what seemed an eternity, I could hear the jostle of the breakfast cart coming down the hallway. Had a whole night passed? Dr. Lebalm had said my baby would be born last night, and now it was morning. Was there something wrong? I didn't have time to worry as another contraction gripped my swollen belly. "Oh-hh-hh…" The nurse immediately started timing the contraction.

At times the pain was almost overwhelming and I found myself recalling the horror stories I'd heard at the baby shower Jan had given me. I remembered Brenda telling about how her baby's heart had almost stopped and her emergency C-section. I relived Connie's trip by ambulance to the hospital in a snowstorm, thinking she would deliver in the car, then she, too, had had a C-section. And I thought again of the stillborn baby another had delivered. I had the same scared feeling now that I'd had that day. How had I coped? What had calmed me?

Libby. I remembered her motioning me into the kitchen with a tilt of her head, sensing that I'd been thoroughly scared by the stories the others had told. Stories about horrible labor pains, trouble giving birth, things that could go wrong along the way. I could almost feel Libby's hands on my shoulders, telling me not to pay any attention to them. She'd told me every mother has a story to tell, because every child is special, and I'd have a story to tell, too. I smiled, remembering Libby's calming words.

"Oh-hh!" A strong contraction caused me to call out, bringing me quickly back to reality and rousing Kevin.

"How's it going?" he asked sleepily.

I panted in and out as the nurse had instructed. "Fine." I didn't sound fine, but Kevin didn't seem to notice. He closed his eyes, his even breathing acting as counterpoint to my labored breaths.

When the contraction had passed, I tried to relax, gathering my energy for the next round. I tried to imagine my soon to be born baby scrunched up in my abdomen, little arms and legs pushed together tighter with each contraction. This couldn't be too comfortable for the baby either. As if hearing my thoughts, a little foot— or was it an arm—pushed against my taut skin. In reply my body responded with another strong contraction, as if to say, *We're working on it. We'll get you out of there soon.*

A hospital aide brought a breakfast tray into my room, the smell of eggs and toast drifting in with her. When she saw me panting through another contraction she stopped in her tracks. "Oooopps, guess you won't want to be eating this, huh?"

As if on cue, Kevin sat up. Breathlessly, I motioned her to leave the tray for him. Even after my long night of labor the thought of food didn't appeal to me.

But it did to Kevin. He polished off my breakfast, then went in search of another cup of coffee.

Mid-afternoon Dr. Lebalm stuck his head into the room. "This child is certainly taking its time," he said good-naturedly. "It'll have a nickname before it gets here. Pokey." He chuckled.

I managed to ask a question between the ever-increasing pains. "Is everything going okay?"

Dr. Lebalm stepped all the way into the room. "Not to worry," he assured me, "most first labors are long. The baby may be slow, but things are progressing nicely. Hang in there, Anne, you're doing fine." He picked my chart off the end of the bed and glanced at it. "If things don't speed up in the next couple hours we might have to consider a C-section. But your vital signs appear good. We're going to let nature take its course for now. Even if it is the slow road."

Libby was right—I was going to have a story to tell about this night and long day. As soon as the next contraction faded I began fashioning our child's tale...

You little stinker, you were supposed to be born in Rochester. The doctors had it all planned out. Daddy and I were going to go there on Monday, and you were going to be born on Tuesday. The doctors were afraid because Mommy had been sick while she was pregnant, so they wanted to have a whole team of doctors ready to take care of you and Mommy.

They thought you might be sick too because of all the medicine Mommy had to take while you were in her stomach. So they told us we had to come to Rochester, where they had the special doctors, for you to be born.

But you little stinker. You had a mind of your own. You decided we didn't need to drive that far. You wanted to be born closer to home. There you were, on a Thursday night, stretching your arms and legs, telling all of us, "I'm coming." But then, "Pokey" (that's what the doctor called you), you were in no hurry once we got to the hospital. Your daddy ate Mommy's breakfast, lunch, and supper before you finally decided it was time to come out and see who your parents were.

Another contraction engulfed my body. The nurse, who'd been in and out almost constantly through the day, talked me through it. "Come on, Anne, breathe with me. Short little breaths. You're doing great." She glanced at her watch. "Almost over. Keep on breathing." The contraction seemed to go on and on. I must have given her a frightened glance, which she returned with a calm smile. "Hang in there, Anne. Stay with me now." The nurse caught my eye and breathed along with me, in, out, in, out. Finally a long, deep breath as the contraction faded. "Whew, that was a hard one," she stated. She didn't have to tell me. "I'd better check you," she said, snapping on a glove.

After quickly examining me she called out loudly, "Okay, it's happening. Time to be a daddy, Mr. Abbot."

Kevin jumped to his feet. Realizing he had nowhere to go, he sat back down. Then he stood up again, not sure where he should be.

"Stand here." The nurse pointed to the head of my bed and Kevin followed orders. She grinned at me. "I'll get the doctor. You're going to be a mommy."

My body seemed to take on a life of its own. I could barely catch my breath before the next contraction took over. It was as though waves on a beach were pounding my body, another one coming before the previous one had time to fade away. Kevin had taken a stance by my head, holding my hand near my ear in some sort of vice grip. It was hard to tell if it was him or me who was squeezing the hardest. I wanted to tell him to let go for just a second to stretch out my fingers—anything to relieve the discomfort I was feeling. But I was afraid to let go, fearing it would hurt even more to have nothing to hang on to, to be completely alone.

Olivia

We sat around the table, our untouched food growing cold, unsure of what to do next. An uneasy silence hung in the air like a heavy blanket. It felt as though something more needed to be said, but we were all talked out.

Somehow I'd managed to throw together supper. I could have saved myself the trouble. After listening to Brian's explanation, the four of us seemed to have lost our appetites. We sat around the supper table in silence, pushing food around on our plates. It wasn't what I would call quality family time.

In the end, Bob grounded Brian. It didn't seem much of a punishment in light of the crime, but what more could you do with a kid who didn't have his driver's license yet?

And who sure wouldn't be getting it anytime soon.

Brian just nodded. We knew his suspension from the football team would be an additional blow. I hoped all this punishment wouldn't discourage him so much that he stopped caring about being on the team at all. That could lead to even more trouble.

I stood to clear our practically full plates. "Do you have any homework?" Even though it was Friday, I asked the question of both kids figuring it would give them something to do with the long evening stretching before us.

Emily and Brian nodded. Bob took the break in the silence as an opportunity to excuse himself to go back to the bank for a couple hours. "Since I missed most of the day today," he added with a pointed look at Brian.

Emily looked around the table, her eyes questioning. It was usually her job to clear the table, Brian often eating after the rest of us, after football practice. I knew she was wondering if the same rules applied tonight.

"Go do your homework; I'll clean up." I didn't have to tell her twice.

Emily scooted from the table with a quick, "Thanks, Mom." Relief filled her voice. Anything to get out of this gloomy kitchen.

Brian sat, pretending he was still interested in his meal. I guiltily scraped our uneaten food off the remaining plates into the sink, thinking of starving children everywhere. The garbage disposal loudly chewed the wasted food. For a moment I thought I'd heard Brian say something. I stopped the disposal to listen, but when I turned, his head remained down, his eyes focused on his plate. I turned the disposal back on, hearing Brian's voice at the same time. This time when I turned to look at him the noisy machine somehow served as backup for his confidence. His mouth moved, but I couldn't understand what he was saying. I flipped the off switch.

"What did you say?" I asked too loud, my voice echoing through the kitchen, overcompensating for the now quiet machine.

Brian cleared his throat, his fork bobbing up and down in cold pasta. "Could I go see Pete?" His voice cracked as he questioned, so soft it was a wonder I'd heard him at all.

Pete. In all my ranting and raving, worry and anger since we'd found out what had happened at school, never once had I wondered how Pete was doing. Yet here was my son—suspended from the football team, humiliated in front of his friends, sentenced with counseling at school and grounded for life at home—he was worried about his friend.

I hadn't wondered about Pete—or how Dr. West was dealing with her son's hospitalization—at all. All I'd done was blame both of them for letting this happen. I felt ashamed. What kind of person was I to not once wonder how Pete was doing? Or how his mother, a mother of a son just like me—how she might be feeling?

The thought that Brian, for all his denials, for all his defiance, even in his brokenness, was worrying about his friend, Pete, made my heart ache. There was a goodness in Brian even teenage troubles couldn't erase. A mixture of sorrow and joy mingled in my heart. I turned to the sink, hoping the sound of running water would cover the emotion in my voice. "I think visiting Pete would be a good idea. Let me finish the dishes, call Dad to check on Emily, then I'll drive you."

We stopped at the information desk to ask for Pete's room number, but we were informed that he wasn't being allowed visitors. Brian scuffed his foot against the desk in frustration. It made me realize how helpless he must be feeling. He was having all kinds of things done to him—suspension from the team, counseling appointments lined up, being grounded—but he could do nothing to help the situation, not even visit his best friend. Brian blew a breath out in frustration as we turned to go.

"Olivia!" I heard my name called and glanced to my left. Dr. West was emerging from the hospital cafeteria just off the lobby, a steaming cup of coffee in her hand. A flash of apprehension shot through me. Would she be glad to see me, or was she, like me, blaming others for what had happened to her son?

"Dr. West." I kept my voice even, not sure how she felt seeing me, or Brian.

"Olivia, I'm so glad you came." She gave me a one-armed hug, holding her coffee away from our bodies. "You too, Brian." Dr. West gave us a welcoming smile. "This way," she said as she walked down the hall, expecting us to follow. I glanced over my shoulder at the receptionist who'd just told us, "No visitors." She shrugged her shoulders.

Dr. West was still talking. "Pete's going to be glad to see you, Brian. You're the first one who's been here."

"But," I tried to explain, "they said no visit…" My words trailed off as it dawned on me that none of the other boys had probably even tried to see Pete, visiting regulations or not. I was glad we'd come, and I gave Brian an encouraging smile.

"How's Pete doing?" Brian asked, sounding more confident than I knew he was.

Dr. West hesitated, stopping outside a doorway. She took a sip of her coffee, then spoke in a low voice, "He's pretty good, now. They've got him closely monitored, EKG, blood gas levels…," she rattled off some technical medical jargon, then said, "You know his heart stopped."

Brian's eyes got wide as the news sunk in.

"No, we didn't know that," I replied with a sinking feeling. It was worse than I'd ever imagined.

"On the way to the hospital." Dr. West looked past us, remembering. "In the ambulance." She shook her head as if to shake off the memory. "But he's doing good now, considering…" Again, her voice trailed off. "Oh, come on," she said as if talking to herself, "he's going to be fine. Let's go in. I know he'll be glad to see you." She pushed open the door and stood back, letting us squeeze past her.

The first thing I saw were Pete's closed eyes. He looked dead. The next thing I saw was the tube in Pete's mouth. Brian saw it too, and stopped in his tracks. He took an involuntary step back, then coughed, speechless.

"Pete?" Dr. West called her son's name. "Look, you've got company."

Pete's eyes opened slightly, then wider as he recognized Brian. His hand, which had been lying lifeless at his side, lifted in a small greeting.

We were still speechless, but I saw Brian wiggle his fingers in greeting, his hand down by his side. I doubted Pete could see it.

Dr. West looked at us as if we were imitating statues. I'm sure we were doing a good job of it.

"Oh my goodness," Dr. West filled the silence, "I forgot to tell you they put Pete on a respirator. His breathing was very irregular after they got his heart started. He needed a little help breathing. It— I mean the tube—should come out tomorrow. I'm sorry," she apologized, "when you work in a hospital sometimes you forget how these things look to other people. It probably looks much worse to you than it is."

Brian was ghostly pale.

Dr. West reassured him with a touch on the shoulder. "The tube is helping Pete. Really."

Brian nodded, but not very convincingly.

"Go ahead and talk to Pete." She gave Brian a small nudge. "It's probably one of the only times he won't be able to disagree with you." She laughed softly, her humor lifting our shaken mood. "I'm going to take your mom back to the cafeteria for a cup of coffee."

Brian gave me a nervous glance, then walked to Pete's bedside. "Hey, Pete." Brian raised his hand in a second greeting, his tone far from the normal guy-to-guy banter they usually spoke in. "Way to get out of practice."

Dr. West and I exchanged a look; they'd be okay. "Let's go get that cup of coffee I promised you." Dr. West led me out of the room as Brian slowly began filling Pete in on what had happened in his absence.

The cafeteria was crowded with visitors and hospital personnel eating a late supper. Dr. West maneuvered her way through the crowd, refilling her cup and pouring an extra one for me. She nodded at the cashier, who waved her through the line. I signaled from the table I'd been able to find near the windows.

As Dr. West handed me my cup I asked, "Is this what they mean when they say 'hospital privileges'?"

Dr. West laughed, holding her cup up in a sort of toast. "Free coffee, our negotiated perk. You don't know how hard we had to fight for this. Enjoy." She blew on her coffee, then took a long sip.

Silence settled between us. I wracked my brain trying to think of what I should say. I too sipped my coffee, trying to buy time. What do you say to someone whose son almost died? The horror of what could have happened struck me again, a sickening feeling passing through me. Pete could be dead. It could just as easily have been Brian. The whole situation still seemed like a bad dream.

"Dr. West," I began, "I just don't know what to—"

"Please, Olivia," Dr. West interrupted, "I think under the circumstances you should call me Ellen. Right now, we're just two mothers wanting only the best for their sons." She gave me a grim smile. "Right?"

"Right." I sipped my coffee. "After all, they're too big to spank."

A laugh burst from Ellen's throat. "You've got that right." Then she sobered. "It was so much easier when they were little. Too bad we didn't know it then."

An image floated through my mind of Brian playing in the park one summer day, years ago. He'd dragged a backpack full of small cars to the park with us, insisting, "I needs to drive them, Mom."

Another small boy joined Brian in the sandbox, helping him build an elaborate maze of sandy roads. I watched as the two miniature road engineers plotted their imagined town. "This is where the daddy works." "Here is where the big kids go to school." "This is the racetrack." Like small boys everywhere, their throats hummed, sounds of roaring engines filling the warm air.

I lay back on the blanket I'd brought, content to relish the few moments when my attention wasn't being demanded. It didn't last long. I'd opened my eyes to find Brian standing over me, his hands flinging sand in my face as he angrily declared, "Tell him they's mine!" He pointed to what amounted to a miniature car lot, filled with small vehicles, lined up, ready for viewing. Brian's playmate sat nearby, one small car in his hand. He was busily pushing it back and forth in the sand, small engine noises coming from his lips. Brian repeated, "They's mine!"

I sat up, ready to referee, when the boy's mother walked over, reached into the bag she was carrying and pulled out a tiny, bright yellow, bulldozer. Holding it toward Brian she said, "Here, Josh will share his machine with you."

Brian grabbed the toy and ran back to the highway they'd built, rumbling sounds emerging from his throat before the wheels were even near the sandy roads.

The mother looked at me and grinned. "Don't you wish you could freeze them at this age? Sometimes it's almost too easy, isn't it?"

Brian had been three then, my first child, and I'd not found motherhood an easy transition. No, it wasn't easy. None of it was, and I opened my mouth to tell this Pollyanna-like mother how I felt. But before I could put my feelings into words, she'd sat beside me on my blanket, gazing contentedly at our happy boys and sighed, "This your first?"

I nodded.

"Thought so." She motioned to Brian's mass of cars. "The car lot there kind of gave you away. Josh is my fourth. All boys. You learn by the second one to let them bring only one or two toys along. Too many things to keep track of, get lost, and drag home at the end of a long day. They're usually cranky then too. My third one's over there." She motioned to the slide at the far end of the park. "The other two are in school, ten and fourteen."

I raised my eyebrows, saying my first words to her, "That's quite an age spread."

"Second marriage," she explained. "My husband has two kids from his first marriage, a boy and a girl. They're fifteen and seventeen." She glanced at her watch. "We gotta get going." She called out, "Josh, give the car back to the little boy, then go find Brad." She stood, brushing herself off. "Do you mind if I give you some advice?" Her tone was touched with the weariness of someone who'd done this before. "Enjoy your little boy. As my mother used to say, 'When they're little, they have little problems; when they're big, they have big problems'. It's true."

Now, in the hospital cafeteria, those words of advice I'd scoffed at twelve years ago came back to haunt me. *When they're little, they have little problems, when they're big, they have big problems.* The memory of my innocent little Brian caused tears to sting my eyes. What had I done wrong that he was in such big trouble now?

I looked across the table. "Dr. West…uh, Ellen," I corrected. "I'm so sorry. I don't understand how this could happen to our boys. They're good kids."

Ellen held up her fingers. "I know they are. Don't apologize, Olivia. There's no need. Believe me, I've spent hours wondering the same thing myself. Of course, at first I was scared silly, but after I knew Pete was going to be alright, I was furious. Not at Pete, but at myself. I'm a doctor! If anyone should be able to spot the signs of drug use it should be me, right? But I missed it." She shook her head in disgust. "Ms. Doctor Know-It-All didn't know enough to save her son from an overdose. Right about now I feel like the worst mother in the world."

"No," I corrected her, "I've got dibs on that title."

Ellen put her elbow on the table and wiggled her hand. "Wanna arm wrestle for it?"

We laughed, a new easiness between us.

"Honestly, Olivia, you don't know how many times I've replayed the past weeks and months in my head, trying to see what I missed. As they say, 'Hindsight is twenty-twenty'. Now I can spot all sorts of red flags. Pete's moodiness, his forgetfulness…But honestly, I'm like that at least once a month. I chalked it up to adolescence."

"I did, too," I echoed, remembering my visit to Dr. West a few short months ago, when I'd been convinced Brian's behavior was just hormones.

"You know," Ellen went on thoughtfully, watching as she swished the remains of her coffee in the bottom of her cup, "ever since Pete's father and I divorced, I thought I'd made a special effort to be close to Pete. I mean, he didn't have his dad around on a daily basis to talk about guy stuff, so I subscribed to a car magazine, sat and watched sports programs with him in the evening, things like that, trying to make sure we had a 'relationship.'" Dr. West lifted her fingers and made quick quote marks around the word. "I thought he could talk to me about anything. That's what upsets me so much; I don't know what more I could've done."

"You mean other than home schooling and putting bars around your house until he turns eighteen?"

Ellen gave a wry laugh. "Believe me, it's occurred to me."

I was feeling helpless, too. I tried to explain my thoughts to Ellen. "I'm beginning to realize that sometimes, no matter what we do or how hard we try, we can't protect our children from every trouble."

"I know what you're saying, Olivia. I just keep wondering what more I could have done. I mean, the kid's got everything in the world that you'd think would make him happy. Designer jeans, the latest tennis shoes...he's already been talking about what kind of car he wants when he gets his license which was supposed to have been next week." She shook her head. "Not going to happen now." Ellen paused, then went on, "He's got a CD player and a television in his room, and every kind of video game on the market." She rubbed her eyebrow in thought. "Maybe this is going to sound odd, coming from someone who's spent her life studying science, but I keep thinking maybe I should've taken him to church more. You know, given him something to believe in, something to stand for besides just *stuff*." She emphasized the word "stuff" as though it were something bad. "When I ran into the hospital yesterday and saw him lying on that bed with the ventilator tube in his mouth, all I could think was, 'Somebody pray for my son.'"

"Anne would do it. Anne would pray for Pete." The words were out of my mouth before I realized I'd spoken. I could feel blood rushing to my face in embarrassment and quickly rubbed at my face as if I were tired. Who was I to be offering Anne's prayers for Pete? The thought caused my heart to beat faster, remembering all the times Anne had said to me, "I'll pray for you." How many times had I rolled my eyes when she'd said that to me? Here was Ellen, wishing someone, anyone, would pray for her son. How many times had I turned down Anne's freely offered gift? What had I been turning away? Something that would have saved me from this heartache? I was offering to Ellen what I wouldn't accept myself.

"Anne?" Ellen's voice held a question.

"Remember my, uh, friend? Anne?" I replied, stumbling over the first explanation to come to mind.

"Ahhh, Anne." Ellen sighed in recognition of the name. "Isn't that your friend with cancer?" When I nodded, she asked, "How's she doing?"

"Oh, fine," I declared confidently. "She's just fine." A twinge of guilt pricked my conscience as I thought of all Anne had been through the past months and my lack of communication with her recently, but I reassured Ellen and myself in a single sentence. "Her cancer's in remission."

"That's good," Ellen said with a satisfied nod.

There was a brief moment of silence as we sipped our coffee, alone with our thoughts.

"Listen!" Ellen's command interrupted my thinking, a welcome break from the scene I was remembering, when I'd screamed at Anne, "I don't need your prayers!" I shook off the memory with a flick of my head, turning my attention back to Ellen.

"Do you hear it?" Ellen cocked her head to one side, cupping her ear with her hand. All I could hear were dishes clanking and the mumble of people's voices. "Can you hear it?"

I strained to listen, but could hear nothing beyond the ordinary. I too cupped my hand over my ear. The whole cafeteria seemed to quiet as others picked up the melody being piped over the hospital speaker system. It was Brahm's "Lullaby".

Ellen smiled. "I love it when I'm here for this." I must have given her a puzzled look because she added, "When they play the lullaby. It means someone just had a baby."

Anne

"It's a girl!" Dr. Lebalm held a wet, wiggly body aloft for us to see.

I heard Kevin's soft exclamation, "A girl," whispered near my ear. Then he turned and kissed me, coming away with a huge grin on his face. "Congratulations, Mom."

"Congratulations yourself, Dad," I laughed. Instantly, the previous hours of labor were a thing of the past. I was exhausted, yet exhilarated at the same time.

The nurse handed me what seemed an incredibly small bundle, considering how huge my abdomen had been the past month. I nestled my baby in the crook of my arm. It was surprising how naturally she seemed to fit there. I pushed back the edge of the blanket to get a closer look at this so-new life.

Kevin leaned in too, as fascinated as I. "She's got your hair," he said, running his fingers lightly over her dark brown hair. It was standing straight up, as if it had been electrified, and sprang back up as Kevin's fingers passed over. We laughed.

"I suppose in fifteen years she'll be standing in front of a mirror blaming us for having a bad hair day." Kevin looked from the baby to me, a grin spread across his face from ear to ear.

Brushing the baby's face with the back of my fingers was like touching a cloud—so soft I almost couldn't feel her. Then she opened her mouth, yawning as though she were a tiny bird in a cartoon nest.

"Okay, Pokey," the nurse said, picking up Dr. Lebalm's nickname, "it's time for me to check you over." She bent down and gently transferred the baby to her own arms. Leaning her head close, she cooed to my baby, passing on information to me in a baby talk voice. "You'll get to see Mommy again in a few minutes. Your mommy and daddy think you're pretty special, don't you know." She walked out of the room, still speaking in her sing song tone.

I leaned my head against the pillow, suddenly exhausted. Kevin was practically skipping around the room. Every now and then he'd stop, rub his hands together like a little kid with a quarter between them, then give a sharp clap and start walking again, grinning the whole time.

"I didn't know it would feel this good to be a dad," he said to no one in particular.

Watching Kevin pace made me feel even more tired. I closed my eyes, dozing off in what seemed like seconds. The next thing I knew, Kevin was putting a phone to my ear. "Your mom wants to say congratulations."

In my exhaustion I'd forgotten all about calling to tell others the news. Kevin had given my mother the vital statistics, including details of my prolonged labor. She had little more to ask other than how I was feeling.

"Tired," was all I could muster. I felt as if I could sleep for days.

"Take care, Anne," Mom said as Kevin reached to hang up the phone.

I should call Libby. An excited thump of my heart caused my eyes to fly open. Then I remembered her parting words to me: *I don't need you, Anne.* Resignedly, I closed my eyes, something more than tiredness filling my heart.

I drifted in and out of sleep, barely listening while Kevin called Andrea, then his brother. Kevin seemed as energized as I felt drained. I conked out completely as he dialed his boss' number.

I woke to find Kevin sitting next to my bed, holding our baby in a rose-colored blanket, a tiny pink knit cap on her head. He was gazing at her with an expression I'd never seen before; a mixture of love, happiness, and pure wonder filled his face. He looked up. "You're awake."

"Barely," I croaked, my throat dry.

Kevin grinned at me. "I've been waiting for you to wake up. Should we do the count?"

"What?" I was puzzled as to what he meant; a sleepy fog filled my head.

"You know," he lifted the baby slightly towards me. "The count. Fingers and toes."

"Oh, that count. If we're going to be good parents, we'd better." I slid over on the bed, making room for Kevin to lay her down and unfold the blanket.

Ten tiny fingers and ten tiny toes wiggled in the air as our baby reacted to being freed from her cocoon. Kevin reached a finger under hers and she grasped his tightly.

"No fair," he said looking at me.

"What do you mean?" I asked.

"She's got your hands, too. Look." Kevin slowly pulled his finger away, stretching out my little girl's long fingers.

"Oh-hh," I exclaimed, taking her tiny hand into mine. "She's going to be a fantastic piano player." I could imagine her hands, grown a bit of course, spread out over my keyboard as I taught her to find middle C.

We stared at our child in awe as she kicked her legs and waved her arms, small baby sounds accompanying her movements. She seemed incredible and unbelievable at the same time. After a long moment spent gazing at her tiny being, Kevin leaned over, put his arm around my shoulders and squeezed me close. "Can you believe we did this?"

I shook my head, hardly beginning to understand the miracle of birth. "We didn't," I replied softly. "We could never make something this awesome all by ourselves." I was practically whispering, overwhelmed by this new life in front of us. "God had a hand in this one."

Kevin, who usually cocked an eyebrow whenever I mentioned anything even halfway religious, just squeezed me again and nodded in agreement, once more reaching out his hand, grasping our daughter's tiny hand in his.

I gave our baby daughter her first bottle. Kevin changed her first diaper. That was going in her baby book. I slept again for what seemed like hours, waking in the middle of the night to find Kevin sitting beside our daughter's crib. At first, I thought it was a trick of the light coming through the window blinds in pale streaks, but the closer I looked I could tell it wasn't light, but tears streaming down Kevin's face. It was such a private moment, I gently turned my head pretending to be asleep. The only other time I'd seen him cry was at his grandmother's funeral, and even then it was the tears one sheds in tender grief. Years of heart trouble had left his grandmother with little quality of life. Death had come as a blessing to her and the family who'd watched her suffer. The tears Kevin was crying now came from a different place. A place I hadn't seen before.

I turned in bed, wanting to do something to ease his emotions, but not wanting to intrude. I feigned sleep. Through my hooded eyes I saw Kevin sink his head into his hands, covering his eyes. His body shook as he silently cried harder, and then through his tears I heard him whisper, "I can't lose her."

At first, I thought he was talking about our baby since he was sitting near her crib in the darkened room, but when he choked out the words again, "I can't lose her," I knew he was talking about me.

During the long hours of labor and the glorious hours after our baby's birth, I'd forgotten what lay ahead. My looming surgery, chemotherapy and radiation had been mercifully erased from my mind, a blackboard wiped clean. Now they were back, crowding out the joy, filling me once again with fear and dread.

"Kevin," I called, my voice sounding sleepy even if I wasn't, "come here." I patted the bed softly.

He rubbed his face, pretending it was tiredness that caused his face to be buried in his hands in the middle of the night. He stood by my bedside, not understanding what I wanted until I pulled back the light covers and slid over, making room for him.

Silently, he slipped off his shoes, gently lowering himself onto the bed beside me. He lay on his back and I nestled next to him, my head on his shoulder, one leg snuggled between his. Wordlessly, his arms around me and mine around him, we drew comfort from each other. In time Kevin's breathing became deep and I knew he was asleep.

I, however, was wide awake. A new feeling worked its way in and around my anxiety, filling the empty places that had made me hollow with fear, afraid to think, afraid to feel. I could feel it rising and bubbling amidst the old terrors, creating a new thought entirely.

My breathing became even as my thoughts and breaths combined in a sort of duet...breathe in...*I'm*...breathe out... *going*... in...*to*...out...*live.* In—out—in—out. *I'm—going—to—live.* I could feel my jaw settling in a determined pose. *I'm going to live.* My eyes focused on my baby daughter, lying innocently in her crib beside my bed. A surge of love, unexpected and powerful, swept through my body. Suddenly I understood why animals in the wild were so fierce in protecting their young.

I was a mother now.

Who would love my baby more than I would?

I had to live.

Olivia

I just knew the lullaby I'd heard played in the hospital cafeteria was for Anne's baby. Before we left the hospital, I slipped Brian some money and told him to go into the cafeteria and buy himself a soda for the trip home. Since he'd never turned down food in his life, it was an easy bribe. I took advantage of the couple minutes he was gone to slip over to the information desk.

"Excuse me?" I asked, my voice filled with innocence. "Could you tell me if Anne Abbot had her baby yet?"

The receptionist held up a finger. I realized she was listening to a phone call over her headset. I glanced over my shoulder, feeling like a criminal trying to get information I wasn't supposed to have. For the first time in my life I hoped Brian was late. The receptionist turned to me, "Yes?"

"Uh, yes." I tried to sound as though I knew exactly what was going on. "I was wondering if Anne Abbot had her baby?"

"Oh, ma'am, we're not allowed to give out that information. But I can tell you if she's a patient here. How do you spell her last name?" The receptionist typed the letters into her computer as I relayed them. "Ah, yes…here she is." She turned to me with a smile. "I'm not allowed to tell you anything about a patient's condition, but…" She shifted her eyes, conspiratorially. "I can tell you that I just heard the lullaby play over the speaker system, and that means a new baby has just been born in the hospital. So…?" Her voice rose in a manner that seemed to mean, *it probably was your friend.*

I nodded, a self-satisfied smile on my face. Maybe I had a career as Nancy Drew in my future.

It wasn't until Brian and I were almost to the car when it dawned on me. I'd thought of Anne as my friend twice within the past half-hour.

It was dark as Brian and I drove the familiar highway between Carlton and Brewster, a half-moon glowing in an otherwise dark sky. I felt an odd excitement when I thought of Anne having her baby.

Is it a girl or a boy?

I quickly cut off the thought, chiding myself for my curiosity.

She would have called you, you know.

Again, my conscience taunted me. Memories of my outburst at Anne standing defenseless on our sidewalk, the crumpled brochure on drugs lying between us, flooded my mind.

She was right.

She overstepped our friendship.

She was trying to help.

I was arguing with a fool and I knew it. Still, my mind churned out its defense.

She had no right.

You were her best friend. She had every right.

You never asked for help.

Of course not; you're too stubborn. But you needed it.

Did not.

Did too.

Argghhh! I practically screamed aloud in frustration. My thoughts were getting me nowhere. I couldn't think about this. I wouldn't think about it.

"So," I asked Brian, stepping on the gas, hurrying us home to break my cycle of self-chastisment. "What did Pete have to say?"

Brian choked on his soda, coughing and sputtering. I realized my poor choice of words even as he replied, "Mom, he had a *tube* down his throat. He didn't *say* anything."

Of course he didn't. "Sorry, I wasn't thinking." I leaned over and turned down the radio. "What I meant was, how did Pete seem? What did you talk about?" I quickly turned my head from the road and glanced at Brian. "And, I do mean what did *you* talk about." I smiled, trying to make up for my gaff.

Brian shrugged his shoulders in the way all teenagers have per-fected, the move that says I-dunno, but really means ask me more. So I did.

"Did it seem as if he understood what you were saying?" I didn't know how Pete really was. Ellen had mostly talked about her reaction to what had happened, not how Pete was doing. I'd left Brian with Pete, forgetting that Pete couldn't talk. Now I was curious as to how they'd communicated.

"Yeah, he understood." Brian said the words slowly, as if meas-uring the weight of them. "At least I think he did." He sounded tired.

"Did you tell him what's been happening at school?"

"Yeah." Again, the word came out with effort.

"Did you tell him about the football team? How the season might be suspended?"

"I tried, Mom, but I don't know if he heard me." Brian looked out the side window, then turned to me. "Pete kept shutting his eyes. At first I thought he was, like, falling asleep, or something, so I just sat there. I didn't know what to do. But then, he'd open his eyes, like maybe he thought I'd left or something, so I'd start talking again. I told him about how Coach Rollins talked to us and about having to see the school counselor. But then, I didn't know what to say any-more, Pete just laid there with his eyes closed. So I quit talking…" Brian's words trailed off. He stared out the window for a long time, the radio suddenly intruding with a nonsensical commercial. I snapped it off, wondering why I'd turned it on in the first place. I wasn't interested in anything a radio announcer could possibly have to say; I only wanted to hear my son.

Brian continued to look out the window. I could hear his breathing filling the quiet car, uneven and shallow. He took in a great gulp of air and blew it out forcefully, a small whimper escaping his throat. I glanced at him out of the corner of my eye, his eyes were blinking rapidly. I didn't know what he was going through, what he could possibly be thinking or feeling. I reached a hand out, touching his shoulder. For once he let me keep it there. I rubbed his arm, feeling the tensed muscles beneath his shirt begin to relax. Then, in a voice so low I could barely hear, he said, "I told him I'm sorry."

I squeezed his shoulder. "We're all sorry this happened, Brian."

It was as though my simple words had opened a dam. A loud sob burst from deep in Brian's chest. "No, Mom, you don't understand; I'm the one who's sorry. I made Pete do it."

Anne

Kevin and I were trying our best to be Mr. and Mrs. Perfect Parents. At the first sign of a whimper, we would rush to our daughter's crib, eager to diagnose the cause of her complaint. After two days at home we considered ourselves experts at diaper changing, feeding, and burping. I'd change her diaper while Kevin headed to the kitchen to warm her bottle, then he'd sit with me while I fed her. When her bottle was drained or she started dozing off, Kevin would gently take her in his arms, patting her back until he heard a satisfying burp. Then we would lock eyes and grin, patting ourselves on the back. Another successful feeding.

The trouble was our innocent baby had us doing these things from midnight until the break of dawn. By morning she was exhausted, ready to sleep the day away. Unfortunately, we were too, but didn't have the luxury of not having to fix meals, wash clothes, answer the phone, and pay bills. Not to mention Kevin, who had to work to pay those bills.

On the third morning, after another long night of tending our time-challenged daughter, Kevin looked at me with red-rimmed eyes. "I don't know," he said, his voice cracking with exhaustion, "this new parenthood isn't all it's cracked up to be."

Lack of sleep was taking its toll on me, too. He'd meant it as a joke, but instead of chuckling I burst into tears. "I know-ow... I didn't think it was going to be like this," I sobbed. "I'm just so tired."

I *was* tired. Bone tired. I found myself dreaming about sleep the few moments my head was on a pillow. Even though I was exhausted from taking care of our new baby, I knew, deep down, my tiredness and lack of energy couldn't be completely attributed to having a newborn in the house. My cancer was back. I could sense it.

Before I'd left the hospital, Dr. Lebalm had consulted my doctors in Rochester, who'd been at first apprehensive, then delighted when he'd assured them we were all just fine. I'd delivered a perfectly normal infant. They had agreed I'd need at least a week to rest up before making the trip to Rochester to face another surgery.

Rest up? That was a joke. I'd never been so tired in my life. Not only were we trying to adjust to this new role of parenthood, we were also driving ourselves to exhaustion trying to figure out how, or what, we were going to do with our baby when we went to Rochester.

The original plan had been for me to have the baby there in Rochester. The hospital had said they would keep the baby in the nursery for several days while I underwent surgery. But now that Pokey had jumped the gun, of course the hospital wouldn't take care of her. Kevin and I discussed our options.

"I don't know what else we can do." Kevin was pacing across the living room, our sleeping baby on his shoulder. "We'll have to take her along."

"But Kevin," I countered for the umpteenth time, "I'm not going to be able to help or hold her while I'm there. Where are we going to keep her bottles and warm them up when we need to? And it can't be healthy for her to be around all those sick people in the hospital, either."

"Oh yeah." Kevin sounded deflated. "I hadn't thought about the bottles." He shifted the baby to the crook of his arm. "Maybe I should stay home." In the same breath he countered, "No, that wouldn't work." He sat down on our worn couch, placing the baby gently on his legs. Sighing deeply he remarked, "I don't know what to do, Anne. I just don't know."

"All I can think of…" I drew a deep breath, gathering my thoughts. "…is to ask my mother if she can come stay here."

Kevin nodded his head slowly, agreeing by his reluctant motion that it wasn't our best option, but our only one. "I'll call her," he announced, gathering our baby in his arms and handing her to me.

"Evelyn! Hi, it's Kevin!" His false cheerfulness made me sad.

Why should we be in the position of having to ask my mother to come stay with the baby? Most mothers would already be here. My mother had never offered to come, she had only offered her congratulations. What would she say now when we truly needed her? *Oh Lord,* I prayed, *we need Your help, and my mother's. Open her heart.*

I could only hear Kevin's side of the conversation.

"Oh, she's fine."

"Yup, baby, too."

"We're both a little tired. She kind of has her days and nights mixed up."

I could hear Mom laughing on the other end of the line. It didn't seem funny to me. Apparently, Kevin didn't think so either. I could see him holding the phone out, grimacing at the receiver. He quickly rolled his eyes before speaking again. "Listen, Evelyn, the reason I'm calling is to ask you a favor. I'm sure you remember that Anne needs to go back to Rochester to have her surgery—"

"Well, yes, the doctors are pretty sure she's going to need another mastectomy."

"No, they don't want to wait any longer than absolutely necessary."

"Evelyn," I could hear Kevin interrupting my mother, "the reason I called is to ask if you could possibly come to Brewster and stay with the baby for a few days while we go to Rochester?"

I cringed listening to Kevin. I knew we would be gone at least a week, maybe longer. There was a long silence as Kevin listened. All I could hear was the muffled chatter of my mother's voice through the receiver. It wasn't a simple, "Yes."

I watched Kevin carefully as he said goodbye and hung up the phone. "What did she say?" I sounded about as hopeful as he looked.

"I'm not sure," he said, shaking his head as if confused. "I think she said she'd come. Something about clearing her calendar. But I do know she said she'd call back tomorrow."

"What does she have to check on? Did she say?"

"It sounded really important." I could hear the sarcasm in Kevin's voice. "Her friend Esther is having a card party next week and your mother was afraid she might not be able to find someone to fill her spot." Kevin pounded his fist on the counter. "I'm sorry, Anne, I don't understand your mother. Who'd even have to think about something like this?"

Who, indeed? My throat tightened as tears threatened my eyes.

"I wish my mother was still alive," Kevin stated angrily. "She'd already be here."

I nodded, blinking back tears. There was no use crying over things that couldn't happen. I bowed my head, looking at my sleeping daughter. *Lord, I don't understand...what are we supposed to do? Help me to trust You to show us.* I shifted the baby onto the couch and walked over to Kevin, putting my arms around him from behind. He brought his hands up and awkwardly hugged me.

"I wish things were different," he whispered.

The phone rang and I snatched it up quickly to keep from waking the baby, but it didn't matter because I heard a loud wail at the same time I said, "Hello?"

It was my dad. All he said was, "We'll be there."

I hung up the phone and put my arms around Kevin. As he turned and slipped his arms around me I felt tears come, tears of relief and exhaustion, tears of joy and sadness. Kevin held me tight as our baby cried on the sofa and I cried in his arms.

Olivia

One of the hardest things I've ever done was sit in my car that dark night, listening while my son poured out his confession. *He* was the one who caused Pete to be in the hospital? I pulled the car over to the side of the highway, too shaken by Brian's admission to drive. In a trembling voice, Brian started talking about how scared he was when he saw the ventilator tube in Pete's throat.

"Honest Mom, I didn't know that could happen from what we did." The lights of a passing car swished by, catching the side of Brian's face in a stark glare. He scrunched up his face against the brightness, looking suddenly like a scared little boy. He confirmed my thoughts with his next words. "I'm just so scared, Mom." His face crumpled as once again he sobbed into his hands.

I unbuckled my seat belt and slid over beside him, unbuckling his belt as I slid my arms around him. He slumped against me, his head falling onto my shoulder. It had been years since I'd held him like this. Years since I'd seen him cry. Years since he'd let me know he needed me.

"I feel so stupid," he cried. "I didn't mean for any of this to happen. I'm so stupid," he said over and over again.

I held him, not saying anything, an overwhelming sorrow filling my heart. I blinked back my own tears. Occasionally, I'd run my hand in small circles across his back, trying to comfort. I remembered the times as a small boy when he'd run to me crying over a real or imagined hurt; I'd held him this way then too. Back then my hugs alone were enough to comfort. Not so now. I felt his body shaking with emotion as he sobbed out his fear.

When he had cried himself out, he rubbed his wet face against the shoulder of my coat, slowly pushing himself away from me as if drained. He slumped down in the car seat, bouncing his head against the seat back as if punishing himself.

My voice was soft when I asked, "Why don't you tell it all to me, Brian?"

He nodded slightly, taking his time before speaking. "It's such a *baby* thing." His voice was filled with scorn.

He paused for so long I finally asked, "What's a baby thing?" All I could think he meant was something to do with Anne's baby, but I knew that wasn't what he was talking about.

He inhaled deeply, his breath coming in shudders filled with tears. "That huffing stuff—it's a baby thing." He hung his head.

"Brian," I implored, "I'm new to this. You're going to have to explain to me. Remember, your dad and I had never even heard of "huffing" until a few days ago. What do you mean, it's a baby thing?"

He shrugged. "It's something little kids do."

A new fear swept through me and I spoke in carefully measured tones, "You mean kids like Emily?"

Brian nodded.

"No, Brian." I could hear panic in my voice. "You don't mean Emily does this too, do you?"

Brian shook his head. "No, I don't think Emily does it."

I could breathe again.

His voice was stronger now. "At least she'd better not, or I'll kill her…whoops, guess that wasn't the best thing to say, huh?" He looked at me, an ironic half-smile on his face.

I half-smiled back. "No, it probably wasn't the best choice of words, but I know what you meant. Can you explain what you mean by it being a baby thing?"

Brian flexed his fingers, clenching his fists tightly in a nervous gesture. "Well, it's just…it's…this huffing…well, lots of the little kids do it. When the older kids find out someone like me is doing it…well, they call us, uh…like, babies. You know, if we're going to get high we should be doing something else. It's just that the stuff is so cheap and easy to get that the little kids do it, too."

My mind was already reeling with the information he'd given me. There was a class system for taking drugs? Where had I been hiding? "What kind of stuff are we talking about, Brian?"

He shrugged. "All kinds of things, well…like, uh, your hair spray, for one."

"And?" I coaxed.

"Some of the girls paint their fingernails with that white stuff you use to make corrections with."

"What would that do?" This wasn't making any sense to me.

"It dries on their nails but it still smells, so they can, like, sit and smell it during school."

Oh. I cringed. I had two bottles of the stuff sitting by my rarely used typewriter. My hair spray. My correction fluid. I was beginning to feel as though I were an unknowing "dealer."

"Some kids smell spray paint. They spray it in a bag and then take deep breaths out of the bag. I never did that, though."

He looked at me as if I should be glad. "That's good, I guess." What was I supposed to say?

"There are all kinds of other things, too. Like a bunch of stuff we have at home. Your dusting spray and the gasoline Dad has in the garage for the lawn mower, and…"

As Brian recited items as if they were a grocery list, my jaw dropped lower and lower. If these kids had put as much effort into their school work as they knew about this topic, they'd all be top scholars. I was amazed, furious, and humbled. Amazed that he knew so much, at least about what would create that "high" the kids seemed to be searching for, not what could happen when something went wrong. Furious that this had been going on right under my roof and I didn't have a clue. And humbled to know my son had a life apart from me. I'd raised him all these years, assuming I knew him, knew just what each door slam meant…*I'm home…I'm mad…You don't understand.* Knew what he liked to eat when he was "starving"… *Pringles potato chips…cold hot dish…a glass of milk in a certain blue mug.* I even knew who he was talking to on the phone just by the tone of his voice. I'd been so smart. I knew my son inside and out. How could I have been so wrong?

"...honest, Mom, I never knew that stuff could cause someone to almost die. I told Pete it would just make him feel good. I'm so stupid!" Brian banged his head with his hand.

"The other day in the locker room," I asked, "was that the first time Pete had tried it?"

Brian shook his head. "No, we'd done it lots of other times, at home, and...places." He must have heard my sharp intake of air as he said "home," because his words trailed off and he turned to look at me. "We mostly did it at Pete's house. His mom wasn't home all that much."

As if that should make me happy—that he didn't do it at our house much. It made me sick to think of him doing it at all, anywhere.

"Mom," Brian was close to tears, again, his voice a whisper, "is Pete going to be...normal again?"

I thought of the way Pete had looked, lying so still in his hospital bed, a tube coming from his mouth, unable to talk, an IV snaking from his arm, a heart monitor beeping softly near the head of his bed. It had scared me—I could understand why a fifteen-year-old would be frightened. "I think so," I answered slowly, "from what his mom told me, anyway. It sounded like they had him medicated to regulate his heartbeat and keep him quiet while he's on the respirator." I realized now how little Ellen had actually said about Pete. She mostly talked about her own shortcomings as a parent. I'd listened to her, never applying her words to myself. What were my faults as a parent?

"Brian," I questioned, not sure I wanted to hear the answer, "what could I have done to make things different?"

He thought for a long minute, rubbing his forefinger in a circle on his chin, then, with a sly grin, replied, "Not use hair spray?"

I looked at him, my mind blank, not understanding his joke. I felt a flash of anger, how dare he treat my heartfelt question so flippantly? And then, in almost the same moment I realized he was just like me, turning a serious question aside with a joke or smart comment. How many times had I done that with Anne? Her asking me a question in earnest, truly wanting to hear my thoughts; me, not willing to examine myself enough to give an honest answer. What had Anne done to get past my defenses? An inner voice seemed to answer. *She kept asking. She kept loving.*

I still felt annoyed over his attempt at humor, but knew any show of it would cause him to clam up. "Bzzzzt," I gently teased, "wrong answer." Growing serious, I asked, again, "Really, Brian, what could I have done to prevent this?"

Brian stared at the lighted dashboard for a long time. When he spoke, his words were slow and thoughtful. "I don't know, Mom. Sometimes kids just do dumb things. I guess you've got a dumb kid, is all."

"You're not a dumb kid!" The words were much louder than I expected, causing Brian to jerk his head up in response. "What you did might have been dumb, but that doesn't make you dumb. As long as you learn something from this and grow from it, you're going to end up a better person." I looked him straight in the eye. "Believe it, Brian."

He nodded, surprised at the force of my words.

I slipped my seat belt back into place. "Let's go home."

That night when everyone was asleep, I found myself wandering through the house, my own words ringing in my ears, *as long as you learn something from this, and grow from it, you're going to end up a better person.*

I couldn't help but think of my fight with Anne. The words I'd tossed at her in anger. In denial. The weeks I'd spent blaming her. The weeks I'd spent missing her. Too rigid to admit I'd been wrong. Too obstinate to apologize.

I'd meant the speech for Brian. *As long as you learn something from this, and grow from it, you're going to end up a better person.* But I found myself wondering, what was I was supposed to learn? Was I, as Brian thought of himself, too dumb?

Maybe we weren't dumb—just stubborn.

I roamed the house, trying to quiet my thoughts. Not knowing if I should be thinking about Brian—would he learn from this? Would he change his ways? Or myself—was I to blame for any of his behavior? Was my anger towards Anne justified? For the first time, I found myself questioning my role in our argument. Had Anne really tried to change me? Or had I, in response to her friendship, started changing on my own?

My eyes lighted upon my computer and my leather office chair. The place I'd spent so many fruitless hours dreaming about writing the great American novel, but in reality, writing absolutely nothing. Who was I trying to kid? I suddenly saw my life in stark reality. My whole life had been a daydream, a fantasy I'd built up in my mind. I'd thought I had the perfect marriage. Instead, I had a husband who was hardly ever home, and when he was, his mind was somewhere else. I'd thought I had the perfect family, a handsome boy and a charming, precocious daughter. Instead, I had a son who admitted using inhalants and had convinced his best friend to do the same, almost at the price of his life. And Emily? Maybe I hadn't been making up a fantasy about her. She was still my young and innocent little girl. But if I didn't start seeing things as they really were, who knew how Emily would turn out?

I paced the room, trying to sort through my racing thoughts. I'd give up writing and concentrate on my family instead. Forget my column. Forget writing a novel. It was time to give up my dream and live in the real world. The thought was like a slap. Get real! Wasn't that what Dr. Phil on the *Oprah* show had said, that I should "get real." Okay, I would. No more writing—make that dreaming—my days away. With Dr. Phil's help, I'd put writing behind me and get real.

I started rummaging through the tapes by the video machine. I remembered recording that show; the tape had to be here somewhere. Maybe an expert could help me. Show me how to start "getting real." I remembered, I'd started taping the program when Emily had run in the house yelling about an ambulance at school. I couldn't remember watching television since that afternoon. I hit the eject button and out popped the tape, still in the machine. It had taped to the end of the reel and then automatically rewound to the beginning. I snapped it back in, fast-forwarding through an old program at the beginning. As I waited for the tape to reach the part where I'd left off, my eyes roamed the room, as restless as my thoughts, finally landing on the shelf above my computer. There, neatly wrapped, was the birthday present Anne had brought to my house so long ago. The present that mocked me at every glance. The present I'd felt unworthy of opening. The present I'd forgotten about the past few days.

A stream of light from the street lamp outside the window made the small package glow as if lit from within. Whereas before I wouldn't go near the package, now I couldn't seem to stay away. I put the recorder on "pause" and crossed the room to get the gift. Returning to the couch, I fingered the wrapping, recalling with chagrin the day Anne had brought this gift to me. It no longer seemed off-limits. Instead, I had an odd sense it held some sort of answer.

A tug brought the silver ribbon away from the royal blue paper. With my thumbnail I slit the tape on each end. Sliding the box away from the wrapping left me holding a hinged, rectangular box. Closing my eyes I slowly lifted the lid. I opened my eyes and found myself looking at…my nemesis? A talisman?

It was an exquisite silver writing pen. As I lifted the pen, turning it to admire its sleek lines, I noticed an engraving on each side of the clip. It was too dark to read clearly, so I walked over to the window to catch the light from the street lamp coming through the window. On one side was etched, "Write on." I smiled; it was a clever play on the encouraging words we'd used as teenagers. I turned the pen slowly, trying to catch the light, just so, to read the engraving on the other side. It read simply, "Love, Anne."

My heart was pounding as I stared at the simple, yet eloquent words engraved on each side of the pen. As quick as the stroke of a pen on paper, the dream I'd just given up, Anne had given back to me.

Anne

I don't know which made me more nervous, the thought of going to Rochester and facing another surgery, or the thought of my mother coming to stay. Exhausted as I was, I spent any free moment I had cleaning every nook and cranny of our small house. My mother never failed to let me know, not so much by her words but by her actions, how she felt about the cleanliness of my house. It wasn't uncommon to find her kneeling on the floor cleaning my self-cleaning oven, or squirting my bathroom counter tops with a second layer of cleaning spritz. Unfortunately, or maybe fortunately, I didn't inherit her cleaning genes.

It was in the middle of one of my marathon cleaning sessions, when the baby was taking her long, should-have-been-nightime sleep in late afternoon, that I sat down on the couch for "just a second." The next thing I knew, Kevin was standing over me. Apparently, he'd arrived home from work expecting supper and instead found Sleeping Beauty, as he laughingly put it.

Finding me asleep, dust rag in hand, was a wake-up call for both of us. We realized we couldn't keep up the schedule we'd been trying to perfect, no matter how hard we tried. The human body was made to work and rest.

"You're exhausted, Anne," Kevin pointed out, "and I am, too. I'm worried I'm either going to fall asleep driving to see my clients, or fall asleep while I'm talking to them. Insurance can be boring enough—they don't need the agent conking out in the middle of his own spiel."

I had to agree.

I swallowed my pride and called the doctor's office. After an all too hearty sounding laugh when I described my problem, the nurse commented, "Oh, Honey, by the time you finally get those kids to sleep through the night, they turn into teenagers and you're fighting with them all over again to get them into bed at night. Believe me, I know. I raised three of 'em, and still don't know how I lived through it." She laughed again as if her advice was the funniest thing in the world.

"That's not very encouraging," I replied, tears at the ready, "considering my husband and I have been awake for the past 72 hours. At least it seems that long."

"I remember those days, Honey, I sure do. Hang in there, it'll get better. Now, here's what you do…" I was all ears as she went on to explain, "Try to get your little one to stay awake a little longer every time she wakes up during the day."

That advice was at odds with everything I'd read, considering all the chapters devoted to Ways to Get Baby to Sleep. But at this point we were ready to try anything.

She went on, "You've got to play with her, you know, kind of tickle her, give her a baby massage, rattle a few toys in front of her. If she falls asleep while she's nursing—you are nursing, aren't you?"

A flash of regret swept through me as I remembered the reason I wasn't nursing and my upcoming surgery. "Uh, no." Once again I felt as though I were a poor mother. I couldn't cope with my baby's sleep schedule and now I could tell by the nurse's tone that she didn't approve of my feeding methods, either. "I have a, uh, health problem," I explained. "I can't nurse."

"Ummm," she cooed, sympathetically, "I'm sorry. That's too bad." She really did sound sympathetic, and I felt a bit better. "Well," she continued, "if she starts dozing off during her feeding, you just jostle her a little to get her to wake up. You keep that up for a couple days, and your little one should have her days and nights straightened out in no time." She sounded so confident, it was hard to doubt her.

"Thank you," I mumbled as I hung up the phone. I didn't feel anywhere near as confident as the nurse sounded.

Kevin and I came up with a plan. We decided it was foolish for Kevin to sit with me each night when I got up to feed the baby. In our excitement at being first-time parents, we'd been eager to not miss a minute of our baby's waking moments.

However, that eagerness was being replaced with weariness. Neither one of us had the stamina to watch our baby practically twenty-four hours a day. We decided I would cover the nighttime hours from midnight until six-ish. That way I could get a few unbroken hours of sleep before midnight, and hopefully the baby would sleep a bit in-between so I could doze, too. Kevin would get an abbreviated but full night's sleep, filling in during the evening and again in the couple hours of morning before he went to work. I promised to take a nap sometime during the day when the baby was sound asleep. As much as we worried about getting enough sleep just to function, we were beginning to worry even more about Kevin's job, or rather the income it provided. He'd missed quite a bit of time from work already and would be missing even more in the coming week.

It wasn't that his boss was putting pressure on him—Kevin did enough of that himself. Kevin had always been a workaholic, putting in hours that were neither required nor expected. He arrived at work early and left late, bringing home paperwork to occupy any remaining hours. His diligence had paid off. He'd cultivated a loyal customer base and had a nice commission check each month. But we were nowhere near easy street. Most of the money we'd saved over the past years had been spent as a down payment on our house. And while Kevin's employer offered a good health insurance plan, it didn't cover the loss of income from my piano lessons or the additional expenses that came along with an out-of-town hospitalization.

"I don't know, Anne," Kevin said, running his pencil down the ledger once again, "we're going to be cutting it close this month. I figure, minimum, four nights in the motel and all my meals eaten at a café…even if it is the hospital cafeteria it still adds up. Plus, we've got gas to get down there, phone calls home to check on the baby—"

"Don't you mean check on my mother?"

Kevin raised his eyebrows. "You said it, I didn't." He looked at the figures again, running a hand through his hair as if his motion would stimulate some creative financing thoughts.

"Maybe we should've taken my church group up on the benefit supper they wanted to sponsor for me," I suggested meekly. Inwardly, I cringed at the thought. The idea of sitting in the church basement watching limp spaghetti being piled onto plates in my honor embarrassed me. I also knew our congregation was not made up of independently wealthy people. Anything they gave would cause their budget to be stretched that much further that month. Our finances didn't seem like anybody's responsibility but ours.

Kevin didn't even have to think about my suggestion. "No" was all he said, then added, "We'll make it somehow."

"I suppose we could ask my parents for a loan. Dad's offered before." Again, my suggestion was weak. I knew how Kevin felt about accepting help.

"Anne, I said we'd make it." Kevin's voice was stern. He tossed the pencil onto the paper in frustration. "If we have to, we'll take out a loan." He'd said the words matter-of-factly, but I knew Kevin had always prided himself on being able to pay our bills as they occurred; I knew things had to be tight for him to be considering that option.

"Maybe we could go talk to Bob, Libby's husband. He's a banker, maybe he'd have some ideas…"

"Anne, stop it!" Kevin's words were harsh. "I'll figure something out."

Just then a wail came from the other room, and just as quickly tears filled my eyes. A sob burst from my throat. "I'm so sorry. If it weren't for me this wouldn't be happening to us. I'm sorry. I can't help it. I hate this! I hate being sick!"

"Ssshhhh." Kevin's arms were around me, his voice soothing in my ear. "Don't cry, Anne. Ssshhhh." He pulled me to my feet, gathering me into a tight embrace.

"I'm sorry if I sounded mad. I'm not. I don't like you being sick, either. If anything, I'm mad about the fact you're sick—that you have to go through this—not about trying to pay for things. When I vowed, for better or worse, I meant it." He slid his arms to my shoulders, pushing me back enough to look into my eyes. "Understand?"

Sniffling, I nodded. "Thanks." I grabbed a tissue, swiped at my eyes and blew my nose. "I'd better get the baby."

As I started towards the doorway Kevin turned me around to face him. "I'll get the baby, you go take a long bath."

The idea of a relaxing bath with a tub full of bubbles was so inviting I started crying all over again. "Now I know I'm too tired," I laughed through my tears, "when I cry over taking a bath."

"Go on." Kevin gave me a playful push as he went to pick up our daughter.

I paused in the doorway watching him cuddle our little girl. He held her in his left arm, chucking her under her tiny chin with his right forefinger. Then he leaned over, kissing her on the cheek. He pulled back a bit and rubbed his nose against hers, cooing to her all the while.

A pang of joy and regret mingled in my heart as I watched father and daughter bond. This was supposed to be a joyous, carefree time. Instead we were burdened with mounting bills and an uncertain future, blessed with a new life to care for. "Kevin," I said softly. He turned to my voice. "I'm sorry."

He gave me a puzzled look. "For what?"

"When we said our vows, for better or worse, I never thought we'd be getting both things at the same time."

Kevin then said something that sounded like a riddle but went straight to my heart. "Don't worry about it, Anne. The better is so much better than the worse is bad."

I turned those words over and over in my mind as I soaked in the steamy, fragrant water.

⌒

Mom and Dad arrived right on schedule, the five-hour drive from Minneapolis getting them to our house by mid-afternoon. That gave us the rest of the day to get them acquainted with their new granddaughter and her still-evolving routine. They hadn't been in the house an hour when I found my mother sneaking a peek in my oven. She wasn't looking to see what was cooking—that wouldn't happen for another hour or so—she was checking to see how clean it was. It must have passed her test, for she made a pleased-sounding murmur and closed the door.

I'd already changed the sheets on our bed where my mother and father would be sleeping. Kevin and I planned to sleep on our old hide-a-bed sofa in the living room. We reasoned that would give us more space to walk the baby in the middle of the night as well as ease preparations for our early morning departure.

My father seemed to have an instant bond with his new grand-daughter, convinced he elicited her first smile by vibrating his lips gently on her tummy. I wasn't sure if it was an actual smile, but she did seem to enjoy it, and they passed a good 15 minutes playing on the floor together.

My mother was more concerned with the nuts and bolts of each day.

"What time does she wake up in the morning?"

"Well, ummm." I hesitated, not wanting to spell it out. *Two A.M. and then usually, three-thirty, and then*...I hinted instead. "She hasn't settled into a regular schedule yet. She's kind of drowsy in the after-noon, then gets a second wind later. I hope she's not going to be too much for you."

"Oh, pooh! I raised you girls just fine didn't I?"

I didn't have the heart to remind her she'd been thirty years younger then. So I agreed, "Yes, you did." I went on, explaining, "The formula is over here. Be careful when you heat it in the microwave; it gets hot pretty fast." I'd learned that late one night the hard way, burning my wrist with just a few drops of the hot liquid. Better me than the baby. I'd had to plunge the bottle in a dish of ice cubes to cool it down, my hungry little baby wailing her lungs out, impatiently waiting.

Mother, however, had other plans. "I never had a microwave when you girls were born. You girls nowadays have things so easy. I always heated your bottles on the stove in a pan of warm water. I'm sure that method still works just fine." Mother glanced confidently around the kitchen. "I think we'll get along just fine." That was the third time she'd said "just fine," and I was beginning to wonder if she was trying to reassure me or herself. "You go finish your packing and I'll get supper started." Mom pointed to the door.

"Listen, Mom," I paused by the counter. "I wanted to talk to you about my surgery…it might be a week or so before we get back, and…"

"Oh, pooh, Anne, don't talk like that." Mom turned her back, opening a cupboard door as if to look for something. "You'll be back before you know it. You're going to be just fine." She closed the cupboard door. "Now go!"

"But, Mom, I want you to know it's not going to be an in-and-out kind of surgery. It's more complicated than—"

"We've got plenty of time to talk about this tonight. If I don't get supper started those men are going to starve to death." She waved a dish towel at me. "Just get!"

"Okay," I reluctantly agreed, knowing she would not find time to listen to me tonight either. I opened the fridge door. "I've got a roast beef with carrots and potatoes all ready to go. Just drain the water off the potatoes and add them to the pot," I instructed. "Put it in at 350. I've already got the meat seasoned."

"Anne, you act as if I've never cooked before." She pulled the roaster out of the fridge, lifting the lid. "Oh." The tone of her voice told me something was wrong.

"What?"

"I see you didn't brown the meat first. Seals in the juices, you know."

I'd made roast beef a hundred times and never had I browned it. Every time Kevin said it was his favorite. I quoted my mother, "It'll be just fine."

"Just go get ready." She shooed me out of the kitchen with both hands.

As I folded the roomy sweater I expected to wear coming home from the hospital, I could hear the sizzle of meat on the stove top. I sat down on the bed, suddenly exhausted with all the preparations. I'd spent the past week trying to adjust to having a new baby in the house, worrying about how we'd care for her while we were in Rochester, cleaning in preparation for my parent's arrival, trying to make backup plans in case my mother needed help. I'd failed miserably at that. Jan was going to be out of town all week visiting her sister; she herself was looking for after school care for her son. I didn't dare ask Connie to fill in. Several women at church had generously offered to babysit "Anytime, anytime at all." But I didn't feel as though I knew any one of them well enough to really ask.

Libby would do it. Yes, there was a time when Libby would have done it without hesitation. But not anymore. *She told you she would.*

We'd stopped at a bookstore following one of my many doctor appointments. Libby sipped a cup of steaming coffee; I'd passed, not sure if I was queasy from chemo medication or a baby who was tap dancing in my stomach.

"Here's one." One-handed, Libby pulled a paperback from the packed shelf, two books beside it falling to the floor. Libby held the book for me to see, *The New Age Book of Baby Care.*

"I'm beginning to feel I need *The Old Age Book of Baby Care.* I clasped my stomach hoping it would calm my rolling child. "What will they think of next?" I bent to pick the books off the floor.

"How about this one?" Libby held another book. *How to Bond with Your Baby.*

"That's a possibility." I took the book from her, skimming it quickly. The closer the date of my delivery loomed and the larger my body grew, the more apprehensive I found myself about raising this child. I blurted out my fear to Libby. "I'm getting scared. I've never even changed a diaper or babysat. What do I know about raising a baby?"

Libby grabbed the book from me and stuffed it onto the shelf. "Give the kid to me for a couple months. I'll handle it." She said it with the confidence of a mother who'd done it before. "I look back on those first few months and compared to having a crabby teenager in the house, it's a piece of cake." She grew serious. "I mean it, Anne. Well, not about giving me your baby for a couple of months, but I'll gladly watch your baby anytime. Really. Anytime."

Back then her words reassured me because I knew she meant them. I knew I could count on her anytime.

Anytime, except now.

I focused once again on my open but empty suitcase.

So many times this past week, as I'd cooked and cleaned and made phone call after phone call, trying to get everything lined up to run smoothly for my mother, I'd thought of Libby and how much easier it would have been to leave my baby with her.

I missed her all over again. Sure, her harsh words had stung. But I knew they'd come from a deep dark place within her. A place of defense and denial. Libby didn't have the strength of prayer to help carry her burdens as I did. She was trying to do it all by herself. I'd thought about her words a lot. I'd come to realize Libby hadn't really meant them for me, even if she didn't know that. She'd been lashing out at her fear, and I just happened to be in the way. If Libby couldn't pray for herself, I could.

I began folding the clothes I'd laid out on the bed, praying for Libby as I smoothed wrinkles. *Oh, Lord, strengthen Libby.* I folded back the arms of a sweater. *Open her eyes to truth.* I bent the sweater in half. *Give her courage to deal with the truth.* I placed the sweater in my suitcase. *Soften her heart enough to let You in.*

By the time my suitcase was full I had Libby surrounded by prayer. It was then I realized that in all my busyness preparing for our departure I'd forgotten to pray for myself. I hoped there were others who were praying for me, much as I'd prayed for Libby, but if there weren't, I figured God wouldn't mind listening a few minutes more.

"Anne, time to eat!" Mom called from the kitchen.

I quickly bowed my head. "Lord, watch over me as I go through this surgery. Grant me your peace and healing. Let your love show through me to the people I meet. You know my needs better than I do, Lord—"

"Anne, come and eat!" This time it was my father calling.

"Amen, I guess." Smiling, I rolled my eyes heavenward as I rose from the bed. I snapped the suitcase shut, picked it up and went to set it by the front door on my way to eat.

Just as I neared the door on my way to the kitchen, I heard a soft knock. "I'll get it," I called, even though I doubted anyone else had heard it. It was probably one of the neighbor kids selling something for school. I swung open the door, fully expecting to see Davy Bell standing on my front step asking if I'd like to buy another roll of wrapping paper. Instead, there stood Libby.

"Libby?" The word was out before I'd consciously comprehended it was her. My voice had risen at least an octave in surprise. I cleared my throat and, remembering, corrected myself. "Olivia!"

"I hope I didn't wake the baby." Her voice was softer than I recalled. She stood, looking me straight in the eye, a cake in her hands.

"No. No, she's still sleeping," I whispered. I felt a bubble of emotion welling within me.

"Ahhh," Libby sounded pleased. "You had a girl."

"Yes, I did," I replied, stunned to see her on my doorstep. And then, just because it felt so good to say her name, I said it again. "Libby."

Olivia

I'd knocked softly on Anne's front door, hoping not to wake the baby.

Or hoping she wouldn't hear your knock at all?

I'd rehearsed my lines over and over on my way to Anne's house, going so far as to say them out loud into the silence of the car. "I hope I didn't wake the baby." I sounded nervous even when I said them to myself. What would I sound like saying them to Anne?

When I pulled up to her house, I noticed a strange car parked in the driveway. My first thought was, "Maybe I shouldn't stop now." My second thought was, "Good, they have company." I could just drop my cake off and leave. My third thought was, "You chicken. You're not getting out of this. Stop the car right now and go in and say what you came to say." I slammed on the brakes before I talked myself out of stopping and almost did away with my carefully baked cake. As it was, I got a finger full of frosting as I grabbed at the plastic wrap covering while trying to stop the cake's slide forward. I licked my finger, then quickly checked my face in the car mirror. That's all I needed—chocolate frosting on my teeth.

Trying to sugarcoat your words?

Again, my conscience pricked.

Just do it, it told me now.

I took a deep breath, picked up the cake, and walked toward the door.

Through their picture window I could see a light in the kitchen dining area and three people sitting around the table. Of course. Her mother would be here now, helping Anne with the baby. I hadn't thought of that possibility. A cold sweat broke out on my upper lip.

This was going to be hard enough; I wasn't sure I needed witnesses. My feet seemed as though they were clad with cement as I slowly moved up the three steps leading to Anne's front door. How many times had I bound up those same steps, eager for a visit with Anne? I'd barely knock before swinging open the door and calling, "It's me!" Now, I stood on the top step, the door resembling the Great Wall of China. Surely no one would hear my knock. I could leave my cake on the doorstep and call to see if they'd found it. I could take it home and let Emily and Brian eat it as they'd begged to do as I was frosting it.

Or you could knock.

I knocked.

Softly.

It was a chicken-sounding knock, much too soft for anyone to truly hear. I lifted my hand to try again, but before I could, the door swung open and there stood Anne. She looked radiant.

A sudden case of nerves made my words come out hoarsely. "I hope I didn't wake the baby." My sentence sounded rehearsed. Probably because it was. I hoped Anne didn't notice.

Without hesitating for even a second Anne breathed my name three times. "Libby. Olivia. Libby."

There was a moment of awkward silence. I took that as my cue. Holding my cake out to her I said, "It looks like you have company. I brought you dessert."

"Thank you!" Anne spread out her arms almost as if to hug me, then brought them in closer and held her hands open in front of me. "It's a cake," she remarked, sounding pleased.

"Well," I replied, pushing it into her hands, "it may look like a cake, but actually, it's humble pie." I'd rehearsed that part too as I was measuring and sifting, mixing and baking. Thankfully, those words came out sounding true.

It took Anne a second to catch my meaning, looking up at me in surprise. Just then Kevin poked his head around the corner. "Anne, are you coming? Your mom has the roast rea—" He saw my silhouette in the doorway. "Oh, hi," he said, interrupting himself. I lifted my hand in a small wave.

"I guess I'd better let you eat." I slowly turned to go. "Oh here, I almost forgot." I pulled the small gift I'd bought for her baby from my bulging coat pocket.

Anne put a hand on my arm. "No, Libby, don't go. Stay. Please?"

"You're eating. I'll come back another time."

"I won't be—" She stopped, started again. "No, not another time. Come see the baby."

Kevin had disappeared. I took a deep breath. "Anne, I do want to see the baby, but I came here for another reason. I really wanted to talk to you, to—" I stopped, cleared my throat. "I need to…apologize."

"Oh, Lib—Olivia, you—"

"No, Anne, let me say what I need to. Please."

She turned and set the cake on a table near the door, the unopened gift beside it, then stepped out onto the front step with me, pulling the door closed behind her. It was a cool night and she wrapped her arms around herself.

I cleared my throat, once again. "Anne, this is hard for me to say. I'm not used to apologizing, you know…because I'm usually so right!" My attempt at humor fell flat. Anne stood there, an unreadable expression on her face. "I just want to tell you, Anne, this whole thing had nothing to do with you and everything to do with me."

I hadn't intended to tell Anne all that had happened over the past few days. About Brian's confession, about the hours I'd spent searching my mind, trying to figure out what had gone wrong. I'd just planned to go to Anne's house, apologize, give her my cake and go home.

Instead, when Anne whispered my name a fourth time, "Oh, Olivia," with such empathy and compassion, it made me stop and swallow the lump that had formed in my throat. I found myself pouring out every last detail of my anguish.

"Anne," I started, "you can't imagine what these past few days have been like at our house. First of all, I have to tell you, Brian is…was…using drugs." That was the first time I'd actually said the words out loud—*my son is using drugs*. Hearing the words spoken out loud caused a shiver to run down my spine, but there was a sense of relief there, as well. A feeling that if I could say it, I could deal with it.

Anne murmured in dismay.

"Have you ever heard of huffing?"

Anne shook her head.

"I hadn't either, but believe me, I know more about it now than I ever hoped to." I explained to Anne what this new huffing sensation was all about. Then I went on to tell her about Brian's visit to see Pete at the hospital. Anne had heard Pete was hospitalized, but hadn't realized the seriousness of what had happened.

"Olivia, you must have been so scared. To think that could have happened to Brian!"

I blinked back sudden tears. Anne knew exactly how I felt without my having to say a word. I nodded. "I was terrified. Mad, too."

Anne gave me a half-smile. "I know you, Olivia. I'm sure you were mad. Is Brian grounded for life, or just until you and Bob move to the retirement home?"

"That's not the half of things." I rubbed my eyebrows with the tips of my fingers. What came next was the hard part. "I don't know how to say this." I paused. "I feel as though I should have some sort of punishment, too. For the way I treated you." In the darkness I could feel my face flaming with shame. Anne was silent, as if she knew I needed to speak aloud my words of regret.

I told it all. How I'd paced the house late at night, wondering what had gone so wrong. How, in frustration, I'd sat down to watch an old *Oprah* show, then had spotted the birthday gift she'd left for me.

"I never did open it," I explained, my voice quavering. "I didn't feel I deserved anything after the way I'd acted."

"You didn't open your birthday present?" Anne was amazed.

"Not then," I explained. "I did later—just the other night. Anne, you have no idea what your gift meant to me—" My voice broke as I remembered the pen, the symbol of my dream returned.

That night, I sat with the silver pen in my lap, watching the tape of Dr. Phil on the *Oprah* show. It seemed as if he were talking just to me, telling me things I didn't want to hear, but that I needed to hear all the same. Tell-it-like-it-is-Phil was telling it directly to me. Instead of denying my faults as I'd done in the past, that night I felt his words cut straight through me. What usually sounded like gobbledygook—psychiatric mumbo-jumbo—all of a sudden made sense. I saw my life as never before.

There Dr. Phil was on tape, going over his life strategies, telling me that I created my own experiences.

I recalled the way I'd lashed out at Anne. I was the one to cause our rift. She had only been trying to help. Trying to warn me of trouble. If I'd listened to her, taken her words and mulled them over, I might have spared Pete, and certainly Brian—our whole family, really—a lot of anguish. And, I would have had a friend by my side to help me through it.

I paused the tape as a scene from my past played in my mind. There was my dad, lying in a hospital bed, dying. There I stood, a stubborn, inarticulate teenager, unable to put into words the last sentence my dad would hear from me. I wanted to apologize for all the times I talked back to him, for all the times I thought of him as old-fashioned and "square." He'd tease me about his being "square" as I'd roll my eyes at another of his imagined foibles. I wanted to apologize for all the times I hadn't said "I love you," when I really did. Then, as now, my experience had been in my hands. Granted, I'd been young, maybe too young to know better, but even now, years later, I hadn't learned anything from my behavior. I'd gone through life being stubborn, refusing to say things that needed to be said to the people who needed to hear them. Some *experience* I'd created.

I fast-forwarded through a commercial, then listened as Dr. Phil spoke, telling me I couldn't change what I didn't acknowledge. I felt as if I'd been slapped in the face as I recalled the times I'd blamed every place, every thing, everyone else for my problems. I'd blamed my father for taking the joy out of every birthday I'd ever had, I'd blamed Bob so many times for my unhappiness and even for my lack of friends, I'd blamed Anne for Brian's problems, I'd even blamed her for changing me. I saw my behavior in a new light—no one, not one single person, was responsible for the way I'd behaved except me.

I clutched the pen Anne had given me, my belated birthday present. Suddenly, that beautiful silver pen seemed my ticket to a different life, a changed life. Once again I paused the tape, walked to my desk and grabbed a legal-sized yellow tablet. I returned to the couch ready to write. Immediately, I realized I needed to start where the problem had begun, with the incriminating words on that baby shower game sheet. I set the pen and paper aside, then tiptoed into our bedroom. I had to dig through the pockets of several jackets before I found it. The paper was folded in a tight little package, as if the words themselves wanted to remain in the dark, just like me. No longer. Unfolding the notepaper, I returned to the couch, pressing at the wrinkled creases as if my motion could erase all that had happened in-between.

There were the words scrawled across the page, "changes everything." The two simple words that had changed so much. I'd let them have such power over me that bad things had happened as a result. Now, I wanted to use the words to cause change for good.

The blaring of the television startled me as the paused tape automatically started up. I pushed the mute button, then Stop. By the flickering light of the television, I started writing—incidents from my past that I imagined had scarred me forever and times when I'd blamed others for mistakes that were mine alone. I didn't even want to try to imagine how many things I didn't remember. I wrote down what had happened, my reaction to it, and if I'd been angry, hurt, or had blamed someone else. Then I paused, rereading what I'd written. After much thinking and soul-searching, I wrote down what a better reaction would have been. It wasn't easy. There were a couple times when I'd thought I might have to take both my hands and force my pen across the page. To see my mistakes right before my eyes was, for lack of a better term, eye-opening.

I could see all too clearly that what I'd thought was justified behavior on my part had done nothing but hurt the person I was lashing out at. Ultimately it had hurt me the most.

It was a humbling experience.

I wrote and thought, and wrote some more. I was still writing when Bob came into the room. "Olivia, what are you doing?"

I jumped as though it was the bogeyman who'd entered. "Oh!" I realized it was only Bob. "You scared me. What time is it?" Only then did I notice he was dressed for work. I hadn't heard him get up, turn on the shower, or walk down the stairs.

"Seven-fifteen. Did you fall asleep watching television? It looks as if your side of the bed wasn't even slept in."

I followed Bob into the kitchen, automatically filling the coffee pot with fresh grounds. "I couldn't sleep," I explained, plugging in the percolator. "I started watching a tape and then I started writing." I stopped. How could I explain what had happened to me last night to this man I was seeing as if with different eyes? "I guess I lost track of time." I yawned, the sleepless night hitting me full-force. "This could be a long day."

Bob nodded, sympathizing with my lack of sleep as he poured himself a bowl of cereal. "Why don't you lay down for a nap after the kids get off to school?"

I looked at my husband. He was the same man I'd looked at yesterday. The same guy I'd been mentally chastising for working so much. The same husband I'd thought took me for granted. But during the night, something had changed. In the early morning light he looked different. There was a soft vulnerability about him I hadn't noticed in years. Suddenly, my heart was full of things I wanted to tell him. But I knew now wasn't the time. I walked to him, wrapped my arms around his waist and gave him a warm kiss. "Would you have time to talk tonight?"

"About?"

What did I want to talk about? I had the whole day to figure it out. I answered vaguely, "Oh, just some things I thought about during my sleepless night. Some of it has to do with Brian and, I guess some of it has to do with…" I was practically tugging the unfamiliar words from my mouth, "…with me."

Bob looked at me strangely, sensing my uneasiness. "Okay," he said, not questioning me further.

By the time the kids left for school I'd gotten a second wind. After showering and getting dressed I felt ready to tackle my whirling thoughts again. I sat down to watch the end of the tape, the tape that had started my introspection. It was then I heard the words that truly changed everything.

As Dr. Phil sat on stage counseling audience members I took notes, thinking they would help me solidify my thoughts. Something I could explain to Bob later that night. I'm sure Dr. Phil had no idea how "Life Strategy Number Nine" would change me, but it was the piece that completed the puzzle of my thoughts. He said it so simply, but it hit me like a thunderclap, the simple phrase falling on my heart like cleansing rain; *there is freedom in forgiveness.*

It was as if I'd been struck dumb. The thought took over my mind. What would it be like to forgive everyone? To say, "Dad, I understand. I forgive you." To sit across from Bob tonight and say, "Bob, I'm sorry I've been crabby about all the time you've been spending at work. I know you're trying to provide a good life for our family. Thank you." To drive over to Anne's house, knock on her door and say, "Anne, I was wrong. Please forgive me."

It was as if a whole new section of my brain had opened. A phrase from a long-forgotten Bible verse flashed through my mind: *Your sins are forgiven.* Where had that come from? I'd gone to church occasionally growing up—we were what I've since heard referred to as C and E members. Christmas and Easter. Church wasn't a priority with my parents, consequently it never had been for me, either. A couple times a year my parents would march my brother and me off to church, often enough that the people in Brewster recognized our church affiliation, but not often enough that it came to mean anything to me personally.

I'd never felt much need for religion. Growing up with a "pull yourself up by your own bootstraps" philosophy had left me with the sense I had to "do it" myself if anything was going to get done.

Now this phrase running through my mind, *Your sins are forgiven*, had me puzzled. If my sins were forgiven, who had done the forgiving? It didn't make sense; I was supposed to be the one in charge.

The words were flowing from my pen as if I were in a speed-writing contest. Previously, I judged and critiqued each word before I wrote it; this time I let the words come from a different place, a place deep inside I hardly dared question. At one point I took a break and called my editor at the paper, explaining—okay, let's tell-it-like-it-is, *acknowledging* that my work had not been up to par lately and asking for a leave of absence for a few weeks. "To clear up some personal matters," is how I explained it. All thoughts of writing my column, much less my novel, were sidelined as I explored new found ideas. By the end of the day I felt like a new person.

Until Bob walked in the door.

The sight of his face caused my bighearted ideas to evaporate. When I was faced with putting them into action, I'm ashamed to say, I chickened out. By the time Bob got home from work it was late, and the courage I'd felt earlier in the day was gone. He didn't seem to remember my morning request to talk, and it seemed easier to let it wait for another time. Besides, I wasn't sure what to say to him, anyway.

Forgiveness wasn't as easy as it sounded.

"How was your day?" At least I could make an effort to get past the "if-you're-not-going-to-talk-to-me-I'm-not-going-to-talk-to-you" way we'd been treating each other.

"Fine." He sounded tired.

"That's good." I mentally chalked up a relational point for myself. Then it dawned on me—point keeping probably wasn't part of the forgiveness thing. I tried to erase it.

We went to bed in silence, each keeping politely to our side of the bed, our backs toward each other. All of a sudden my day of insight seemed for naught. If I couldn't put to practice anything I'd learned what good was it? "Bob?" I whispered, half-hoping he wouldn't hear me.

He didn't. Which was a good thing considering I had no idea what I'd planned to say. I punched at my pillow, vowing to try again tomorrow.

I spent the next day trying to make amends with my father. It's not exactly as if I chickened out again, but I was stumped. How could I ask for forgiveness from someone who was no longer alive? I wrote out my thoughts and feelings about the times that troubled me, but I still felt as if I'd missed something.

Unable to go further I turned to the problem with Anne. I looked at those scribbled words once again, acknowledging that Anne hadn't "changed everything," as I'd accused her. She had brought about some changes in my life to be sure, but it was me who had done the changing in response to her. My old, familiar, hands-off way of dealing with people didn't fly with Anne. Anne questioned me and challenged me in ways no other person ever had. She made me reach deeper. Shared her joys and struggles with me. She made me care. I found myself longing for that friendship again. A friendship that wasn't just on the surface. A friendship with Anne. It hadn't always been comfortable, but I could see what I'd been missing. And I wanted it back.

I realized Anne had done nothing, absolutely nothing, wrong. It had all been my fault. It was clear to me the ball was "in my court," so to speak. That's when I headed to the kitchen to bake my humble pie.

I explained all this to Anne as we stood shivering on her front steps. Once, her mother had poked her head out the door asking if we weren't getting cold, but other than that, I was able to tell Anne what had happened to me over the past days, uninterrupted. Anne listened in silence, occasionally shaking her head, making a sympathetic humming sound deep in her throat. It sounded somewhat like a mother comforting a child and only served to make me tell her more.

"Anne," I ended by saying, "you were so right and I was so wrong. Can you ever forgive me?"

Anne opened her arms and drew me in. "Oh, yes." She pressed my head into her shoulder as a mother does to comfort a small child. "I've missed you, Olivia," she whispered as she held me for a long, healing time.

As Anne held me, I remembered all the years I'd gone without a close friend. All the years I'd held people at bay, vowing not to get close enough to get hurt. As I felt the warmth of Anne's arms around me, I realized how much better it felt to have a friend. I was beginning to learn that people could argue and be hurt, yet still be forgiven. There really was power in forgiveness. I could feel it.

Into Anne's shoulder I spoke, my voice muffled by the cloth of her shirt. "Could you please call me Libby?"

I felt Anne chuckle, then she said again, "I've missed you, *Libby.*"

It was the first time I'd felt a bubble of joy in weeks.

Anne

To say I was surprised to see Libby on my doorstep would have been an understatement. Shocked would have been a better word. No sooner had I prayed, "Lord, you know my needs better than I do," than He'd sent Libby knocking on my door. You'd think I would have learned to trust God's ways, but He kept surprising me.

Listening to the emotional upheaval Libby had gone through in the past weeks was difficult. How I wished I'd been there to help her as she'd helped me through my diagnosis and treatments. I knew the healing power of friendship firsthand, but was unable to offer it to Libby in her time of need.

There was a time when I was afraid Libby and I would never be friends again. That I'd overstepped our bond and severed our ties completely. How good it felt to have our connection restored. When she softly asked, "Anne, could you call me Libby?" I felt the knot of our friendship bind tighter than before. God does work in mysterious ways.

Libby came in the house to see the baby, but since she was sleeping, we sat with my mom, Dad, and Kevin, who had gone ahead and eaten supper without me. We had a piece of Libby's chocolate cake while we waited for the baby to wake up. There was a slight stiffness to our conversation, as if we were testing the boundaries of our recreated bond. At the first sound of a cry from the bedroom Libby jumped to her feet, announcing, "I'll get her!" Then she turned to me. "Is that okay?"

"Go on." I nodded my head toward the sound, giving my permission. I carried our plates to the sink, then went to join Libby and my new daughter. I found Libby standing over the crib, looking at my baby, listening to the soft baby sounds she was making, grunting and stretching her tiny arms, trying to wake up.

"She's gorgeous," Libby whispered when she felt me by her side.

"I know." It wasn't parental pride talking. I felt I was giving God a compliment for so carefully forming this precious child, then giving her to us to raise. "Go on," I urged, "pick her up."

Gently, Libby leaned into the crib, sliding her arms under the tiny body. "Oh," she marveled as she straightened almost too quickly. "I forgot how small they are." Then she laughed, speaking softly as she recalled, "I remember when we brought Brian home from the hospital; he seemed like a doll, almost weightless. But after we'd walked the floor with him for hours that first night, trying to get him to quit crying, it seemed as though he'd gained fifteen pounds."

"Believe me," I chimed in, "at three in the morning she feels like she weighs a lot more than she does after a long nap. We've had a few of those nights too."

Libby and I stood in silence, watching the baby make small sucking motions with her mouth, feeling our way back to friendship, using my daughter as a bridge.

Libby took a huge breath, then let it out with a sigh. "I'm sorry I missed it," she said, glancing at me, sounding wistful.

"Missed it?"

"The call," she said, matter-of-factly, as if I should know what she was talking about.

"The call?" I questioned, not catching on.

"You know, the phone call. The one you make to your favorite people right after you have the baby. You pick up the phone and call everyone you've ever met, even if it's four in the morning, just because you're so excited, and you know they will be, too. I wish I could have been there for that." She moved her eyes from the baby to me. "I'm sorry, Anne."

"Me, too," I replied, recalling those long hours and the joy that followed. "I thought of calling you, but I didn't know if you'd...if I..."

"You don't have to say it, Anne. I know it was my own fault I didn't get that call. I'm sorry," she apologized again.

"If it makes you feel any better, I was so tired after my long labor that Kevin did all the calling. I actually slept through that part."

"Thanks for thinking of me, anyway." Libby ran her finger lightly down the baby's cheek. "She's so beautiful." She looked at me, asking softly, "What's her name?"

I hesitated, not knowing how Libby would react to the name we'd chosen. I'd decided the day of the baby shower, when the others had suggested fanciful names with unusual spellings. It was Libby who calmed my fears that day, then suggested a name that seemed so right. Honest and strong. Qualities I wished for my daughter. "We named her Jane."

I could see a flash of remembrance pass over Libby's face—a sudden clouding, almost a pain. I imagined she was recalling that baby shower as the beginning of our time apart. Then quickly, her face softened, and understanding filled her face. "I like Jane," she said simply, repeating the exact words I'd said at the baby shower in response to her suggestion.

We looked at each other then, all awkwardness falling away, the space between us filling with acceptance and forgiveness.

"Yes," Libby stated as if there were no doubt about it, "I like Jane."

I went and warmed a bottle, then rejoined Libby in the nursery. Libby had taken over the rocking chair, insisting on feeding Janey, so I sat on the floor and told her "all the gory details," about my labor as she'd asked. As Libby rocked the baby, I poured out my story. Telling it made me feel I'd joined some vast universal women's club. Libby nodded in recognition as I described my first labor pains, our rush to the hospital, then the long wait until Janey was born. She sighed in pleasure as I described my first glimpse of the baby, then told me she'd been at the hospital and heard the lullaby played at the moment of Janey's birth.

"We were kind of together after all." Libby sounded pleased. "Even if we didn't know it."

"Even if we didn't know it," I repeated. After a moment I added, "God let us share it anyway." I glanced at Libby, not sure if she would appreciate my insight. But she nodded thoughtfully, without a pause in her steady, rhythmical rocking.

Libby changed the subject. "Open the gift I brought for Jane." She continued rocking. "I didn't know if you had a boy or a girl, so it's kind of generic. I hope she likes it."

I untied the yellow ribbon, then pulled the pale green paper from the small box. Lifting the lid, I could see nappy white fur filling the space. "Oh," I smiled, pulling the small stuffed animal from the box, "it's a little lamb. How darling."

As I lifted the lamb from its tissue paper bed, a tinny tinkling sound accompanied it. "What's that?" Libby seemed surprised.

I turned the lamb over, spotting the gold turn key right away. "It's a music box, too. How perfect. You know, my piano and all." I wound the ring tight and let it go.

As the tinkling notes began, Libby apologized. "I didn't realize it was a music box. I just pointed to it in the store and the clerk wrapped it for me. I hope it doesn't play that "It's a Small World" song. That's enough to drive a person nuts. If it does, I can return—"

"Libby." I stopped her with a finger to my lips. "Listen."

*Jesus loves me this I know...*the familiar tune drifted through the room, settling on us like a gentle, soothing hand. I kept my finger to my lips as we listened to the tinkling melody in comfortable silence.

When the song had slowed to its last few notes, Libby asked, "It's okay, then?"

"It's perfect," I replied, winding the lamb up one more time, letting the simple tune remind me that Jesus did love me. After all, he'd returned my friend to me.

Although I didn't want Jane to fall back to sleep right away, I didn't have the heart to take her from Libby's arms. She looked so right lying there, held securely by my friend.

After a time Libby slowly got up. "I guess I shouldn't stay the night," she whispered, gently laying Janey into her crib. "I'd better get home before they send out a search party." She straightened, then turned to face me. "Thank you, Anne. Thank you for…"

I held up my hand; she didn't need to say any more. I knew exactly what she meant.

"…everything," she finished.

I closed my eyes and nodded, just once, sealing our friendship without words.

I walked Libby to the door. Mom, Dad, and Kevin were in the adjacent living room watching television, the sound drifting around us, filling the silence as we searched for words to sum up the night.

I reached out, giving Libby a hug. "Thank you so much for coming over tonight. I know what you had to say wasn't easy, and I want you to know that—"

Libby stopped me with a "ssshhhing" sound in my ear, saying simply, "I'm glad I came."

We stepped back, smiling at each other, glad to be friends again.

"Well," Libby said, reaching for the door, "see you tomorrow, okay?" She spotted the suitcase by the door. "I see your folks must be leaving tomorrow, huh? That'll work out—I can help you with the baby."

I could feel the smile fall from my face. "You don't know, do you?" My five words sounded as though they were being spoken by a statue. I remembered all that had happened in these past weeks, the weeks Libby and I had been apart. Not only had I had my baby, I'd also been scheduled for another mastectomy.

My hesitation must have tipped Libby off, for when she replied her voice held a combination of curiosity and wariness. "What don't I know?"

"Oh Libby," I sighed, "I don't know how to tell you."

"Tell me what?" I could hear a hint of fear in her voice.

"My folks aren't leaving tomorrow. Kevin and I are." I paused for a deep breath, gathering courage.

Libby stood with her mouth open, as if to ask a question.

"Kevin is taking me to Rochester tomorrow." I answered Libby's unasked question, adding, "I have to have another mastectomy, Libby." My voice held a hint of fear. "My cancer is back."

Olivia

I knew what it felt like to get punched in the stomach.

Once, when I was about eight, I was playing catcher in a backyard baseball game my brother had scraped together. I knew they were desperate for players when my brother asked me to play. He stood me behind home plate and commanded, "Just catch the ball." After a summer spent watching them play from the crab apple tree foul marker, I felt proud to be asked to play. I crouched behind home plate, determined to prove myself. I was going to be the best girl-catcher they ever saw. I could see the ball coming toward me. Danny Jordan had thrown a way-too-high pitch, but if I kept my eye on the ball, I was sure I could catch it. The too-big leather glove they'd given me led the way as I rose up to reach for the ball. Just as I stood, the batter decided he might as well try to hit the slow-moving meatball coming his way. His backswing hit me right in the middle, causing me to double over and fall to the ground, gasping for air.

It was remarkably similar to how I felt now—hit in the gut with a baseball bat. Hard. The only difference was, this time I was still standing.

If someone had asked me if it was possible to experience joy, shame, and fear, all at the same time, I would have said, "Absolutely not!" But that was before I felt those emotions in combination myself at Anne's that night.

As I drove away from Anne's house, one part of me felt as light as a feather, filled with a gladness I hadn't known was possible, knowing Anne had forgiven me and we were friends again. Another part of me felt filled with shame as I recalled the glib, self-assured way I'd convinced myself over these past weeks that Anne hadn't needed me, that my accusing words hadn't really mattered. I'd only fooled myself and for that I felt awful. But there was another part of me that felt even worse—the part of me that felt I'd been punched in the stomach when Anne had said the words, "My cancer is back."

It was a physical sensation I felt to the very core of my body. My mind kept screaming, "No! It can't be true!"

And then I'd hear her words again, "My cancer is back."

"No! No! No!" I pounded the steering wheel in anger. It couldn't be true.

Just minutes ago, I'd been standing by Anne's front door, feeling like a queen whose kingdom had been restored. Now I felt as if the whole earth had been knocked from under me. When Anne told me her cancer was back, I felt as though my face had frozen into an "I'm trying not to look shocked" expression. "Oh, no," I'd said, sounding as if she'd told me my shirt was unbuttoned one button too many. As if it were a simple, easily-fixable problem. Inside, I felt as if my heart had dropped to my feet. "Are they sure?" I'd asked dumbly, like they scheduled mastectomys for practice, or something.

Anne had nodded, her lips pressed together in a grim line.

I felt tears prick at my eyes. "I don't know what to say, Anne. I thought you had this beat."

"I thought so too," she replied.

"What can I do?" I asked, my mind numb, feeling totally helpless, unable to think of a tangible thing to offer.

"Can I leave your number with my mom? In case she needs help?"

What she was asking was nothing. My phone number. I felt like a heel having nothing more to offer. "Oh, Anne," I begged, "there's got to be something more than that."

"Libby, you don't know how good it will make me feel to know Mom has a backup. Just in case." She glanced furtively towards the living room, and speaking *sotto voce* she added, "You never know what might rattle my mother."

I clearly remembered Evelyn when I'd met her during Anne's first surgery, jabbering a mile a minute, doing everything she could to avoid facing the problem at hand. Maybe serving as backup wasn't such a small thing after all.

"Okay then," I responded, "I'm the official backup." I reached out to hug Anne, still hardly comprehending that this was happening. "Promise you'll call me after...after the surgery?"

"I will. Promise."

The air in the car felt dead. Cold and lifeless. It was as if all the life-giving qualities it usually contained had been snuffed out. I forced myself to breathe, not convinced it would sustain me. I felt physically sick. My fun times with Anne flashed through my mind, followed by the empty stretch of time when our friendship had almost ended because of my stubbornness. Tonight it had all been restored to me—Anne's forgiveness and the promise of friendship. Then with one word, *cancer*, it felt threatened again.

"No!" I yelled the word into the empty car again as if by screaming it out I could stop what was happening. I heard the word echo back to me, heard by no one, no real help at all.

I drove around town for maybe an hour, trying to absorb Anne's news, waiting to make sure everyone in my house was asleep before I went home. I knew Emily was wild to hear about the new baby, but I didn't feel I could talk right now.

Silently I slipped into bed, not wanting to wake Bob and possibly have him ask how the night had gone. As I lay on my back, a cold blue-gray shadow played across the ceiling, looking as icy and bleak as I felt. There was nothing I could do to make this go away. Nothing I could do to make it better. Absolutely nothing I could do.

You could pray.

My eyes snapped around the room. Where had that come from? I examined the unexpected thought, realizing it hadn't been an actual voice I'd heard, but I'd heard it as clearly as if it had been spoken.

You could pray.

There it was again. I rolled onto my side, trying to shake the words from my mind. I tried to concentrate on the good things that had happened while I was at Anne's—seeing her new baby, the long, cleansing talk we'd had, rocking Janey to sleep while Anne talked to me—but all the good things kept getting pushed out of my mind by one word. Cancer.

Pray. The other word was just as insistent.

Cancer.

Pray.

I rolled onto my back again, staring at the ceiling. Cancer.

Pray.

Hesitatingly, I closed my eyes, keeping them open just a slit, one eye firmly on what I knew was reality. I opened my eyes again, sliding them in Bob's direction. I didn't need him to be asking me what I was doing. He was sound asleep. I turned my head toward the ceiling and closed my eyes all the way this time, my hands folded over my rib cage.

"Okay, Lord, I'm going to try this…" I opened my eyes once more. I felt awkward thinking these thoughts to someone, to *something* I wasn't sure was even there, much less listening. I tossed onto my side.

Pray! The word came again. If God, or whoever, was going to keep me up all night until I obeyed, I figured I might as well go ahead and do it.

"Okay, okay, I will." I found myself trying to placate the impatient voice as I rolled once again to my back. I folded my hands, but this time kept my eyes wide open. "Listen Lord, or God, or Whoever you are, I'm not sure how to do this. But, well, I don't need Your help, but my friend Anne does. Could You just…umm, just…be with Anne? And, ummm, let her know I'll be there for her, too?" My eyes roamed around the bedroom. "Uh, I don't know if You can hear me or not, but if You can, thanks." Now I closed my eyes. "Amen, I guess."

I didn't feel weird, but it wasn't as if some big, peaceful feeling entered my body, either. One thing I did notice was that the word cancer was no longer running through my mind like a mantra. I closed my eyes again, this time to sleep. And I did.

Until about three hours later when I found myself dreaming I was back in high school, the fire alarm insisting I leave the classroom.

The ringing persisted, even after I'd run out of the building. I looked around, wondering where my classmates were, finally feeling someone tap my shoulder. It was Bob, poking me out of my sleep. "Answer the phone."

I fumbled for the receiver, noting that my bedside clock read three-thirty four. I groaned. I knew both kids were in their rooms asleep, but this couldn't be good news. "Hello?"

"You're an aunt!"

"What? Who is this?" My voice was filled with sleep, the words coming out as a croak.

I could hear laughter at the other end of the line. "Libby, it's me, Anne. You said you wished you could have been there to get the call when Janey was born. Well, here's your call."

I felt a rush of pleasure, as if Anne really had just given birth to her baby. "Congratulations, then," I replied, feeling excited even though the news was belated.

"I was up feeding Janey," Anne explained, "and I kept thinking about you. Thanks for being here for me tonight."

Her choice of words was odd. Isn't that what I'd prayed, *Let Anne know I'll be there for her?* I felt a small tingle up the back of my neck. Now I did feel weird. I could hear Janey crying in the background. "You'd better go be a mom," I advised.

"Easy for you to say," Anne replied, "your kids sleep through the night."

"Goodnight, Mama." I hung up the phone and turned in bed, punching at my pillow, ready to go back to sleep. I smiled into the night, remembering Janey's soft cry behind Anne's voice. I turned onto my stomach, trying to get comfortable, picturing Anne rocking Janey to sleep. I turned once again, lying on my back, watching as light from the full moon sent shadows dancing across my bedroom. I replayed the middle-of-the-night phone call in my mind. What was it Anne had said? *Thanks for being here for me tonight?* That part I'd heard loud and clear. But there was something else my sleepy mind had barely registered when I'd picked up the phone. Suddenly, I heard the words as if Anne was standing right beside me. *You're an aunt!* Yes, that's what she'd said. *You're an aunt.*

I turned onto my side, pulling the covers up to my chin, creating a warm cocoon. I snuggled my head into my cool pillow, and just before I fell asleep my heart gave an extra little thump, as if just for a moment, it couldn't quite hold all the joy.

Anne

I knew leaving Janey was going to be hard, but I wasn't prepared for the rush of maternal feelings that came over me when I tried to say goodbye. Intellectually, I knew my being gone was not going to bother Janey one iota. She was going to be fed, get her diaper changed on a regular basis, and even get rocked to sleep, but it wasn't going to be me doing it. That's what bothered me.

"Ooookay, say goodbye to Mommy now." My mother held Janey in the air, wiggling her body as though she were a performing puppet. It was supposed to make me smile, but only made me feel like grabbing my child into my arms and holding her forever.

Which is exactly what I did. Well, not the "hold her forever" part, but I did snatch her out of my mother's arms for one last squeeze. Janey's skin felt so soft as I rubbed my nose into her cheek, smelling one more time her sweet baby smell. Before Janey had been born, I'd worried if I would be a good mother, if I'd love her enough. I didn't have those worries any longer. I loved her more than enough.

"Anne," Kevin eased Janey from my arms, "we have to get on the road." He held Janey to his chest, pressing his head to hers in a gentle hug. With a sigh he handed her back to my mother. "If we're going to make it in time for your appointment, we've got to go right now."

I knew he was right. I reached to rub Janey's back. "Bye. Mommy loves you." Tears welled in my eyes. It was so hard to say goodbye to her.

"Tell Mommy we're going to be just fine." My mother spoke in that high-pitched I'm-talking-for-the-baby talk that was supposed to be funny, but just made me feel worse. I should be the one doing that kind of talking. I should be reassuring my mother that Kevin,

Janey, and I would be just fine. My mother should be the one leaving, not me.

Kevin opened the door and held it with his foot as he grabbed the suitcases. "I'll call," was all he said as he walked out to the car.

"Mom, you be sure and call Libby if you need anything." I had one foot out the door. "Did I remember to show you where the doctor's number is?"

"Anne," my father said firmly, "you go do what you need to do to get better." The calm in his voice settled my thoughts. "The faster you get started, the sooner you'll get home."

"Yeeesss," my mother squeaked, holding Janey in front of her as though she were a rag doll, "your grandma and grandpa are going to take good care of you. Yeeesss we are!"

My father leaned forward and hugged me. "Good luck, honey." I could hear emotion in his voice as he whispered, "I love you."

"I love you, too." I hugged him back. I waved over his shoulder at my mother. "Bye, Mom. Love you."

"Say 'bye' to your mommy." Mother had turned Janey around so she faced me, waving one of her tiny hands in farewell. "Drive careful," she called, hiding any emotion behind her high-pitched, false-sounding voice.

If I thought I was unprepared to leave my new baby, I was just as unprepared to face another surgery. Last time I hadn't known what to expect; this time I knew everything. The first whiff of air inside the hospital doors sent my heart hammering. I remembered all too well the thin hospital gown, the sharp stick in my vein to start my IV, the calming voice of the anesthesiologist as she told me to count backward from one hundred. "One hundred," I'd repeated, asleep before I could form another number.

I also recalled the recovery room, the nurses calling out other patients' names, trying to get them to wake up. "George!" The nurse kept calling to the patient next to me. "George! It's time to quit snoring and wake up."

"Yes," I thought, "quit snoring. It's disturbing my sleep."

Then, through my own fog I heard, "Anne? Anne! It's time to wake up." "Oh no, I'm much too tired," I thought, turning my head from the sound. "Let me sleep."

But, of course, they didn't.

There were only two things different between my last surgery and this one. Last time the patient next to me had been George; this time it was Helen who the nurse was telling to wake up. And this time, instead of waking up with one breast, this time I had none.

Olivia

I felt Anne's absence as if something cold and hard had taken up residence where my heart had once beat. Even though I'd gone for weeks without speaking to Anne, it felt as if that time had been mercifully cut away from the fabric of our friendship. Her absence made it feel as though a huge hole had been torn in the substance of my days.

In a way, it was as if everything had returned to normal. Anne was back in my life, Pete was out of the hospital, Bob still came and went, leaving early and returning late, the kids left for school, and I had the long day to fill with household tasks and errands. But what had seemed routine and normal now chaffed like a huge rock in a too-small shoe.

The cool relationship Bob and I had developed felt empty. We communicated on a "need to know" basis only.

"I'll be working late tonight," he'd say as he left for the day.

"Emily has a birthday party to go to after school. I'm driving," I'd say in response.

I didn't like the pattern we'd fallen into, but I didn't know how to change it. I knew *what* to do, I just didn't know *how* to do it. Through all the journaling and introspection I'd done during the past week, I knew I needed to apologize to Bob. I needed to acknowledge my mistakes, my faults, and make a concerted effort to change them.

"Easier said than done," I muttered to myself as I stocked the refrigerator with fresh fruit, vegetables, and milk. At the grocery store, I'd tried to forget all the things I needed to say to Bob, but instead found myself wandering the crowded aisles mumbling, "I'm sorry, Bob. I need to tell you some things. I've been an idiot." That last phrase popped into my mind after I saw the look an elderly woman gave me as I absentmindedly squeezed tomatoes. I realized I'd been talking out loud—to vegetables, no less. I quickly finished my shopping, determined to talk to Bob that night. Talking to tomatoes was getting me no where at all.

But that night I understood anew how they'd come up with the saying, "Easier said than done." Sitting together watching the news, then again later on as Bob and I got ready for bed, I opened my mouth several times to start with the words, "Can we talk?" Just as many times I closed my mouth without speaking. The words stuck unsaid in my throat. Bob and I were becoming like brother and sister. Most siblings had a more emotional relationship than the one we'd fallen into.

While Emily seemed to be back to her usual talkative self, there was an unsettled quiet that would come over her at times, as if a portion of her innocence had been taken away, and she was trying to figure out what would replace it. The older brother she had idolized had fallen from his pedestal, and she wasn't quite sure where he stood in her eyes anymore. My heart went out to Emily as I watched her watch Brian, measuring his words and actions to see if he deserved her trust. I felt unable to guide her to the new place she was trying to find.

But my heart went out to Brian even more. He seemed to have taken on sole responsibility for what had happened to Pete. Even though Pete would be back in school next week, apparently no worse for the ordeal he'd been through, Brian walked around the house with the weight of the world on his back. He put on a good act, pasting a "regular guy" expression on his face when he came down for breakfast. But the minute he thought I wasn't watching, his brows would furrow and he'd start chewing on his lower lip. I tried to explain to Brian that Pete held some guilt in this matter. After all, he could have said no. But Brian persisted in taking full blame. He wasn't antagonistic, but he wasn't exactly Mr. Great Communication Skills either. He mumbled goodbye before he left for school in the morning, returning within twenty minutes of dismissal according to the agreement we'd made. He ate a snack, did his homework, watched some television. Things all kids do. Actually, he was acting much as before, minus most of the attitude. But there was a melancholy about him that tore at my heart. I'd expected him to rail against the grounding we'd imposed, but he'd seemed almost relieved to have his schedule curtailed. He was acting like the ideal kid. Well, an ideal kid with the weight of the world riding on his shoulders.

Yes, it seemed my home life was back to normal. But what had become normal wasn't what I wanted anymore.

Anne

I was wrong. There was something else different about my surgery this time. After my last mastectomy, the nurses, the doctors, and even the aides were constantly reminding me to do my exercises. My breathing exercises were designed to get my lungs working properly after the shock of surgery as well as to get my muscles back into condition after the removal of my breast. And my arm exercises were intended to help me regain the use of the muscles near the area where my breast had been. With Libby's coaxing—actually her drill sergeant-like insistence—I'd faithfully done the exercises and recovered almost full use of my right arm.

This time was different. There was an eerie silence from everyone. No one suggested I breathe deeply, no one even hinted that I should be moving my left arm. The nurses monitored my blood pressure and temperature like clockwork, even taking me for a short stroll down the hospital hallway. Some of them worked in concentrated quiet; others jabbered a mile a minute, asking me about my husband, squealing in delight over my new baby, asking what my favorite television programs were. But no one said a word about my recovery.

After my last surgery, someone had showed up at my room—a recovering breast cancer patient—to talk about possible reconstructive surgery. Not this time. It was as if there was a sign posted on my door: DO NOT TALK TO HER ABOUT CANCER!

I tried to convince myself this silence was because they all knew I'd been through this before. I didn't need to hear it all again. I knew the "drill." But there was more to their silence than that. I could feel it. When Dr. Adams and Dr. Payne came to my room at the same time, I knew right away something was wrong.

"Anne. Kevin." Dr. Payne, my surgeon, nodded at us. "We've got good news and bad news," he said, not wasting any time. Dr. Adams nodded in agreement. Dr. Payne continued, "As I told you yesterday, Kevin, the surgery went well." Dr. Payne smiled at me. "I talked to you too, Anne, but you may not remember."

I shook my head; he was right, I didn't.

"The surgery went as we expected," he explained. "We got everything we could see. The tumor was fairly large, but the surrounding tissue looked healthy. Your breast was somewhat engorged from your pregnancy, but everything stitched into place quite nicely. I did have to leave a small opening on the outer quadrant where we removed the larger portion of the tumor, but that should heal over fairly quickly."

He made it sound so routine. As if he performed second mastectomies on young women who'd just given birth every other day. For a moment I felt reassured by his words.

"Unfortunately…" he continued.

I had known he was going to say more. After all, he'd started out by telling us he had bad news, too. But still, the word caused my heart to sink.

"…uh, I think Dr. Adams may be able to explain this better." Dr. Payne nodded at my oncologist.

"Yes, well," Dr. Adams flipped some papers on the clipboard he was carrying. "We've received the lab tests back from your surgery, and I'm afraid the news is not what we hoped." He ran his finger down the page, stopping near the middle. "The tests show you have infiltrating ductal carcinoma. Your hormone receptor assays were negative, and unfortunately…"

There was that word again. My heart started pounding.

"…all eleven of the lymph nodes we removed were node positive." He said the words matter-of-factly, but there was an expression around his eyes that made me feel he did not deliver this kind of news every day. I felt a wave of compassion for him. Certainly his job held its rewards, but I could see all too clearly that it held many sorrows, also.

Please, Lord, I breathed silently, *encourage him in the healing work he does.*

"…so we're going to want to hit this with everything we've got." Dr. Adams' first words had been lost through my prayer, but I knew he was referring to my treatment. "We're going to give you a few days to heal up, but we don't want to wait any longer than we have to—"

"Doctor?" Kevin interrupted. "Will we…uh, Anne, need to take all of her treatments here? In Rochester? We live a long way from here, and with the new baby and all, it's kind of hard to work things out. I was wondering…" his words trailed off, uncertainty clinging to them.

"We're definitely going to need to get her started on the chemotherapy here. We'll be using some fairly new and potent drugs. I rather doubt they would be available back in…" he paused, consulting his chart. Not finding the answer, he asked, "Where is it you see Dr. Barrows?"

"Carlton." Kevin and I answered in unison. "Ah yes, Carlton," Dr. Adams repeated. "How far is that, again?"

Kevin and I again answered together. "Forty miles."

"From Brewster," Kevin added, breaking our duet. "Not from Rochester. Rochester is several hundred miles from us."

"Well, we'll see if we can't work out some arrangement with the hospital there after we get your treatment regimen finalized. We should be able to administer the bulk of your treatment close to home. I hope you understand there is some urgency involved here."

I stared at him, not fully comprehending what he was inferring.

Dr. Adams picked up on my blank expression. "Let's put it this way…if it's the kind of cancer we *hope* it is, waiting a few days to start treatment isn't going to matter. And, if it's the kind of cancer we hope it's *not*…well, waiting a few days isn't going to matter." He paused, giving us a chance to comprehend what he'd said, then continued, "But we want to make the best use of the time we have. Do you understand?"

I turned the words around in my head—*the kind of cancer we hope it is…the kind of cancer we hope it's not*. Either way, waiting a few days for me to heal before starting treatment wasn't going to matter. At first the words didn't make sense. It sounded as if it didn't matter if we started treatment now or waited until later. For a fleeting moment I closed my eyes, imagining myself going home tomorrow, savoring how it would feel to hold Janey in my arms, to nuzzle her warm, sweet-smelling neck, to rock her to sleep. I could almost feel her resting next to me, a comforting weight in my arms. Then, just like that, realization dawned and my eyes flew open. I looked into my empty arms, then at Dr. Adams. I could read the meaning of what he'd said in his eyes. He was trying to tell me that time may be running out.

Olivia

All it took was a phone call for my seemingly normal life to change.

"Hello, Libby? Is this Libby Marsden?" The voice was extremely friendly, but unfamiliar.

I answered with guarded wariness. "Yes, it is." Probably a telemarketer. I tucked the phone under my ear and started folding warm-from-the-dryer clothes I'd just dropped on the couch. I'd make quick work of this caller. "I'm busy right now." My tone was businesslike; she didn't have to know I was busy doing laundry.

"Oh, well, I'm sorry to disturb you, but this is *very* important. I wouldn't be calling but I don't know what else to do."

This was a pitch I'd never heard from a phone solicitor before. My curiosity was piqued. "Oh-hh?" I asked, egging her on with my tone, hoping she would get to the point quickly.

"It's about the baby. I just don't know what to do."

I'd never heard of someone trying to play on a client's sympathies using babies. If this woman didn't explain her point now, I was going to hang up and call the State Attorney. "Uh-huh," I remarked, sounding as if I'd caught on to her scam. "The baby. Right."

"Libby?" The woman truly sounded as though she knew me.

It was then I realized most everyone, even rude telemarketers, called me Olivia; it was only Anne who called me Libby. But this wasn't Anne. "Who is this?" I asked, still wary.

"It's Evelyn," she explained, as if I should have known all along. "Anne's mom."

Ah, yes. Dumb me. I'd never talked to this woman on the phone in my life. Pardon me for not recognizing her voice. I could feel my hackles rising. There was something about this woman I did not like. For Anne's sake I hid my feelings.

"Evelyn," my voice was sickly-sweet. "Hello, how are things going?"

"That's just it." She pounced on my words. "Things aren't going well at all."

Instantly I was worried. "What's wrong with Anne?" I asked, not even trying to mask the fear in my tone.

"Oh, we haven't heard from them yet. Well, of course, they called when they got down there, and again this morning, but Anne wasn't scheduled to have her surgery until later today and, well, you know how those things can drag on. And then to try and find a phone and I suppose they—"

"Is something wrong with Janey?" I interrupted Evelyn. I couldn't help it; her babbling was serving no purpose but to make me nervous. Spit it out, lady.

"No-oo, nothing's wrong with Janey. She's doing just fine." Evelyn's voice held an edge that led me to believe there was more to her call than there appeared to be. "It's just that a small problem has come up and, well…I just don't know what to do, and Anne did leave your number. She said to call you if I needed anything and I'm afraid…I was wondering? You see it's just that…well, we got this phone call a little bit ago, and I thought of you and…"

Good grief, say it already! To Evelyn I said, "Anything, anything, at all. Don't worry about it. What can I do to help?"

"Oh, thank you! Thank you!" She was gushing and I didn't have a clue what I'd done. Or was going to do.

Care to clue me in, lady? What I said was, "You're welcome, I guess. But Evelyn, you're going to have to tell me what it is I can do to help." I sounded much nicer than I felt.

"Oh, Libby, thank you. I just didn't know what we were going to do. I'll bring Janey over within the hour. Thank you so much."

Bring Janey over? There was something here I wasn't getting. I could hear her start to hang up the phone. "Evelyn, wait!"

"What?" She sounded almost curt, as if she was afraid I'd back out on her. "Evelyn, it's fine if you bring Janey over," I reassured. "But can you tell me what's going on? What happened?"

"Didn't I tell you?" She sounded incredulous. "Andrea just called—Cari fell and broke her leg. She needs me. I have to go home."

⌒

As Evelyn promised, within the hour I found myself surrounded by a bulging diaper bag, a half-dozen baby bottles, a brown paper grocery bag stuffed with stuffed animals and assorted other toys, a detailed rendering of Janey's schedule in Anne's handwriting and of course, Janey, herself. Anne's dad stood in the doorway, his mouth pressed into a disgusted frown.

Evelyn could hardly talk fast enough. "I think I got everything. The baby's formula is in the diaper bag and I threw some extra sleepers in there too. You know how fast kids can go through clothes in a day."

I pointed to my now folded stack of laundry. "I know."

Evelyn hadn't waited for my response, but kept talking. "She can be a little fussbudget at night. Well, at least she was last night, and I didn't figure out any tricks to get her to settle down, so I hope she's not too much trouble for you. You know, Andrea's Cari, she's three now, and she fell out of her swing and broke her leg. Oh," Evelyn cried, barely stopping for air, "I just can imagine how frantic Andrea is."

"Andrea can handle this on her own, Evelyn." Anne's dad gave an exasperated sigh, even as he handed me a pink plastic rattle. Obviously he knew this was a battle he wasn't going to win.

As if she hadn't heard him, Evelyn went right on talking.

"She's really Grandma's girl, you know—Cari, that is. Do you have any questions? No? Okay then, we'll be going—bye." Her last sentences were said in one fast breath, and then just like that, she backed out the door, not giving Janey so much as a squeeze.

I felt I'd been hit by a whirlwind, and apparently so did Janey. She reclined in her car seat, eyes open wide, her little mouth forming a small, surprised "Oh." She stared at me.

"It's just you and me, kid," I tried to joke, staring right back, hoping I didn't look as startled as she did. It had been many years since I'd mothered an infant. A swift panic descended as my mind frantically searched its recesses trying to decide—what do I do now?

I heard the car carrying Evelyn drive away at the same moment it dawned on me that she hadn't left the key to Anne's house or access to anything of Janey's that Evelyn may have forgotten. Like a Girl Scout trying to earn her survival badge, I rummaged through Janey's meager luggage, trying to determine if we had enough to sustain life. A stuffed dog. A small bear. A teething ring. (I hoped Janey wasn't going to be here long enough to need it). Five sleepers. Fourteen diapers. A large can of powdered formula. Baby wipes. A tube of diaper cream. And the small white stuffed lamb I'd given her. As I pulled the lamb from the bag a couple of tinny-sounding musical notes clinked from inside the lamb. Twisting the gold ring until it grew stiff, I let go, listening to the high-pitched, harp-like tune...*Jesus loves me this I know.* Janey started waving her little hands. I found it hard to believe that a barely week-old baby would respond to a song, but when the tune stopped Janey let out a small whimper. In a let's-see-if-this-works reflex, I wound up the toy again. The music instantly quieted her. After what had to be the tenth time winding up that little lamb, I decided *I* would start crying if I had to listen to it one more time. I stuck the lamb in Janey's seat with her. If the mean old baby-sitter wouldn't let Janey listen to it, she could at least look at it.

Janey began fussing, so I eased her out of the well-padded car seat into my arms. I had no idea when she'd eaten last, but decided it wouldn't hurt to try offering her a bottle. But first, I checked her diaper. Soaked. Her tiny feet kicked at the air as I folded up the old diaper and replaced it with a dry one.

I gazed at the small body lying in front of me. How did she get to be so perfect?

When you were in your mother's womb I formed you. There was that voice again, the same one I'd heard the other night lying in bed. I looked around, trying to convince myself I wasn't really hearing things. Of course, there was no one else in the room. Unless little

Janey had become a ventriloquist in her spare time, I had nothing to blame for what I'd heard except my own mind. This was getting a little weird. Ignoring the voice, I slipped Janey's little legs back into the sleeper and went to prepare her bottle.

I sat on the couch to feed Janey, propping my arm against the throw pillows for support. I surveyed her belongings strewn about the living room. We may come into the world with nothing, but it sure doesn't take us long to accumulate stuff. Janey's stuffed animals, diapers, and sleepers dotted the room. Even though Evelyn had brought the basics, I realized there were a lot of things she hadn't brought that would be kind of nice. A crib, for instance.

I recalled the rummage sale I'd had about seven years ago. I remembered thinking I could either save Emily's crib, high chair, and baby swing for my someday grandchildren, or I could gain a whole section of my attic for at least fourteen years. In retrospect, fourteen years wouldn't have been *that* long to store the stuff. I wished I hadn't been so hasty. What was I going to do?

Janey was sound asleep in my arms, and I was lost in a daydream, wondering what the neighbors would think if they saw me carrying baby furniture into the house. Emily slammed the door. "I'm home!" she screamed, letting the world know school was out for the day. I jumped in surprise and Janey startled in response, then fell right back to sleep.

"A baby?" Spotting Janey in my arms, Emily's voice dropped to a whisper as she rounded the corner. In exaggerated tiptoe steps, Emily crept to my side. "Ohhh," she whispered. "Who is it?"

"It's Janey," I whispered back. "Anne's baby."

Emily looked on, wide-eyed. "Can I hold her?"

I patted the couch with my free hand. "Sit here," I instructed softly.

In slow motion Emily slid gently onto the couch, and I transferred Janey into her stiffly-waiting arms. "Be sure and support her head," I cautioned, moving Emily's arm so her hand cupped the baby's head.

Emily sat as still as a statue, staring down at the sleeping baby. "She looks like a doll," Emily whispered. "But heavier."

I could see her arms start to sag under Janey's relaxed weight. "Do you want me to take her?"

Emily shook her head, so I eased two small pillows under her arms for added support. "When is Anne coming to pick her up?" she asked, assuming this was a short-term baby-sitting job she was getting in on.

"Anne's in the hospital, remember?" As soon as I said it, I remembered I hadn't told Emily about Anne's latest surgery. I was still trying to come to grips with the news myself.

Biting the inside of her cheek, something Emily did when she was trying hard to remember something, she shook her head. "I don't remember that. Is Anne sick?" Emily looked down at Janey, already feeling sorry for this small baby whose mommy was in the hospital.

"Kind of. Maybe." I wasn't sure how to explain things to Emily when I didn't understand them myself. Maybe the doctors would find out this new tumor was benign. Maybe she was already on her way home. Maybe Anne wasn't sick at all. "I'm not sure," I ended up telling Emily. "Anne had to go back so the doctors could check up on her, after the baby and all…" I finished lamely. "But lucky us!" I forced some enthusiasm into my voice. "We're going to be taking care of Janey until Anne and Kevin get back," I explained, not quite believing the fast turn of events myself. "Won't that be fun?" I sounded as if I was trying to convince myself as much as Emily that taking care of a newborn baby was going to be a piece of cake.

Emily smiled at me. "Can I help?" Just then the door slammed once again, and Janey let out a loud wail. "Mom!" Emily looked up at me, an expression of terror on her face. "What do I do?"

I could hear Brian toss his book bag on the counter, then open the refrigerator. It only took a few more seconds until he poked his head around the corner. "What's that noise?" His eyes traveled to me in question, then landed on Janey for his answer. "A baby? A baby!"

Whereas Emily had been in awe, Brian sounded incredulous. For a second, I considered telling him it was his new sister, but April Fool's Day was long past and Janey's cries were getting piercing. It didn't seem the time for a joke.

"Here, let me take her." I scooped Janey out of Emily's arms, explaining to Brian, "She's Anne's baby. Jane." I couldn't hear if Brian responded; Janey's cries slit right through my eardrum.

No matter in what position I held her, the crying continued. I recalled Evelyn saying Jane could be a little fussbudget, but this was getting on my nerves. Just to top off all the commotion, the phone rang.

"It's Dad," Emily called. "He needs to ask you something." Emily held the phone at arm's length, as if I'd hand this screaming baby to her if she got too close. She made it clear she wanted nothing to do with this part of our task.

I shifted Janey to one hand and picked up the receiver with the other. "YES?" I practically screamed into the phone, trying to hear myself talk over Jane's surprisingly loud theatrics.

"What did you say?" Bob's voice over the phone line was weak competition for what was occurring in my other ear. "I can't hear you!" I sounded as though I were a person whose hearing aid batteries have quit working. "Say that again!"

Bob repeated his sentence. I heard every other word, making Bob sound like a nervous obscene phone caller. "I… you…pick… pants…me."

"Just a second," I hollered into the phone. "Here." I turned and plopped a screaming Janey into Brian's arms.

"What's that, again?" I screamed into the phone, then realized my voice was as startling as a firecracker going off in church. I turned to see what had happened. Janey had quit crying as quickly as if someone had flipped an "off" switch. There she lay in Brian's muscular teenage arms, looking as if she were on a relaxing vacation in the Bahamas. Her little feet were kicking as if swayed by a gentle breeze, her arms splayed out as if to catch the last of the sun's rays. But it was her eyes that captivated me most. Her eyes were wide open, focused as if on a treasure she'd found in the deep dark sea. I followed her gaze to see what was so fascinating. Janey was gazing into Brian's eyes as if mesmerized. The same way he was looking at her.

Anne

I was frantic. Something was wrong, and neither Kevin nor I knew what to do. At that moment I forgot all about any problems with my health. All I was concerned about was my daughter. Where was she?

After we'd talked with the doctors about the results of my surgery, Kevin tried calling home to let my parents know what was going on. No answer. He waited a while, then tried again. And again. And again. Still no answer. I felt physically sick. It seemed impossible that my parents would have taken Janey on an extended outing for the day. I ran every possible scenario through my mind. Had Mom run out of diapers? Hardly possible after only a day and a half—we'd left five boxes of disposables neatly stacked in the corner of Janey's room. Had they run out of formula? Again, we stocked so much formula in preparation for our trip, that there were enough cans in the cupboard to last until Janey grew teeth and was begging to eat at Burger King. Had Janey suddenly gotten sick? This was the only reason I could think of that would cause them to be away from the house for the past five hours. Still, we had left the phone numbers to several areas of the clinic and hospital. I couldn't imagine they wouldn't be able to track us down and give us any news. Kevin left to find another phone and try our house once again, while in desperation I called Libby.

"Hello!" Emily's cheerful greeting caught me off guard. In my harried search for my daughter, I'd expected a worried, adult voice to answer my call. Instead, Emily's clear, sweet voice filled the air.

"Emily?" Immediately I adjusted my tone so she wouldn't pick up on my fear. "Are you home from school already?"

"Is this Anne?" I could hear Emily trying to place my voice, following her mother's instructions not to talk to strangers.

"I'm sorry," I apologized. "I should have told you right away. Yes, it's me, Emily." I would have loved to visit with her for a moment. Even though she was only ten, Emily was one of the best conversationalists I knew. But worry about Janey cut through any thoughts of an extended conversation. "Is your mother there, Emily?"

Picking up the worried tone in my voice, Emily questioned, "Are you sick?"

I didn't know what Libby had told Emily about me, and I wasn't sure just how much a ten-year-old should know about her friend and piano teacher who had cancer. It was hard to know what to say. Other than being stiff and a little sore from the surgery, I actually felt pretty good. I decided to err on the side of the positive. "No, Emily, I'm not sick, but the doctors want to check on me for a little while yet."

"Oh, good! We get to keep Janey for a while then!" Emily giggled, then quickly stopped herself. "Ooops. I don't mean I'm glad you're in the hospital." She stopped speaking and I could imagine Emily quickly covering her mouth with her hand. She gave another giggle. "But I am glad we get to keep Janey. Oh, Anne," Emily squealed, "I love Janey! Mom let me hold her and she's so soft. Now Brian is holding her. She was crying and then when Brian held her she got quiet, just like that!" I could hear Emily click her tongue, letting me know just how fast this transformation had occurred. "She's like a doll, but I know she's not really a doll, so I'll take good care of her. Mom said I could help and I've read lot's of *Babysitter's Club* books, so I know how to babysit, and—"

None of this was making any sense. Libby had told Emily she could babysit for Jane? Brian was holding my baby? I interrupted this little chatterbox who seemed to know so much about my missing baby. "Emily. Slow down, do you know where Janey is right now?"

"I told you, Anne," Emily sighed in exasperation. "She was crying and when Brian held her she got quiet, just like that!" There was that emphatic tongue click, again. Emily jabbered on while I tried to make sense of what she was saying. "…And I've always wished I had a baby sister, so I'm going to pretend she's my little sister. Is that okay?" She paused, waiting for my answer.

"Of course," I answered, still not fully understanding what was happening. "Can I talk to your mother?" I was hoping Libby could clear up my confusion.

"Oh, she's not here," Emily announced, as if everything was perfectly normal. "She had to go pick up some pants at the dry cleaner's for my dad, and then she was going to go get Janey some more diapers. But don't worry, 'cause Brian is sitting down, and Mom changed Janey's diaper before she left, and we'll take really good care of her 'til you get home, and—"

"Emily." Once again I interrupted. "Back up for a minute, why is Janey at your house?"

"Because," Emily sighed, sounding as if I should know this already. "You're in the hospital getting checked over and Janey needs somebody to take care of her." Emily sounded as though she were talking to a dim-witted child.

"Oh," I replied, sounding as though I were a dim-witted child. "I see." Which I didn't. But I did know Janey was fine. Sort of. "Ummm, Emily?"

"Yes?" At this point she was sounding more adult than I.

Sounding as if I were asking permission for a sleepover, I asked, "Could you have your mother call me when she gets home? Right away?"

"Okay," she answered, sounding distracted. "Anne, wait! Mom's home—hang on." I could hear a clatter as Emily laid the phone down, yelling loudly to her mother in the garage, "It's Anne!"

You couldn't have pried the phone out of my hand.

"Anne?" Libby's voice had never sounded so wonderful. "How are you? Is everything alright?"

"What is going on?" My worry and frustration of the past hours came out in my voice. I sounded mad. "What does Emily mean, she's babysitting for Janey? Brian is holding her? Where is my mother?" Finally, my voice softened. "Is Janey all right?" The questions that had been running through my mind spilled out of my mouth in one long breath.

"Anne. Anne. Calm down, Janey's just fine," Libby assured me. "Didn't your mother call you?"

"Call me about what?" I was losing patience trying to solve the riddle of what was happening to my daughter.

Libby must have sensed my worry, for again she assured, "Anne, Janey is perfectly fine." Libby's voice sounded calm and sure. "You should see her." Libby's voice filled with pleasure. "I think your young daughter has fallen in love. Brian is sitting on our beige checked chair, you know, the one by the window? The sun is starting to set behind Brian's shoulder and Janey is staring into his eyes like a puppy dog. It's right out of a painting."

I knew just the chair Libby was talking about and could see the scene in my mind. Instantly, I felt calm. Everything was all right. *Thank You, Lord.* I could feel His constant care for my daughter, even when I forgot to ask.

"Libby, tell me what's going on. Emily said she's going to be babysitting for Janey. What happened to my mother?"

"You really don't know any of this, do you?" Libby chuckled.

"No!" I recalled our frantic hours of wondering. "Tell me, please."

Finally, Libby filled in the details of the past question-filled hours. That my mother abandoned her post to go tend Cari didn't surprise me. But I felt awkward knowing Libby had Janey thrust on her so suddenly.

"I don't know why my mother's acting like this. I feel I should apologize, but I don't know what's going on with her. I'm so sorry this had to fall on you."

"Anne, don't think about it for even one second. Remember when I offered to help out? I meant it."

"But what about your writing? And, you've got Brian and Emily to—"

"If you could see my two kids, you'd think Janey was the best thing that ever happened to either of them. Emily seems to think Jane is a dreamy doll come to life, and Brian is acting as though Janey is the only other person on earth besides him. I'm actually afraid they may start arguing over who's going to get up with her in the middle of the night."

"Oh Libby, I feel so bad this happened. I thought I had everything taken care of. And now this. I really don't know when we're going to make it back and—"

"Anne, I told you not to think about it for a second. I'm glad to be able to help." Libby's voice was matter-of-fact. "Now tell me what happened with you? Did you have surgery? What did the doctor say?"

Suddenly, that old, scared feeling was back. In my worry over Janey, I'd been allowed to forget about my own situation. No longer. My voice was a whisper as I spoke the reality of what the doctors had told me. "It doesn't sound good."

"What doesn't sound good?" Libby repeated what I'd just said in a flat tone, all previous joy gone from her voice.

"My tumor." I felt my throat tighten and paused to clear it. "It's cancer." Saying the word was harder than I'd thought. "It's…it's…it's not good." Those three words were all I could force through my lips. I swallowed the lump that had formed in my throat.

"No." Libby said the single word in a way that made me feel she was trying to stop the cancer by force of will.

There was a long silence as Libby absorbed my news. I could hear Emily talking in the background, her high-pitched singsong voice lilting up and down as she cooed to Janey. I looked around my stark hospital room, suddenly realizing I was alone. All alone. No one else was going to be able to go through what was ahead for me. It was going to be me. Alone. All I wanted was for it all to go away and for me to be in Libby's living room holding my baby. My arms actually tightened as I thought of holding Janey. A small whimper escaped my quivering lips. I hoped Libby hadn't heard.

"Are you okay?"

I nodded my head, knowing she couldn't see my response. Tears streamed down my cheeks. I felt so alone.

"Anne," Libby seemed to sense my longing, my emptiness. "I'm going to take care of Janey as if she were one of my own kids. Okay?"

Again, I nodded. And again, Libby seemed to understand.

"Okay," she said, as if it were settled.

I breathed deeply, trying to gather my emotions, suddenly grateful for a friend like Libby. I knew I could count on her to watch Janey for me. "Thanks." My voice came out high and squeaky.

In a take-charge voice, Libby redirected my sad thoughts. "What happens now?"

"Well-ll," again my voice cracked. "I know I have to have some kind of treatments. The doctor said he'd come back tomorrow and explain what he has planned. I'm not really sure what happens next." I felt the weight of a future filled with uncertainty. "Oh Libby," I whispered, "I'm scared."

Libby didn't waste a beat. "Listen to me, Anne. You are going to be fine. You hear me? You are going to be just fine."

I leaned my head back against the pillow, tears filling my eyes. How I wanted to believe her. If only I could believe the words she said so firmly.

Am I going to be fine, Lord? Am I?

As if in response to my prayer, through the silence of the phone line, ever so softly in the background I heard a small sound. I strained to hear the familiar, yet elusive music. Finally, it came to me, the tinkling sounds of Janey's music box lamb, the gift Libby had given her. Silently, I hummed along with the faint tune, tears streaming freely down my face. *Jesus loves me this I know.* The familiar words filled my heart, and I clung to them, as if to a promise. *We are weak, but He is strong.*

"Thanks, Libby," I croaked. My throat was clogged with tears, and I knew she could tell I was crying, but I wanted to be sure she knew. "Thank you for being my friend."

After a short silence, Libby cleared her throat. "No problem," she said as if I'd thanked her for running a simple errand. I had a feeling being my friend was not going to be so simple, but Libby went on as if it were nothing. "You do what you have to do to get better. I'll hold down the fort here. Okay?"

Once again, I simply nodded, knowing Libby would hear my unsaid goodbye. As I hung up the phone, I could hear the little music box playing in the background. A smile played on my lips even though I was still crying. Yes, Jesus did love me. He gave me a friend like Libby.

I laid my head on the pillow. *He loves you too, Libby.* I imagined Libby rocking my little Janey. *Even if you don't know it yet.*

Olivia

I was scared. All my cool confidence of a moment before vanished the second I removed my hand from the phone. It was the first time I'd heard actual fear in Anne's voice, and it frightened me. The doctors usually couched their reports in positive terms. *We got it all. You've got youth on your side. There are all kinds of new medications.* But if Anne had given in to her fear, then the doctor's report couldn't have been good.

I looked over at Janey lying content in Brian's arms, Emily hovering near, attentive to her every move. As I watched Emily gently curl Janey's fingers around an index finger, a horrible question hit me with almost physical force. Would Anne be here to raise Janey? I felt sick as the realization swept over me. Anne might not see her daughter grow up. Closing my eyes, I tried to imagine what missing those years would be like for a mother, but I couldn't begin to fathom the idea of not being there for your children.

In clarity born of hindsight, I suddenly realized how I'd nonchalantly taken the years I'd had with my children for granted. I stared at Brian and Emily, trying to imagine what it would have been like to not see them grow up. I couldn't imagine it. All I could visualize were the passing years; time passed so slowly while we lived it, but looking back, it had flown by in an instant. I remembered struggling to slip wiggly feet into newborn sleepers that would soon be replaced by toddler sizes. Pushing the kids higher and higher each year on the swings in the park. Cheering along with them as first Brian, then Emily, passed their swimming tests, darting around the city pool as if they were big fish in a little pond. The world was theirs, and like the winner of a gigantic prize, I'd been given a free ticket for the ride. The trouble was, I hadn't known I was a winner. Until now.

How many times had I wished time away? *Hurry and grow up!* I'd been trying to run a wet washcloth over Emily's jelly-filled face while she darted around my kitchen pretending to be a jack rabbit. *How many years,* I'd figured in my head, *until she can wash her face by herself?* She'd been washing her own face for several years now. Where had those years gone?

Now stay there! I recalled saying not that many years ago as I plopped Brian into bed for the fourth time in the same night, wishing he were old enough to put himself to bed. With sudden clarity I realized how many times in the past year I'd suggested to Brian, "Why don't you stay home with us tonight?" I knew I'd lie awake, waiting to hear his bedsprings squeak, signaling he was home safe in his bed. The time I'd so brazenly wished away had passed without me being aware of it.

Seeing tiny Janey, wrapped in her soft pink blanket, a miniature version of Emily ten years ago, made me realize how elusive time had been. Emily looked huge standing next to Janey. Where had the time gone? And here I was, wishing it all back, wondering if Anne would have any time at all.

Of course she will. I shed the previous thought with a swift shake of my head. I didn't have time to think about this now. "Okay, kids," I clapped my hands like a modern-day Mary Poppins, "everybody get busy. I know you two have homework to do, and I've got supper to make, so let's get at it." Activity had always been my way of coping with stress, and I knew how to handle my unsettled thoughts. Move.

"Mom!" Brian and Emily protested in unison. "What about Jane?"

Ah yes, what about Jane? In my efforts to forget about Anne's future, I'd momentarily forgotten about little Janey, too. Fortunately, it didn't take more than a second to recall all the meals I'd cooked with a child on my hip. "No problem," I announced, reaching for the baby. "Give her to me; I did this many times with you kids." I transferred Janey onto my shoulder. "You two go do your schoolwork. I'll call you when supper's ready."

Mumbling, they shuffled off. I marched confidently to the kitchen.

I'd forgotten how pliable a baby can be. When I imagined making supper while holding Janey, I thought of a toddler who could wrap her legs around me and grab on with her arms. Little Janey was like a big glob of slippery gelatin. I propped her up, high on my shoulder, but the smallest movement would cause her to go into a slow but sure slide down my chest. Up I'd hoist her, down she'd slide. Every time I tried to put her into her car seat she'd start to fuss. I was afraid to let her cry, knowing Brian and Emily would come running to see what was wrong. I finally sat down on a kitchen chair in defeat. How had I done this before?

"Mom, I'm really hungry." Emily poked her head around the kitchen doorway. "I can't think because my stomach keeps growling." She spotted me sitting, holding Janey. "I thought you were going to make supper," she declared, sounding put out that a baby could take precedence over hunger.

"I'm trying," I replied, looking at the empty saucepan on the stove. It didn't look as if I'd attempted much. "Janey's not cooperating," I explained, feeling like a heel for blaming my ineptness on a defenseless baby. "Go do your homework, and I'll call you when it's ready."

"But, Mo-om, I'm starving to death!" Emily whined in an all too babyish sounding voice.

"You are not going to starve in an hour," I snapped, wishing Emily were a few years older and could do the cooking for me. *There you go again, wishing time away.* My voice softened as I instructed Emily, "Come here and hold Janey then, while I get something started."

"But, Mom, my homework!"

"Do you want something to eat or not?" Once again I sounded irritable.

Her bottom lip protruding in a silent pout, Emily pulled out a chair and plopped into it. Stiffly, she held out her arms, relaxing them as I placed a squirming Janey there.

"Now sit still," I cautioned, turning to fill a kettle with water. I decided to scrap the idea of the roast I'd planned to start two hours ago and whip up a quick batch of macaroni and cheese instead.

Before the kettle was even half full, Emily's piercing shriek filled the air, "Ick! Ick! Icky! She pooped on me! Get her off! Mom, take her!" The room filled with sound as Janey started wailing an off-key duet with Emily. "Oh, ish! Phew!" Emily continued to shriek.

Drenching my shirt sleeve, the kettle clattered into the sink as I grabbed for Janey, afraid Emily would knock her to the floor with her theatrics.

"Gross! Oh gross!" Emily continued to shout, holding her hand in the air as if it were contaminated. "This is so gross!"

"Act your age!" I commanded, trying to hold Janey in a way that would keep the offending material off my clothes as well. As the words left my mouth, I realized the only person in the room not acting her age was me. I took a deep breath, trying to calm myself. "Listen, go wash your hands with soap," I instructed. I pulled a bag of potato chips from the cupboard. "Then you can take these to your room and snack on them while you work on your homework. I'll get Janey cleaned up and then I'll try to get something made for supper."

Emily stomped from the room, holding the offending hand in front of her.

"I'm sorry," I apologized to her retreating back, "it's been a long time since I've had a baby to take care of."

Emily stopped, but didn't turn around. "I liked it better when I was the baby," she said, wishing like me for a time that was no more.

⌒

Eventually, we all got cleaned up. Emily hadn't been exaggerating when she'd declared Janey gross; I'd ended up having to give her a quick bath. Bob walked in as I snapped Janey into a clean sleeper.

"What's this?" he asked, sounding surprised.

"I'm so glad you're home," I declared. It was the first time in months I'd greeted Bob warmly. "Could you please hold her while I run and change? I got kind of wet." I held out my arms, modeling my soaked shirt.

"Sure," Bob said, bending over the couch to pick up Jane. "I hope I remember how to do this." He plucked the baby up expertly, settling her comfortably against his chest. "How come she's still here?"

I'd briefly told him over the phone, when he'd called about his dry cleaning, that I was watching Janey, but apparently he thought it was a short-term job. I explained, "Anne's mother had an emergency and had to go home. We've got Janey until Anne and Kevin get back from Rochester."

"This should be fun," Bob said, eyeing me to see if I agreed.

"It already has been," I replied, my tone letting him know there was more to the story. "I'm going to change." I slipped from the room, listening as Bob murmured to Janey. The soft slightly higher pitch of his voice brought back memories of our own kids' first days with us. How young and inexperienced we'd been then. Of course, we hadn't known it. Our whole life lay before us, an endless adventure just waiting to happen. Where had time gone?

I turned and peeked back into the room, watching as Bob gently jiggled Janey, cooing to her, smiling at her, making funny little faces for her. For a moment he looked exactly as though he were the young man I'd married. Face a bit thinner, hair a bit thicker, an openness I hadn't seen in a long time. I walked to our bedroom wondering, when had it disappeared?

As I slipped out of my wet shirt and pulled a fleece sweatshirt from the closet, I found myself longing for those early days. Nostalgia tugged at my chest as I recalled the joy Bob and I had found simply being in the same room together. What had changed?

I imagined walking into the living room, giving Bob a smile that came from my heart and not just the muscles around my mouth. I'd wrap my arms around him, and as his arms wrapped around me, I'd pour out my apologies for the time I'd wasted in sarcasm and one-upmanship. I'd tell him my fears about Anne and how I didn't want to waste a moment more of life's allotted time.

How had we gotten into this rut? What had happened to us?

Many waters cannot quench love.

As if in answer to my question, the words I'd heard at a recent wedding came to mind. "Many waters cannot quench love," I recalled the minister saying to the young couple. The couple looked too young to be getting married, but weren't more than a year younger than Bob and I had been when we'd said our vows. They'd looked as naive as we'd been too.

The minister had given the usual sermon about holding onto love during the tough times. Just wait, I'd found myself thinking, it might not be water that quenches your love, but it'll be something. Kids. Work. In-laws. You just wait. When you're young and in love, you can't imagine anything bad enough to test your love. But wait.

I'd glanced at Bob sitting in the pew next to me. He looked tired. I was tempted to reach out and take his hand, to squeeze it, to let him know I could see his exhaustion, but something held me back. A stubbornness filled my heart. *I'm tired too, you know. You're not the only one who works hard. You could reach out to me.* I looked at Bob again, this time seeing only the wall between us. As if to avoid any temptation, I clasped my hands together tightly and turned my attention back to the service.

I'd thought the minister's sermon had fallen on deaf ears—mine anyway. I'd stubbornly passed the time chalking up all the times in the past weeks Bob had ignored me, had to work late, or had fallen into bed too exhausted to even say goodnight. But here were the words again. *Many waters cannot quench love.*

Bob and I had certainly been through many waters over the past fifteen years. Maybe this last year was just a trickle in the stream. A dry spot to get through. As Bob devoted himself more and more to his job I'd let resentment build up like a dam inside me. Maybe if I dug a little deeper and tried a little harder, my relationship with Bob would get flowing again.

I eased the sweatshirt over my head, resolve building in me. That's what I'd do— I'd go to Bob and act as I used to. I'd ask him how his day was and really listen. If he told a joke, I'd laugh instead of rolling my eyes. And I wasn't too old to flirt a little either. I just hoped I hadn't forgotten how. Yes, that's what I'd do—I'd be the Olivia he'd met, not the Olivia even I didn't like anymore, the Olivia filled with resentment and stubbornness.

I glanced in the mirror, running a hand over my hair, smoothing it into place. I was going to really try to make our relationship better. I didn't know what had happened to us, but whatever it was, I could change it. That's what Dr. Phil, on the *Oprah* show had said—that I create my experience. Okay, so I would recreate it. Yes, that's just what I'd do.

"Are we ever going to get something to eat around here?" Brian's crabby voice echoed down the hall, interrupting my thoughts.

"Yeah!" Emily chimed from her bedroom.

"Olivia?" Bob called, "I think this kid is hungry. Besides, I've got a meeting to get to, so hurry up."

Instantly, my nostalgic emotions and resolve fled as reality thumped me on the head. *I can tell you what happened.* I yanked the hem of my sweatshirt into place, anger and resentment back in full force. *Real life happened, that's what.*

Defenses firmly in place, I marched into the living room. "Bob, could you run out and get us a pizza?" I scooped Janey out of Bob's arms. "And please hurry, we're all starving."

Anne

I tried to quell the rising panic I felt as I listened to Dr. Adams outline the treatment schedule he'd planned for me.

"Anne. Kevin." Dr. Adams addressed us both as if we were going to be taking the treatments together. "At this point we need to be aggressive. The lab reports suggest a very aggressive Stage Four cancer..."

Stage Four. My mind clamped on the words. Stage Four. From the reading I'd done I knew Stage Four was about as bad as you could get. The doctors had said the same words after my last mastectomy, and yet they'd assured me they'd gotten it all. I'd believed them. But here I was, months later, lying in bed hearing the same words all over again. Stage Four. I tried to refocus, tuning in to Dr. Adam's moving mouth.

"...along with the chemotherapy, we're going to want to hit this with radiation as well. We'll bombard the disease from both directions..."

It sounded as though he was planning a war.

"...then we'll have to..."

Dr. Adams—all the doctors, really—seemed to talk in plural. "We." "Us." "We'll." "We're." As if they were in this battle with me. Yet their choice of words only served to emphasize just how alone I was. It would be only me having the needle full of potent chemicals stuck into my arm. Only me lying on the table while a technician hid behind a barrier as radiation bombarded my body. Only me feeling the fatigue. Only me feeling the nausea. Only me.

I am with you always.

The words stopped my frantic thoughts. "Oh, Lord," I prayed, "why do I always forget you're with me?"

I am with you always.

Again the words filled my mind. I grasped onto them as I watched Dr. Adams speak of my coming treatment. His mouth moved, but I didn't hear a thing he said. It didn't matter. I knew I was hearing all that was important.

I am with you always.

In some perverse way, I found myself looking forward to starting treatments. It seemed the only way the doctors would let me get back to Brewster. Back to my baby. Back to Libby.

So when the technician said, "You might feel a burning sensation when the chemo starts infiltrating." I actually said, "Good."

He looked at me as if I'd lost my marbles.

During my previous round of chemotherapy, Libby had sat by my side, passing the time in quiet conversation or companionable silence. Kevin, however, was too nervous to sit with me for the time it took to administer the potent drugs.

"I'm sorry, Anne, I want to be there for you, but—" He ran a shaky hand through his hair. "I can't sit there and watch them put that…that *stuff* into you. I can come in and see how it's going, but I'll crawl out of my skin if I have to watch." He was trying his best to explain his reticence to me. "Maybe it's the same kind of thing…you know, the same reason they don't let doctors operate on their own family. I'm sorry, Anne, I don't think I can do it."

I understood. I really did. Sometimes, if I thought about it, the whole process made my skin crawl too. Drugs so powerful they'd kill cancer—surely they could kill healthy cells as well. I didn't try too hard to understand. I just took the doctors' advice and clung to the promise I'd been given. *I am with you always.*

I found I couldn't concentrate enough to read during my chemotherapy, so I used the time to pray. Even then my thoughts were scattered. If I thought of Janey, I'd pray for her. *Lord, let her feel Your love and mine.* If Kevin poked his head into the cubicle, I'd pray for him. *Calm his fears, Lord. Let him continue to find challenge and reward in the work he does.* The technician seemed to check on me every few minutes, so he got prayed for too. *Bless him in the work he does. Give him a heart of compassion for the patients he's working with today.* And of course, I couldn't help but think of Libby, who'd sat with me almost every minute of my last round of treatments. I missed her by my side. *And Lord, bless my friend Libby. Open her heart, so that she may know You as her Comforter, just as You are mine.*

Olivia

I talked on the phone with Anne every night during the time she was in Rochester. She'd call to check on Janey and always ended up apologizing for what she was convinced was a huge imposition on me.

"They started my first treatment today," Anne told me, sounding upbeat. "The doctor ordered some baseline scans yesterday, but they're going to let me wait to start radiation until I get home. Of course, I'll have to take the treatments in Carlton, not Brewster."

"I'll drive you," I offered automatically, "just like always." I hoped my words would erase the memories of those awful weeks when I'd blamed Anne for everything that had ever gone wrong in my life. I felt I'd come a long way since then.

"I'm going to have to find a sitter for Janey. I'll be having radiation every day for a couple weeks."

I looked at Janey lying content on a blanket on the floor. "Don't bother," I told Anne, "we can take her along. I'll hold her while you have your treatment; that way you won't have to be away from her for very long."

"Oh Libby," Anne sighed, "I couldn't ask you to do that. I mean, you've watched Janey for half her life already. If you're going to drive me to my appointments and watch my baby, maybe you could come clean my house and cook meals too."

"Sure," I teased back, "but I draw the line at windows and ironing."

Anne laughed, the lighthearted sound making me feel as though she were at home, just a few blocks away, not hundreds of miles away in a sterile hospital.

"They're discharging me tomorrow." Her hopeful tone made me wonder if she'd read my mind, wishing her home.

"Tomorrow? I thought you had to stay long—"

"I do," Anne interrupted, anticipating my thought. "But you know how insurance regulations are; they won't let me stay in the hospital any longer. I'll be staying at the hotel with Kevin. We'll walk over to the hospital for my treatments in the morning. I should be home by the end of the week." She paused, as if she'd just thought of something wonderful. "Home by next week—that felt so good to say."

"Then say it again," I urged.

"I'll be home..." Anne's voice trailed off, as if she had something more to say. She took a deep breath, then said the words again, as if she really believed them. "I'll be home."

There was a comfortable silence as we savored her words.

"We'll be waiting for you," I added, just so she knew.

"Libby," Anne said, "thanks again for—"

"Don't. You don't have to say it anymore."

"But I feel so bad that you—"

"Anne, I said *don't*, okay?"

"But it's such an imposition on—"

"Goodbye," I said, my tone telling her that if she didn't stop thanking me, or apologizing, I was going to hang up.

"Tell Janey I love her."

"I will."

"You, too."

I'd lost Anne's train of thought. "Me too, what?"

"I love you, too."

I'd never had a friend say those words to me before. As the four words flowed effortlessly from Anne's mouth, my throat clamped itself shut.

Anne didn't wait for me to reply. "Bye, Libby. Talk to you tomorrow. Give Janey a hug from me."

It's a good thing Anne hung up without waiting for my goodbye. I couldn't have forced any words past the lump in my throat.

Time and again I tried to explain to Anne how much we enjoyed having Janey in our house, but Anne insisted that a baby's presence had to be a major upheaval in our lives. Actually, having Janey in the house was the best thing that had happened to our family in ages. Janey served as a focal point for our increasingly dysfunctional relationship. We couldn't get into a loud argument for fear we'd wake the baby. If Bob wasn't home, taking care of Janey filled the hours I used to sit and brood about his absence. Having Janey in the house gave Brian a new focus as well.

"Hey, Mom," Brian would say bursting through the door after school. "Where's Jane?"

Not the usual, "What's to eat around here?" Or, "What's for supper?" Not even griping about homework his math teacher assigned. There was anticipation in his voice, as if he was looking forward to what the rest of the day had to offer.

Even Emily had come around. Her initial bouts of jealousy over being usurped as the baby of the family had been put aside in her eagerness to play with a real baby. She no longer needed her dumb, old dolls, which she declared were "for third graders."

Janey gave me a new focus too. Gone were the hours I'd thought should be spent writing. The monkey on my back that used to cry out every time I passed my desk saying, "Sit down. You should be writing. You're letting time slip by. Don't you have anything to write about?" thankfully was silent.

Every now and then I'd pass my desk and see the silver pen Anne had given me glinting in the light. But instead of an inner voice harping at me each time I walked by, laying a huge guilt trip on my shoulders, I felt a quiet calm that said, "Wait. The time will come. Wait." So I did. For now, it seemed enough to take care of Janey.

And take care of her I did. Not in the way I'd hurried my own kids through their days, following a rigid schedule as though I were a drill sergeant. This time was different. It was as if I had been given a second chance of sorts with Janey.

When Brian and Emily were babies, taking care of them had felt as if it were a chore. Sleepless nights were followed by jam-packed days. I tried to follow a schedule only a superwoman could maintain.

Morning baths, followed by dressing and feeding. Short naps while I rushed around the house dusting and collecting laundry. Lunch time followed by play time that consisted of surrounding the kids with toys while I tried to cram in a few more household tasks. An hour of *Sesame Street* captivated them for a time while I started supper and maybe snuck in a chapter of a book, trying to fold laundry at the same time. Evening brought another round of baths, sleepers, a bedtime snack, and a quick goodnight.

This time however, everything was different. A morning bath that had felt like fifteen minutes of solid drudgery years ago now turned into a half-hour play time. I soaped Janey's tiny body, then leisurely scooped the warm water over her, washing off the bubbles. She relaxed in my arm as if to say, "I like this."

I recalled trying to fit my own kids' slippery, kicking legs into sleepers that always seemed much too big or way too small. How many times had I lost my patience, just wanting to get them dressed so I could get on with my agenda? Now, if Janey wanted to lie and kick for a while after her bath, I was content to sit with her on the bed while she stretched the kinks out of her skinny little legs.

Time seemed as if it had taken on a new dimension as I tended to Janey's needs. She added a newfound structure to my day, but I also found myself with a lot of time to think. After all, no matter how precocious a two-week-old baby is, she's still not much of a conversationalist. I found myself thinking and talking out loud.

"What could little Janey be thinking?" I asked as I smoothed lotion over her arms after her morning bath.

"Are you wondering where your mommy is?"

I waited, while in my mind she answered, "Yes I am."

"Your mommy is at the hospital getting all better so she can take care of you for a long, long time." I slipped a rose-colored sleeper underneath Jane.

"Are you wondering who I am?"

"Well, of course," I answered for her, zipping the sleeper closed.

"My name is Olivia. Your mommy calls me Libby. No one else calls me that, but your mommy is my special friend, so I let her call me by a special name."

The first time I found myself talking out loud to Janey, I actually stopped and looked around, wondering if just possibly someone was on their way with a net to take me away. Since no one in the room seemed to mind, I kept right on talking. After a while our conversations came to feel perfectly natural, and Janey began to seem less a wordless infant and more a really good listener.

"What would Janey like to do now?" I asked, slipping her into my arms.

"A warm bottle would be nice, thank you."

"Since you asked so politely, that's just what Libby will get you." I placed Janey in her car seat on the kitchen table while I readied her bottle.

I settled on the couch with Jane, a pillow under my arm for support. "Here you go, a delicious mid-morning snack of warmed, pre-mixed formula. Yummy." The "yummy" part sounded forced, but I thought Janey would understand.

"I suppose you're wondering what Libby's thinking about today."

I ignored the, "No, not really," she tried to say and continued. "Well, let's see. I'm wondering if Emily is ever going to quit wanting to practice piano. You know, she's trying to impress your mother when she gets back. And I'm wondering what Brian is going to do when you go home to live with your mom and daddy. And I'm wondering if Bob still loves me."

I glanced at Janey to see how she'd reacted to my last comment. Convinced she had given me a tell-me-more look, I went on. "Bob hardly talks to me anymore. Well, I hardly talk to him either. But," I defended myself, "it's hard to carry on a conversation when someone doesn't talk back."

"Oh, really?" Janey seemed to say. "You don't seem to have a hard time with me."

I ignored her comment.

"He's at work all the time. And when he is home, he seems pre-occupied with something. He might as well be a million miles away."

"Ask him about it."

"I shouldn't have to ask."

"If he's preoccupied, maybe he's forgotten he hasn't told you his thoughts." Janey was showing surprising maturity for a two-week-old.

Her bottle empty, I lifted Janey onto my shoulder and patted her back. "He should know I'm not a mind reader."

"He can't read yours, either."

"Well, that's a good thing, because most of the time what I'm thinking about him, he wouldn't want to know."

"That's not very nice."

"I know, but—"

"But what?" Janey was interrupting me." It's not very nice." She burped loudly.

"But—"

"No 'buts.' Do you love him?"

"Of course," I answered automatically.

"Do you really?"

"I think it's time for your nap." I scooted forward, struggling to get off the couch.

"Oh sure—whenever the questions get hard, it's time to do something else."

"You're getting kind of mouthy for someone who can't even talk."

Janey wiggled sleepily as I placed a blanket over her. "Just think about it."

"Go to sleep," I said, trying hard to sound as though I were a nice baby-sitter, instead of a woman who had some soul searching to do.

Did I love Bob?

Of course I did.

How would he know? I glanced at Janey, seemingly asleep. Oh sure—now she was a ventriloquist who talked in her sleep.

I refused to let a sleeping baby tell me what I was supposed to think about, so I sat down and flipped through the stack of yesterday's mail. Bob had brought it home with him from work late last night and it had gone unnoticed until now. Bills, catalogs, a hardware store flyer...and a letter addressed to Libby Marsden. Except for Christmas cards, I rarely exchanged personal notes with anyone. Christmas was two months away. I held the letter up to the light, trying to figure out who it was from. Probably cousin Karen. I recalled our family joke that her cards came so late she might as well save them and mail them the following Christmas. Maybe she'd taken our advice.

"Why don't you just open it?" I startled myself. I didn't even need Janey for an excuse. Now I was talking out loud to myself. Get the net.

I stuck my thumb under the flap and tore the gold envelope open. Sliding out the card I quickly flipped it open. I should have known; only Anne called me Libby. But why would she write? We talked on the phone every night. Still, it felt good to be holding something in my hand that was from her. I poured myself a cup of coffee and sat at the kitchen table, pretending Anne was with me.

The front of the card showed an empty chair; underneath, in a gently scrolling cursive, were two words: "Something's missing..." Inside, one word: "You."

Just like that, I missed her. I closed the card and then, as if for the first time, read it again. Even the second time, though I knew exactly what it would say, I felt a pang of loneliness when I read the word, "You." Not that I hadn't missed Anne before now. I had. But not in the physical way I felt now. It was as if she'd been here, sitting beside me, then suddenly she wasn't. There was an absence to the room I palpably felt. Or maybe it was an absence in my heart. Either way, it didn't feel good.

I turned to the left hand side of the card, filled with Anne's tight, neat script. It was odd to see her handwriting. In the time I'd known Anne I'd only glanced as she'd filled out a hospital questionnaire, signed an occasional check, or wrote small little notes on the corners of Emily's piano books. I'd never seen a page filled with her writing. It was unfamiliar, yet familiar at the same time. I examined the way her letters were formed—a friendly roundness to them, in perfectly straight lines. Just as I would have imagined Anne's writing, had I ever thought about it.

I took a sip of coffee, savoring the words to come.

Dear Libby,

Time is passing slowly today. I know we talked last night, but I'm wishing you were here today. I know the hours would fly by if you and I could talk them away. I thought I'd "talk" to you on paper.

I had my blood work at 7:00 this morning. My actual treatment won't be until 1:00. How to fill the time in-between? Kevin has been trying to keep up with paper work and spends quite a bit of time on the phone talking to clients, etc. I get up and walk a lot, but the hallway kind of looks the same after the tenth time down. (That was supposed to be funny.) I've been getting many cards from the people at church. There is one older lady who has sent me a card every single day. It's funny, because I hardly know her. But it's comforting to know that even almost strangers are praying for me. (I'll take all the prayers I can get!) Kevin went out and bought some tape for me. I made him tape all the cards up on the...

Taking another sip of coffee, I flipped the card over to the backside. I smiled in anticipation; the whole back was covered with more of Anne's writing.

...walls around my bed. I have the card that Emily sent smack dab in the middle of the wall where I look about 50 times a day. (Be sure and tell Emily.) I like to think of the cards around me as symbols of being surrounded by prayer. It's a good feeling.

I still can't believe this is me sitting amongst all these sick people. I feel fine. Maybe once I'm at the hotel with Kevin this will start to feel more routine. Right now, I go down to the treatment area, and the other people don't look all that sick either. Some of them are wearing mink coats, expensive dresses, and jewelry that's got to cost a fortune! It's as if we're all waiting for a fabulous party, instead of chemotherapy treatments.

When I'm waiting, I usually end up visiting with the people around me. Libby, believe me, I won't have trouble thinking of "something worse," for a long time. You can't believe what some of these people have been through. I'll tell you about some of them when...

The writing ended, but the sentence wasn't finished, and Anne hadn't signed it. The letter seemed incomplete. I turned the card over, as if I expected another page to magically appear. It didn't. I picked up the gold envelope and looked inside. Sure enough, there were two more folded pages stuck inside the envelope. Eagerly grabbing them out, I poured myself another cup of coffee and then, smoothing the crease in the middle of the paper, I read on.

...I get back. I have to keep telling myself that God does not put a burden on us which we cannot handle. But this is a load! With His help, we'll come through this ordeal the way He has planned.

In my devotional time today I read a passage from the Song of Solomon. It's really a passage about the love between a husband and a wife, but one phrase struck me as it reminded me of our friendship. It said, "Many waters cannot quench love."

An eerie, tingling feeling went down my spine. It seemed a very unusual coincidence that the same odd verse had been in my mind just a day or so earlier. My arms were covered with goose bumps.

It reminded me of that "time apart" we spent. (Sorry, I never know what to call it. I'm just glad it's over!) I don't think there was a day that went by,

Libby, when I didn't pray for you. I was reminded again today how faithful God is, allowing you back into my life. How lucky I am to have a friend like you! "Many waters"—or arguments, or hospital stays—cannot "quench" the love I have for you. God has given us a special bond.

All kinds of blessing on you today, Libby!

Love you,
Anne

I placed the letter on the table and laid my hands over her writing, as if by doing so I could give to Anne the same warm feeling she'd given me. I lifted my hands and peeked again at her final words. "Love you." Not the same old, "Love," that others used to casually sign off, but "Love you."

It amazed me how Anne could so easily say those words. *Love you.* They weren't words I'd heard often in my life. Occasionally my mother would say them; maybe two or three times I'd heard the words from my dad, and only once, as we hugged after Mom's funeral, had I heard them from my brother. Of course, over the years Bob had uttered them now and then, although not lately. No, not many people had ever said those words to me.

How often have you said them?

There was that chiding voice again. It had been easy to blame Janey for the pointed conversation I'd had this morning, but since I wasn't in the same room with her now, I knew I was only fooling myself.

How often have you told other people that you love them?

"Okay, okay," I scolded myself, "I admit it, I haven't said it much either. Are you happy now?"

I paused, realizing I'd asked myself a question. A not-so-easy-to-answer question. Was I happy now that I understood there were two sides to the question? That I could have said the words too?

Not really.

It wasn't easy to admit that I was as much at fault as those I'd been blaming. Just because my parents, or Bob, hadn't uttered, "I love you" very often, didn't mean I was off the hook.

So, okay, maybe I should have said, "I love you" more to my mother and dad. But they were gone. What was I supposed to do now?

Tell the people you can.

This was really getting irritating. Since when did my conscience get so smart?

Okay, I could easily tell the kids. Emily would eat the words right up. Brian, well, Brian might be as uncomfortable hearing the words as I would be saying them. But I could try. It might be harder to tell Bob. I wasn't even sure I wanted to say the words to Bob. He hadn't been very loving lately.

Have you?

I looked once again at Anne's closing; *Love you.*

Why do you always do this to me Anne? You don't even have to be here, and you make me think about things that make me squirm.

Even though I'd rarely heard the words from my parents, it still seemed natural that they should have told me on occasion. But never, never had I heard the words "I love you," from a friend.

Until now.

It had never occurred to me to tell a friend, someone I wasn't even related to, "I love you."

Until now.

I peeked at Anne's closing one more time. Then, even though I'd been talking out loud to myself all morning, I looked around my kitchen to make extra sure no one was there.

The words came out in a whisper, as if I were just trying them out for size, not yet sure if they fit. "I love you, too."

I let the unfamiliar words hang tentatively in the air as I went to check on Janey.

Anne

Kevin and I decided to stop by our house and unload things from the car before going to Libby's to pick up Jane. As I waited on the doorstep, while Kevin unlocked the door, I recalled the last time I'd stood there, talking to Libby. Another lifetime ago. In the two weeks since that night it was as if the time of estrangement between Libby and me had melted away. As if it had been told to me by a friend and then almost forgotten.

I had talked with Libby every day since I'd been gone. Our conversations had ranged from the mundane ("Emily got a B on her spelling test") to more serious things, ("I'm worried about Brian, he's been a different kid since the drug episode").

It was as if our friendship hadn't skipped a beat. If anything, it was stronger than before. We knew we could weather hard times.

All other thoughts vanished as Kevin swung open the door to our house. Its well-remembered smell flooded over me. Even before I set foot inside, it felt good to be home.

The house was stuffy from being closed up for almost two weeks, but I hardly noticed as I walked through the rooms, touching all that was familiar. I bounced on the edge of our bed, wondering if hospital bed manufacturers ever slept on their own creations. Even though it felt as if I'd spent most of the past two weeks in a reclining position, I couldn't wait to climb into my own cozy bed in a few hours.

I walked into Janey's room, opening the blinds to let the last rays of late-afternoon fall sun fill up her room. I ran my hand over the taut sheet covering her crib. I wondered if she had missed her bed too? A little tee shirt lay across the arm of the rocker, as if Janey had thrown it off in a rush to get somewhere. I knew my mother must have tossed it there, probably meaning to bring it along to Libby's, but then changed her mind. I folded the tiny garment and put it away in a drawer.

It felt good to be doing normal household tasks—opening blinds, folding clothes. I gathered up the few soiled pieces of clothes in Janey's hamper, actually looking forward to doing a load of laundry. I walked back to our room, intending to pull the dirty clothes from Kevin's suitcase and my own. I found Kevin simply standing in the doorway, his back to me, looking into our bedroom. I went up behind him and gently placed my hand on his back.

"Looks good, doesn't it?"

"Um-hmm," Kevin hummed. "Really good."

We stood together, looking at our familiar room. Savoring being home.

"Anne," Kevin said turning, taking me and Janey's dirty laundry into his arms, "I didn't realize how much I missed this. Missed being—" His voice cracked and he cleared his throat. "Missed being here. With you."

I nodded in agreement, my head buried in his shirt. I could feel his chest rise and fall as he breathed deeply, as though relishing every molecule of the air around him.

"I love you, Anne Abbot." He squeezed me to him even tighter.

The stitches from my surgery tugged from the pressure, but not enough to make me want to end our embrace. "I love you, too," I said, turning just a bit to relieve the strain on my incision.

⌣

I was tired already. The washer was going, filled to the top with a load of whites. I walked into the living room as Kevin pushed his arms into the sleeves of his brown leather jacket.

"Ready to go get Janey?" he asked.

"Just let me rest a minute," I replied sinking onto Kevin's old college couch. "Ouch!" I jumped up and scooted over a few inches. "That popped spring got me. Right where it hurts, too." I rubbed my upper thigh where it had poked me.

"This thing has seen some days, hasn't it?" Kevin caressed the back of the sofa, apparently recalling fond memories.

"*Better* days, I'd say." I rubbed the spot on my leg that was still throbbing.

"Tell you what," Kevin sat down beside me, avoiding the spot where the recalcitrant spring resided. "If you feel up to it in the next few days, why don't you shop for a new couch? I think it's time for this one to be put out to pasture. After all, we can't have a couch that pokes my wife or baby daughter." Kevin lowered his voice so he sounded menacing: "It's *dangerous.*"

I laughed, then brought our discussion back to reality. "As much as I'd like a new couch, I think we have enough bills to worry about without adding new furniture to the list."

"I know." Kevin sounded resigned. "But I think we can swing it. Insurance will cover most of your medical treatment, and I should be getting a year-end bonus in a couple months. That should cover the couch, anyway."

"But," I protested, "we've got all those hotel bills, and eating out, and gas—"

Kevin covered my mouth with his hand. "Anne, go shop for a new couch. I want you to have it. Okay?"

His hand still over my mouth, I looked into his eyes. They told me this meant more to Kevin than just getting new furniture, as if it would offer some sort of tangible hope for our future. Only after I nodded in agreement did Kevin remove his hand, leaning down to give me a gentle kiss where his hand had been.

"Let's go get our baby." Kevin stood, reaching two hands out to me, lifting me out of our old couch, into what he thought was hope.

Olivia

I'd been watching for Anne and Kevin out the window half the afternoon. Anne hadn't been sure what time they'd get back; she was scheduled for her last chemo treatment in Rochester early in the morning. They planned to leave for Brewster as soon as possible after that. I'd suggested they stop by their house first to get the car unloaded before they picked up Janey. That way they wouldn't have to try to manage a possibly cranky baby along with luggage. I'd had a casserole in the refrigerator that I'd intended to send home with Anne. I knew her fridge was empty. As the afternoon wore on, I'd put the dish in the oven, assuming they'd get here before supper. Now, I was beginning to wonder if something more had happened. Surely, Anne would have called if they'd been delayed.

I peeked in the oven for no earthly purpose other than to assure myself the casserole was still in there. I'd bathed Janey after her afternoon nap and put her into a clean sleeper, which had miraculously stayed clean the rest of the afternoon. I had her four other sleepers clean and folded in her bag along with her toys, extra formula, and diapers. I shook my head, wondering how those five little sleepers had survived their almost daily washing. I looked at Janey, kicking contentedly on her blanket in the middle of the living room floor. I was going to miss her.

I'd been so busy these past days patting myself on the back for restoring my friendship with Anne that I hadn't noticed how things with the rest of my family were, or rather weren't. Little Janey had been a welcome diversion. Our lives had circled around her like wagons circling for protection. Unlike a wagon train, however, we weren't on the alert for an unexpected attack from without, we were avoiding attack from within. I wanted to change that attitude.

After my day-long conversation with myself, I'd vowed to tell each of the kids, this very afternoon, that I loved them. I figured I had to start somewhere, and the kids were an easy target.

Emily came charging through the door, her usual minute by minute account of the day spilling from her lips.

"You should have seen the awesome jeans Wendy had on today."

"Awesome jeans?" I asked. I never could understand how the kids could distinguish one brand from the next as they walked past each other in the hall. Jeans all looked "blue" to me.

"Oh yeah, they were so *fat*." Emily shot me a look, trying out her new word.

"*Fat?* What's that supposed to mean?" All I needed was for Emily to develop an eating disorder.

"Umm, well," Emily bit the edge of her lip. "I'm not sure, exactly, but I know it means something *good*. Like, '*Oh!*'" Emily pitched her voice higher, imitating a classmate passing on the newfangled compliment, "'you look so fat today.'"

What next? In my day that remark would have been cause for a fight.

"So if I said, 'It would be really fat if you'd do your homework now,' that would be pretty cool, huh?"

"Yeah! Well, no! I mean, I don't want to do my homework right now." Emily put her hands on her non-existent hips. "Mom! That was a trick."

I grabbed her to me, laughing. Here was my chance, "I…" The next word was stuck in my throat. I tried, again, "I…"

Emily pulled back, the smile still on her face. "I…what, Mom?"

I tried. I really did. But the best I could do was, "I…think you're fat."

Emily squeezed me around the waist. "I think you're fat, too."

Brian walked in just then, overhearing our mutual compliment session. "Do you guys even know what that means?" He chuckled as though he'd overheard us speaking Czechoslovakian or some other language we didn't know.

"Not really," I replied, releasing my hold on Emily. "But we think it's something coo-oool." I did the best cool person imitation I could muster. Obviously, it wasn't very *fat*. Brian rolled his eyes.

"It's not like being fat, it's phat. Pretty Hot And Tempting." He swung open the fridge, then closed it.

"Pretty hot and tempting?" I asked. Now he was the one speaking Czechoslavakian. "What's that mean?"

"Phat. P.H.A.T. It stands for pretty, hot, and tempting. Something that's really coo-oool." Brian did a much better imitation of a cool person than I had done.

"Oh-hh!" It was as if a light bulb had gone off in Emily's head. She'd just been granted the keys to become tomorrow's recess time center of attention.

I still didn't get it. Taking the chance of branding myself an old fuddy-duddy, I ventured, "I thought fat meant you were...well, *fat*."

Brian shrugged. "So maybe that's why kids say it. It's opposite of what parents think it means."

"Oh-hh!" Emily grinned, understanding settling around her. She was getting more of an education in our kitchen than she did at school.

Brian had better things to do than explain teen talk to his mom and his little sister. "Where's Janey?"

"I get to hold her first!" Emily quickly put in her claim.

"I was just going to get her bottle ready." I poured the formula into the bottle as I spoke, expertly popping it in the microwave, hitting the timer for a minute. Janey was starting to wiggle, trying to wake up from her nap. "Emily, why don't you go see if she's awake?" I knew if Jane was awake we'd have heard her by now, but it would give me a chance to be alone with Brian. Emily skipped into the living room.

"So, how was school today?" I asked, trying to sound casual, as if I wasn't that interested. It was the only way I knew to get him to actually talk.

"Fine." His usual answer. A tightly closed door.

"Do anything phat?"

Brian couldn't help but smile at my question. Apparently my joke had opened the door just a crack, because he answered, "Well, kinda."

He said it tentatively, as if he didn't want to tell me out right, but wanted me to ask more. So I did.

"So tell me, what does a sophomore think is something kinda phat these days?"

"We had an assembly today. There was this pro football player who gave a talk." Brian poured himself a glass of milk. "Most of the time those things are so lame. But this guy was really interesting. Even the seniors were listening."

"What did he have to talk about?" I tested the formula against my wrist, acting as though I wasn't trying to pry information out of him.

Brian took a gulp of milk, downing half the glass in one big swallow. Wiping his mouth with the back of his hand, he went on. "He talked about how some people think sports are just for dumb jocks. That when he turned pro, lots of people acted like he was going to make a fortune just from hitting other guys with his body. But he knew that with one wrong hit, his whole career could be over. So he made sure he finished college first. Then, with the money he got when he signed, instead of spending it all over the place like people were telling him he should, he started making business investments. After a few years, his business investments were worth more than the sports contract he'd signed. He said lots of his teammates thought he was nuts because he didn't go buy a new sports car, or that kind of stuff. He said he saw guys get all messed up on drugs—" Brian stopped, looking as if maybe he'd said too much, taking another swallow of milk to cover his silence.

"Um-hmm," I answered nonchalantly, as if I were just kind of listening instead of hoping with all my might he would keep talking. It was the most I'd heard Brian talk in months.

"Well," Brian continued, twirling the glass around in his hands, "he said those guys were the dumb jocks—the ones that let the money take control of their lives. He said you gotta have something in control of your life that makes you a better person. Not just a better athlete, or a better student, but a better all-around person. He said the way he did that was by his faith."

Like Anne, I thought, just now putting together that her faith was what made her so different from other people. Better.

"I don't know if the principal liked that part very much," Brian continued. "All of a sudden Mr. Harris walked out by the guy and said, "We're almost out of time." The football guy grinned, kind of goofy-like, like he expected that or something, then he said, 'Sometimes time runs out before we get everything done in life that we want.' He said some more stuff after that, but I got to thinking about Pete and how he almost ran out of time before he was ready. Mom?" Brian looked right at me, as though he really wanted me to hear this part. "Sometimes I still get scared about that."

I looked right back at him. "Me too."

"Pete seems different now. He's so quiet, and he never wants to do anything. Well," Brian added quickly, half-smiling, "not like either of us can do much. We're both grounded. But I mean, he doesn't even talk like he wants to do anything." Brian shook his head. "I wish I could do something to make him better."

"You can," I added. "Keep being his friend."

He could pray.

Oh yeah, I was supposed to tell Brian that? Me. Little Miss Prayer Expert. I'd thought that voice was just for me; now it was giving me advice for others, too. I grabbed a cloth and started wiping the kitchen counter, doing my best to ignore my thoughts. Instead I remembered my vow to tell both kids I loved them. I'd already blown it with Emily, the one person I thought would be easy to tell. I couldn't imagine how I'd ever get the words out to Brian.

Silently, Brian got up and stood near me at the kitchen sink, rinsing his glass under a stream of water. He saw the bottle in my hand. "Should I go feed Jane?"

Tell him now.

I opened my mouth, then closed it.

"That would be nice," I replied, handing him the warm bottle. "I need to get the table set. I think Anne and Kevin will be here for supper."

Tell him now.

Again, I opened my mouth. Nothing came out. I took a deep breath, pulling dishes from the cupboard. Maybe my plan wasn't so great after all.

Brian paused by the table, looking at the baby bottle in his hand. "I'm going to miss Janey when she goes."

"Me too," I said. A picture of Brian leaving home three years from now flashed through my mind. "A person gets kind of attached to certain kids."

As he turned to go, the words that had been stuck in my throat earlier slipped out so unexpectedly, so easily, it was as if they'd been waiting there all along. "I love you."

I was surprised. I hadn't struggled. I hadn't even thought about it. Yet, there they were, three little words for Brian and me and all the world to hear.

Brian turned, a puzzled look on his face, as if he wasn't sure he'd heard me correctly.

"I love you," I said again, smiling, a curious tingle near my heart. One corner of his mouth turned up in return. "Phat."

Brian and Emily were holding vigil over Janey, talking silly baby talk, acting as if it were just another night to play with our resident baby, not the night she would be leaving. There was an old-fashioned innocence about my children as they pretended to smell Janey's "stinky" feet, then keeled over as if knocked out by the smell of baby lotion. As anxious as I was for Anne to arrive, some small part of me said *don't hurry.*

I settled into a chair, content to watch the three of them play, knowing Anne would come as soon as she could. I closed my eyes, remembering the feeling I'd had moments ago when I'd said to Brian, "I love you." Why had it been so hard? Why hadn't I said it more often? For all my worry and fretting, it had been so easy to say those words.

Many waters cannot quench love.

There was that verse again, popping up like a jack-in-the-box, surprising me every time. I opened my eyes, letting them linger on Janey, then Emily, and finally Brian.

Maybe there was truth to the words. For all my failings as a mother, my kids still seemed to love me. In my heart I repeated the words, *many waters cannot quench love.* This time—for this moment anyway—it seemed something I might be able to believe.

But I wasn't going to hold my breath about it.

Anne

"Absolutely not! Can you imagine Kevin trying to take a nap on that couch?" Cradling Janey, Libby flopped herself onto the two-cushioned sofa, demonstrating what she meant. "Look." She motioned to her lower half. From mid-calf down, her legs dangled in midair. "See what I mean?"

"I think my chemotherapy has erased my decorating brain cells," I said, picturing six-foot Kevin trying to fit himself between the arm rests.

"Oh, but it is comfortable." Libby sighed.

Even Janey looked relaxed in her horizontal position astride Libby's chest. A friend of my mother's had sent a front-carry baby sling which I wasn't going to be able to wear until my surgery site healed, so Libby had strapped it on her body when she'd arrived to pick us up for lunch and an afternoon of couch-shopping.

"It'll be much easier than lugging that heavy car seat all over the store," Libby declared, picking up Janey, already in the seat, and bringing her out to the car. Buckling Janey into the backseat, she pushed aside my apologies and protests. "Don't worry, you'll be doing this yourself soon enough. Believe me, it gets old. Fast."

Libby had suggested a mid-morning trip, right after my treatment, but I'd found it was all I could do to get up the gumption to do anything by noon. It wasn't that Janey was disrupting the schedule I tried to keep. It was me. I was finding myself so exhausted that whenever I laid her down for a nap, I would collapse within minutes on the nearest comfortable surface.

I'd started my radiation treatments on Monday, and while at first it seemed I would be able to breeze through them without many side effects, by the end of the week I felt as though they were zapping any strength I had left.

When Kevin and I had arrived in Brewster after our trip to Rochester, I'd felt as if I were, in a sense, walking backward—from a place of sickness into my home, a place I knew would be filled with life. Back into Libby's welcoming friendship. And when I took my child into my arms, hugging Janey to me as tightly as I dared, I felt as if I were embracing life itself. It felt wonderful.

Although I was sure Janey had no particular knowledge of who her mother actually was—Libby had, in fact, spent more time with her since birth than I had—Janey nestled into my arms as if I'd never been away. It was as if my arms were a familiar place, a place she wanted to stay for a while.

I couldn't begin to describe how wonderful, how normal it felt to be in our own home, just the three of us. I don't know how long Kevin and I sat on the couch, taking turns holding Janey, reminding ourselves how lucky we were to have this tiny infant, yet in the same breath, remarking on how much she'd grown. Her whole existence seemed a marvel, and we didn't want to miss one minute more of it.

I was glad when Libby insisted on taking Janey along to Carlton for my radiation treatments.

"Are you kidding?" she cried when I suggested finding a babysitter. "I'm having Janey withdrawal the way it is. No way! That kid is coming with us."

And so she did. Jane became the darling of the waiting room. Apparently, it's not often they get barely one-month-old babies in the radiation treatment area. Young mothers, either. There we sat, Libby, Janey, and I, surrounded by pale-faced men and women old enough to be our grandparents or great-grandparents. At first they looked at us as if we were visitors, assuming we were accompanying some other older person, envying us our youth and our health. But when they realized the sick person was me, they accepted us into their select group, instantly adopting Janey as their mascot.

"How is Miss Jane today?" Mr. Eiseman asked daily as we entered for my eight-thirty appointment. His granddaughter was expecting his first great-grandchild any day now. He'd told us his goal was to get well enough to go to Colorado for Christmas to see her.

"Look at little Chaney this morning," Mrs. Bauer cooed in her thick German accent "all dressed in pink." She was on her third round of radiation. She'd had one breast removed twenty-five years ago, followed by radiation and twenty years of remission. "Of course they tolt me I was cured. Then, at my checkup five years ago, boom! There it was, back on the other side. Now it's in my lungs, and I've never smoked a day in my life."

The waiting room was filled with people, each eager to share their stories with anyone who would listen. I was grateful for the way they looked out for each other. Had Mrs. Bauer slept well last night? Did Mr. Clark's son stop by yesterday afternoon? Did Mr. Eiseman have plans for Thanksgiving?

"And how about you, dear? How are you feeling?"

It was my second day of treatment, and Libby had gone to grab herself a cup of coffee from the cafeteria (My taste for coffee was dulled from the chemotherapy I'd received). I was passing the time eavesdropping on the waiting room conversation. It was a lesson in caring ministry to listen to people, each sick in their own way, tend to the concerns of others.

It was only after Mrs. Bauer asked a second time, "Dear, how are you feeling?" that I realized she was talking to me.

"Me?" I pointed at myself. When she nodded, I automatically answered, "Great!" Then realized I was being less than truthful. "Actually, tired," I amended.

There were knowing nods all around.

"Does it make you really tired too?" I asked, figuring I'd get a straight answer from these people who'd been through this before. "I thought maybe it was just because I had the baby and haven't gotten my strength back yet, and then with the chemotherapy, and all—"

"Oh, dear," Mrs. Bauer patted my hand, "dat's your baby? I thought it wass your friendt's. My goodness, no vonder you're tired." She went on to explain, "Don't let those nurses tell you nothing. Everybody reacts to this stuff different. I've seen some come in here and you'dt tink they were going to a coffee party, talking and laughing and saying they're going right back to vork after their treatment. Then there's folks like me, and Chake over there," she pointed to a sallow-skinned man across the room, "those treatments zap the zip out of bott of us. Don't they, Chake?"

Jake nodded in exaggerated slow motion, as if agreeing with Mrs. Bauer more than once. "Yup," he finally added.

"So you chust do whatever you got to to keep up your energy," she advised. "Whatever you got to."

By the time Libby arrived with her coffee, I had learned the names of most of the waiting room residents, and Janey had been chucked under the chin by almost all of them as well.

"You don't waste any time, do you?" Libby whispered after I'd introduced her to everyone. "I leave for five minutes and you've got a whole new set of friends by the time I get back. Even found a boyfriend for Janey, I see." She inclined her head towards Jake who was making slow motion faces at Jane.

I elbowed Libby in the ribs, then leaned my head back and closed my eyes. It felt good to have her beside me again. Making wisecracks. Acting like this was just another day. A regular day. As if sitting and waiting for a radiation treatment was just another way to have fun with your best friend. If I hadn't been so tired, I would have told her what I was thinking.

No matter where I was, I found myself closing my eyes every chance I had. It wasn't that I was sleeping my time away. In fact, that was part of the problem—I couldn't sleep. At least, not well. My nights were spent tossing and turning, my dreams filled with dark clouds and disturbing impressions that left me lying awake in the dark, wondering if it was my dream that woke me or a cry from Jane.

I'd heard radiation treatments could cause your energy levels to drop, an idea that hardly seemed possible considering I had zero energy before starting them. Libby had picked up on my listless state and had started staying at the house with me for a couple of hours after my treatments. As soon as we walked in the door, she practically forced me to lie down while she either tended to Janey, dusted the house, threw in some laundry, or started something for supper. She tried tiptoeing around, determined to give me a chance to rest. Sometimes it worked. Having another person in the house sometimes lifted the anxiety I felt enough to allow me to drift into a half-aware kind of sleep. Most of the time it didn't.

"Libby," I'd call from my reclining position on the couch, "you don't have to brown the hamburger on low just because you think it's quieter. I'm awake."

"Close your eyes," she'd command, refusing to talk to me.

"They are closed," I'd call back, quickly shutting them. "I feel so bad that you—"

"I can't hear you," she'd respond, although I knew very well she could.

"Did Jan ever put those plum-colored highlights in her hair?"

Libby poked her head around the corner. "Yes! You can't believe how different she looks."

"See," I taunted, "I knew you could hear me."

And before either one of us knew what had happened, Libby would be sitting on the end of the couch with my ankles draped over her lap, feeding Janey her bottle, talking an hour away.

"I'm going to refuse to come over any more if you don't get a new couch." Libby rubbed the spot on her thigh where I knew from experience that spring would poke.

The fact that Libby always got the end with the sprung spring was the reason we were out shopping for a new couch.

"This one would be perfect." Libby ran her hand along the slightly curved back of a beige sofa. She walked around and stood in front of it, measuring with her eyes. "Kevin would definitely fit, and look, there's a cushion for each of you." She used three fingers to point out the three cushions on the seat of the couch. "Go on, try it out," she urged.

I sank into it, grateful for any excuse to sit. This outing had been more taxing than I'd expected. "Oh, it is comfortable." At that point a hard oak bench might have felt good, but I knew this felt better. "You try it, too." I patted the cushion beside me.

Libby sat at the far end. "I'd better try this end. After all, it's probably where I'll be sitting the most."

"Can I help you ladies?" The salesman who'd been not-so-discreetly following us around the store approached. "Excellent taste," he remarked, waving his hand over the couch as if he were some sort of game show model. "Did you notice it's on sale?"

Actually, I hadn't. At this point, I would have been willing to pay most any kind of money just for a place to sit.

He began to rattle off the virtues of the couch, its manufacturer, and the store itself, which "would be glad to take your old couch off your hands and donate it to charity. After the new one arrives, of course."

The salesman had intuitively guessed I was the one looking for a new sofa and directed his comments towards me. Libby didn't let the opportunity pass, silently mouthing his words behind his back, contorting her face and waving her hands to make his description seem like an out-of-this-world deal.

I sucked in my cheeks, trying my best to look attentive, trying my best not to laugh.

"What do you think?" The salesman had caught me looking at Libby and turned his head to include her in his question.

Quickly, she snapped an extra-serious expression on her face. "Um-hmm," she hummed, sounding as though we were discussing nuclear physics instead of a couch. "Very interesting. What do you think, Anne?"

Libby tossed the question to me, forcing me to wipe the grin from my lips. "Uh, ummm," I stammered, "does it come in other fabrics?" I knew the light beige fabric was impractical for a family with a baby, and the question seemed a perfect way to send the man on a mission, giving me time to think about the purchase. Time to sit a bit more, too.

"Of course," he said. "I'll go find the samples."

"You rat!" I laughed, tossing a throw pillow Libby's direction. I couldn't throw it too hard; Janey lay snug against Libby's chest, dozing comfortably.

"I couldn't help it. He was taking his job a little too seriously. Good grief, telling us that the store was founded by German immigrants in 1898, and that it had started out as a combination mortuary and furniture store? Just what I need to know to make a furniture purchase." She grew serious. "Really though, the couch seems a good price. And it is comfortable. What do you think?"

I knew Libby was asking about the couch, but another thought had captured my attention. When I'd listened to the salesman describing the people who founded the store, I hadn't given them a thought. It just seemed like a nice story. But hearing Libby repeat the salesman's words about the store's beginnings made me realize that they were all dead. The people who had started this store with such high hopes and dreams were all gone. This store, and in a way this couch itself, was their legacy.

Isn't it odd what we pass on to others I thought, looking at Libby and then Jane, wondering if I would have time to pass on anything to them.

"What do you think?" Libby interrupted my thoughts.

"I think…" I replied, remembering how badly Kevin wanted me to replace our old sofa with a new one, "I think I want Kevin to have this couch. Even if I'm not around to enjoy it, he should have a comfortable couch to sit on. Janey, too."

"Anne!" Libby scolded. "What do you mean…'if I'm not around to enjoy it'?"

She would have gone on, but I interrupted, "Libby, I'm just so tired—"

She interrupted right back, "Of course you're tired. You had a baby barely three weeks ago, and then you had a second mastectomy and a week of chemotherapy. And you just finished your first week of radiation treatments. What do you expect? To be doing cartwheels in a furniture store? Lighten up, Anne. No one expects you to be Superwoman except you."

When she put it that way, my worry seemed foolish. I wouldn't expect anyone else who had gone through what I had in the past weeks to be tending a baby, cleaning house, and shopping for furniture. Why did I expect it of myself?

"You're right," I told her.

"Of course I am. I'm always right," Libby quipped. Then quickly added, "Almost."

I glanced at Libby; it wasn't like her to qualify her statements.

"It's the new, humbler me," she explained, picking up on my unasked question, waving a hand as if revealing another side of her personality.

"Here we go, ladies." The salesman was practically stumbling under the weight of five thick sample rings, stuffed under his arms and hanging from his hands. He tried to ease them down to the floor, but ended up dropping two of them right at my feet. "Sorry about that," he apologized. "Maybe you want to start with that one." He motioned to the one nearest my foot as he tried to organize the other four.

I bent down to pick it up, realizing almost immediately that it was too heavy for me to chance lifting it. Before I could even think of what to do or say, Libby had slid from the couch, settled herself on the floor by my feet, and started flipping through the samples. "Nope."

"Nope."

"Nope."

The salesman looked as if he wanted to ask just who was buying this couch, anyway, but Libby beat him to it by explaining, "We have two bodies, but one brain." As if it were the most normal explanation in the world.

"Would you ladies mind if I go check on another customer?" It was obvious he had two Looney-Tunes on his hands.

As if to prove our point, and maybe his, we answered in unison: "Nope."

Olivia

"Can you come over? Right now?" Anne's voice sounded weird.

I looked at the clock on the kitchen stove: eight fourteen A.M. The kids had barely left the house for school, Brian refusing to wear a cap, even though snow was in the forecast. It was a good hour earlier than Anne ever called, and hours before I usually dropped by her house.

"Sure. Give me a couple minutes to run a comb through my hair. I'll be right over." I poured myself a second cup of coffee and headed to the bathroom. What could be wrong? I gave my hair a quick fluff and a spray. Anne had been scheduled to start her second week of radiation today, but the doctors had decided to give her a few days off as the radiation site was showing signs of burns. I had told Anne I'd stop by after lunch to visit, but obviously this was something that couldn't wait until then. I quickly patted at my face with a powder puff and brushed some blush quickly over my cheeks. Good enough. I'd put on lipstick in the car.

Anne met me at the door. She looked great, but one glance told me what was wrong. She was wearing her wig. The wig she'd stored proudly in the back of her closet. The wig she had never had to wear. Until now.

"Oh Anne," I sighed, pulling her into my arms, "it happened." I could feel her head nodding slightly against my shoulder, her breathing irregular, on the verge of crying.

She pulled away, pressing her hands against her eyes, pushing back impending tears. Taking a deep breath Anne fingered the different, coarser hair. "Libby, it was so gross."

I couldn't help but smile. "You sound just like Emily when Janey pooped on her."

Anne's mouth turned up a little. "Well, if I were Emily's age that would be gross. But Libby, you can't believe this. Come look."

Anne led the way to the small bathroom off her and Kevin's bedroom. She bent and opened the cabinet door beneath the sink, pulling out a white garbage can. Holding the can with both hands she thrust it toward me. "Look."

I did. It seemed as though the small, white container was almost filled with Anne's long, auburn hair. I'd never seen that much hair in one spot. My chest tightened as I imagined all of that hair falling from Anne's head. I couldn't help but reach out and touch it. "Oh, Anne," was all I could say as I fingered the damp, brown locks lying limply in her garbage.

"I know," she answered, looking at the hair piled in the can, understanding my unsaid thoughts.

Anne turned to place the can under the sink, but I grabbed it from her hands. "We're dumping this." I marched to the kitchen, dumping the dead hair into her larger garbage can, then tugged the bag out of the can and tied it shut tightly. "Make a pot of coffee," I ordered. "I'll be back."

I waded through a couple inches of snow, stuffing the black bag into the metal can by the alley. "So there!" I said, not sure who I was talking to, but feeling better knowing the hair was out of Anne's house.

The comforting smell of coffee filled the air as I stomped back into Anne's kitchen.

"I thought I'd try a cup," Anne said, motioning to the two mugs setting near the coffee pot. "I need something to settle my nerves. Libby, you can't imagine what it was like."

Anne was quiet as she filled the two mugs. She handed me my cup, then we each pulled out a chair at the table and sat down. She held her mug with both hands for a minute, absorbing warmth through the glass, then took a small sip. "Ummm," she murmured, "it actually tastes good today."

"Good—we can start actually drinking coffee together when we get together for coffee." Lately, I'd been drinking my cups alone as

Anne said most everything left a metallic taste in her mouth, a side effect of her treatments.

Anne took another sip of coffee, then stared into her cup. "When I woke up this morning there was hair all over my pillow." She paused, looking into the liquid as if reliving the scene. "It was more than I'd ever noticed before, but I didn't think much of it. Kevin left for work while I was feeding Janey, so after she went back to sleep I got in the shower. Oh, Libby," Anne shuddered, shaking her shoulders as if shaking off a bad dream, "when I put my head under the shower I could feel hair running down my body with the water. I looked down and there was hair all around my feet. You know what I did?" She looked at me, an almost amused expression on her face.

I shook my head. I couldn't even guess.

"I grabbed the shampoo bottle, poured a huge amount in my hand, and then I scrubbed my head. Scrubbed and *scrubbed*." Anne's voice sounded as if she were scouring the words. "I didn't want to watch my hair fall off a few clumps at a time. I just wanted to get it all off. Do you know what I mean?"

Anne sounded as if she wanted approval that what she'd done was okay.

I imagined standing in my own shower, looking down at my toes and seeing the hair from my head all over my feet, clogging the drain. Just the thought made me feel cold. Naked. As if I wanted to hide myself away. What courage it must have taken for Anne to purposely scrub the hair from her head, to pull that wig from the back of her closet where it had been kept in silent storage and put it on her bare head.

"I am so proud of you," I told Anne. "Rather than denying that your hair was falling off, you went ahead and tackled the problem head-on."

"Libby!" Anne scolded, looking at me wide-eyed, a slow grin spreading across her face.

"What?" I had no idea what she was chiding me about.

"Do you realize what you just said?"

"Of course, I said I was proud of you for tackling the situation head-on."

Now I got it. All of Anne's hair had just fallen off her head, and I was unintentionally making a joke of it. I slapped myself on the forehead with the heel of my hand. "Just a minute," I explained, "I'll see if I can fit the other foot in my mouth, too."

Anne chuckled. "At least we can still laugh about things. I guess that counts for something."

"Let's hope it does," I replied. I sipped my coffee, but finding it too cool for my taste, I set it down. "As I was saying before I put my foot in my mouth, I really can understand what you mean. Why should you walk around wondering if a clump is going to fall off now or a little later, or look down and find your sweater covered with hair? If it's going to fall out anyway, might as well get it over with."

"Exactly." Anne grabbed our mugs, and dumping the cooled coffee down the drain she refilled them. "I could see myself at the grocery store, old Mr. Lehr tapping me on the shoulder, saying, "Excuse me, miss, I think you dropped something." There he'd be standing by the vegetables, pointing at a clump of hair lying on the floor. I'd rather wear this wig than walk around with bald patches."

"I agree," I stated, watching Anne as she returned with our cups. I wondered what her head looked like under that wig. Was she totally bald? Did she look like some of the kids at the mall in Carlton who shaved their heads? I wanted to ask, but among all the topics we'd discussed during the course of our friendship, for some reason this one seemed too personal.

It had been odd to walk in today and see Anne with straight brown hair. I'd been so used to her wavy, auburn locks. The wig was shorter than her normal hair and made her look older in a mature, almost professional way. "You do look nice," I commented.

Anne rolled her eyes.

"No, really, you do," I assured. "And you know me—I don't say stuff to be polite." I had proven that moments ago.

"That's true," Anne said, stopping to catch her reflection in the microwave door. "You really don't think it looks weird?"

"Not at all. In fact, you probably won't like this either, but I actually like it better than your other style."

"Libby! You didn't like my hair?" Anne was aghast. "Why didn't you say something?"

"I did like your hair," I back pedaled. "It's just that this straighter hair is more modern-looking."

Anne brushed at the synthetic bangs, hanging just a touch longer than her normal cut. "At least I can look with-it." Anne sighed, sitting down again. "But I feel like a little old lady, wearing a wig, so tired I can hardly keep my eyes open. And the past couple days, my back has been hurting, too. Sometimes I feel I'm a hundred."

Just then we heard a cry from the bedroom.

"I'll get her," I said getting up, motioning for Anne to stay right there.

Janey was really wailing.

"See," I pointed out, hurrying towards the bedroom, "here's proof you're not a hundred. I've never heard of any centenarians having babies."

"Then you haven't heard about Sarah," Anne called to me in the bedroom.

I quickly changed Janey's diaper, wondering what dumb rumor was going around the town nursing home now.

"I'm sure," I announced, carrying Janey against my shoulder into the kitchen. "Some old gal at the nursing home is having a baby. As Emily would say, 'Duh'!"

Anne laughed. "Libby, it's a story from the Bible."

"Oh," I remarked, feeling foolish. I handed Janey to Anne. "I suppose you're going to tell me about it?"

"Only if you want to hear it."

"Might as well keep me entertained while I get Janey's bottle ready."

"I can't remember exactly how old Sarah was when she found out she was going to have a baby. But she was *old*." Anne said the word in a way that made Sarah sound ancient. "And this was after years and years of being humiliated because she was childless...."

Janey finished off her bottle about the same time Anne finished telling me the story of Abraham and Sarah.

"You're right," I stated when she was done, "that would be worse."

"Worse? What's worse?" Anne asked, not getting my point.

"I thought that's why you were telling me the story—you know, something worse?"

"Libby, I have no idea what you mean. What does the story of Abraham and Sarah have to do with that?"

"Sarah," I explained, "you know, being a *hundred* and having a baby. Now that would be worse."

Anne gave an exasperated sigh. "That has nothing to do with the story."

"So your point is?" I still didn't get it.

"Well, there really wasn't a point. You asked me to tell you the story about the hundred-year-old lady that had a baby. Remember? But I suppose the point is that when you believe in God, there's always hope."

"Oh," I replied, carelessly brushing aside her interpretation. "I thought this was supposed to be the 'something worse' thing. You know, you could have this little baby and really *be* a hundred."

A look I couldn't read passed across Anne's face, then was quickly erased. "I don't think the story of Abraham and Sarah counts as something worse. But you're right, we need to think of something worse for my hair falling out. Let's see..." Anne pressed her lips together in thought.

"Look at it this way," I countered, "since your hair fell out, at least this time we know something is happening in your body. The treatments must be working—"

Anne interrupted, "But that's not something worse, that's good."

"Oh, I know," I responded, "I'm getting to the something worse part. Something worse would be if you had bought that Orphan Annie-like wig. Now *that* would be worse!"

After helping Anne fold a load of laundry, I gave Janey a kiss on the cheek. "You take good care of your mommy today," I instructed.

Out of habit I almost answered, "I will," but managed to catch myself.

Turning to Anne I cautioned, "Try to take a nap this afternoon; you've had a big day already."

"Aye, Aye, Captain." Anne gave me a mock salute, accidentally flipping her new bangs into disarray. She reached out, giving me a quick hug. "Thanks for coming when I called."

"No problem. See you tomorrow," I replied, sounding as if it were any old day.

But it wasn't. I hardly saw the passing road as I drove through a light dusting of early November snow, my mind filled with images of Anne. I didn't want to face my empty house, so I turned the car toward the highway. Maybe I'd drive over to Carlton and roam around the mall. Anything to keep from thinking about what was happening to Anne. But on the drive to Carlton all I could see was Anne. Anne's pillow covered with hair. Her shower drain, so plugged with hair the water wouldn't drain. The white garbage can half-filled with her auburn locks. Anne in her new wig. I tried to imagine Anne without hair. I recalled my confident words earlier this morning, "At least we know something is happening because your hair is falling out." I'd meant them to sound positive, but now they seemed more of a warning. I vaguely remembered Anne saying something about hope, but for the life of me I couldn't remember what it was. All I recalled was somehow making a joke out of what she'd said. A sick feeling swept through me. What was happening to my friend?

Libby was a rock. There I was, falling apart because my hair had dropped out, and she was pointing out that having my hair fall out was a good thing. It sounded like something Martha Stewart would say, "Yes, hair falling out—it's a good thing." I'd have to remember to tell Libby. Another thing we could laugh about together.

When I thought about my situation the way Libby described it, it didn't look near as bad as I'd been thinking. Maybe something different was happening inside my body this time. Obviously, the chemotherapy hadn't stopped the cancer last time. Maybe this time, with the combination of chemotherapy and radiation treatments, things would be different.

After Libby left, I held Janey and looked at the two baskets of laundry Libby had folded, trying to get the gumption to put the clothes away. I hadn't had the energy to fold more than a couple washcloths, but Libby seemed not to notice. She just jabbered away as if folding your friends' laundry was what all girlfriends did to pass time.

I shifted Janey onto my lap. It was getting harder and harder for me to hold her against my chest. The radiation treatments had left a couple of fiery-red patches of skin on my chest, and even though I had gauze over the spots, they burned and itched whenever I happened to rub against them. Libby was going to drive me to Carlton for my checkup the next day. The doctor wanted to take a look at my burns to see if I could continue my treatments.

I knew I'd be spending the morning with Libby, which brought to mind a dilemma I'd been struggling with. We were having Janey baptized over the Thanksgiving weekend—three weeks away—and I still hadn't decided who Janey's godparents would be. Although

Kevin had suggested a first cousin of his as a godfather, he'd left the final decision up to me. I knew propriety would say I should chose my twin sister, Andrea, as godmother. After all, I was godmother to Jimmy Jr., but my heart wasn't agreeing with my head on this one. My heart was telling me to choose Libby. But whenever I thought about asking her, my head was in conflict. I knew Libby was not exactly a dedicated Christian. Even though she did belong to a church in Brewster, she never attended services. When I'd asked Libby about her beliefs, she'd managed to artfully change the subject.

I remembered how, in the heat of anger over Brian, Libby had shouted that she didn't need my prayers, but at times since then I'd sensed a softening and a new openness about her. After all, just today she'd asked me to tell her the story about Sarah. She had listened too, even if she'd misinterpreted the point.

But then again, my head argued, wasn't the point of having a godparent to lead the child spiritually? I could hardly expect Libby to do that. On the other hand, as wrapped up as Andrea was with her children, would she care enough about Janey to truly look after her spiritual welfare if something were to happen to me?

Suddenly, it was as if I were viewing the room from afar. There was the chair, the old worn couch, the end table and lamp, even the two neatly folded baskets of laundry. And there was Janey, lying alone on the floor. It seemed a cold, empty place. In my mind I saw Janey, as if a year from now, toddling across the room to an empty chair.

"No!" I shook my head, shaking off the morbid thought. I refused to think about that. I was supposed to be picking a god-mother and that's just what I would do. Libby. Andrea. Libby? Andrea? No matter how much I thought about whom to choose, a clear answer didn't surface.

Oh, Lord. I prayed as I carefully propped Janey in a corner of the couch and then went to put the laundry away. *Show me whom You would have me choose.*

Olivia

I didn't like the look on the doctor's face one bit.

Anne had insisted that Janey and I come with her into the examining room.

"That's us," Anne said, rising as the nurse called her name. "Come on."

"Anne," I explained, "it's called a *waiting* room for a reason. We can *wait* for you out here. Look," I said in an exaggerated tone, waving my hand towards the children's play area, "there have been other children in this very room before." Toys and books littered the corner, proving my point. "Don't worry, we'll be fine."

The nurse stood patiently by the door, holding Anne's chart.

"But," Anne protested, "time goes so much faster if you come with me. I get in that cold room, and put on that paper-thin gown, then just sit there and shiver while I wait for the doctor…who always takes forever, I might add." Her eyes pleaded with me to come along.

We marched along, a short parade—the nurse leading the way, Anne in the middle, and Janey and I bringing up the rear.

"If you'd get undressed and put that gown on." The nurse ushered us into the room, pointing at the waiting gown. The nurse looked at Janey. "If she gets fussy you can take her out to the waiting room. We have toys out there."

I gave Anne a see-I-told-you-so look.

"Don't worry," Anne explained, "the only one who gets fussy is Libby, and she doesn't care much for toys."

The nurse chuckled and closed the door.

"That sounded like something I would say," I countered, amused at Anne's quick remark.

"Must be spending too much time together." Anne turned her back as she slipped off her sweater and into the thin gown.

"Here, let me get that," I said, seeing Anne grimace as she turned her head, trying to reach the ties at the back of her neck. I quickly laid Janey on the examining table. Anne held a hand on Jane as I knotted the wrinkled strings together. "There." I patted Anne's back, feeling the bone of her shoulder blade poking out. I'd never noticed it before. I looked at her arms, hanging out of the shapeless hospital gown. Since fall, we'd all been wearing long-sleeved shirts and sweaters, defending ourselves from the onset of winter. Even Anne's arms had thinned out in the few months since I'd seen them uncovered. Anne was beginning to look as though she were an advertisement for starving foreign people. An uneasy feeling settled over me.

"Okey-dokey," I said, sounding like a demented kindergarten nurse trying to convince her patient that surgery without anesthesia really wouldn't hurt. "All tied up tight. A bug in a rug." I could feel myself flush with nervous heat.

Anne turned, raising one eyebrow. "Are you okay?"

"Oh," I fibbed, trying to hide my growing unease, "I'm used to talking to Janey. Sorry." I patted Anne's back. "Done."

I picked up Jane as Anne lifted one hip onto the examining table.

"We should do that more often," Anne commented, expertly sliding onto the spot where Janey had lain. "It's nice and warm."

She rubbed her thin arms. "See what I mean? How chilly it is in here?"

Actually, the room felt fine to me. "Ummm," I hummed non-committally, noticing anew Anne's thin limbs.

Now that I was noticing, even her face had thinned. Her cheekbones more prominent, her eyes a bit sunken. Or was I just imagining? I pretended to be engrossed by an ear canal poster on the wall over Anne's shoulder. How could she have gotten so thin without me noticing? Had she really lost weight, or was it the flimsy gown that made her look pale and stick-like in contrast?

Anne was gazing out the second-floor window. I shifted my eyes back to her.

Usually a model for good posture, Anne sat with her arms wrapped around her body, her back and shoulders curved as if preserving any warmth her body could generate.

She looked small and frail, years older than she was.

"See what I mean?" Anne asked. "It always seems like years until the doctor gets here." She rubbed her hands together, keeping them close to her body. "I'm just freezing. Aren't you cold?"

"Not when I carry my own portable heater," I tried to joke, adjusting Janey in my arms. As if in contrast to Anne's failing body, I could feel a trickle of moisture running from the back of Janey's neck down my own moist arm.

"Okay," I said, determined to change my thoughts, "what if...?"

Anne interrupted, "You hate that game!"

I'd forgotten, I really did hate that game. But in an effort to lift the veil that had descended over my mind, I'd grasped at whatever was handy.

I looked at Anne, she was smiling.

I could hardly complain since I'd done it to myself. "What if...what if someone yelled, "Fire!" Would you get dressed, or run out in that ugly gown?"

Anne appeared to be thinking hard. "Well-ll, considering that you have Janey taken care of, I'd grab my clothes and try to put them on as I ran. Okay, my turn."

It was good to see Anne happy, her arms finally relaxed and at her side. "Ask me anything."

Leaning forward, she asked, "What if...what if someone came up to you and said they were a publisher, and they heard you were a writer and they were wondering if—"

"Anne," I sighed heavily, "this is supposed to be fun and you always take it so seriously. Besides, you've asked me this before, remember?"

"Not exactly like this. You said I could ask you anything, so I'm asking. So, anyway, they were wondering if you had any ideas for a good book lately. What would you say?"

"Who wants to know? The publisher or you?"

"The publisher, of course." Anne sat back, a smug look on her face. "This is just a game you know."

"Okay," I rolled my eyes, letting her know I was playing, but not happily. "I'd tell the publisher I'd taken a break from writing for a while. That I'd had some trouble with my teenage son and I wasn't sure if my marriage was going to make it, and that—"

It was as if I were foaming at the mouth. I couldn't believe the words coming from my mouth, in my own voice no less. Anne's mouth fell open as I told her about Brian, how withdrawn he'd been. How having Janey in our house had opened him up. Shown me a side of Brian I'd thought was lost. How it was still a struggle to get him to talk, and when he did, it was usually about the vision of Pete in his hospital bed, hooked up to a respirator, unable to speak. My son was weighed down by guilt and seemed unable to find his way out.

"Oh, Libby." Anne's voice was a sympathetic murmur, serving only to make more words tumble from my unstoppable mouth.

"And, I don't know what to do about Bob. I mean he treats me fine. But he's distant. When I ask him what's wrong he says, 'Nothing.' But I know something's wrong. For a while, they thought someone at the bank was embezzling funds. Some examiners came in for a few weeks, but Bob never said anything more about what happened. So much of that stuff is confidential. I don't know how much I dare ask him or how much he simply can't tell me."

"I am so sorry, Libby," Anne said then, her voice filled with emotion. "I've been so absorbed in my cancer and every little ache and pain I've been feeling, and you've been going through all this stuff with your family. I never even thought to ask you about any of it. I feel terrible."

No, actually, I was the one who felt terrible. I looked at Anne, her frail body perched on the examining table, leaning forward, trying to absorb every word of my self-centered complaint. Here I was sitting in a doctor's office. A *cancer* doctor's office. Waiting for my best friend to find out if she could continue her radiation treatments, and I was pouring out my problems to her as if I were lying on a psychiatrist's couch, paying money to have someone listen to me complain.

"Getting back to my writing," I started, trying to steer this game-gone-awry back to the original question. I acted as if I hadn't interrupted my initial response ten minutes ago and confessed to Anne all my worries of the past weeks. "I don't know what to tell you. I have it here…" I pointed to my head. "I want to write. I turn words and phrases around in my mind all the time. But right now, I don't have it here…" I pointed to my heart. "My emotions have been a jumble for months. Frankly, I haven't thought much about writing a novel lately."

I didn't tell Anne about the journaling I'd been doing with the silver pen she'd given me. I'd been so proud of myself and the break-through I thought I had after watching that Dr. Phil on the *Oprah* show. Somehow, I'd expected to become a changed person by simply watching a TV program. I was finding out it wasn't that simple.

Until now I'd done nothing but congratulate myself for going to Anne's house to apologize. Yet seeing her sitting in front of me and offering her listening ear, knowing all she'd been through, I realized it was Anne who had offered friendship back to me. I remembered standing on her door step, afraid even to knock. If Anne had so much as blinked wrong that night, I could have just as easily changed my apology into another attack. How did Anne do it? How could she offer me this unconditional friendship?

I looked away from Anne. It wasn't easy to remind myself of the turmoil I'd put myself through, separating myself from Anne's friendship because of my stubborn denial of the facts. Brian's drug use. My rejection of Anne's friendship. The fact that she'd done nothing to hurt me, everything to help me. Even continually asking me about my writing. She knew it was my heart's dream, and she'd been encouraging me to follow it. It was me who had turned her away, turned my dream away, had even been turning my family away—all because of my unwillingness to face my fear. The fear that Anne's continuing unfailing friendship made me see. The fear I could finally name, but not tame. I could identify it, I just couldn't seem to do anything about it.

It was the fear of letting go and loving. Truly loving. Loving without counting points. Loving without expecting love back. Loving without walls in place. Even I was getting tired of trying to keep those walls built up. Walls high enough, strong enough to prevent ever getting hurt were getting hard to keep in place. Walls high enough and strong enough to keep me from ever feeling true love were starting to feel thick and oppressive. I was beginning to realize the very walls I'd built to protect me were the same walls that were hurting me.

Other than going to Anne's that one night, the only progress I'd made in my resolve to change had been telling Brian I loved him. Even then, I'd practically needed the Heimlich maneuver to get the words out. What would it take to be like Anne? I didn't have a clue.

"Hello, ladies." By the time the doctor finally entered the room, I felt I should pay him for the silent counseling session I'd been through. But since I didn't have any answers to my questions, I didn't offer.

"Okay, Anne, let's take a look." As usual, Dr. Barrows was all business. "The chart says you've been experiencing some difficulty at the treatment site."

Dr. Barrows tugged the string at the back of Anne's neck, sliding the gown down her right arm. All I could see was Anne's sharp shoulder blade and Dr. Barrows' grim face. He slid the gown from her left shoulder as well.

"I don't like the looks of this," he declared. "See, here... here..."

Anne tilted her head so that her chin was against her chest, looking down where Dr. Barrows was pointing. I could see her nodding slightly in understanding.

"We're going to need to debride that dead tissue—get it off there—before we continue treatments." He slid the gown back over her shoulders, not bothering to retie it. "You're not from Carlton, are you?"

Anne answered, "No, from Brewster."

"They have a nursing home over there, don't they?"

Anne nodded.

"I'm going to make arrangements for you to go there and take some whirlpool treatments in the big tub they have. Warm, swirling water is the easiest way to get that skin off. After you're done with each session, you're going to have to take a clean cloth and try to rub as much of that loose skin off as possible. Do you have any questions?"

"Will it hurt?" Anne asked, her voice sounding small.

"The whirlpool part should feel good, but getting the skin off is never a comfortable job. I'm sure you know the burns hurt, too."

Again Anne nodded.

I pretended to be entertaining Janey, but inside my stomach clenched. Anne had never said a word about being in pain.

Dr. Barrows went on, "So yes, it may hurt, but the faster we get this cleared up, the sooner you can resume treatments. We don't want to waste any time. Understand?"

Anne's head moved up and down.

"Any other questions?"

Anne shook her head, but for the second time that day, I found my mouth spilling forth words. "Then what?"

Dr. Barrows shot me a look that seemed to say, *You really don't know?*

I didn't, so I asked, "I mean, when Anne does finish her radiation treatments? Then what?"

"Then we wait," Dr. Barrows said simply.

"Wait for what?" My big mouth just kept talking.

"To see if the cancer comes back."

After that, my big mouth had nothing more to say.

Anne

Libby had volunteered to watch Janey while I went to my whirlpool treatments, but the thought of sitting alone in that big therapy room at the nursing home made me feel apprehensive, the whirlpool tub was barely shielded by an opaque curtain, and I never knew if someone would walk in on me during my session.

"I don't know," I explained to Libby over coffee after my appointment with Dr. Barrows, "it seems like it would be creepy. What if some old man comes wandering in while I'm sitting in the tub? Or even if an aide came in? I'd feel weird."

"I guess I would, too," Libby agreed.

It was Libby who came up with the perfect solution. Since my four whirlpool treatments weren't scheduled until late afternoon, Brian and Emily would watch Janey, while Libby went with me to my treatments. After the first one, Libby had invited Kevin and me to join her and her family for supper.

"I'll have Brian pop something in the oven while we're at the nursing home," Libby said. "Besides, it'll give us something to look forward to when the treatment is over."

I knew what she was doing. I'd seen Libby flinch when Dr. Barrows so bluntly told me it would hurt trying to get that dead skin off my chest. I'd also noticed how quiet she'd gotten after Dr. Barrows told us the only other thing to do was wait. Libby was trying to turn these sessions from something to be dreaded, into something resembling a good time—if that were possible.

I was so glad Libby was with me during that first session. A nurse had shown us into the room where the large circular tub had already been filled with warm water. She showed me how to operate the water jets, letting me know this was a huge disruption in her busy schedule. "We have patients to feed this time of day, you know." Then she left.

The room was huge and cold, and the humidity from the tub made the therapy room feel clammy.

Libby was leaning over the tub, running her hand through the water. "You know, if we weren't here for a treatment this could actually feel kind of good. We could bring bubble bath and—"

"Oh yeah," I laughed, "and have nurse Ratchet throwing mops at us to clean up afterward too."

"Oh, no," Libby deadpanned, "we'd sneak out while she was busy feeding her patients. Long before she saw the mess."

"Well, I suppose I should get in." I looked around, expecting to see some sort of instructions on whirlpool protocol. "Am I supposed to leave my panties on? Maybe I was supposed to wear a swimsuit or something. I never thought about how this was going to work."

"Anne," Libby instructed, "get undressed and get in. You couldn't wear a swimsuit or the water wouldn't get at your burns. See?" She made swirling motions with her hands by her chest.

Following Libby's command I unbuttoned my sweater. When I reached to pull off the T-shirt I'd been wearing underneath, Libby said, "Here, let me get the water going for you." She played with the handles, turning different jets on at varying speeds, sending the water into a noisy whirl. "This could be kind of fun."

Again, I knew what Libby was doing. Turning her back to me, she used the water jets as an excuse to give me privacy. I slipped into the moving water, letting my body become enveloped by the swirls and warmth. Dr. Barrows had been right—the water did feel good as it brushed against my burns, soothing them in a way my own touch only irritated. The water not only eased the pain on my skin, it also caused the incessant ache I'd been feeling in the small of my back to let up as well.

"Ahhh." The sigh escaped my lips, nearly engulfed by the roar of the water.

Libby heard and turned. "It must feel good."

"It does." I felt as though I was screaming trying to speak above the sound of the whirlpool jets. I leaned back, closing my eyes, letting the healing water sweep my body.

Libby explored the large room, stepping on the treadmill, peeking out the closed Venetian blinds, checking out the daily therapy schedule posted on the wall. Finally, she pulled a small chair near the whirlpool, sitting almost shoulder to shoulder with me, so her eyes gazed forward instead of directly at me. Again I felt her respect for my privacy. We settled into comfortable silence, letting the sound of the water fill the air, much as our conversation normally did.

At one point Libby noticed me shifting, trying to relax further down into the warm water. Wordlessly, she folded a towel into a pillow of sorts and set it behind my head. Again I closed my eyes, comfortable in silence with my friend.

Oh, Lord, use this water to bring healing to my body. And, use this time to bring healing to Libby too. She's hurting, Lord. She's worried about Brian and about her marriage. Show her the way to healing. I feel so inadequate, Lord, but if you can use me in any way to show Libby your plan for her, I'm willing.

As if in *Amen*, the whirlpool timer clicked off and the room filled with what sounded like noisy silence. In surprise, Libby and I said, "Oh!" Our joint word echoing in the damp air.

I sat for a moment, not anxious to get to the next step. Libby mistook my hesitation for modesty. She quickly got up from her chair and walked to the far corner of the room, acting totally fascinated with the treadmill she'd checked out earlier. Finally, she turned to me. "Listen, Anne, I'm not sure what to do right now. I'm sure you don't need me staring at you while you try to get that skin off, but if you need any help, just ask and I'll do what I can. Okay?"

I knew Libby could be squeamish about this sort of thing. She'd often told me she wasn't much of a nurse when it came to her kids being sick. I knew what it must have taken for her to offer to help.

"Thanks," I told her, then asked, "Could you hand me that gauze in my bag over there?"

Cotton gauze in hand, I eased onto the edge of the tub. The warm water had caused much of the skin that had been burned to turn a milky-gray color, making it easy to know just where I should be working. I took a deep breath, then tried a few tentative swipes. The first pieces of skin came off easily and without pain, but as the numbing effects of the water wore off, and I reached the edges of the skin that needed removing, I gasped softly, reacting to the scouring of the gauze against my skin.

"Are you okay?" Libby asked, her back to me as she pretended to study the daily therapy schedule.

"Libby, I hate to ask you this, but do you think you could help me?" Each time my hand neared my body I tensed in anticipation, instinctively drawing away from what I knew would cause pain. "I just don't know if I can get it all myself." My voice was high and near tears.

"Sure." Libby responded without hesitation, sounding as if she did debriding as a hobby in her spare time.

I knew she'd never seen my chest since my operations. But when she walked toward me, her face was filled, not with shock at the sight of my scarred and burned skin, but with concern.

"Let me," Libby said, gently taking the gauze from my hand. She placed her left hand behind my back, supporting me in a way I couldn't myself. She pulled my damp body next to her, so that my shoulder rested against her chest. Then, with her own body cradling mine, she began lightly dabbing at the edges of loosened skin, working them away with a soft rolling motion.

It certainly wasn't painless, but since I didn't have to administer the treatment myself, I was able to look away, and let my mind wander, trying to think of something else besides the present.

"Could you tell me that story about Sarah and Abraham again?" Libby asked as she daubed gently at my skin. "It seemed interesting, but I was so busy trying to figure out the "something worse" thing I thought you were trying to tell me, I totally missed the point."

Once again, I saw completely through Libby's motives—she was trying to get my mind off what she was doing. That was fine with me.

I began reciting the familiar story of Sarah's barrenness. How other women had laughed at her. Sarah's unbelief when told she would finally bear a child. And then her laughter. Maybe first in unbelief, then in delight. Finally, she had a promise, a hope she could cling to. As I retold it, Sarah's story spoke to me in a way it never had before. In some ways, Sarah and I were much alike. We were both afraid of what the future held for us. Sarah, a barren childlessness; me, cancer. Yet God had given us both promises we could cling to.

Sarah, *you will bear a child.*

Anne, *I will be with you always.*

Hope.

God's promise and Libby's loving touch combined to make me feel as if I'd been cleansed inside and out.

Before I knew it, Libby straightened and said with satisfaction, "There, that looks nice and clean." She made it seem as if I had been to a spa, instead of our town's nursing home.

Olivia

My knees were shaking before I even turned around. I knew what it must have taken for Anne to ask for my help in debriding her skin. I also knew I had to help her. Just how I was going to manage that, I didn't know. Even cleaning off one of my kids' scraped knees caused my stomach to clench; I wasn't sure how I'd react to seeing Anne's chest after two surgeries and radiation burns. I took a deep breath and pasted a look of concern on my face before I turned around.

It wasn't near as bad as I had imagined. The two surgery scars were curved in a smooth, almost smile-like, way. It wasn't at all the jagged, red skin I'd pictured. The burned skin, however, looked dead. Well, of course it did—it was. And that was my task—to get it off.

I worked as gently as I could and still be effective. I knew the quicker we cleaned it up, the faster Anne would be able to resume treatments and get better. The area under the skin I removed was raw and sore looking. It sent chills down my spine to imagine how it must feel to Anne as I rubbed the edges of skin away. I'd asked Anne to talk to me, to tell me a story—anything to keep from imagining the pain I might be causing.

As Anne recited the story of Abraham and Sarah, as odd as it seemed, I noticed a similarity between Sarah and me. When Sarah at age ninety—Anne said she'd looked it up—was told she was going to have a baby, she laughed. From the way Anne described it, it sounded as if it was a kind of sarcastic laugh. A, "Yeah *right*, I'm going to have a baby," kind of laugh. It sounded like something I would do.

All of a sudden this Sarah lady seemed real. God told her she was going to have a baby and she laughed, "Okay, tell me another funny tale." And even though she laughed, God's promise came true. Maybe there was hope for me and all my doubts yet.

I anticipated supper being a disaster. I imagined Brian forgetting to put the roast, carrots, and potatoes waiting in the fridge into the oven. I was positive Bob would call at the last minute and say he had to work late. And if he did make it, I was convinced he and Kevin would have absolutely nothing to talk about. I thought Anne might be too worn out to sit at the table. And I even imagined Emily and Brian fighting through the whole meal, accompanied by Janey's cries. So much for worrying.

It was as if a modern day Emily Post had orchestrated the meal. The smell of hot roast beef and roasting vegetables filled the air as Anne and I walked into the kitchen. Emily had set the table, including a coffee cup saucer and her old baby spoon at a spot for Janey. She had dug out bright yellow linen napkins from the bottom of some drawer and, wrinkles and all, had stuffed them haphazardly into our everyday drinking glasses. The center of the table held the stubs of one white candle and one light blue candle, remnants of an unremembered burning, in the only good candle holders we owned, silver and tarnished. They flanked a pink plastic flower ring, meant to surround a large candle, but instead encircling a picture of Janey we'd taken during her stay with us. Anne gushed over it all, and even I had to admit the table had a childlike charm about it.

We followed the sound of voices into the living room. Kevin and Bob were visiting as though they'd known each other for years, explaining they'd discovered they had belonged to the same college fraternity. The fact that it was different colleges and several years apart didn't seem to diminish their common bond. Brian was sitting on the floor, holding Janey in the crook of his crossed legs, talking to her and making silly faces. Emily was playing piano, her huge grin not even trying to disguise the fact she was trying to impress Anne. When she heard us enter the room, Emily played all the louder, nodding her head in time with the music.

Although I could tell Emily was practically crawling out of her skin, wanting to greet Anne, she patiently played to the end of her piece. When the last notes were played, Anne began clapping and we all joined in, even Brian. Emily scooted off the bench, hopping across the floor to Anne.

Just before falling into Anne's embrace, Emily stopped short. "What happened to your hair?" she asked, her hands grabbing at her own hair.

During my daily visits, I'd gotten so used to seeing Anne in her straight brown wig, that I never thought of her as looking different anymore. I'd forgotten Emily had not seen Anne since she'd started wearing her wig.

"Oh Emily, I'm so glad you asked about that." Anne answered as if it were the most natural question in the world. She put an arm around Emily and led her back to the piano bench. "Sometimes I feel like other people are looking at me and wondering what happened to my hair, but they never say anything, and it's so strange. I know they must notice that I look different."

"You do," Emily confirmed. "But it's nice."

"Thank you," Anne responded. "I'm wearing a wig." She said it as if it was no big deal, but I remembered how shaken she was the day her hair fell out.

"Why?" Emily asked.

"You know I'm taking treatment for my cancer, don't you?"

Emily nodded solemnly.

"Well," Anne explained, "the medicine is very strong, and sometimes it makes your hair fall out. Like mine did."

"Did it hurt?"

"No." Anne smiled. "I never even thought about that. See, Libby," she looked my way, "it could have been worse." She went on speaking to Emily. "Did you know in the Bible it tells us that God knows the number of hairs on our heads?"

I found myself shaking my head along with Emily, imagining the garbage can half-filled with hair.

"Well, He does," Anne explained.

"God must be a good counter," Emily said.

I was thinking the exact same thing.

"The Bible also tells us that if God cares even about the number of hairs on our heads, just think how much He cares about the rest of us."

"That must be a lot," Emily said.

"Exactly." Anne gave Emily a squeeze.

I excused myself to the kitchen. *What kind of God sits and counts the hair on people's heads?* I plopped the roast on a platter. *He wouldn't have time to care about anyone; all He'd be doing is counting.*

Sure Sarah, laugh, my conscience reminded. *The promise still came true.*

～

Brian insisted he could hold Janey and eat at the same time.

"I'll be super careful," he stated, demonstrating how he would eat. He held Janey off to the side in his left arm, leaning way over his plate to put food in his mouth with the fork in his right hand.

I could see Anne watching Brian throughout the meal. Not in a worried sort of way, but with an expression of awe on her face. She seemed amazed that someone could love her baby almost as much as she did.

"Brian, you're a natural," Anne said as Brian finished up his meal without a peep from Janey and not so much as a cake crumb dropped on her blanket.

I could see Brian trying to hide a proud smile. "Do you think she's hungry?" he asked, diverting the compliment.

I pushed back my chair. "I'll get her bottle."

"That's okay, Mom." Brian stood up, holding Janey like a football in the bend of his arm. "I know how to do it."

Jumping from her chair, practically tripping over Brian's heels, Emily asked, "Can I burp her?" Emily took great pride in the fact that she could get such a tiny baby to make such a loud noise.

Anne opened her mouth to answer, but before she could say anything, Brian said, "We'll see. Come on, twerp."

I found myself with a stupid grin on my face and a proud, swelling feeling rising in my chest. I turned back to the table and found myself gazing straight at Bob, the same silly grin on his face. Slowly and deliberately his left eye closed, then opened. He'd winked at me. I couldn't remember the last time he'd done that. An electric current passed between us, along with a feeling I hadn't felt in a long, long time. I liked it. A lot.

Suddenly, I found myself laughing out loud.

Sarah laughed in delight. The words of Anne's story came to me as the others joined in my laughter, the joy of our children and each other filling us.

My eyes took in the laughing faces around me. Anne had said something else when she'd told me the story that first time. What was it?

As if in instant answer to my thought, the single word popped to mind.

Hope.

Ah, yes. My eyes met Bob's, then Kevin's, and finally, Anne's. That was it. Another bubble of laughter filled my throat.

Hope.

Anne

Libby was wrong. She didn't look one bit out of place sitting in the pew of our church. Out of the corner of my eye I glanced into the row behind us. The royal blue wool suit Libby wore made her look elegant, like the banker's wife she was. Bob looked just as distinguished in his suit. I'd told Libby at least a dozen times that Brian "absolutely" did not have to wear a suit to Janey's baptism. But apparently my words had fallen on deaf ears. Emily too was wearing what I knew was a new dress. Libby had assured me Emily would be wearing the dress to the school Christmas concert as well. Still it looked to me as if Libby had bought the whole family brand-new clothes—something I'd pleaded with her not to do.

"Honest, Anne," Libby had vowed in the foyer of the church, "Bob has had that suit for at least three years, Emily had outgrown every dress in her closet, and it was a good excuse to get Brian used to dressing up. He'll probably be going to the prom next year; he might as well learn how to tie a tie this year as next."

Libby didn't say one word about the new outfit she had on.

My mother was in the pew with Kevin and me, holding Janey. Right beside her was my dad, then Andrea, Jim, Jimmy Jr., and Cari. I'd been anticipating this day for weeks, but now that it had arrived I was finding myself so distracted with details that I was having a difficult time enjoying it.

My mom, Dad, Andrea, and her family had arrived the night before. Although Libby had helped me get the house ready for their arrival, and Kevin had left work early so he could help prepare dinner, I still felt unprepared.

"Good grief," Andrea exclaimed as she walked up the steps into our house, "what did you do to your hair? Color it, cut it, *and* straighten it? It must be fried!" Jimmy Jr. and Cari barreled past us. Cari's leg wasn't broken, after all, just sprained.

Self-consciously, I touched my wig. Libby had assured me time and again that it looked great. Now I felt unsure. "Andrea," I explained, "it's a wig."

"Well then, no wonder," she stated, marching past me with her suitcase.

Mom was right behind her. She reached out and hugged me, whispering into my ear, "It looks very nice, Anne. How have you been feeling?"

A scream from Cari interrupted my answer. Mom started laughing. "Oh, those two, they've been at it the whole way here."

I turned to see Jimmy and Cari struggling, each pulling on a leg of Janey's little lamb music box. Quickly, I went to them. "Hey, you two," I said softly, laying a hand on each of their shoulders, "you have to be very gentle. This is a special toy of Janey's, and it has a secret to share if you listen quietly."

Jimmy Jr. and Cari stopped their tugging, but neither was willing to let go of the special lamb. They looked at me skeptically.

"Stuffed animals can't have secrets," six-year-old Jimmy stated confidently.

"Tell me first," Cari pleaded.

"I'm first, I'm the oldest," Jimmy declared, even though he had just said the little animal couldn't have a secret.

"You can both hear it at the same time," I told them, taking the lamb from them and discreetly winding the music box ring. "Sit right here." I motioned to the floor. I held the lamb so that it was right between both of their ears, letting go of the winding stem. The tinkling strains of "Jesus Loves Me" played between their heads.

Three-year-old Cari's eyes grew wide, a grin covering her face. Jimmy rolled his eyes. "Big deal," he said. "She can have it." He got up and stomped off.

Softly I sang along with the music, "Jesus loves me this I know…"

Cari joined in, chiming along whenever I sang the word, "me," adding a "me, too" every now and then.

I rewound the lamb, gazing around at my family. Kevin was showing my dad and Jim the television channels we received in Brewster. I could hear Mother opening the oven door, either checking to see what was for supper, or if it was clean. Andrea was digging Matchbox cars out of a backpack for Jimmy Jr. No one had asked where Janey was or how my treatments had gone. How could I feel so alone in a room full of people? A wave of self-pity washed over me. Didn't anybody care about Janey? About me?

I felt Cari tugging my sleeve. "Do again," she said, poking the little lamb with her stubby finger.

I let go of the winding stem, the song starting up midstream. *Yes, Jesus loves me. Yes, Jesus loves me. Yes…*I listened to the music, singing the words softly to Cari. As I sang the simple tune, it seemed, in some odd way that the words were being sung back to me. *Yes, Jesus loves you.*

You.

Jesus loves you.

I closed my eyes and took a deep, comforting breath. *I hear You. Thanks.*

⁓

"Would the family of this child please stand." The minister's words cut through my thoughts. I quickly glanced at the bulletin to see what I'd missed. My mother stood up, handing Janey to Kevin. Her motion caused my whole family to stand, one by one, in a straggling array. Dad popped up beside Mom, then Jim. Andrea stood, at the same time frantically motioning to Jimmy Jr. He reluctantly slid off the pew, a miniature car in each hand. Even little Cari slowly climbed up on the seat of the pew and stood.

"Would the parents and godparents bring this child forward to be baptized." The minister's command pushed us out of the pew.

I could feel the eyes of the congregation on us as we filed out of the pew toward the front of the church. Janey was awake, eyes wide open, seeming to enjoy her special moment. I tried to concentrate on Jane, but instead found myself wondering if Mrs. Burns was whispering to

Mrs. Jans that she thought I was wearing a wig. My head itched and I reached up to try to scratch my scalp through the webbing. I had a wild fleeting thought about what Mrs. Burns would do if I were to suddenly tug this hot itchy patch of hair from my head. As often as Libby bolstered my confidence about how my wig looked, she couldn't do a thing about how it felt. But then I remembered, she had tried to help me in that way, too. I tried to focus on the minister, instead I found myself thinking back…

"Anne, you don't have to wear that just for me, you know." Libby had her chair pulled up next to me as I reclined in the whirlpool tub. It was my second treatment and the hot, swirling water was causing my scalp to sweat profusely under my wig. A steady stream of sweat ran from under my wig, down my cheeks, dripping into the twirling water.

My scalp had been soaked the day before too, but since the whole process was new, I hadn't realized the moisture was from me and not the damp atmosphere. Just the thought of taking my wig off made me feel cooler. But I was concerned about Libby. She'd already seen my scarred chest; did I need to subject her to this sight too?

"Anne," Libby said, "watching you sweat is making me more miserable than anything your head could possibly look like. Take it off."

"Are you sure it's not going to gross you out?"

"Take it off," she repeated.

"It really is hot."

"Take it off, already!"

"Give me a towel, first," I said.

I used the towel Libby handed me as a sort of shield, slipping the wig off with my right hand, rubbing the towel over my head with my left, revealing it slowly. I handed the wig to Libby. "Here."

"Oh, this is gross!" she said.

Embarrassed, I spread the towel over my head.

"Not you," Libby scolded, seeing my covered head. "I meant this wig. It's soaked. Ooooo."

The damp hair hung limply as she held it at arm's length. It looked something like a drowned long-haired animal.

"Give me that towel, I need it more than you do." Libby swiped the towel from my head, stuffing part of it inside the wig. "Much better," she declared, holding the white towel and wig over her hand in a way that made it look as though it were a ghost with hair.

She eyed me, a smile playing on her lips.

"What?" I asked. I sank to my ear lobes in the swishing water. "Go ahead, tell me. I look bad."

"No, you don't," Libby responded, still smiling. "You look like my grandma."

"Gee, thanks," I muttered, sinking lower.

"Anne," Libby reminded, "you've never seen a picture of my grandmother. She was a beautiful woman. Thin hair, but beautiful."

A warm feeling flooded me. Not warmth from the water, but warmth that came from somewhere deep inside. It had been a long time since anyone had called me beautiful.

Yet, it happened again, within the week.

~

I'd taken a look through my closet, and knew that not one item in it would be appropriate to wear to Janey's baptism. Ever since I'd had my first mastectomy I had put off buying clothes, not sure what size I'd be after my pregnancy or surgeries, not feeling much like shopping after my treatments. Even though I was still dragging, I was looking forward to Janey's baptism and wanted to make it a special day.

I knew I was pushing her christening a bit. Most people in our church wait until the baby is several months old, but I felt an urgency I couldn't explain and told Kevin I wanted to hold it as soon as we could arrange it. Tying it into the Thanksgiving weekend worked well with everyone's schedules.

Libby insisted we stop at Elizabeth's, an old house turned boutique in Carlton. I'd been there once, but found the gift items too tempting and the prices too steep for my budget. I'd never even looked at the clothes.

"We'll just get ideas here," Libby promised as she pulled to a stop by the curb in front of the mansion-like house. "Sometimes these out-of-the-way places can surprise you."

"Let's go to the mall," I protested, even though Libby was already out of the car. Just the thought of wading through crowds of people at the mall made me tired, so I followed Libby up the walk. "I'd better not like anything here," I warned, talking to Libby's back. "I can't afford much, you know."

"Olivia, hi!" The owner of Elizabeth's greeted us with a smile. "You're just in time—I'm marking all the fall things down. Would you believe I'm starting to get spring shipments in already? They push these seasons closer every year," she said with a shake of her head. "I don't have much storage space, so this stuff has to go." With a black Magic Marker she underlined, *30 Percent Off All Fall Merchandise.*

Libby turned and gave me a "see I told you so" look that I pretended not to see. As Libby explained our mission, I paged through the rack of winter dresses, enjoying the feel of fine fabrics against my skin. Party dresses were mixed in with more practical clothes, all of them way too dressy for my life. I couldn't help but smile, imagining myself waiting *elegantly* for radiation treatments in a forest green silk pant suit, wondering how I'd get formula stains out of it when I got home.

As Libby joined me at the rack, I whispered, "There's nothing here that looks like me. Let's go."

"Let me look," she said, expertly slipping the clothes past her appraising eyes. She paused briefly at a royal blue suit, then paged it by. "This!" she declared, pulling a jacket from the rack.

"Libby, brown is not my color," I whined. "It blends with my hair and makes me look washed out."

"This isn't brown," she stated, sounding like a fashion designer. "This is *toast*. And besides, you'd wear this under it." She pulled a thin-knit sweater from the rack.

"Orange?"

"It isn't orange," Libby emphasized, "it's *pumpkin*, and it will look fabulous on you."

This time I raised my eyebrows. "I've never worn anything *pumpkin* in my life."

"Well then, I'd say it's about time you start," Libby stated, looping the jacket, skirt, and sweater hangers over a finger. "The dressing rooms are over here."

I knew I'd never get out of there without trying the outfit on, so I followed without protest.

The dressing room was no more than a large closet in the old house, too small for even a mirror. As I stepped into the skirt, then carefully slipped the sweater over my head, I could feel the perfect fit of the fine clothes. The silky knit of the sweater felt as though it were a soft touch against my bruised skin. I looked down, trying to gauge my appearance. Even with my navy blue socks on, I could tell the colors were a great combination. I felt almost pretty. I slipped off my socks, then grabbing the jacket, self-consciously stepped from the dressing room, walking on my toes, pretending I was wearing heels. Libby was conversing with the owner and a handsome older gentleman, so I tiptoed to the three-way mirror for a final judgment of my own.

My daydream shattered. What had looked so promising in the dressing room hung on me like a limp sack. The pumpkin sweater I'd thought had caressed my chest clung to my body in a way that made me appear concave. I could see the outline of the tube top I wore over my burns. I turned, catching myself in profile. I looked even worse from the side. Wan and tired. How could I have ever thought I looked pretty? I stood flat-footed, wanting only to be out of these clothes that weren't mine. In frustration, I closed my eyes and turned my back to the mirror, only to feel Libby's hands on my shoulders, turning me around to face myself again.

I knew it was childish, but I kept my eyes closed as Libby adjusted the sweater, pulling on the shoulders, sliding the hem into a smooth line over my hips.

"Here," she said.

I turned to her voice, refusing to look in the mirror. She held out the jacket for me to slip into. Libby pulled a tortoiseshell head band from a nearby shelf. Holding the band between her lips, with both hands she reached up and gently pushed the hair of my wig behind my ears, slipping the head band onto my head, fluffing the hair behind it a bit. I felt her hands on my shoulders, turning me once again.

"Now look," she said.

I opened my eyes, ready to head to the dressing room, but found myself rooted in front of the mirror. Even my unpracticed eye could see this outfit was made for me. The fall colors enhanced my sallow-looking skin, making me look more a powdered model and less a cancer treatment patient. The jacket made my chest appear fuller, the lapel lines hiding the rumpled tube top under the sweater, drawing my eyes up to the turtle neck. I smiled at Libby in the mirror. "Thanks," I mouthed.

"We'll take it," she called to the owner, smiling back at me.

I turned back to the mirror, standing once again on tiptoe, turning this way, then that. Libby walked back to the counter while I took one more quick glance. I turned, ready to head back to the dressing room, and found myself face to face with the gentleman who had been standing across the room only minutes earlier. The man's eyes traveled my body, slowly appraising me from head to toe. I wondered if he could tell I was wearing a wig? If he noticed the rumpled area over my chest? I could feel myself flushing in embarrassment under his silent gaze. Just when I was ready to ask him to please move, he opened his mouth and said one word. "Beautiful." He turned and continued his shopping.

I stared after him, a silly grin plastered across my face. I'd never seen this man before, and yet he'd declared me beautiful. I turned back to the mirror. It was the first time since I'd been diagnosed with cancer that I'd felt something close to pretty. As if I were a little girl all dressed up for a party, I stood in front of the mirror, imagining all the good times ahead. I would wear this suit to Janey's baptism. I could wear it again for Christmas, maybe with a gold sweater.

Maybe I'd have enough energy in a month so we could plan something special for New Year's Eve.

~

I felt a nudge in my ribs, along with a sharp whisper, "Anne, that's you!"

My scattered thoughts focused.

"By what name shall you call this child?" The minister was asking the question for a second time.

I looked around and saw with new clarity all the people who were so important to me. They were gathered in this church for Janey's baptism—my parents, my sister and her family, Libby and Bob, Brian and Emily. Kevin.

They're beautiful, I thought as I observed their smiling faces. I looked into the congregation, noticing the faces of young children straining to see the baby at the front of the church, watching the older people glad to be welcoming a new child into their midst. *Beautiful.*

Suddenly, I didn't feel scattered at all. I looked at Kevin, holding Janey in his arms, imploring me with his eyes to answer the minister's question. I knew what I was supposed to say. Kevin and I had long ago decided to name our daughter Jane Anne Abbot. But standing in the church, surrounded by love, filled with hope for all the future held for my child, I surprised even myself when, in a strong clear voice, I answered the minister's question by saying, "This beautiful child shall be called Jane Hope Abbot."

Olivia

I would love to have a picture of Kevin's face when Anne changed Janey's middle name during the baptism. First his eyes widened, then he cocked his head, looking at Anne in the way a dog does when it wants the last bite of your hamburger. I almost burst out laughing. Finally, Kevin's eyes crinkled in a smile, and he nodded agreement. Somehow, changing Jane's middle name to Hope seemed entirely appropriate. Anne's radiation treatments were over without any further burns. Her energy seemed to be returning. And finally, there was a true sense of hope about her situation. I'd have been entirely content to kick back and enjoy the day if I hadn't felt Andrea's eyes boring a hole through my back. Right through my new royal blue suit, no less.

I'd asked Anne at least fifty times if she was sure she wanted me to be Janey's godmother.

"Absolutely positive," Anne declared, drying the saucepan I'd handed her.

It was the last day of her whirlpool treatments and the final night of our family suppers together. We'd developed a routine of sorts, Brian and Emily in charge of Jane, Kevin and Bob talking current events in the living room, Anne and I finishing up in the kitchen.

I'd been sitting by the whirlpool that afternoon, content with my own thoughts. Anne's chest burns had cleared tremendously over the four days of her therapy, the dead skin falling away; new clear skin forming underneath. Sometimes, a sharp wince would cross Anne's face, but she assured me it was only a crick in her back from sleeping wrong. She too was pleased with the way her burns had healed. I was almost sorry to see this relaxing time together come to an end.

"What if...?" Anne's question cut through my dream-like state.

"No, Anne," I sighed heavily, "please spare me."

"What if…?" she said, ignoring me.

"No, really, I don't want to play that game," I told her emphatically. "Last time we played I could have just as well slit open my stomach and handed you my guts." I recalled the way I'd foamed at the mouth, revealing my concerns about Brian and my marriage. I was not going to do that again. I was determined not to put my troubles on anyone but me.

"Just one more time, Libby. Please?" Anne raised herself a bit from the swirling water, damp tufts of hair sticking up like a funky hairdo. "I'll just ask one more question and then never again. Promise."

"Hallelujah!" I answered, knowing Anne would keep her vow. "Ask away." I trilled my tongue in a mock drum roll. "Brrrr-rrrr, here it is folks, the *final* 'What If…' question."

"What if…" Anne asked, her voice rising over the noise of the water, "what if I asked you to be Janey's godmother?"

"Paaaaah!" I burst out laughing. "Me?"

"Don't sound so surprised," Anne answered. "I've given this a lot of thought. Prayer too."

"I'm sure you have, but are you sure you heard the right answer?"

"Yes," Anne replied, sounding positive.

"I'd be honored to be Janey's godmother. I love that kid like one of my own. But I've got to warn you, Anne, I'm not that hot when it comes to all that spiritual stuff. If you want to change your mind I won't be offended."

"You know, Libby," Anne went on as if she hadn't heard my protest, "you remind me of Martha."

"Martha?" I wracked my brain trying to place the name. "Martha who?"

"Martha. From the Bible."

"I told you, Anne, I'm not big on that Bible stuff. You can still change your mind, you know."

"Martha and Mary were sisters," Anne went on, again ignoring me. "Mary loved to sit and listen to Jesus as he taught, but Martha, even though she believed, always felt as if she had to be doing something." Anne leaned her head against the side of the metal tub. "That was her gift. Kind of like you."

"I have a gift? Yeah right."

"I've told you before, Libby, you have the gift of words. You know that, so quit fighting it. But you also have the gift of works. Like Martha."

As usual, I didn't like the direction this dumb game was taking. I should have known better than to agree to play. Even one last time. "Works," I muttered. "Another thing to feel guilty about not doing, in addition to writing."

"There's nothing for you to feel guilty about. You're using your gift all the time. Right now, for instance."

"Oh, yeah, just sitting here." I was underwhelmed.

"Think about it, Libby. You've driven me to countless appointments, helped me get prepared to have a baby, baby-sat for Janey, made me meals, questioned my doctors when I was too numb to do it myself, helped me shop for a new couch, listened to me talk for countless hours...I could go on and on, but I think you understand. It's a gift, Libby. A true gift. You don't wait around to be asked. You don't even ask if you should do it. You just see something that needs doing and you go ahead and *do* it."

"But that's what friends do," I protested.

"Not all friends," Anne replied. "I don't see anyone else volunteering to sit here with me. Do you?"

I didn't answer. But she had me thinking.

"There's a verse in Proverbs..." Anne went on, "I've read it several times and it never meant much to me until I read it again just yesterday. It says, 'There is a friend who sticks closer than a brother.' That's you, Libby. You've been like a sister to me through this whole thing. Closer than a sister. That's your verse, Libby. You're that kind of friend to me."

An unexpected lump had formed in my throat.

"You say you're not big on spiritual stuff. Well, you may not have the words *yet* to express your beliefs. But believe me, Libby, your actions speak louder than any words you could possibly say. So will you be Janey's godmother?"

I felt totally inadequate to be the godmother of Anne's child, but I nodded my head anyway. "I'll try." My voice was a croak. Anne pretended not to notice.

"Good! So, what if…"

"Anne! You promised!"

"No, no…I didn't mean it like that. I was just going to ask, what if I asked Brian to be Janey's godfather? What do you think?"

Tears sprung to my eyes. I looked toward the window, blinking rapidly. "I think—" I had to stop and clear my throat. "I think…" I paused, once again. "I think you're wrong about that gift of words. I'm speechless."

I cast a sideways glance at Brian standing tall at my side. Anne had asked that our whole family come to the front of the church with them during the baptism. So here we stood, Brian and I in the middle, Bob and Emily on either side of us. Andrea glaring at my back from her pew. Emily was clutching her piano book. Anne had asked her to play "Jesus Loves Me" at the conclusion of the baptismal ceremony. I wasn't sure I could stand to listen to the song one more time. Emily had done nothing but practice the piece since Anne had asked. The simple tune seemed to run through my mind even now in a never-ending loop.

My eyes traveled to Anne, her face beaming as she stood by Kevin's side, seemingly the picture of health. She looked fabulous in her new outfit. I doubted anyone even noticed she was wearing a wig. If I hadn't known she'd just finished radiation treatments, I'd never have guessed she'd even been sick.

As much as we had looked forward to Anne's treatments being completed, for some reason I was finding the time now harder to bear. Waiting didn't seem much of an activity. I much preferred the days I spent driving Anne to appointments, visiting with her while we waited…at least we were doing something. Now we were simply waiting for time to pass until her next appointment, right before Christmas. Then Anne was scheduled for a couple days' worth of tests in Rochester to "see where we stand," as the doctor put it. We all knew he really meant, "To see if the cancer has spread." It was hard to believe this day was part of the waiting. That even as the minister blessed Janey, her mother could be manufacturing cancer cells. It didn't seem possible that something so awful could be happening in the midst of this day.

I watched little Janey as she was calmly transferred from Kevin's arms to the minister's. Her tiny mouth formed a small "oh" as he scooped water from the basin over her head. I recalled my own children's baptism. They'd been baptized just because that's what everyone did. I'd stood as a young mother and promised to raise my children in the church. Even though I'm not the kind of person who makes a promise lightly, I'd broken my promise to God without a thought. Anne's question, "Will you be Janey's godmother?" had caused me to examine my conscience. Could I keep a promise to Anne I hadn't kept to God?

I'd been thinking about my pledge to Anne for two weeks. I knew Anne took her request very seriously. Could I do any less? I even went to a bookstore to see if there was a book on godparenting. There wasn't. I didn't know exactly what my promise entailed, but I figured I had plenty of time to figure it out. After all, Janey was only a couple months old; I'd be her godmother for life. I'd bought Janey a children's book as a christening present and reasoned that I had plenty of time to figure out the rest.

⌒

"Mom?" Brian tapped softly on my bedroom door. He'd just hung up the phone in the hallway. I knew Anne was planning to call him tonight to ask Brian to be Janey's godfather. I'd heard his stunned voice saying, "Sure!" Then later, as he put the receiver back in place, I'd heard him whisper, "*All right!*"

Now he was knocking on my door. "Mom?" He was grinning from ear to ear. "Did you know about this?"

I couldn't play dumb. "Yup." A smile played on my lips, too. It was wonderful to see Brian excited about something.

He entered the bedroom, his still-growing feet shuffling along the carpet. Brian plunked himself onto the edge of the bed. "I suppose we should start going to church, huh?" My son cut right through any pretenses I might have had about fudging on this task.

"Uh..." He'd caught me off guard. I knew my promise to Anne was going to involve some effort on my part, but I had been thinking more in terms of gifts and cards.

"I mean," he went on, "Anne said godparents are in charge of seeing that a kid is raised to believe in God and stuff. Like going to Sunday school and saying your prayers." He paused, scuffing his foot over the carpet. "Do I have godparents?"

I squirmed. He did, but obviously they'd never taken their job near as seriously as Brian was taking his—he didn't even know who they were. Not wanting to cast my brother or my cousin in a bad light, I avoided Brian's question with one of my own. "This is a big responsibility; do you think you're ready for it?"

Brian was thoughtful for a moment, then said slowly, "I think so, if you'll help me."

Oh, God, I thought offhandedly, then stopped and realized I really was praying. *Only if You'll help me.* I reached out and squeezed Brian's arm, repeating the words to him. "Only if you'll help me."

As Brian stood and stretched before leaving my room, a familiar phrase ran through my mind. *A little child shall lead them.* I'd heard that phrase somewhere before and in this case it seemed true. Brian was leading me, and Janey was leading both of us. Into what, I wasn't quite sure.

"Do you, as godparents, promise to raise this child to love and serve the Lord? If so, answer, 'We will.'" The minister waited for our answer.

Brian looked at me, nodding slightly. I grabbed his hand and held on tight. We were in this together. In unison we responded, "We do," unsure of the task we were committing to, but committed all the same.

⌒

Anne may have been sure about her choice of me as Janey's godmother, but I had the distinct impression Andrea wasn't too pleased. Nor was her mother. They breezed into my house after the service, like two cats with their claws out.

"Libby," Andrea addressed me, the familiar name coming from her mouth, grating on my nerves, "it's so sweet of you to have our family over for Janey's christening dinner. You must have worked hours getting everything ready. Of course, you don't work, so you probably love doing this kind of thing. I tell you, my little Cari," she paused for a quick breath, "that's C-a-r-i, pronounced 'car' and 'eee.'" Andrea spelled the name, then pronounced it. As if I hadn't heard her the twenty times she'd told the kid to quit running around my living room. "So many people pronounce it wrong, but I wanted her to have a different sort of name. Not something ordinary like my name, or Anne, or Libby. Did Anne ever tell you we had a cat named Libby? Anyway, my little Cari keeps me so busy I couldn't possibly get a dinner like this organized. But I'm sure being a banker's wife, you have help for this sort of thing."

I more or less interrupted, "No, actually, I don't." It took every effort on my part to unclench my jaw and speak civilly to the woman.

Evelyn, Anne's mother, chimed in, "You're just a little Martha Stewart."

It didn't sound like a compliment. I faked a smile.

Evelyn went on, "Take my Andrea, for instance. She is the most wonderful mother. She doesn't need a lick of help. Of course, she doesn't have time for entertaining like you do, what with all the projects she has lined up for her children. Did she tell you that Cari is signed up for dance lessons? Can you believe it, three years old and already going to classes? She's so smart. And Jimmy Jr., he's in peewee wrestling. Now granted, I wasn't too happy about that at first. I mean, it seems so rough for those little boys, but you should have seen him at his first match. Why he had that Nelson boy down on his back so fast, the whole place was standing on their feet cheering. Weren't they Jimmy?"

Little Jimmy stopped pushing his Matchbox car into my bookshelves for a second to smile up at his grandma.

"Now, my Anne, here…" Evelyn turned her head toward Anne, who was standing near the punch bowl talking with her father, Kevin, and Bob. I hoped she wasn't hearing any of this. "I just don't know what kind of mother Anne will be. She's always been so one-track minded. Take this piano business of hers. She didn't want anything to do with sports, like Andrea. Anne just sat inside and pounded away at that keyboard. Well of course, she got very good at it. But it got so we couldn't go anywhere. Anne was always supposed to be playing for somebody's wedding, or funeral, or for church. It didn't seem normal for a teenager to be satisfied with that. Maybe if she would have been more active when she was younger she wouldn't have this little sickness she's going through now."

It was the first time I'd ever heard Evelyn acknowledge Anne's illness.

"Didn't Anne look wonderful today?" I asked, attempting to replace the monologue I'd been listening to with normal conversation.

"I guess so." Evelyn sounded doubtful. "Brown has never been Anne's color. Of course, now that she's wearing a wig, it may be a color she can wear more often. But her hair will grow in soon, and then what is she going to do with that expensive suit? A foolish waste of money if you ask me."

"Janey was sure good during the service, wasn't she?" I tried again.

Andrea answered, "What do you expect from a child who has no stimulation? I mean Anne just sits on the couch and waves a rattle in front of the kid's face. Of course Janey's going to be content to lie around. I could never get by doing that with my two."

I excused myself to the kitchen. *Martha had to get to work.* An unflattering vision of Martha Stewart floated through my mind as I pulled a deeply-browned turkey from the oven. I popped a basket of rolls into the oven to warm. As I arranged meat slices on a platter, it occurred to me Martha was also the name of the woman in the Bible to whom Anne had compared me. "Martha," Anne had said, "she had the gift of works. Like you."

"Well," I thought, jabbing the knife roughly through a leg joint, "this Martha's going to have to have the gift of tongue-biting to get through this meal without exploding!"

Dinner conversation was more of the same. Andrea bragging about her children, Evelyn bragging about Andrea. Anne sat wordlessly, taking it all in. Twice I saw the now-familiar wince cross Anne's face. I wasn't sure if it was from the conversation or the crick in her back that Anne claimed was from sitting on her old couch. In-between my irritation at her mother's and sister's conversation, I wished that new couch would hurry up and get here.

I cornered Anne in the kitchen when she came to help with dessert. "No offense," I spit out in a harsh whisper, "but have you ever noticed how your sister dominates the conversation? All she can talk about are those two darling kids of hers. And your mother sits there and agrees with her. She hasn't even held Janey since we got to the house."

Anne shrugged her shoulders. "That's just the way they are." She pulled dessert plates from the cupboard while I cut the pie. "I guess I'm used to it."

"Used to it? How can you get used to people being rude?"

"They don't mean to be rude, Libby, it's just their way."

"Well, I think their way is the wrong way." I slammed a piece of pumpkin pie onto a plate. "If I were you I'd give them a piece of my mind."

"Libby, I agree with you. Sometimes Andrea does get on my nerves. Mom too." Anne sighed as she scooped ice cream onto a plate. "Don't get me wrong—there have been plenty of times when I've spoken up, but they can't see anything they've said is hurtful, and I just feel bad afterward. I've learned to accept them as they are."

"What they *are*, are *mean*," I spouted, immediately realizing I sounded like a little kid, not much better than the people I was criticizing. "That didn't make sense, did it?" My voice softened, "I'm sorry, but I don't understand how you can listen to them talk like that."

"To tell you the truth, Libby, I don't really notice what they say anymore. I just try to remind myself the Bible tells me I am to honor my family—especially my parents. I don't have to like everything they do or say, but I'm commanded to love them. So I do. At least I try my best to." Anne picked up two plates heaped with pie and ice cream, my criticism of her family already forgotten. "Ready?"

I lifted two dessert plates as well, pretending our conversation was over. "Oh, go ahead," I said, setting one of the plates down, "I want to grab the coffee." It was a feeble excuse to stay in the kitchen, but Anne's words had struck a nerve, and I needed a moment to think. I stood by the sink, thinking about what Anne had said.

Even I knew one of the commandments was to honor your parents, but I'd never thought about how difficult that command could be to apply in real life—assuming a person took the command to heart, that is. How many commands or promises had I heard, or made, and never taken seriously? I recalled the many times I'd blamed my parents, especially my father, for my inability to have close friends. To act lovingly toward Bob. To tell my children I loved them. I blamed my parents for all my inadequacies simply because they hadn't verbalized their feelings. I didn't love my family the way Anne loved hers. I blamed them instead.

What made Anne so different from me?

She lives her beliefs. The answer slid easily to mind. I had watched Anne for a year now, living each day, trying her best to follow what she believed.

Life would be easier if you knew what *you believed.* My, "I think you know better" conscience had ready answers today.

What exactly did I believe? I was the only person who could answer that question, but suddenly my conscience was silent.

Anne's simple question, "Will you be Janey's godmother?" had made a Pandora's box out of my mind. It seemed every aspect of my life was in question. Why had I chosen to live as I had? Was I worthy to be Janey's godmother? Would I have the courage to make the changes it would take to be a mentor to her? Could I?

I had made a promise today. A promise to Anne. A promise to God. If I hadn't thought much about it before, I was thinking about it now. If Anne could love her mother simply because God commanded her to do so, even though the woman was enough to drive a saint nuts, was any less expected of me in my responsibility to my family? To Janey? A feeling of stark terror swept over me. I was in over my head, swimming without a life jacket. How in the world could I be Janey's godmother when I had a hard enough time being Olivia? I wasn't like Anne. I was critical of guests in my own home. I practically choked trying to tell my kids I loved them. I had a big mouth. I was unworthy of—

"Mom?" Brian poked his head into the kitchen, interrupting my diatribe. "Is there dessert for the rest of us?"

"Uh, yeah," I sounded flustered even to myself, so self-absorbed that I'd forgotten about my company in the other room. My mind was spinning with doubts about what I'd committed to do. About my life. I could see ice cream beginning to melt in puddles around the pie. "Here," I motioned to Brian, "grab a couple plates."

"Are you okay, Mom?" Brian picked up two plates in each hand.

I stared at his hands. When had his hands grown that large? How much had happened in this house that I'd never noticed because I'd been so wrapped up in myself? "I'm fine," I answered, not feeling fine at all.

As I walked into the dining room I wondered, "Can a person be made an un-godparent?" That action seemed the easiest way to still my swirling thoughts.

⁓

I was never so glad to have two people leave my house. Actually four, if you counted Cari and Jimmy, Jr. I wasn't counting Jim Sr. and Anne's dad—they could have stayed as long as they liked. It was all I could do to keep myself from jumping in the air in celebration when I closed the door behind Andrea and her mother. I thought they would drive me nuts. How Andrea could possibly be Anne's twin sister I didn't understand. Surely there had been an undiscovered mistake at the hospital. Maybe Evelyn wasn't really Anne's mother either.

After everyone left, I headed to the kitchen, ready to use the clean up time as thinking time. I thought I had worked through so many issues during the time Anne and I had fought. I'd come to the conclusion that I needed to forgive, and that would solve all my problems. While my actions had led to my reconciliation with Anne, I still felt my life was a mess. Anne asking me to be Janey's godmother had caused me to question my ability to serve as a role model, not only for Jane, but for my own family as well. If I felt so confused, how could I possibly be a mentor to anyone else? I had some serious thinking to do, as well as some serious cleaning. The evening stretched before me. I kicked off my heels and rolled up my sleeves. Lots of time to sort things out.

Brian and Emily had cleared the table and loaded the dishwasher, but there was still plenty to do. Crystal goblets to wash by hand, a coffee pot, sauce pans, and a turkey roaster to scrub. A table cloth and napkins to throw in the wash. Plenty of time to think.

I ran a sink full of soapy water, carefully immersing the crystal glasses Bob and I had received as wedding gifts almost sixteen years ago. This was supposed to have been a joyous day, yet I felt agitated, as if there was something I'd forgotten to do. I carefully wiped the rim of each glass, trying to think what it could be.

Know what you believe.

There was that voice again.

Chiding me?

Instructing me?

I scoured brown bits from the sides of the roaster until I'd worked up a sweat. Maybe cleaning my pots and pans would put order to my thoughts. It didn't.

As I gathered up the tablecloth and napkins, I reviewed the day in my mind. I'd daydreamed through Janey's baptism, worrying more about what Andrea was thinking than about my accountability as a godmother. I'd criticized Anne's mother and sister, not only in my mind but also to Anne. This day had found me doubting my ability to follow a commandment, much less a promise, and had me questioning my ability and worth as a mother and a wife. No wonder I felt at odds with myself. The day had only served to emphasize how inadequate I was to be Janey's godmother.

Too tired to carry my large roaster to the basement where I usually stored it, I swung open the oven door, intending to leave it in the oven overnight. There, in the middle of my still-warming oven, sat the basket of rolls I'd placed to warm hours ago, hard as rocks, staring at me like a basket of brown, accusing eyes.

"Let's face it," I muttered, stuffing the cement-like rolls one by one down the garbage disposal, "you're not going to make it as a cook. You're no great shakes as a wife. Or a mother." I jammed a fourth roll down the disposal. "You might as well face up to it, kiddo, you're never going to make it as a writer either." I listened to the rolls tumble and grind, feeding in more. It was a satisfying sound, in line with my tumbling thoughts. I rammed the last roll through the drain. "And you're certainly not godmother material."

As I washed the last of the bread crumbs down the drain, I didn't feel much like Martha Stewart or Martha from the Bible. I just felt like unworthy, unchangeable Olivia. I'd have to figure out my life some other time. Right now, all I wanted was to go to bed and get this long day over.

Anne

I tried my best to get everything ready for Christmas. I knew once I returned from my tests in Rochester, scheduled just days before the holiday, there would be no time for any further preparations. I pushed myself to continue a somewhat normal routine. But just getting dressed in the morning was enough to make me ready for a mid-morning nap along with Janey. I more or less gave up the idea of dusting, and vacuuming was out of the question. It took up too much of my limited energy. I focused what I had on Janey and a few batches of Christmas cookies.

"This too shall pass," I whispered as I sank into the familiar corner of our old worn-out couch. I was too tired to do more than sit and dangle a rattle in front of Janey. Even the thought of rearranging the throw pillows behind me to help alleviate the pain in my back seemed too much of an effort. I sat, dreading the sound of the oven timer which would mean I'd have to get up again.

With Kevin's help, I'd decorated Janey's first Christmas tree, placing the "Baby's First Christmas" ornament front and center where Janey could see it if Brian came over and held her near the tree. Brian had given the ornament as an early Christmas present. He knocked on our door one day after school, bundled up against the cold, holding the clumsily-wrapped present in his gloved hands. With a stocking cap pulled to his eyebrows and a scarf wrapped around his chin, he looked as though he were a swaddled wise man bearing a precious gift.

"This is for Janey." He held the gift out to me, almost turning to leave at the same time. I could see a friend waiting in a running car at the curb.

"Can you come in for a second?" I asked. "Janey would love some company."

One side of Brian's mouth turned up in a half smile. "I'm supposed to go right home after school—you know, I'm still grounded."

"That's right, I'd forgotten."

So often I forgot about the scare with drugs Brian had had just months earlier. He was so gentle with Janey, it was hard for me to imagine him doing anything dangerous. "How about if I give your mom a call and tell her you're here? I've got Christmas cookies in the kitchen." It was a shameless bribe.

"Maybe I'd better not, Pete's in the car." Brian tossed his chin in the direction of the curb. "He just got his license." His eyes looked over my shoulder into the house, as if trying to get a glimpse of Jane.

"I'll bet Pete eats cookies too," I invited.

Within a minute both boys were stomping their huge feet inside my door, draping their coats, caps, and scarves over the arm of my old couch.

"Hey there, Janey." Brian squatted in front of Janey, who was lying on her back on a blanket on the floor. He rubbed his hands together, warming them, then picked her up in an easy motion.

How I wished I could lift my child that easily. It was getting harder and harder for me hold her for any length of time, my back aching with the added weight.

"This is my friend, Pete." Brian turned Janey to face Pete, sticking her right arm out in a baby handshake.

Awkwardly, Pete stuck out his hand, then curled his fingers, all except his index finger which he threaded through Janey's fist. "Uh, hi."

"Come and have some cookies, boys," I instructed, quickly arranging an assortment of cookies, caramels, and fudge on a platter.

Brian washed down his second cookie with a glass of milk. "Maybe you could open her gift now." He had Janey balanced securely on his leg. "I mean, it's kind of something you could use."

"You don't have to ask me twice to open a gift." I smiled, already tearing at the wrapping. I carefully removed the gift tag on which was printed:

To: Janey.

From: Your Godfather, Brian Marsden.

I set it aside, mentally taping the tag into Janey's baby book. I could imagine Brian trying to squeeze all the letters onto the small tag. "Oh, look Janey," I cooed, pulling the ornament from the box. "Look what your godfather gave you for your first Christmas!" I dangled the porcelain ornament from my finger. Janey's eyes followed intently as it swayed in the afternoon light.

Even Pete grinned as Brian ducked his head in an embarrassed blush, a smile plastered across his face.

"Is it okay?" Brian asked, his recent growth spurt belying his youthful self-consciousness.

"I just *love* it!" A high squeaky imitation baby voice came from Pete's mouth, and we burst out laughing. Even Janey seemed to pick up on the joke, waving her arms in a burst of joy.

Brian gave a satisfied nod, then started to stand. "I'd better get home."

"Just a minute." I motioned him to stay sitting. "You might as well open Janey's gift to you. I'm not sure we'll be here for Christmas."

I'd mailed gifts for my family to my mother's house just in case the weather turned bad and we weren't able to make the long drive to spend Christmas with them. But I was hoping we'd be able to spend a few days there. I had my other gifts piled under the tree, ready for giving when I returned from Rochester. I'd wrapped a book, along with a scarf in shades of royal blue and purple, for Libby. Small gifts for Brian and Emily were under the tree, along with gifts for Kevin and Janey. I grabbed Brian's gift and returned to the table. Pitching my voice somewhere near where Pete's had been, I laid the gift in front of Brian, "Hope you like it."

Instinctively, Brian seemed to realize it was hard for me to hold my daughter. In a graceful exchange he handed Janey to Pete, who looked at her as if a hot potato had been dropped into his lap. "Hi!" Pete squeaked in the same goofy voice he'd spoken with moments before, then cleared his throat and repeated, "I mean, hi." He looked at us, explaining, "I've never held a baby before."

Brian unwrapped his gift, cradling the framed photo of himself and Janey that had been snapped after the baptism in his large hands. "Pretty cool." He continued to stare at the picture, not seeming to notice the wooden frame I'd debated about for fifteen minutes in the department store.

"Uh, Mrs. Abbot?" Pete sounded uncomfortable. "I think, uh, that Janey, uh, well, she kind of smells like she…"

Just then the air currents in my kitchen must have swirled because I knew exactly what Pete was getting at. "I guess this is a mom thing, huh?" I remarked, pushing myself away from the table. "Here I'll take her."

"I'll carry Janey into the bedroom." Brian jumped up and deftly transferred Janey into his arms. "Then we'd better get going."

"Oh sure," I teased, following him, "when the going gets tough, the tough get going. If you know who I mean."

Brian gently laid Janey on her changing table. "Bye, girl," he said, running the side of his index finger under her chin. "Thanks for the present." Brian looked at me.

"The cookies, too," Pete chimed from the doorway. "They were awesome."

As I changed Janey's diaper, I heard the boys stomp through the snow to the car, their teenage banter muffled, but loud enough to filter through the walls. A feeling of contentment filled me as I thought of Brian's visit. I was glad we'd chosen him to be Janey's godfather. He was turning into a special young man.

I was grateful, too, for the short break Brian had given me. Resting for ten minutes between cookie batches hadn't been doing much to restore my energy. And, the heating pad hadn't seemed to make a difference on the crick in my back. If Janey needed attention, I'd been forced to kneel beside her on the floor. Holding her was becoming a painful task. Brian's visit had not only given me a chance to rest; he'd entertained Janey, as well as lifted my sagging spirits.

It was hard not to get discouraged when I compared this Christmas season to previous ones. Thinking back, I could hardly imagine how effortlessly I'd trimmed the tree, shopped for gifts, spent days in the kitchen baking and frosting, preparing plates to give away, then baking some more. This year was a contrast in opposites.

It seemed that no matter which way I slept, I was waking up with a backache every morning, one that continued throughout the day. I tried not to worry about the pain, but since it had gone on so long I couldn't help but think it might be a tumor. I'd called Dr. Barrows, who had suggested aspirin and a heating pad. "Your tests will tell if it's anything we need to do something further about. Until then, see if you can't get your husband to give you a good back rub." He didn't seem concerned, so I tried not to be either. But it was hard not to worry when the dull ache was so constant.

I gathered Janey from the changing table into my arms, determined to finish baking the rest of the almond crescent cookie dough I'd stashed in the fridge when Brian had arrived.

"Then Mommy's just going to relax and wait for Christmas to come," I cooed to Janey.

Suddenly, my back spasmed so tightly that my grip on Janey loosened. I could feel her falling from my arms, but was helpless to stop her. I tried lifting my knee to slow her descent, but even that slight movement caused my back to tighten more. *Lord,* I prayed as Janey slid down my legs toward the floor, *protect my child!*

Janey lay on the floor, unhurt but wailing. I was curled in a ball beside her, crying myself. Whether because of the pain or because I was unable to tend my daughter it was hard to know.

Help me, Lord! Help me…

"Mrs. Abbot?" Unexpectedly, Brian's voice called from the front door. "Uh, Anne? Pete thinks he forgot his cap. I'll look for it if you're still busy with Janey."

Brian practically tripped over us as he walked toward the couch where the boys had thrown their winter wrappings. He stopped in his tracks. "What's…? Are you okay?" Then without waiting for an answer, he said, "I'll call my mom."

Olivia

Anne almost seemed glad to be in the hospital.

By the time I arrived at her house, Brian had helped Anne onto the couch and was pacing across the living room, patting Janey's back, repeating softly, "You're both okay. You're both okay." Anne was lying on her side, eyes closed, a heating pad propped against her back with pillows. When I approached the couch, she raised her eyelids half-mast. "Merry Christmas," she offered weakly. Then she closed her lids, adding, "I think you should take me to the hospital."

Gingerly, Anne stood while I threaded her arms through her bulky winter coat. She was sweating by the time it was on. "Maybe we should take this off," she joked in a tired-sounding voice. "I'm hot."

"And I suppose when we get outside you're going to tell me you need to go to the bathroom." I tried to make my words sound light-hearted, but I was scared. Anne was pale and shaky, unable to straighten. Any movement made her wince, and when I helped her stand from the couch I heard her try to cover a gasp with a small cough. I was beginning to wish Brian had called an ambulance instead of me.

A step at a time we inched toward the door, leaving Brian to wait with Janey, instructing him to send Kevin to the hospital in Carlton.

"Oh, one more thing, Brian." It was an effort for Anne to talk.

"Just go, already," Brian urged, scared for Anne, too. "I know how to warm a bottle and change Janey's diaper, and if she cries I'll just walk around with her until she stops."

"No, it's more important than that." A corner of Anne's mouth turned up. "If you're hungry, eat that cookie dough in the fridge. I think I'm done baking for this year."

Dr. Barrows was waiting for us when we arrived at the hospital, surprised to see Anne looking so weak and vulnerable. Uncharacteristically, he joked, "You two will do anything to get out of cooking supper."

Anne barely nodded, sinking into the wheelchair a nurse had produced. Politely, I tried to look amused. Dr. Barrows had hardly acknowledged my presence during previous visits, and I wasn't in the mood to get acquainted now. The forty-mile drive had been long and silent. Anne had dozed fitfully during the trip, moaning occasionally. At one point she opened her eyes and mumbled, "You're a good driver," then had fallen back to sleep. It was a hard drive, keeping one eye on snowy roads, another on Anne.

Uncomfortably, Dr. Barrows rubbed his neck. "Let's see what's happening. I'm going to want to get some blood drawn, we'll do a scan, and then...well, we'll see from there." I had the feeling he felt out of his league.

Kevin joined me in Anne's room about two hours later. Anne was in another part of the hospital having tests done.

"I took Janey and Brian over to your house," Kevin explained. "Bob was home and said they'd manage for the night. If you want to head home..." His words trailed off and he pressed his hands against his eyes. "What's happening to her?" His words were almost a whisper. Kevin's shoulders sagged. He leaned forward, hanging his head for a moment. "This kind of stuff isn't supposed to happen at Christmas." He swore. "It's not supposed to happen at all. Not to people Anne's age. We've got a baby to raise. Doesn't God know that?" Kevin looked at me with desperate eyes, repeating loudly, *"Doesn't God know that?"*

I felt as if I were being grilled for an answer to a test I hadn't studied for. My mouth opened and shut, no magic words appearing.

"Of course He knows, Kevin." Anne's gentle answer filled the silence as she was wheeled into the room. Her voice was stronger now. "I don't know what question you were asking, but whatever it was, God knows."

Anne chattered away cheerfully for about a half-hour after returning to the room, apologizing for all the trouble she'd caused Brian and me. Kevin too. Color had crept back into her face and the grimace she'd worn all the way to the hospital had been replaced by her usual smile.

"I think I'm going to close my eyes for a little bit." Anne was fighting to keep her eyelids open. "They must have given me something in that medicine to make me sleepy—" She yawned in the middle of her sentence. "Oh, goodness, don't count on me being the life of the party tonight." And, just like that, she was asleep.

A nurse poked her head into the room and whispered that Dr. Barrows would like to talk to Kevin. Kevin cocked his head towards me in a "let's go" gesture, so I followed him out. Dr. Barrows was waiting by the nurses' station, a grim look on his face.

"It isn't good." As usual, Dr. Barrows didn't mince words.

"But she looked so good after the tests. She sounded happy, like she always does." Kevin was saying the same things I was thinking.

"That's because we gave Anne a blood transfusion. Her counts were extremely low, which is probably why she had this trouble today. The transfusion will perk her up for a while, but I can't tell you for how long. I'm afraid we have a more pressing concern..." Dr. Barrows paused, as if he couldn't quite believe what he had to say. "There is a large tumor at the base of Anne's spine. That's what has been causing the back pain she's been having. I'm going to consult with her doctors in Rochester, but my best guess is that it's too large to operate on at this point. I'm certain they will recommend a course of radiation treatments to try to shrink the tumor before doing anything else."

My mind was tumbling, trying to absorb everything.

Dr. Barrows clicked his pen, nervously. "I don't want to be the one to cry 'wolf' here, but I would consider notifying any family members of her condition—"

"What?" My voice came out in a panicked croak.

Dr. Barrows looked at me, a sympathetic expression crinkling his eyes. "Anne's a very sick young woman. I can't predict what will happen. As Anne herself told me, 'Only God can do that.'"

"She knows?" My voice sounded as though it belonged to someone else.

"Yes. Anne asked, so I told her what I'm telling you." Dr. Barrows looked down the hall toward the nurse coming from Anne's room. "Anne's condition is very serious. Then again, we never know in cases like hers. She's young. Her heart is strong. She has a lot to live for. She could snap out of this. But I want you to be prepared. We'll give her another transfusion later tonight if you want us to, but that's another thing we're going to have to discuss. The transfusions will give Anne some energy, but in the long run they may just prolong the inevitable."

Kevin and I were gaping at Dr. Barrows as if we were two fish out of water. I could not believe Anne's condition was as serious as Dr. Barrows was indicating. Why, just a couple hours ago Anne had been baking and telling Brian to eat her cookie dough. Was Dr. Barrows really trying to tell us Anne could be dying?

I'd always thought Anne would be cured. Her faith was strong, her sense of humor intact…it seemed her case would be one of those uplifting stories people talked about for years. Even when Anne lost her hair from the chemotherapy and had been burned so badly by the radiation, neither of us had taken it as a sign of worse things to come. It was just something to get through on her way to being normal again.

I'd never thought about life after Anne. For some reason, I thought we had all the time in the world to continue being friends. Recently, I'd gone so far as to daydream about a time far in the future when Anne and I would be old widows together. We wouldn't be lonely. No, we'd sit on the porch of the house we shared, laughing our days away, remembering our husbands and sharing stories about Brian, Emily, and Janey. Now Dr. Barrows was telling us that Anne might not be here for Christmas. It didn't seem possible.

"I'll talk to the people in Rochester in the morning," Dr. Barrows concluded. "And you might want to talk this over with Anne. She indicated to me she may not want to have too many blood transfusions."

I knew the situation was bad when Dr. Barrows reached out his hand and squeezed Kevin's shoulder. It was the first gesture of emotion I'd seen Dr. Barrows show, and it scared me more than the words he'd just said.

"I have to make a phone call," I told Kevin. "I'll be back in Anne's room in a few minutes if you want to go call her folks then." I practically ran to the phone in the hospital waiting room.

It wasn't until the phone was ringing that I noticed the time. It was almost 10:00, a time at night I hated for the phone to ring, but tonight it didn't seem to matter.

"Hello." Dr. West's calm, confident voice at the other end of the line helped focus my jumbled thoughts.

"Ellen? It's Olivia. Sorry to call so late, but it's important."

"Is it Brian? Is he okay? Pete's in his room." It was a typical mother's response to a call that time of the evening. I'd almost forgotten there were other worries in the world besides the ones on my mind.

"No, no, it's not the boys. Sorry, I should have known you'd worry if I called this late."

"It's no bother. I was just going through some medical journals. What's up?"

I took a deep breath and plunged in. "It's my friend, Anne. Anne Abbot. Remember I told you about her this fall?"

"She had breast cancer, if I remember correctly."

"Yes," I replied, "she did. She does. Well, uh, that's why I'm calling. I'm here at the hospital. Anne had a sort of attack this afternoon, and the doctor is telling us we should maybe call the family. But I talked to Anne a few minutes ago, and she seems fine. A little tired maybe, but fine."

I went on for almost forty minutes, telling Dr. West about Anne's appointments in Carlton and Rochester, recalling what I could of the medical jargon the doctors had used, the drugs they'd used for chemotherapy, the radiation treatments Anne had had and winding up with the report Dr. Barrows had just given us.

"The reason I'm calling," I finally told Ellen, "is that I need your professional opinion. What would you say is the prognosis in this case?"

There was a long silence before Dr. West responded. "Olivia, if you were calling me to hear a better report, I'm afraid I can't give you one. From what you've told me, your friend's condition doesn't sound promising."

An icy coldness started spreading through my body, beginning from my ear, pressed hard against the phone receiver.

"If I were Anne, I would do whatever I'd dreamed of doing very soon. She might want to make a videotape for her little girl."

I stared straight ahead at a hole in the green vinyl chair across the room. Anger rose in my chest. What kind of friend was Ellen to be telling me this? Didn't she know I'd called her for a different opinion? I didn't want to be hearing this. What kind of doctor was she anyway?

"I'm sorry, Olivia." There was true compassion in Ellen's voice, but I wasn't willing to accept it.

I clenched my teeth together, trying to keep my bottom lip from quivering. I was freezing.

"Olivia? Are you still there?"

"Yes." My voice sounded as cold as I felt. "Thank you. I need to go."

"Call me anytime, Olivia, really."

I hung up.

⌒

When I got back to Anne's room, Kevin was slumped in the room's only chair, his head thrown back, mouth open, a loud snore emanating on every breath.

"Poke him for me, will you?" Anne lay on her side, eyes open. A small tuft of newly-grown hair was cocked at an odd angle over her ear. Even though her hair had begun to fill in, Anne had been wearing her wig each day until bedtime. I hadn't seen her without it recently, and it gave me a start to see Anne lying in bed, the wispy, thin hair making her look years older than she was.

I gave Kevin a gentle nudge, causing him to turn slightly, close his mouth, and stop the irritating noise.

"Are you going to go home now?" Anne asked, her voice soft and a bit weak.

"Depends," I said, shrugging my shoulders. "Got anything good to talk about?"

Anne smiled. "Always."

I moved to the side of her bed, resting one hip on the mattress. "Tell all."

"Did you know the older lady in the room next to me has been in the hospital almost a month? She fell and broke her hip, then she got pneumonia, and now she's—"

"Good grief, Anne," I interrupted, "I thought you had something interesting to tell."

"I thought that was interesting. I feel sorry for her. I've been lying here praying for her."

"You would." I shifted both hips onto the edge of the bed, hooking my feet on the side rails for balance. "Let's talk about something really interesting, for instance…how about the fact that Brian may have a girlfriend?"

"No! How do you know?" Anne's eyes lit up, wanting every detail.

"Well, Emily told me she's seen Brian talking to Kimmy Peters at school. And some girl has been calling our house almost every night asking for Brian. He races to the phone, then stretches the cord as far as it will go so that he can sit on the basement step and close the door so we can't hear a word of his conversation. Nancy Drew here put two and two together." I was quiet for a moment, imagining my son, who up until now had only been interested in sports, having a girlfriend.

"How do you feel about that?" Anne asked.

"You know, I surprised myself—I'm really okay with it. Brian's changed a lot in the past months."

"I've noticed," Anne confirmed. She slowly shifted her position in the bed. A wince of pain flickered across her face. She blinked hard, then settled back, picking up the conversation. "He's really matured."

"I thought maybe it was from that counseling program the school offered for the athletes that got caught in that drug thing, but I asked Brian about it, and he said it was 'worthless.' His word, not mine. He said all they do is watch some lame videos and then they're supposed to talk about them, but nobody does. So the counselor says things they already know and then excuses them. I don't know what, but something has caused him to grow up lately. I'm actually thinking of un-grounding him."

"I'm sure he'd be happy about that." Anne closed her eyes for a minute.

"Are you getting tired?"

Anne opened her eyes. "No, just thinking. Brian has shown a lot of maturity lately. I especially notice it when he's around Janey. He takes over with her as if he's been around babies all his life. Did you know he brought her a Christmas present today?"

I hadn't. As Anne told me how touched she'd been by Brian's gesture, describing his modest embarrassment as well as his pride in introducing Janey to Pete, I saw with sudden clarity the reason for Brian's newfound maturity. It was because Anne had asked him to be Janey's godfather. She'd put her trust in him. I hadn't even considered it. I'd been punishing him for his transgression by grounding him, giving him extra chores, restricting his time with friends. Anne, however, saw past his fault into the goodness of his soul and entrusted her daughter's care to him. Much as she'd done with me. I had to admit Brian had thought much more about his responsibility towards Janey than I had. I felt chagrined. Here was Anne, going through one of the worst trials anyone could, and even now she was helping my son grow up and listening to my problems.

"Do you ever get tired of being my friend?" After the words were out of my mouth, I realized I had interrupted Anne. "See," I went on, "that's exactly what I mean. Sometimes, I act like an insensitive, complaining jerk."

Anne shifted her body, raising her head to rest it upon her bent arm. "Do you know that you are the only person I still feel normal around?"

Anne had answered my question with one of her own. I did likewise. "What do you mean?"

"Everyone else treats me as though I'm some fragile cancer patient. Either they act condescending toward me, afraid I'm going to fall apart if they move too fast, or they say the wrong thing. Or else they pretend they don't know I've had cancer at all. It's as if I'm watching them walk on eggshells. You can't believe the way people will dance around a conversation, trying to avoid the mention of anything having to do with being sick. It's almost funny sometimes. And you'd be surprised how often words like 'sick', 'hospital', and even 'cancer', come up in normal conversation. Even Kevin," Anne made a slight movement with her chin towards her sleeping husband. "All we talk about anymore is cancer. How am I feeling? When is my next doctor appointment? What was my blood count? It makes me feel as if that's all I am to people—Anne Abbot, cancer victim. You're the only person, Libby, who treats me just like you always have. You don't know how many times I've thanked God for sending you to be my friend."

I let out an unbelieving laugh. "Oh yeah, God would send a mixed-up, middle-aged housewife with an indifferent marriage, a troubled son, and a daughter who talks too much to be your friend." I stood up and stretched. "That's a good one, Anne."

"Oh, Libby," Anne smiled, turning onto her back, a small grimace crossing her face as she moved, "you're going to be surprised at all God can do some—" A spasm of pain interrupted her. When it had passed Anne asked, "Could you call the nurse for me? I think I might need some medication." As we waited for the nurse, Anne whispered, "Get some rest, Libby. I'll see you tomorrow. Give Janey a kiss for me, okay?"

⌒

As I crossed the snowy parking lot heading toward my car, images of how Anne had looked over the past several hours ran through my brain. Pale. Weak. In pain. Asking to be taken to the hospital. Asking for more medication. So unlike the indomitable Anne I knew.

With a press of the key chain I unlocked the car door, the chill of the stiff seat matching the inner chill I felt. I was scared for my friend. As I drove home in the dark, a Christmas carol played on the radio. "Joy to the world" a choir sang out. I snapped it off, recalling Brian's description of Janey and Anne crying on the living room floor.

"Where's the joy, Lord?" I challenged. "Huh? Where?"

As I turned into my driveway, the porch light glowing a welcome, Anne's words echoed in my mind. *You're going to be surprised at all God can do.*

"Okay, God," I challenged once again, "surprise me."

Anne

It wasn't the best day I'd ever had. I'd been wakened from a restless sleep by the nurses doing their morning duties. Temperature, blood pressure, and more blood to be drawn. Kevin came awake slowly, stretching the kinks from his chair-shaped body. A grizzle of whiskers spread across his face, making him look haggard and still tired. I had a few bites of scrambled eggs before pushing the tray over for Kevin to finish. The pain medication made me feel a bit nauseous.

Even before Dr. Barrows came back with my blood counts, I knew they weren't good. I felt weak and tired.

"I'm going to give you another blood transfusion, Anne," Dr. Barrows told me, before going over my test results. "It'll give you some energy. I understand your parents are coming to see you today."

"And my sister." My voice sounded stronger than I felt.

"Good. Good," Dr. Barrows said, sounding distracted. "Mr. Abbot, could I talk to you for a minute?" He headed for the doorway, Kevin springing from his chair in pursuit.

"Please." My one word stopped them both. "If you're going to discuss me, I'd prefer to be included." They eyed each other in silent communication. "Please, Kevin?" I pleaded. "Dr. Barrows? I want to know what's happening to me. I'm not afraid."

Dr. Barrows stepped to the end of my bed. Kevin came to stand beside me, taking my hand in his as if bracing for a blow. Dr. Barrows began, "I talked with your doctors in Rochester this morning." Dr. Barrows stopped, blowing out his cheeks with a puff of air. "There's never an easy way to say this, so I'll just say it. There's not much we can do for you, Anne." He hurried on, not giving us time to absorb what he'd just said. "The doctors did offer the possibility of a bone marrow transplant—there's been some measure of success with the procedure in breast cancer patients. But at this point it's doubtful you'd qualify. You'd have to be in remission before the procedure could be attempted, providing a match could be found, of course. But we're a long way from that point right now. You need to get through the next few days first, Anne. You're weak, your blood counts are very low and the tumor at the base of your spine is causing you a great deal of discomfort. We're going to concentrate our efforts on keeping you comfortable today. I'm going to increase your pain medication; we want to keep on top of the pain, not struggle to catch up with it. We'll get that blood transfusion going as soon as we can, and depending how you feel, we'll try tackling the tumor with some radiation in a day or so. In the meantime you get some rest and enjoy your time with your family."

It didn't take a rocket scientist to figure out that Dr. Barrows was trying to tell me I should maybe say my goodbyes. He left the room, leaving Kevin and me in a heavy silence. I looked at Kevin who was blinking rapidly, trying to hold back tears and at the same time swallowing as if he had something stuck in his throat. I laid my head on the pillow, a sense of peace and calm passing through my body.

Do not be afraid, I am with you.

No matter what happened over the next few days, at least I had that assurance.

Olivia

Kevin met me in the hospital hallway when I arrived the next morning. "We should talk," he said. He grabbed my elbow and practically pushed me down the hall onto a waiting room couch. The morning stubble on his face made him look like an incognito movie star, his rumpled clothes doing nothing to discourage the young woman I noticed eyeing him from across the room. Kevin, however, was focused on Anne.

"It's not good," he burst out without preamble. "It's terrible. I mean it's pretty bad when even the doctor tells you there's not much more he can do."

Again, that creeping, freezing sensation started up my body. I listened to Kevin, nodding as if I understood what he was saying, but the whole time my brain was screaming, "NO!"

Kevin scrubbed at his face. "The doctor did talk about a bone marrow transplant, but I got the feeling it's not a great option. I don't know what else to do. I mean, Anne knows all this, and she accepts it. She's not ranting and raving; she's not even crying. She acts as if it's meant to be. I want to shake her and yell, 'Fight!' But I know it wouldn't make any difference." His voice cracked. "What am I supposed to do?"

I thought for a moment Kevin was going to start crying. Actually, having him cry would have been easier. At least then I would have known what to do. I could've taken his hand, rubbed his shoulder, or murmured some say-nothing phrases until he'd cried himself out. Instead, he stared at me dry eyed, questioning me again, "What am I supposed to do?"

"You're a Martha," I found myself inexplicably telling him. The words surprised even me.

Kevin gave me an "Okay, you've officially flipped" look.

"It's what Anne told me I was," I explained. "When something is happening I want to *do* something. Like Martha from the Bible. I'm more comfortable putting myself into action to help things along, rather than just sitting and waiting to hear the outcome. You're like that, too."

He nodded in astonished agreement.

"Here's the plan. I'll go talk to Anne for awhile." Acting like Martha, I gave myself something to do first. Then, in a most Martha-like voice, I instructed Kevin, "You find a razor and get cleaned up for the day. Call your office and tell them you won't be around for a few days. Call your pastor and tell him to come here." And then, in a voice I still didn't recognize as mine, I added, "Then go to the chapel and pray."

As I entered Anne's room, the nurse was unhooking the bag that had held Anne's blood transfusion. Anne's color was good. However, without her wig, and dressed in a faded hospital gown, she looked even more frail in the morning light. Her eyes were large against chiseled cheekbones—another thing I hadn't noticed during our daily visits at home.

"Morning," Anne said as she spotted me in the doorway. "This stuff is almost as good as coffee." She held out her arm to show where the energizing blood had entered.

"Think I'll stick with the regular kind," I rejoined, holding aloft the Styrofoam cup I'd poured in the waiting room.

"Lucky you," she said, laying her head on the pillow. "Did you see Kevin?" When I nodded, she went on, "Then you know."

I nodded again, crossing the room, settling myself on the edge of Anne's bed. Finding my voice, I asked, "Is there anything special you want?" What I meant was if Anne needed an extra pillow, or a glass of juice. Maybe she wanted to listen to some of her many piano CD's. Whatever she needed I was ready to provide.

"I want you to sing," she replied, fixing me with a look I couldn't quite read.

My vocal range had been a standing joke between us ever since the first true night of our friendship when I'd proved that some people really can't sing. I'd told her that night I could sing three notes at the same time—just not in harmony. Then I'd gone ahead and done it. I knew Anne wasn't asking me to sit at her bedside and sing a lullaby. She continued to give me a steady look, her face serious, with the barest hint of a twinkle behind her eyes, as if asking a very important favor. Suddenly, I understood. She meant at her *funeral!* I froze, a flush rising in my body with the force of a tidal wave. My mind raced. I would do anything for Anne. Anything. But certainly she wouldn't ask that of me. I scrambled for something to say. A polite way to refuse her dying request. Maybe I could sing and people would assume I was choked with emotion. Maybe—

Anne burst out laughing. Combined feelings of sheer panic and hilarity swept through me as I realized she'd been joking. About her funeral, no less.

"You rat!" I swatted at her with my hand. "I can't believe you said that!" I was as warm as a menopausal woman and fanned out the bottom of my sweater in order to cool off.

"You have to admit it was a good one though." Anne was still laughing.

"That it was," I admitted, starting to chuckle myself.

Anne had broken the ice around the topic and grew pensive. "Really, Libby, I want to wear that new outfit we bought for Janey's baptism. The *toast* color, remember?"

"I remember," I said. My voice sounded remarkably normal. Meanwhile, my whole being felt as if it were in a surreal movie. Did people actually sit around and talk about their funerals ahead of time? Apparently so since Anne went on, "I think it would be nice if Emily would play her "Jesus Loves Me" piece. Don't you?"

"Um-hmm," I agreed, wondering how Emily would feel about Anne's request.

I could hear chattering voices coming down the hallway, sounding totally at odds with what we were discussing.

"And if you have anything to say about it, I don't want any gladiolas. They've always seemed like creepy flowers to me."

"I'll call the florist," I replied, remembering one of Emily's first piano lessons when she'd jumped in the car and rattled off facts about her new piano teacher. *And she hates gladiolas.* I remembered wondering what kind of piano teacher this Mrs. Abbot was to fill my daughter in on such mundane details of her life. No longer did the details seem mundane. They were the essence of Anne, and I didn't want to lose even one of them.

"And I want my pastor to give an evangelistic sermon. I know where I'm going—I think it would be nice if others had a chance to get there too."

Instinctively I knew Anne meant heaven. "When you get there..." I paused, not sure how to ask my question. I wasn't exactly an expert on this subject. "Uh, if you see my folks, could you tell them that...well, that I'm—" I stopped, suddenly feeling foolish, not sure why I felt compelled to convey this ridiculous notion to Anne. "Tell them I— that I love them. Okay?"

"Okay," Anne replied with a satisfied smile, acting as though my request was not anything at all unusual.

Suddenly the commotion that had been confined to the hallway burst into Anne's room in the form of Evelyn and Andrea, along with Anne's dad, Jimmy, Jr., and Cari. The five of them stopped dead in their tracks midway into the room. The sight of Anne, pale, frail, and without her wig took the chatter right out of them. Eventually, three-year old Cari lifted a stubby finger and pointed it at Anne. "Funny!"

Andrea slapped at Cari's hand. "Sush!" she warned. "Talk nice."

Instantly my hackles rose, my dislike for these two women rearing up full force. I needed to get out of there, yet felt guilty leaving Anne to deal with them alone. I knew, however, that just as Anne and I'd had time alone together, they too would want to spend time with Anne.

"Hello!" I made every effort to sound as if I welcomed their presence. "You must have started out early this morning to get here already."

Andrea launched into a mile by mile description of their long drive to Carlton. I could tell by the mindless manner in which she was prattling, she was trying hard to cover up her shock at seeing Anne. Jimmy Jr. didn't waste any time; he'd already punched the nurse-call button and raised the foot of Anne's bed with the remote control.

"Listen," I said, interrupting Andrea, "why don't I take the kids to the cafeteria and get them a snack. Anne has been telling me some things I think she might want to share with you too."

Anne pushed her shoulders up near her jaw line in a thoughtful stretch, as if preparing herself for a difficult conversation. After she'd slowly lowered them, she nodded her head. "Libby's right—I need to talk to you."

Jimmy was reluctant to let go of his new found toy, flipping the television on and off in a gesture of defiance before his mother grabbed the control away from him. Cari willingly took my hand and followed along, out of the room.

I don't know if we were in the cafeteria even fifteen minutes before Evelyn came storming over to our table. "I can't believe what that daughter of mine is talking about." She plopped her large purse in the middle of the table, then yanked out a chair, dropping herself into it. "Her funeral! Can you believe that? Her funeral! I refuse to listen to such talk! Get me a cup of coffee," she ordered.

As I walked away from the table to fulfill Evelyn's request I could hear Cari ask, "What a fuun-ral?"

Within ten minutes Andrea had joined us, her eyes red.

"She told me—" Andrea sputtered, pausing to draw a short breath. "She told me she didn't blame me for her thumbs. I thought she forgot about that a long time ago. It was an accident. Remember Mom?" Andrea looked at her mother, wanting confirmation about an incident that was obviously etched in all their minds.

"Well of course it was, Honey." Evelyn reached over and patted Andrea's hand. "You were just trying to help clean the living room, dusting the piano while Anne played. You didn't mean for the piano cover to fall down on her hands. Remember how Anne cried?" Evelyn hurried to add, "Surely that did hurt, even if you didn't mean to do it. Two broken thumbs." Evelyn shook her head as if she still didn't quite believe it had happened.

I shuddered inside, recalling again Emily jabbering about her piano teacher's crooked thumbs. How often had I watched Anne's hands flying over the keyboard, or holding Janey with what Anne referred to as "my funny, backwards thumbs," never dreaming how they'd come to be shaped that way.

Again, I needed to get away. I pushed myself from the table. "I'm going to swing by Anne's room, then I need to run some errands. I've got some Christmas shopping to finish up. I thought I'd run over to the mall. That is, if you guys plan on staying with Anne this afternoon."

"Well, yes," Evelyn said, "we planned to spend the day. But I certainly hope that she gets that funeral business out of her head. I will not sit there and listen to that kind of talk."

As I walked away from the table, once again I heard Cari ask, "What fuun-ral?"

⌒

Already Anne's color had faded. Her arm seemed weak as she barely raised it off the bed to wave me into her room.

"You lasted about as long with them as they did with me," Anne stated, sounding tired. "Dad went to get a snack."

"And to think," I responded in an exaggeratedly nice voice, "you get to spend the whole day with them."

"They are going to stay then," Anne murmured more to herself than me. "I wondered." She turned her eyes toward me. "I can't believe I'm getting tired again. It seems all I've done since I got here is sleep."

There was silence in the room as Anne closed her eyes. I tried to think of something positive to say. Nothing came to me. A feeling of helplessness surrounded me. There was nothing I could say. Nothing I could do to make things better.

"Anne, I'm sorry," I said in desperation, "I just don't know what to do."

Anne's eyes shot open. She didn't waste a second in replying. "Put it in the book." Her eyes looked directly into mine, not wavering an iota.

I knew immediately what she meant. She wanted her story told and she wanted me to tell it. I wasn't sure I was ready to accept that responsibility. But then again, what choice did I have? I was the only one who truly could tell it. Anne's request settled around my shoulders, feeling somewhat a cross between a burden and a blessing.

"Did you hear me?" Anne's voice was weak but her gaze pierced.

"I heard," I replied, my heart thumping wildly with the thought of trying to fulfill her request.

"Then do it." Her eyelids drifted down.

"Right now?" I asked, making my voice light.

"I suppose you can wait a little bit." Anne's voice was frail, but held a hint of teasing.

Footsteps pounded down the hall, the sound followed by Jimmy Jr. and Cari flying past Anne's doorway, on down the hall. From the opposite end of the corridor Andrea yelled, "You two stop that running right now."

I raised my eyebrows towards Anne. "I think I'm going to run over to the mall and finish my Christmas shopping. Can you handle them alone for a while?"

Anne smiled. "I can always pretend I'm sleeping."

"Good idea," I responded, turning to go.

As I reached the doorway Anne stopped me. "Libby, wait, we forgot to think of something worse."

My heart sank to my stomach. What could possibly be worse than the doctor telling Anne there was nothing more he could do for her? I was speechless—the woman of words wracking her brain for words that didn't exist. I could hear Andrea and Evelyn approaching.

Finally, Anne spoke. "I know!" she said, sounding as if she'd made a grand discovery.

I waited to hear what it could possibly be.

"What would be so much worse would be if Janey were going through this instead of me."

Just then Evelyn stepped around the corner, a look of false cheer pasted on her face. Instantly, I understood the discovery in Anne's words. As tragic as it would be for Anne to watch Janey suffer through an illness such as this, that was *exactly* what Evelyn was doing—watching life seep from her own daughter.

For the first time since I'd met her, I could have hugged Evelyn. A warm feeling of compassion swept through me as I looked at her. Instead of seeing a talkative, flighty, self-centered woman, I saw a suffering mother. I reached out and squeezed her shoulder. "Take care, Evelyn."

"We'll be fine, won't we, dear?" She looked at Anne as if for assurance. "Just fine."

⌒

I drove toward the mall, determined to finish my Christmas shopping. My animosity towards Anne's mother and her sister had all but evaporated. I understood now why they were denying Anne's tenuous thread to life. I passed a manger scene set up outside a church. Mary, Joseph, and baby Jesus were frozen into the snow-covered grass.

I watched my child suffer too, Mary seemed to cry out as I drove by. A mother like Evelyn. Mary had been a mother who had watched her child hurt. I thought of Brian. A mother like me.

I know, too.

It came as a quiet whisper and I knew, without question, it was a thought from God. Yes, I thought, Anne would say God too knew what it was like to watch His child suffer.

Almost in reflex, I slammed on the brakes, made a U-turn at the corner, and pulled to a stop across from the church. Without thinking, I climbed the church steps. Finding the door unlocked, I tiptoed into the church, the swish of the door closing echoing through the high-ceilinged foyer. A makeshift stable stood at the front of the church. Green paper palm-shaped leaves were taped to tall carpet rolls stood on end. Three shepherds' staffs were laid neatly near the manger.

I stood at the back of the church, staring at the silent tableau. I'd attended many Christmas programs, the one time of year it seemed fitting to go to church. Always before, by the time I'd arrived at church, the sanctuary had been filled with people. Gold-tinseled angels roamed the foyer; pajama-robed shepherds shifted nervously, waiting for their cues. A miniature innkeeper glared from his inn, waiting impatiently to say his two important words. "No room!"

This late afternoon, all looked different. There were no angels hovering, no shepherds attending imaginary sheep. No innkeeper with ready refusal on his lips. All distractions were missing. It was just me and an empty stable. The stable looked as my heart felt. Lifeless.

Without warning, hot tears began streaming down my face. *What am I supposed to do? I feel so helpless. Am I supposed to want to exchange places with Anne? Isn't that what a true friend would do?*

Images of Brian and Emily flashed through my mind. A picture of Bob as he'd looked when we'd first met came to mind as well. *I don't want to leave them. My time with them isn't done. I have too much to teach them. Too much I need to tell Bob. What's worse, to be Anne, facing death? Or to be me, unable to do anything but watch my friend suffer? What can I do?*

My breath shuddered as I gasped for air, trying to control my suddenly out-of-control emotions. I stood in the center of the church aisle, silently crying until no more tears would come. I closed my eyes, drawing a deep breath. Raising my chin in a gesture of bravery, I opened my eyes and found myself looking directly at a huge cross hanging from the wall above the empty stable.

Okay, God, You tell me—what am I supposed to do? Who am I supposed to talk to if Anne is gone? Why are You...

"Can I help you?" A woman's voice called out. I must have jumped in alarm, as she quickly added, "I didn't mean to startle you. We just finished our program practice and I was in the back hanging costumes. Are you looking for the pastor?"

"No, no. I'm sorry to bother you," I apologized. "I just stopped to—" What had I stopped here for? I took a step backwards. "I've really got to get going." I wondered what I must look like, a strange woman crying over a manger scene. Just so I didn't appear completely crazed, I made an attempt at normal conversation. I motioned to the manger scene. "That looks like a lot of work. Did you make it?"

"Well, I did—and about ten other mothers. It seems every year someone gets new carpeting and we get to add another palm tree." She smiled, swinging her arm toward the surprisingly realistic-looking trees. "We joke about it, saying we'd rather recarpet and get a forest up there than try to make a new baby Jesus every year. We use a doll," she explained.

"Very practical," I commented, wondering why I continued to stand there, talking to a stranger.

The woman had walked halfway down the aisle as we'd been talking. Now she extended her hand and walked rapidly toward me. "Katie," she said. "Katie Jeffries. And you are?"

Automatically I thrust out my hand. "Olivia, uh, Libby. Libby Marsden." I'd corrected myself without conscious thought. It was the first time I'd ever introduced myself to someone as Libby.

"Pleased to meet you, Libby." Katie turned and faced the front, putting her hands on her hips, surveying her handiwork. *And ten other mothers,* I mentally added. "This is one of my favorite times of the season," she stated softly.

"What do you mean?" I asked, still wondering why I was continuing this conversation. Normally, I would have turned on my heel and been out the door the minute I had discovered someone else there. Heck, normally I would have never stopped in the first place. Yet there I stood.

"I love being alone in here after everyone leaves," Katie explained. "It's so quiet. Like the hymn—all is calm, you know?"

"But it's so empty."

"Oh, that's the beauty of it," Katie marveled. "I stand here and I look at that simple stable and I know it's just waiting to be filled. With the Son of God, no less."

Like your heart?

Was that my thought? Or had it come from somewhere else?

Katie's voice filled with a tone of wonder. "Imagine."

"Yes," I echoed, feeling a small bit of wonder myself. "Just imagine."

Katie walked me to the church door. "Our program is at seven-thirty on Christmas Eve. Don't expect wonders; it is just a children's pageant, after all. But I always feel as if something of a miracle has happened by the time we're done. You're certainly welcome."

"We'll see," I offered meekly, knowing full well I wouldn't attend.

"It was nice to meet you, Libby. Take care."

Take care. The same words I'd used to comfort Evelyn.

The small bit of wonder I'd felt in the church stayed with me as I drove to the mall. "All is calm," Katie had said. And that was how I felt. Calm. Not anxious and worried as I had been the past two days over Anne. Was this Anne's secret? Was this what God provided for her?

But my inner critic chided, *I thought you didn't believe in Him.*

Maybe it's you I shouldn't believe in, I said back to my critical voice.

Well now, getting soft, are we?

Maybe I'm getting smart.

Since when did you decide you needed a crutch? I thought you could handle things all by yourself.

My sense of wonder was starting to be replaced by the knot of worry I'd carried around all my life. I pushed it away, determined to hang onto the feeling I'd captured while standing in front of the empty stable.

Just waiting to be filled?

This time it wasn't my critical voice speaking—it was a whisper filled with longing. Filled with hope.

I entered the mall, prepared to zip from store to store, picking up a sweater for Bob at Eddie Bauer, new jeans and a Vikings jersey for Brian. Emily had a list a mile long that included items from most any store in the mall. She would be a snap to please. And I hadn't yet purchased a gift for Anne.

The mall was packed with late-afternoon, last-minute shoppers like me. I realized my plan of zipping through the mall wasn't going to happen as I threaded my way through throngs of shoppers, no one looking particularly pleased to be there. Even though the mall was crowded, there was an emptiness there I'd never noticed before. The signs calling out, "Big Sale," seemed instead to say, "Big *Deal.*" Christmas music that previously had served to add excitement to the air only sounded false when I imagined Anne lying in her hospital bed. The prices on the merchandise didn't seem to matter as I thought of Anne and her medical care. Anything, anything at all if it would make Anne better.

What do you buy for a friend who may be dying? I wandered through the stores, picking up items that turned into meaningless trinkets in my hands. I couldn't get Anne anything to wear—who knew if she'd ever leave the hospital? A book seemed pointless; would she live long enough to finish it? Pushing aside my gloomy thoughts, I decided to look for a gift for Janey first. I wandered into a children's shop I'd always bypassed, never finding a need for the toddler-sized clothes the windows featured. I found myself pulled away from the little clothes I'd thought to buy to a small selection of unique toys and knickknacks, displayed on a high shelf. My eyes were drawn to the figure of an innocent little girl, encased in a child's snow globe. It was one of those toys where an elaborate scene is captured forever in water. This one contained only the little girl, wrapped tight in a ragged, red winter coat, looking up into the sky as if expecting something miraculous to appear any second. When I shook the globe, a sprinkling of fairy dust spread through the watery sky as if coating the little girl's world in magic powder. Who would want a straggly urchin like this? I turned the globe over, expecting to read a name describing the scene, saying something inane like, "Santa's On His

Way." Instead, I found six unexpected words. "Have hope…A Child is Born."

The stable will be filled.

"Can you wrap this for me?" I asked the clerk who had suddenly appeared at my elbow.

"Certainly," she replied. "And whose name should I put on the gift tag?"

"Anne," I said simply, forgetting all about a gift for Janey.

Anne was sleeping when I stopped by her room after my trip to the mall. Her family had left. Kevin held a lonely vigil by Anne's bed.

"She's slept almost all afternoon," Kevin told me, not even trying to keep his voice down. I had the feeling he was hoping Anne would wake up.

"How did things go with her mom and Andrea?" I asked, pulling a chair close to Kevin.

"They finally decided to leave." Kevin sounded stunned, as if he couldn't believe he was living through this nightmare. "All she did was lay there." He motioned toward the bed. "Like that."

It seemed as if Anne had barely moved since I'd left several hours earlier. Her funky auburn hair stuck up at odd angles from her head, making her face appear that much paler against the stark white hospital linens. The plastic hospital ID band hung from her skinny wrist as if it were a piece of bad jewelry. Somehow Anne had managed to kick one of her legs out of the covers, her flimsy hospital gown riding high on her hip. I got up and slid Anne's gown down over her hip, tucking her leg back under the thin covers.

"It's almost supper time," I said to Kevin. "Go to the cafeteria and get something to eat. I'll stay here with Anne."

"I'm bringing Janey tomorrow," he announced, speaking more to Anne than to me. "She needs to see her mom."

I rubbed Anne's thin arm, it felt cool. I fought back a sudden closing sensation in my throat. "Yes, Janey should see her mom," I agreed. "And Janey's dad needs to eat. Now go."

Kevin rose, his clothes hanging from his body. He'd lost weight. I'd been so focused on Anne I hadn't thought much about how Kevin might be handling the situation. I hadn't even given much thought to my own mixed-up life. Just days ago I'd been obsessed with myself. Worrying if I had the ability to write a novel. Worrying what I could possibly write about. I'd worried about Brian and the encounter he'd had with drugs. And I'd fretted about the state of my marriage. Nothing had really changed, and yet everything had. After my short time in a crowded shopping mall and an empty church, I saw my life through different eyes. There was hope to be found for an urchin girl. Hope in an empty stable. I could see now it was the people in my life who made it worth living. I was determined to let them know what I had discovered.

With my foot I pulled the chair to Anne's bedside. I sat down, continuing to hold her hand, rub her arm. Anything to stay connected to this friend of mine.

"Anne," I said tentatively, not sure I should be waking her up. When I received no response I said her name again, louder this time. "Anne!" She didn't respond, but I kept talking anyway. "It's me, Libby. Anne, you've got to get better. Do you hear me?" She lay there, unmoving, except for the steady up and down motion of her flat chest. "I went to a church today." I thought for sure that would get her eyes open. It didn't. "I'm thinking about all that stuff you've told me. About prayer, and gifts. I don't have it figured out yet, and that's why you need to get better, Anne. So you can help me. Do you hear me, Anne? I need you to get *better*." My voice echoed in the silent room, the steady movement of Anne's chest the only indication she was still there.

For a long time after Kevin returned I sat by Anne's bedside, holding her hand. Unwilling to let go.

∼

By the time I pulled into the driveway, all the lights in the house were off. My talk with Bob would have to wait for another day.

At least we had another day.

I wasn't so sure Anne did.

Anne

Almost as fast as I'd landed in the hospital, I was home. Even pragmatic Dr. Barrows couldn't explain my sudden recovery. He'd given me one more blood transfusion, only because Kevin insisted he was going to bring Janey to the hospital, and he wanted me to be able to hold her when he did.

I knew it wasn't logical, but I hadn't wanted to see Janey while I was supposedly dying. I knew she'd have no conscious memory of me lying in that hospital bed, but I just had this strange sense I wanted her to remember me at home, playing with her. Maybe it was me who didn't want to be reminded of what I was losing.

I was sitting up in bed, holding Janey on my lap, when Dr. Barrows came into my room.

"I can't explain it," Dr. Barrows said in greeting, his flat voice not sounding at all amazed. "Your blood work is quite good today. How are you feeling?"

I hadn't thought about how I was feeling. I'd been more concerned about being strong enough to hold Janey. Preparing myself emotionally to see her. I had wanted to be cheerful and loving, with no hint of illness to cloud our time together. I realized now, when Dr. Barrows asked, that I was feeling surprisingly healthy. The pain in my back, while not gone, had subsided considerably, and the overwhelming urge I'd felt to sleep almost constantly was gone.

"Actually, I'm feeling quite good." I clapped Janey's hands together, emphasizing the word 'good.' Janey produced a squeal of delight, and I continued to clap her hands together, repeating, "Good! Good! Good!"

Dr. Barrows removed the stethoscope from his neck. "Could you hold your child a moment?" he asked Kevin, leaning to listen at my back. "Deep breath, please." He moved the instrument several times, listening intently. "Like a drum," he remarked under his breath. "Steady as a drum." He straightened, placing his stethoscope in the pocket of his white lab coat. "The only explanation I have is that in some fashion your tumor has shifted position slightly, so the intense pressure you were feeling has been alleviated. For now. It must have been pressing against the nerves in your spinal column to cause your back to spasm in such a manner that—"

Kevin broke in. "Is she getting better? Is that what you're trying to tell us?"

"No." Dr. Barrows raised his hand in a "hold on a minute" gesture. "I'm sorry if I led you to believe that. Cancer doesn't just disappear. No, Anne's tumor is still there, that I can assure you. It's just that it seems to have..." he paused, searching for an explanation for my renewed body. "Anne seems to have... well, let's just say she's been given a Christmas gift." Dr. Barrows actually smiled at me. "I'm sending you home, Anne." Then he was right back to business. "I want you back here, starting tomorrow. As long as this tumor is cooperating, I want to get you started on radiation treatments. Maybe we've been given another chance. We'll shrink that tumor as much as we can, then we'll see what your doctors in Rochester have to say. Chemotherapy, possibly surgery, could be an option. We'll see."

~

It was a weird feeling to return home, to see everything as I'd left it. I'd been through so much the past couple days. "On the brink of death," Dr. Barrows had told Kevin. It seemed as if the things around me should have changed in some undefined way, but there they were just as I'd left them.

The cookies I'd been baking the day of my hospitalization were still sitting on my kitchen counter, hard as rocks. Kevin apologized for not putting them away, but since Janey had spent the past two days at Libby's house, I knew Kevin hadn't been in the house for more than a change of clothes, if even that by the wrinkled look of him.

The Christmas tree stood straight and tall, and the lights Kevin plugged in as we'd walked in the door blinked out a welcome. Presents under the tree, arranged just so. The ornament Brian had given Janey lay on the kitchen table, the bright and crumpled wrappings surrounding it. I grabbed the ornament off the table and hung it, front and center, on the tree.

"You'd better rest," Kevin reminded as I walked to the kitchen to figure out what to do with my cement-like cookies.

I had to agree. I was feeling sluggish. It seemed impossible that two days of sleeping could have made me tired. "I'll lay down on the couch as soon as I get these cookies taken care of."

Kevin grabbed the cooling rack where the cookies lay and with one swift motion tossed them into the garbage can. "Voila!" he announced. "No more excuses. Go lie down."

I lay back on the couch, a pillow propped under my head. Kevin covered me with a quilt his grandmother had made for him as a high school graduation present, then spread another blanket on the floor near the couch, laying Janey on the floor beside him. Without warning, I felt a pain in my upper back. *Oh, no*, was my initial thought, until I realized it was the bulging spring in the cushion.

"Kevin," I said, "no matter what happens I want you to—"

"Anne!" Kevin cut me off sharply. "Please don't talk about that now. Let's just have a regular day at home."

"No, it's not about that. What I was going to say is, no matter what happens, keep the new couch when it comes. This thing is a pain in the back. My hospital bed was more comfortable than this couch."

Kevin jumped up and brought another pillow to put under me. After I was comfortable, Kevin sat down. Threading his finger through Janey's, he jiggled her tiny fist until she kicked in glee and let go, then they started over again. After a time, Kevin handed Janey a rattle, then turned to face me. "Anne," he said, "I know I just said I didn't want to talk about this stuff but…" He closed his eyes for a moment, then looked at me. "There's something we have to discuss."

I knew it must be something serious and nodded, encouraging him to go on.

"I don't know how much longer I can do this."

What did he mean, do this? Play with Janey? Sit on the floor? Stay married to a woman with cancer? My heart started racing.

My face must have mirrored my thoughts as Kevin quickly elaborated. "I mean live like this. I mean—I'm sorry, I'm not saying this well." He turned to pick up the rattle Janey had dropped, using the time to focus his thoughts. "What I'm trying to say, Anne, is that we are...well, I am, running on empty. I can't keep spending days at the hospital, trying to fit in an hour or two of work here and there, and trying to keep track of Janey. My job is on the line. I hate to even tell you this; you shouldn't have to worry about it. But we've got to have money to live on. That's just fact." He stopped as if he'd run out of air.

"Do you have any ideas?" I asked slowly, knowing what he said was true.

Kevin nodded, deliberately. "I even hate to mention this, but it's the only idea I can come up with." He paused, then spoke quickly, "I think we're going to have to move. If we move nearer to your folks, Andrea and your mom could help with Janey, and it's a whole lot closer to my main office. I've been talking to my boss, and he said they could arrange things so I could be in the office more rather than out on the road. At least until things stabilize with your health. I'm sorry, Anne, I don't know what else to do."

I lay, letting his words sink in. "Can I think about it?" I understood the practicality of his suggestion, but needed time to absorb what he'd said.

"Sure," he answered, then added with a twinkle in his eye, "I wasn't planning to start packing for another hour or so." He heaved a huge sigh. "I thought you'd be upset."

I shook my head. I knew Kevin's suggestion was our only option. I wasn't able to keep up with the day to day tasks of caring for an infant. And who knew how long it might take for me to get well? I could see how the past few days had drained my husband physically and emotionally. How could I disagree when he was trying his best to take care of us?

"No," I replied, "I'm not upset. I'm just glad God gave me you for a husband." I reached out and stroked his cheek. "I love you, you know."

Blinking rapidly, he nodded.

"I'm just going to ask you one tiny favor, okay?"

Again, he nodded.

"You tell Libby and Brian."

His eyes widened, a look of sheer panic flashing across his face. "I never thought about that part."

I let him off the hook. "I was joking," I told him, not smiling at all. "If it's possible to joke about that part."

"I hear you," Kevin empathized. And, I think really he did.

~

We spent a regular day, as Kevin had wished, lying around the living room, eating popcorn, watching Christmas movies on the VCR. Late in the afternoon, Kevin started my absolute favorite Christmas movie. *It's a Wonderful Life* flashed across the screen. Janey settled into a nap, Kevin leaned against the sofa in a spot where I could lace my fingers through his hair. It felt good to be close to him.

As the angel in the movie bumbled his way into the plot, Kevin asked softly, "Have you ever wondered why?"

I knew immediately what he was asking. Why me? Why us? I massaged my fingers against Kevin's scalp, his head rotating toward my hand like a dog needing love from his master. "I've only asked once, and I knew instantly what the answer was. I haven't had to wonder again."

"Well, could you tell me?" he asked, moving his head into my hand in an effort to get closer. "Because I don't understand."

I remembered the day when I'd prayed, asking God the question Kevin was asking me now. *Why, God? Why me? Why should I, a young wife and mother, be diagnosed with cancer when there were all kinds of people who surely had less to live for? A hopeless drunk. A homeless person. What about a child abuser, or a murderer? Why me?*

The answer floated into my heart, my mind, almost as an assurance of God's great love. Why *not* me?

I understood. In God's eyes we were all equal. No one more deserving, no one less. He loved us equally. He would be with each of us, no matter our goodness, no matter our sin. Whatever our earthly trials, He would be with us. This cancer was my burden to bear, but God would be with me no matter what happened to my earthly body. I only needed to ask.

"And," I explained to Kevin, "He'll be with you. Janey too."

Kevin climbed onto the couch, sliding around behind me so that I rested against his strong body, his arms holding me close. Halfway through the movie I could hear his light snores. Apparently, all my sleeping in the hospital had caught up with me; for once I was wide-awake. As the late afternoon sun sunk into the horizon, the multi-colored lights on our Christmas tree filled our home with a warm glow. I watched Jimmy Stewart, playing the character of George Bailey, as he saw what life would have been like in his home town if he'd managed to escape its confines as he had hoped. It became clear to him that everyone he'd known, everyone he'd loved, would have been profoundly different if it hadn't been for his involvement in their lives.

As the credits rolled, I found myself praying. *Lord, thank You for showing me through this movie that even when I can't see Your purpose, You are there. I know You have used my illness as a blessing in my marriage. Thank You for the closeness Kevin and I have shared. I don't know if our relationship would have grown as much without the challenge of my illness. Thank You, Lord. Continue to pour out Your blessings on Janey. Thank You for Brian and the way he has taken on his role of godfather to Jane. Use this relationship for Your purposes. Bless Emily. Lord, keep her close to You, let her hear Your call. Work in Bob and Libby's marriage as well. Smooth out their rough spots and draw them close. And Lord, I especially pray for Libby. I ask that You would use me in whatever way You can to show her Your great and boundless love. Use me Lord, to bring her to You.*

I had often prayed for Libby. I'd been pleasantly surprised to see her in our church the Sunday after Janey's baptism. Brian and Emily had come too. Libby caught my eye as she walked down the aisle after the service, but didn't stay to visit. She quickly donned her coat, then herded her family out the door. Emily turned and gave me a quick wave before the door closed behind her. When I asked Libby on Monday how she had liked the service, she politely offered, "It was nice," then changed the subject. While Libby didn't seem open to a discussion of her spiritual life, I did sense a softening that hadn't been there before. Other than offering my friendship and prayers, I didn't have much else to contribute. Especially in my current condition, which was flat on my back.

All I could do was to continue to pray.

Use me Lord. Use me.

An Ending...of Sorts

Olivia

Anne got home from the hospital the same day she and I had originally been scheduled to leave for her tests in Rochester. It seemed ironic; there certainly had been no need for us to drive that far to find out her cancer had returned.

Dr. Barrows was his usual cautious self, not calling Anne's sudden rebound anything other than, "a shifting of tissue mass." Even Anne didn't call it a miracle, although I heard several others call it that. Anne admitted she still had pain in her back, just not as much. Hopefully, the radiation treatments would take care of it.

Without missing a beat, we were on the road to Carlton the next day to start Anne's series of radiation treatments. Anne was somewhat subdued during our time together. I chalked it up to apprehension over her treatments and the bad reaction she'd had during her last series. I didn't mind filling the silence. After all, I had almost three days worth of news to tell her—things I hadn't told her while she was in the hospital.

The second day, after Anne's treatment, she suggested we stop at Applebee's for lunch before heading back to Brewster. I was glad to oblige; glad Anne had not started feeling any side effects from the radiation treatments.

We ordered, then sipped our coffee. Janey was content with a bottle in her infant seat. Again, Anne was uncharacteristically quiet.

"Is there something wrong?" I asked, reaching my hand across the table, not quite touching her.

Even though Anne didn't use cream or sugar, she picked up her spoon and stirred her coffee. The soft tinkling of the spoon against the cup was the only sound she made. Finally, after what seemed forever, Anne looked up, her eyes filled with tears. "We have to move."

For a fleeting second I thought she meant we had to switch booths. I shifted my eyes, looking for the reason Anne felt we had to sit somewhere else. In another second her true meaning struck. "What?" The word escaped just before my throat closed. Uncharacteristically, my eyes too filled with tears.

Anne nodded, one tear rolling down her cheek. "I didn't know how to tell you."

"No." My brain wasn't grasping what Anne had said. But somewhere, deep down, it seemed as if I had known it was inevitable. Anne was going to be leaving.

"We have to." She reached forward and grabbed my outstretched hand. "I don't want to, but we have to. We need help, Libby. Kevin has to be able to work. And I'm just not able to take care of Janey all day, much less if Kevin has to go out of town."

I wanted to interrupt and say, "I can help. I can watch Janey." But I knew the kind of help they needed was more than I alone could give.

Anne squeezed my hand. "We need to be closer to my treatments, to doctors. It takes too much out of all of us to be driving so far for appointments." She paused. "After all, we have no idea how long this could go on. It could be years. And I hope it is," she added with an optimistic smile, her eyes glistening.

"Where are you going?" I was blinking back tears myself.

"I know you're going to think this is nuts, but we're going to move closer to my folks and Andrea."

"But—"

"I know," Anne stopped me. "I know they haven't seemed that supportive, but they will be if I'm there. They just haven't been around enough to know how to help. There's a good hospital there, and it's where Kevin's home office is. He's talked to his boss, and he can have a job in the office until things settle down."

I slumped in the booth. I thought I'd been prepared for Anne to die, but this felt almost as bad. "What am I supposed to do without you here?" I asked, my voice a pitiful whine.

"I feel the same way," Anne said just as our food arrived.

We pushed our salads from side to side on our plates, pretending to eat.

I laid down my fork. "Okay, answer this, who is going to give Emily piano lessons? Who am I supposed to go shopping with? Or have coffee with? Or complain to about my kids or Bob? Tell me." I sounded mad.

Anne shook her head. "I've thought about all that stuff. I don't know. We'll call. We'll visit. It's not that far." Her eyes filled again.

I rolled mine, trying to keep my own tears from falling over. "I'm sorry. I know you have to do this. It's just that I don't want you to—" I broke off, unable to talk anymore.

We were silent as the waiter cleared away our almost-full plates. "Was there something wrong with your meals?"

Solemnly, as if someone had died instead of saying she was moving, Anne and I shook our heads.

The waiter waited for us to say something. "Whatever," he finally said, and left.

The sound of voices and clinking dishes filled the restaurant, but our booth was cloaked in somber silence.

Anne spoke first. "Do you realize we're sitting here pouting like two little kids? Let's try to be mature about this. Let's think of something worse." Then, before I even had a chance to breathe much less think of something, Anne pointed out, "I could be leaving *in* a box, instead of *with* boxes."

For a brief moment Anne's irreverent comment hung between us, then we burst out laughing at her macabre joke, nervous tension easing away.

"Now *that* would be worse," I observed, in the understatement of the year.

I had made up my mind to enjoy the time I had left with Anne before she moved. I vowed not to even think about what life would be like without her to talk to every day. I remembered with chagrin the horrible fight I'd had with Anne. How empty my days had been during the time I'd stubbornly refused to speak to her. How wasteful that time seemed now. No, I wasn't even going to think about her leaving until I was forced to. After all, Anne and Kevin weren't going to look for a place to live until after Christmas, and Anne's latest round of radiation treatments were over. In the meantime, I was glad to volunteer to drive Anne to her appointments, determined to enjoy every moment we had together. I no longer felt my usual angst, torn between getting things done around the house and the thought that I should be writing something, anything, just so I could call myself a writer. For now I'd been given a reprieve. For once in my life I felt as if I was doing exactly what I'd been put on this planet to do—help Anne.

Christmas was in four days, and Anne and I had decided she would come to my house after her radiation treatment for our gift exchange. I could hardly wait to give Anne the snow globe I had purchased so impulsively while she had been in the hospital. In light of Anne's recovery, its message seemed even more confident. *Have hope.* Hope, not only for Anne's health, but also for their upcoming move and for our friendship. Just because she would be moving didn't mean our friendship would have to end—it would just be different.

I wanted to make the afternoon special, so I dug out my only linen tablecloth, passed down from my grandmother to my mom and from my mom to me. At the time, I accused my mother of giving it to me only because she hated to iron. She didn't deny it. As I diligently pressed the wrinkles from the creamy white cloth, I wondered how soon I could pass the tablecloth on to Emily.

Keeping one eye on the clock since Anne was expecting me to pick her up late morning, I spread the crisply-ironed cloth on my dining table, smoothing the warm fabric with my hands. I had to admit there was a gratifying sense of satisfaction seeing the heirloom, the *hand-pressed* heirloom, on my table. I pulled my wedding china from the cupboard—two dessert plates, two cups and saucers, real silverware, and two crystal water goblets. I set two more plates off to the side, knowing Brian and Emily would be home from school before Anne's and my gift exchange was over. They would want to visit with Anne and Janey, and it wouldn't hurt them to practice their company manners at the same time.

I pulled my silver candlesticks from the cupboard, groaning to see how tarnished they were. Fortunately, since I polished them so seldom, I had a lifetime supply of polish on hand. I was going to have to put things in high gear if I was going to get to Anne's on time. I swiped the gooey cream on and wiped it off almost in the same motion, marveling at the memory of my aunt's always-gleaming silver tea service sitting on her dining room buffet. Obviously, the woman had no hobbies. I rinsed the now-shining metal under hot water, wiped it down, then jammed two white candles into the openings, quickly placing them on the table. I needed to leave *now*. As I threw on my coat, I looked over the table. The old-fashioned linen was the perfect base for my gold-trimmed plates. My crystal and polished silver glistened in the overhead light, turning the snowy gray morning into a sparkling retreat. Even though I'd read it was improper to light candles during the day, I had resolved to break that rule, deciding a Christmas gift exchange with the best friend I'd ever had in my life was an exception. Daytime or not.

Just as I reached for my bulky winter coat the phone rang. No, I didn't have time to answer it. We did have an answering machine, after all; let it do its job. The phone rang again as I quickly zipped my coat. Tossing my scarf around my neck, I reached for my car keys on top of the fridge. Not there.The phone rang a third time. I patted my pockets—nothing but crumpled tissues. The answering machine clicked on, Emily's recorded voice saying, "This is the Marsden's. We can't answer the phone right now. Please leave a message." And then, as an afterthought, she quickly blurted one long word, "Afterthebeep." I chuckled to myself, making a mental note to have Emily re-record the message. There the keys were, practically buried beside a pile of mail. My hand was on the doorknob when I heard the caller speak, "Hiiiiyiii, Libby? Oh, please don't be gone."

It was Anne.

I snatched up the receiver. "I'm on my way!"

I had the phone practically hung up before I heard Anne say, "Wait!"

I looked at the receiver in my hand. I had been in such a hurry to get going I still felt as if I should slam it down and take off for Anne's. I was in "go" mode.

"Libby?" Anne called into the receiver as if I wasn't on the other end, shaking me out of my momentary inertia.

"What's up?" I asked, finally putting the phone to my ear, then turning and leaning against the counter. For the first time since the kids had left for school, their last day before vacation, I looked out the window. Huge flakes of snowman-making snow were falling to the ground in a thick haze.

"We're going to have to go to 'Plan B,' Anne explained. "Janey's running a temperature. I hate to drag her all the way to Carlton if she's not feeling well. I was wondering if I could drop her off at your house?"

"What about your appointment?" A heat wave enveloped me inside my down-filled coat. "I was just on my way out the door to pick you up." I unzipped my coat, fanning myself with the ends of my scarf. "Are you sure you feel well enough to drive there and back by yourself?" I had driven Anne to practically every appointment she'd had in Carlton. It seemed strange to think of her going there alone. What would Anne do without Janey and I there to while away the time?

"I'm feeling really good," Anne declared. "I don't think it will be a problem at all if you don't mind watching Janey. I have to warn you, she's kind of crabby. I thought when I get back we could do our gift exchange. Does that work for you?"

"Sure does," I replied, relieved to be shrugging out of my furnace-like coat. "Bring her over. That'll give me time to fix some fancy little sandwiches for our party." I was glad I had rushed through the morning, setting the table before I planned to leave. This new arrangement would leave me a few hours to wrap last-minute Christmas gifts and make something special for our Christmas coffee later in the afternoon. It was a good idea, anyway.

Ten minutes later Anne drove up. I could hear Janey screaming from outside the door.

"Don't say I didn't warn you," Anne shouted over Janey's wails. Wet flakes of snow clung to her coat and the blanket covering Jane. "I called her doctor, and he said to give her some baby aspirin…well, not *aspirin*, but baby medicine. I just gave her some, so hopefully she'll settle down in a little bit. If she's not better by tomorrow I'm supposed to bring her in; she could have an ear infection, he said." Anne handed Janey to me. Even through the thick quilt covering her head, Janey's cries were piercing. Anne slid a large diaper bag off her arm onto the floor. "Oh no!" she moaned, spotting the fancy table I'd set for our party. "I forgot your gift. It's lying right by the front door."

"Swing by and pick it up when you get back to town this afternoon. It'll only take you a second," I pointed out, unwrapping Janey as best I could with one hand.

"I'll do that." Anne leaned over and kissed Janey's red cheek. "Now be good for Auntie Libby." Anne gave me a wide-eyed look, speaking with her teeth clenched, as if she didn't want Janey to hear. "I hate to leave her with you when she's being so fussy."

"Don't worry," I assured. "We'll be fine. Get going, then you can be back sooner and we can have our Christmas party."

Janey cried continuously for the next two hours, only stopping to draw in a long breath for another round of wailing. I walked her and rocked her, I wrapped her tightly and laid her down. I tried holding her over my shoulder, in my arms, across my swaying legs while sitting. She wanted nothing to do with a bottle, and the three times I checked her diaper only once was she wet, and then not enough to cause that kind of commotion. Needless to say, my fancy little sandwiches didn't get made; neither did my gifts get wrapped. I was beginning to think something was seriously wrong with Janey, when suddenly, as if a switch had been flipped, she stopped crying and fell into an exhausted sleep in my arms. In relief, I closed my eyes, too.

The next thing I knew, Bob was standing at the foot of the couch, looking down at me. My first reaction, which I managed to stifle for Janey's sake, was to jump up and deny I'd been napping. I *never* napped, but since Bob had caught me in the act it was hard to plead innocent.

My second reaction was to over-explain. "Anne had to drop Janey off because she wasn't feeling well, and then Janey cried and cried and nothing I did made her stop, and I wanted to get things ready for the party Anne and I were going to have when she gets back but I couldn't get—"

It was about then it dawned on me that Bob looked as pale as a snowman, and that it was two in the afternoon. He never came home in the middle of the afternoon, unless he was sick.

"Please don't tell me you're sick," I pleaded. I didn't know how I'd muster the energy to tend him all afternoon, not to mention the interference it would cause in my gift exchange with Anne.

Slowly, Bob shook his head. He sat beside me on the couch, rubbing his hand, absently along my forearm.

"Why are you home?" I asked. He was acting really odd. "Did you get fired or something?" I knew things were still unsettled at the bank, but Bob had remained closemouthed about details. It was the only logical explanation I could think of for him to be home in the middle of the afternoon.

"Olivia?" Even his voice sounded odd. "I have to tell you something." He stopped, closing his eyes. At that moment I knew something terrible was coming. All sorts of thoughts ran through my head. He was going to tell me he got fired. He was going to tell me he was having an affair. He was going to say he'd decided to sell our house and move to Istanbul.

Later, when I thought back on that moment, it seemed as if I had thought of every terrible thing in the world he could tell me, except for the thing he actually said. "Anne is dead."

I had no details, but I knew to the very marrow of my bones, what he'd said was true. I carefully placed Janey into Bob's arms, walked to the bathroom, and threw up. Then I started shaking as though I were a leaf caught in an icy winter wind.

As I sat, staring numbly into what had once been my cozy, warm living room, Bob related what he knew in a voice that sounded hollow and strained. "Dan Jordan called me at the bank. He heard the news on the scanner in his office, called a friend of his in the police station in Carlton, and found out it was Anne. I called the police station in Carlton, then the hospital. It's true, Olivia. I didn't want to believe it, but it's true. They let me talk to Dr. Barrows—he'd heard about the accident and was there when they brought Anne in. When I told him I was your husband, he told me all he knew. They're still trying to track down Kevin. His office said he was scheduled to be on the road today."

Like a automaton I nodded. I knew this was a travel day for Kevin.

"Anne was driving through that intersection in Carlton—you know the one where we always comment they should move that sign?"

I cringed. I knew just the intersection Bob was referring to. I could imagine Anne in a hurry to get to her appointment, the heavy snow falling, her thoughts on fussy Janey and the party we were planning. In my mind's eye I visualized Anne absentmindedly cruising through the intersection. "She's such a lousy driver," I croaked. "It's my fault; I was supposed to drive her."

"Olivia, it wasn't your fault and it wasn't Anne's either." Bob rubbed his hand over my knee in a circular motion, trying to comfort. "The light was green. She was behind a pickup, and a delivery van was following her. She was just in the wrong place at the wrong time. It was an elderly man who ran the light on the other street. Didn't even hit the brakes—ran right into her side of the car." Bob moved his hand to my back, rubbing hard across my shoulders. "Olivia, I am so sorry. I know what a good friend Anne has been to you."

With all my heart I wanted to cry, but no tears came. My eyes remained dry. My heart turned to stone—a solid hard lump in the center of my chest. I couldn't imagine how it could possibly keep beating. But it did.

Like a robot, I got off the couch and started clearing the table I'd set for our party. I put the cloth napkins back in the drawer and carefully turned the crystal goblets upside down in the cupboard. The plates and saucers went back on their stacks, the coffee cups nestled together as if they were two best friends.

About forty-five minutes later Kevin called, frantic to find Janey, devastated over Anne. A highway patrolman had stopped him on the interstate and had told him his wife had been in an accident. Only after he arrived at the hospital had they told him the truth. Bob offered to drive to Carlton and bring him home, but Kevin insisted he wanted to be alone for a while, wondered if we could keep Janey. He said he'd call later that night.

Brian and Emily burst through the door, stomping snow from their feet, flushed with the excitement of no school for the next ten days.

"Mom!" Emily yelled, not noticing Bob and I standing together across the room. "Look what I got from my teacher. And our only assignment is to read one book, and we don't have to do a report."

Brian had stopped his foot stomping the second he saw Bob holding Janey. He seemed frozen to the entry rug. Finally, he gave Emily a nudge with the palm of his hand as if to say *be quiet* and then, as if he already knew the answer, asked, "What's wrong?"

Bob and I looked at each other, eyes hooded with pain. What words could we say to our children that would spare them the same anguish we were feeling?

Bob spoke. "Something very bad has happened, kids. I think you'd better sit down so your mother and I can talk to you."

"Are you guys getting a divorce?" Emily queried in a tremulous voice, her eyes darting quickly between us.

Without a word, Brian pulled a chair from the kitchen table and sat down, folding his hands before him, hanging his head as if poised to hear something terrible. Emily's eyes had filled with tears, scared of the unknown. Bob and I joined them at the table, Janey cooing quietly in Bob's arms. He cleared his throat. "I know this is going to be a hard thing for you to understand, kids, but Anne was in a car accident today—"

"Is she hurt?" Emily was almost shouting.

Brian's head shot up, his eyes keenly on his dad, waiting to hear more.

"Yes, Emily," Bob answered, his voice reassuringly calm. "Anne was hurt very badly." Bob waited a moment to let the kids absorb the news, then continued, "She was hurt so badly the doctors couldn't save her. She died this afternoon."

"Noooo!" The word escaped from Emily in an anguished sob. She threw herself out of her chair, into my arms, weeping uncontrollably.

Brian blew out a huff of air, puffing his cheeks in an effort to control his emotions. Slowly he pushed his chair from the table, walked to his dad and gathered Janey into his arms. "I'm going to be in my room for a while," he said, carrying his motherless goddaughter against his heaving chest.

The rest of the night passed in a sort of blur. Bob went and sat with Kevin for a couple hours, bringing home a duffel bag full of clothes, toys, and diapers for Janey. I gave Emily some tea, then ran her a warm bubble bath in an effort to calm her down. Before going to bed she sat at the piano and softly played the "Jesus Loves Me" song Anne had taught her. A huge lump formed in my throat as I watched Emily, in her flannel nightgown, play her favorite piano piece. But still no tears would come from my heart of stone.

Brian would not let go of Janey. I heard him talking to her in his room; later he carried her into the living room, spending most of the evening in the rocker-recliner, steadily rocking himself and Jane. The rhythm was soothing just to watch.

I paced the floor, first waiting for Bob to return with any new scraps of information, then when he arrived with news only of Kevin's great sorrow, I paced, hoping movement would keep me from thinking about what had happened.

It didn't.

My mind raced, thinking of all the things I would miss. Anne's funny, "Hiiii-yiii!" on the phone. Her never-failing optimism. Her sense of humor. The way she could help me sort through a problem just by listening. Her love for my kids. Her love for me.

It wasn't that I hadn't imagined life after Anne in recent days. I had. I'd imagined her dying just a few days ago when she'd been in the hospital. I'd imagined her moving from Brewster, leaving me without a friend. But in all my imagining, I'd always thought I had more time. There would be one more day, one more hour, to tell Anne how much she meant to me. How she had changed me. What a difference she'd made in my life.

Now, as I paced across my living room, through the dining room, into the kitchen, and then back, again and again, I had to face the truth—there was no more time. It was gone. Every second of it. Anne was dead, and I never told her how much she meant to me. How much I had loved her. And what was so ironic was that I'd known Anne was probably going to die, and still I hadn't spoken. Once again, my silent tongue had returned to haunt me.

My heart thumped in my chest, a drummer gone mad, as realization came to me. It could have been anyone in that car. Not just Anne. Bob. The kids. Me. It hadn't been the cancer that killed her, but a car accident. *A stupid car accident.* I walked to the kitchen and stared out the window; a sliver of moonlight reflected starkly off the chunks of snow Bob had shoveled from the driveway. In some way I'd been prepared for Anne to die in the hospital, and yet, when it happened this way, how unprepared I was. Had Anne been ready?

I didn't have to think about that question for a millisecond. I knew exactly what Anne would say. She had been ready to die even before she'd been diagnosed with cancer.

The night seemed endless. None of us could sleep, not even Janey. Brian rocked her through the night. She wasn't fussy, just awake, as if holding vigil along with us for her mother. Around midnight I suggested to Brian that he try to get some sleep, but he shook his head and kept rocking. I didn't have the energy to argue, so I sat there with him.

Emily wandered from her bedroom, rubbing her eyes, complaining she couldn't sleep. "I really tried, Mom. But every time I closed my eyes I kept thinking about Anne and then I'd have to open my eyes to make sure I wasn't having a bad dream."

I patted a spot on the couch beside me, and Emily gratefully nestled in, laying her head on my lap.

After his visit with Kevin, Bob had gone to the bank to clear his desk of some paperwork. He seemed distracted, not at all in his usual work mode. Bob had told Kevin he'd help him sort through some of their financial papers over the next couple days, and he wanted to free up as much time as he could for that project. Bob returned home about the same time Emily joined Brian, Janey, and me, keyed up from work and the strain of the day. "Mind if I join you?" he said, seating himself in an overstuffed easy chair near the couch where I was sitting.

The creak of Brian's rocking chair was the only sound in the room for a long time, creating a rhythm that was oddly comforting. In time, Emily's heavy, even breathing joined in, followed by the slowing of Brian's rocking and his own measured, sleep-filled breath. Janey too had let her heavy-lidded eyes close. It was just Bob and me, awake in the silent room.

Bob broke the silence, speaking softly, "I don't know how Kevin can stand it. If something like that happened to you…" He was quiet a moment. "I don't know what I'd do." He shook his head, as if shaking off a bad dream. "I want to start spending more time at home, Olivia. More time with you and the kids. All this stuff going on at work…it's nothing. In the long run it means *nothing*." His words sounded as though they were a whispered curse in the darkened room, surprising me.

Our relationship lately had been cordial at best. Bob had been distant for some time, but I'd grown comfortable with our separateness. While Bob and I had never had what I would call a soul mate relationship, we enjoyed a comfortable companionship. The fact that Bob was immersed in his work was a lifestyle I'd grown to know. My own father had spent most of his time engrossed in business either at work or at home. The fact Bob wasn't home much, or seemed distracted when he was, felt normal to me. It had never occurred to me to question the way he spent his time. And then this past year, Anne had filled whatever emotional void I might have felt. Bob's vehement statement made me realize just how empty my time would be now that Anne was gone.

"I can't believe how much time I've wasted," Bob said, pressing his lips together in a grim line. "All that time at the office and then, just like that—" He snapped his fingers. "In a second I could be gone. Any of us could be gone. And what would we have to show for it?" He answered his own question. "A clean desk? Files in order? A boss who no longer had someone to cover up for him? What about you and me, Olivia? What about us?"

"Just a minute," I said, waving my hand in a backward, circular motion. "Back up a minute—what do you mean by *a boss who doesn't have someone to cover up for him*? What's going on?" I felt as if the hair on my neck were standing on alert, waiting for Bob to explain his unusual statement.

Bob glanced at the kids, checking to make sure they were asleep. "I've been sick about this, Olivia, just sick. But I didn't know what to do about it. You know how John hired me at the bank? Took pity on this kid who had just graduated from college, but didn't have a lick of experience or a penny to his name?"

I nodded, remembering the day more than fifteen years earlier when Bob had returned from his interview at the bank, saying he wanted to be just like John Erickstad someday. President of a small-town bank, respected in the community for helping those in need. Generous with his time and money for the good of the town. Bob had spent many years trying to live up to John's expectations, trying to model himself after his mentor. Now the tone of his voice was telling me something I wasn't sure I wanted to hear.

"Do you remember when we had those auditors at the bank a year ago last fall? Stayed forever, then came back again a few weeks later? I was putting in extra hours, trying to get records lined up for them?"

I remembered.

"They found some discrepancies in our books. Loan documentation not matching up. Asked me lots of questions I couldn't answer. Told them I'd find out." Bob was speaking in half-sentences, as if filling in the blanks in his mind. "I did some digging. Found out John had put bogus loans on the books. Just made up people. Made up information about them. Used the money for himself."

My heart sank. I knew how much Bob had respected his boss, his mentor. To find this information about John would have been devastating. "What did you do?"

"For a long time I didn't do anything. Somehow John managed to convince the examiners the loans were on the up and up. Friends of his he hadn't bothered to get financial statements from. I sat right there in the meeting with them while John assured the auditors he'd get right on it, get the paperwork up to regulations. At first I believed him. I'd go back at night and look through the files to see if the financial statements had come in, or any other documentation that had been pledged on the loans. Nothing ever showed up. A couple of times I asked John about it. He'd say things like, 'Oh yes, well, the Johnsons are on an extended vacation right now. I've got a note to get in touch with them as soon as they get back.'" Bob rolled his eyes. "I was making excuses to the examiners, promising to follow up with John and get back to them. I believed him, Olivia, I really did. He had never done anything to make me doubt him. I sat right there and told the examiners the same lies John had told me. The loans were such a small part of our portfolio, I think the auditors got tired of trying to follow up on them. I suppose they'll check on the loans the next time through. But the discrepancies got me to wondering, and I kept watching. And then I noticed something—all of the loans that weren't properly documented had names that were combinations of John's kids, close friends, or relatives. Their middle names, married names...some combination that would sound familiar. They just weren't anybody real."

I was stunned, unable to fathom Bob's longtime friend and mentor doing something so unethical. Emily shifted slightly, a sad moan escaping her lips. I stroked her forehead, trying to soothe her dreams along with my disbelief over what Bob was telling me.

Bob hung his head, shaking it slowly in disbelief. Raising his head, he looked me square in the eye. "Olivia, tonight I decided it wasn't worth it. After what happened to Anne, I realized life is too short to live like this. I couldn't pretend I didn't know what was going on. I confronted John tonight, and he didn't deny a thing—just swore he meant to pay back every cent. Funny thing though, he never apologized for lying to me, for making me part of his deception. I'm resigning Olivia. I don't want to work for someone with a character I don't respect."

"I think of all the hours I spent this last year, trying to find out where the errors were, trying to help the auditors, the bank, when in fact it was John's own greediness I was uncovering. I want to spend my time—our time—better than that. I'm sorry, Olivia, for all the time I've been at work, for all the time with you I've missed."

Bob got off his chair and sat on the floor by my feet. Taking my hand in his, he vowed, "I promise I will be a better husband."

I wasn't accustomed to hearing confessions such as Bob's, much less the promise he'd made. I didn't know how to respond. What would our marriage be like if Bob were home more? A lot more? In a way the thought frightened me. Certainly our relationship would have to change. Become closer. Was I ready for that? I didn't know. In response I simply squeezed Bob's hand, leaving my fingers entwined with his. Letting him know I wasn't going anywhere.

We sat in silence, hand in hand, for a long time.

⌐

Much later I awoke, my neck stiff from the awkward angle in which I'd slept, my head perched almost straight back along the top edge of our couch. Sometime during the night, Brian had pushed back the rocking-recliner, settling in for the night with Janey on his chest. Emily's head rested, warm and heavy, in my lap. Bob lay curled on the floor by my feet, his head on one of the couch throw pillows, his fingers encircling my ankle like a warm, beautiful bracelet. I looked at Bob, lying at my feet much as a devoted puppy would. Despite the meager scraps of attention I'd given him over the years, he was still here, loving me, promising to be a better husband. What had I done to deserve him?

At that moment I felt a surge of love so strong I wanted to jump from the couch and embrace Bob, but in doing so I knew I would wake Emily from her troubled sleep. Instead, I rubbed my free ankle against Bob's hand, grateful for his touch. In his sleep, Bob squeezed my ankle, the unconscious gesture causing my heart to ache all the more. I had lost my best friend this day, yet her death had, in some unusual way, returned Bob to me.

"Thank you," I whispered into the cool night air to whomever listened to that sort of thing. "Thank you for giving me Bob."

Then I too made a promise. "I will be a better wife to you, Bob Marsden. I promise I will."

The ringing of the phone woke me the next morning. For the briefest of moments I imagined it was Anne, calling to check on our plans for the day. With thudding clarity the events of the day before came rushing back to me, a sickening sensation washing over me as I eased Emily's head from my lap and dashed to the phone. As I reached for the receiver I noticed Bob was gone from his uncomfortable makeshift bed on the floor; Brian and Janey were still glued together on the recliner.

"Hello?" I found myself whispering, not wanting to wake my children after their late-night watch.

"Libby?" It was Kevin. "Could you come over here? Right now." It was more a statement, than a question. I could hear voices in the background and assumed it was family. Possibly Kevin needed help dealing with Anne's mother. I wasn't sure I was in any frame of mind to handle Evelyn either, but said I'd be over as soon as I could.

Hanging up, I glanced at my watch; it was almost ten, an unheard of hour for me to be sleeping. I rushed to my bedroom and threw on fresh clothes, splashed some water on my face, brushed my teeth. A quick swipe of blush and lipstick and I called it good. Gently I nudged Brian, telling him I was going to run to Anne's, then catching my error I told him, "Kevin's." An already familiar stomach plunge accompanied my correction.

Pulling to the curb in front of Kevin's, I could see through the large picture window there was some sort of commotion going on inside. Our pick-up truck was parked a couple spots ahead of me, which meant Bob was here, too. It wasn't until I walked toward the front door that I noticed the furniture delivery truck in the driveway, mostly hidden by the house. I knew exactly what awaited me inside.

I stood at the closed front door, unsure of what to do. I'd been in the habit of giving Anne's door two quick raps, then letting myself in, listening for Anne's welcoming, "Hiiii-yiii, Libby!" Even though Anne had known I was coming, and seen me walk up the steps, she always sounded surprised and delighted to see me, greeting me with a glad hug. Today I stood on my friends' step, my arm frozen in midair, a statue awaiting release. I knew my knock would not bring the greeting I wanted so badly to hear. It would not bring Anne.

Bob freed me from my indecision. Without waiting for a knock, he opened the door, his voice an intimate welcome of its own. "Olivia." He smiled, memories of our closeness last night in his eyes. "Did you sleep?"

"Eventually." I wiggled my head. "I have a stiff neck to prove it. What's going on?" I nodded to the crowd of people inside.

Bob motioned me in from the cold, closing the door behind me. "People have been stopping by with food since early morning. Anne's folks got here about an hour ago. Then this." Bob waved his hand toward the center of the room.

As if in response to a magician's gesture the crowd parted, leaving my view filled with only Kevin and the red checked couch Anne had ordered months ago.

Words burst from my lips. I couldn't help myself. "It's perfect!" I said to no one in particular. Maybe it was to Anne, wherever she was.

"Perfect?" Evelyn spat the word. "Perfect? What was that girl thinking? My sakes, I have never in my entire life seen a red, much less *checkerboard* couch!" She plopped her hands on her hips. "It's ridiculous! You've got to send it back." Evelyn glared at Kevin.

"It's perfect," I said again, this time moving to put my arm around Kevin. "It's perfectly Anne-like."

"It is, isn't it?" Kevin had tears streaming down his cheeks.

"I wish Anne could be here to see it," I said. "She wanted you to have it, you know."

"I know."

"Uh, Mister?" The high school-aged delivery boy and his young partner looked as uncomfortable as Evelyn. "Uh, what do you want us to do?"

Kevin rubbed the tears from his face in a quick swipe. Composing himself, he gave Evelyn a steady look, then turned to the boys. "Take the old couch and deliver it to a charity. Can you do that?"

"Can my brother be the charity?" the older of the two boys asked. "He just got married and they don't have nothin'."

"Anything," Evelyn corrected. "They don't have anything."

"How'd you know?" The boy stared at Evelyn as if amazed at this stranger's insight.

Our small group chuckled at the misunderstanding.

A flustered Evelyn quickly regrouped. "I suppose it's just as well someone in need gets that old ratty thing. Go on," she directed the boys with a wave of her hand, taking control. "Go on, take it." Evelyn sat down. She watched the boys carry off the old couch, not seeming to realize she'd sat on the previously offending red couch. Absently, she rubbed her hand over the tightly-woven fabric. "It is comfortable, I have to say that. Anne always was one for making people comfortable." At the very end of Evelyn's sentence I heard the tiny catch in her voice. Anne's dad sat down beside her, taking her hand in his.

For the second time since I'd known Evelyn, I had an urge to hug her. She'd obviously had a long night and looked defeated, her eyes red-rimmed, as were Anne's dad's.

I walked behind the couch to stand beside Bob, then reached over the couch back, rubbing my fingers against Evelyn's surprisingly soft shoulder. "We all miss her, you know."

Fumbling for a tissue, Evelyn nodded.

I felt Bob lace his fingers through mine, a gesture of comfort. His gift to me at the start of another difficult day.

We were in this together. All hurting. All dealing with our loss as best we knew how.

⁓

The next two days passed in a hazy blur. I felt as if my brain had been put to sleep in that numbing deadness one feels when they've sat on their leg too long. Occasionally someone would make a remark that would cause the fog to lift momentarily, giving me hope for the days to come. But just as quickly the clouds would roll back, enclosing me in my aloneness. My heart continued to beat as if it were a piece of molten lead, hot and heavy, defying any law of science known to man.

Bob was a rock, not pressing me to speak my thoughts, but ever ready with an arm around my shoulder or a gentle touch on my back. Letting me know he was there, keeping his promise.

Janey stayed with us. Kevin was inundated with relatives and locals dropping by with food and condolences, all well-meaning but draining just the same. I shuttled between Kevin's house and ours, producing Janey for various relatives to coo over, then returning her for Brian and Emily to watch. My kids were troopers, glad for the chance to help.

Jan and Connie, who had virtually disappeared during Anne's illness, now appeared as if by magic, wanting exacting details of Anne's accident.

"I was in shock when I heard the news," Jan said, the whites around her eyes showing as she sat on Anne's new couch. "Absolute shock. Wasn't I, Connie? I mean, I called you immediately, didn't I?" Connie didn't have a chance to respond before Jan continued, "I was at Jacob's getting my hair trimmed when I heard. Why, I didn't even let him finish with my bangs; I just walked right over to the phone and called Connie."

"Yes," Connie said. "I feel so badly that I didn't get over to visit Anne much these past couple weeks."

Weeks? Try months! Anne had never commented, but I had noticed the absence of people who called themselves Anne's friends. At the beginning of Anne's illness many people stopped by or sent cards, but as her condition continued those efforts had all but ended, leaving only a handful of people to offer support. As I listened to Jan and Connie's feeble excuses and condolences I burned inside. Where were you when Anne really needed you?

I remembered a day when I'd stopped to spend the afternoon at the hospital with Anne. As I approached Anne's doorway I could hear her telling the nurse a funny story about Emily that I'd told Anne on the phone earlier in the morning.

"How nice," I'd thought at the time. "Anne thought so much of my little story she wants to repeat it."

But now, listening to Jan and Connie tell me how busy they'd been all winter, I understood; Anne had spent so much time dealing with her illness, she didn't have experiences of her own to tell. She'd had to repeat mine. She had been living, in a sense, through me.

It made me sad to realize that at the end, besides Kevin, Anne had had only me.

And Me.

The unexpected inner voice startled me. But I knew it was true—Anne had had God. It was an oddly comforting thought that my doubting troubled mind mulled over more than once as I politely nodded at Jan, then Connie, not really listening at all.

⁓

Christmas Eve morning found us in church. Unfortunately, it wasn't to sit through an interminable children's program, while my kids counted down the minutes until they could open presents. This time it was for Anne's funeral.

On our way out the door that morning Emily balked. "I don't want to go," she announced, then amended, "Well, I do...but, I don't. Mo-ommm." She burst into tears. Through her sobs Emily explained, "It's just that I've never known... anyone who's died before...except Grandma...and then I was too little to really know about it." She paused, hiccupping a breath. Emily rolled her sheet music into a tight roll. "What if I cry while I'm playing my song?"

So that was the problem. I rubbed her neck, lifting her hair away from her head. It was damp just like her cheeks. "It's okay if you cry, Emily, just keep playing."

"But what if I can't see the music?"

I couldn't help but smile. "Emily," I reminded, "you have played that piece so many times you know it by heart."

"I know I do." Emily breathed deeply, tears continuing down her cheeks.

"Anne loved the way you play that song."

"I know, she told me lots of times."

"Remember how happy Anne looked when you played "Jesus Loves Me" for Janey's baptism?"

Emily blinked her eyes rapidly, gave me a half-smile and nodded.

"Then play it one more time, just for her. Okay?"

Emily unrolled the music, smoothing it flat against her stomach. "Okay, but then do you think I could, like, not play it for a while? It kind of makes me sad."

"I think that would be fine."

How many things would we find in the next days that would remind us of Anne? Make us sad? Make us miss her all over again?

⌒

Anne's funeral was just the way I had listened to her plan it. There wasn't a gladiola in sight. The pastor and I made sure of that. As if we were thieves at a funeral home, we removed eight yellow gladiolas from a large bouquet sent by Kevin's office. The pastor said he'd take them to a parishioner in the retirement home who would be thrilled to get them. Anne would have liked that.

Anne was dressed in the toast-colored suit she'd worn so beautifully the day of Janey's baptism. A flood of memories washed over me as I recalled the day we'd shopped for that outfit, how I'd had to convince Anne to try it on, the way her face lit when she saw how perfect it was. She'd looked so alive the day of Janey's baptism.

Unlike now.

A weight pressed on my chest. My eyes remained dry and scratchy, as if I'd been caught in a dust storm.

The organist played an unfamiliar hymn as we followed Anne's casket into the church. Kevin had asked that our family sit directly behind him. "Anne would want it that way."

The service had barely begun when Janey started fussing. Brian leaned forward and tapped Kevin on the shoulder, holding out his hands in an "I'll take her" gesture. Kevin passed Janey back, and she settled down immediately.

Emily played "Jesus Loves Me" in a slow, heartfelt rhythm I'd never heard her use before, tears streaming down her cheeks through the whole song. She told me later, "I made sure not to cry on my fingers so they wouldn't get slippery." Anne would have liked that too. Brian cried. So did Bob. Everyone was crying it seemed, except me. My heart of stone continued its slow, illogical thumping as the minister stepped into the pulpit.

"I want to start my comments today by reading one of Anne's favorite scriptures. It's from First Corinthians." Anne's pastor adjusted his wire-rimmed glasses, then ran his finger down the page of his Bible, stopping halfway. Raising his head he looked out at the congregation and spoke from memory. "If I speak in the tongues of men and of angels, but have not love, I am only a resounding gong or a clanging cymbal…"

It was as if someone had pulled plugs out of my ears. I'd heard those verses many times before at weddings, but never before at a funeral. Somehow, the words seemed to take on new meaning in the unlikely setting.

"…but have not love, I am nothing. Love is patient, love is kind. It does not boast, it is not proud. It is not rude…not self-seeking. It keeps no record of wrong."

I started squirming in my pew. Over the course of our marriage, my behavior to Bob had been all of those things, and more. What kind of a funeral was this, anyway? I had expected Anne's funeral to be different—after all, I'd helped plan parts of it—but I hadn't expected this. I felt as if the pastor had designed his sermon just for me. He was supposed to be talking about Anne. I shot a sideways glance at Bob, wondering if he was picking up the same message I was. He looked engrossed, not uncomfortable.

The pastor closed his Bible. "And now these three remain: faith, hope, and love. But the greatest of these is love."

He stopped, letting the words settle over the congregation like a comforting quilt. Stepping from behind the pulpit he walked to stand near Kevin, who was sitting in the front pew with Anne's mother and father, Andrea, Jim, and their children.

"These three things…" the pastor repeated, holding up his fingers, counting them off. "Faith. Hope. Love. If you knew Anne, you knew she had faith." He looked at Kevin and I could see Kevin nod in affirmation. "You couldn't be with Anne for more than a few minutes without Anne making some comment that revealed her deep love of God. Many of you may not know this, but Anne's middle name was Faith. She certainly lived it."

I glanced at the minister in surprise. Of all the things I'd known about Anne, I hadn't known her middle name was Faith. How could I not know that? I remembered watching Anne fill out countless medical forms, watching her print A-n-n-e F. A-b-b-o-t. We'd been so busy talking, I'd never thought to ask what the "F" stood for. Knowing Anne, it made perfect sense. Faith. What else did he know about Anne I didn't?

"And, then there's hope. Many of you were here the day Anne and Kevin had their daughter, Janey, baptized." I noticed Brian and Emily listening intently. "You may remember Anne saying her child's name loud and clear that day." The pastor's voice boomed through the church. "Jane Hope Abbot. Hope. That's one gift Anne always had—hope. If not for her physical health, then hope for her daughter, as well as hope for Anne's own eternal well-being."

He paused, walking out to the center of the aisle, standing in front of the burnished oak casket where Anne lay. He stood for a moment looking at the casket, then turned to face the congregation. When he spoke, his voice was filled with tenderness. "And, finally, love. You couldn't know Anne and not know love. *That* she had in abundance. For everyone. If you ever felt Anne's love—and I think it's safe to say everyone sitting here today did—multiply the love you felt times the largest number you can imagine. That amount will only scratch the surface of the love Anne's heavenly Father has for you. I remind you, think on these three things. Faith. Hope. Love." Then after a brief pause he said. "Let us pray."

I felt a restlessness I couldn't identify, a feeling something was waiting for me just outside my grasp. It was a yearning. A longing. For more than Anne—it was for what Anne had. Faith. Hope. Love. But how could I, Olivia Marsden, ever hope to have Anne's faith? Her hope? Her love? I was too weak, and at the same time, too stubborn to ever give myself over to God. I couldn't see a way I could possibly overcome my faults, my failings, my hardheadedness, and simply believe. I shifted, uncomfortable in my seat.

Or was it my skin?

The minister was winding down, thanking everyone for coming, inviting all to stop downstairs for lunch and fellowship. "In closing," he added, "I would like you to open the Bible that's in the pew in front of you to Ezekiel 36, verses 26 and 27."

No one moved.

"Go ahead, I'll wait. You might have to share with your neighbor."

I could hear a few people rustling through pages. The minister stood patiently, smiling at the congregation. I could hear more people pulling Bibles from the holders as questioning whispers filled the air. The Bible in the pew before me glowed as if it were a hot ember, seeming to challenge, *open me*. Like a hardheaded mule, I folded my arms across my chest, trying to hold a feeling akin to fear at bay.

The minister waited calmly.

Finally, Bob grabbed the Bible in front of us.

The minister encouraged, "For those of you unfamiliar with Ezekiel, it's in the Old Testament, page six-hundred thirty-two in your pew Bible."

Louder rustling as the congregation *en masse* turned to the proper page, grateful for the minister's help.

"Ezekiel is a book of prophecy," he announced. "These verses are for those of you who are here today, mourning the death of Anne, wondering if you could possibly be as faithful as Anne. Wondering, 'Is there hope for me?' Wondering how you could get that hope."

Okay, now I knew he was talking to me. I shifted in my seat. Would this service never be over?

"Well folks, here it is. Here is your hope." He lifted his chin, raising his eyes to the stained glass window at the rear of the church. Bob held the Bible so that I couldn't help but read along as the minister confidently spoke the words from memory. "I will give you a new heart and put a new spirit in you. I will *remove* from you your heart of stone and give you a heart of flesh. And I will put My Spirit in you and move you to follow My decrees and be careful to keep My laws."

Logically, I knew everyone else in that church was hearing the same words I was. But it was as if the minister was speaking directly to me. To my heart. To my heart of stone.

I will remove your heart of stone and give you a new heart.

He couldn't possibly mean me. He didn't know me. How stubborn I could be, how hard my heart was. I'd spent my whole life building my defenses, keeping myself apart from others, not ever showing too much emotion. Never feeling too much.

Until Anne.

No, I wasn't going to think about that. With Anne gone I was glad for my defenses. My hard heart.

If I started crying now, it was possible I would never stop.

⌒

Returning home, our mood was glum. It had started snowing big, fluffy flakes, falling straight down, the picture of a perfect Christmas. Just not this one. I plugged in the lights on the Christmas tree, but left the other lights off. In the gathering twilight, the tree was a beacon for our family, drawing us close, much as a lighthouse in a storm. We sat together staring at the tree and the gaily wrapped presents beneath it. Under normal circumstances, Emily would have been begging for hours for us to "pleeeaase" let her open just one. Today she hadn't said a word. The room seemed strangely quiet without Janey. Her soft gurgles and grunts and an occasional fit of crying were missing. Kevin had decided he needed Janey with him tonight. I didn't blame him, I wished for her too. Anything for a bit of Anne.

Even Bob noticed the quiet, getting up and turning the stereo on. The blaring chorus of a Christmas song burst from the speakers, jolting us all out of our *ennui.* Quickly, Bob turned down the volume just enough so the music filled in the too-quiet spots. We settled back into glum silence.

"I don't feel like opening presents." Emily's chin rested on her chest, her arms hung limply at her sides.

"Me neither," Brian said.

A huge lump gathered at the back of my throat. If my kids missed Anne this much, what was I going to do without her? I felt trapped, wanting to cry, but knowing if I did I would never stop. I had to move. Do something. Anything to make this feeling go away.

Our program is at seven-thirty on Christmas Eve. Katie Jeffries' invitation popped into my mind, along with her warning. *Don't expect wonders; it's just a children's pageant after all.*

I didn't need wonders this night, I just needed something to do. Something to get us out of the house. Something to keep my mind off the words the minister had said. Words that wouldn't leave me alone. Hope. Love. A new heart.

I stood up. "We're going to church."

"Olivia," Bob looked at me as if just maybe I was losing my grip. "We just got home from church."

"No, I mean we're going to a Christmas Eve service."

"Mom?" Emily too seemed to be checking my sanity. "We don't even know when one starts."

"And besides," Brian chimed in, "it's only—" he looked at his watch, "five-thirty. No church in Brewster has a program at five-thirty."

"We're not going to church in Brewster," I said. "We're going to church in Carlton."

"Carlton?" The three of them spoke in unison, looking at me as if I really had finally flipped.

"Yes, Carlton. Now everyone get freshened up; by the time we drive there it will be almost time for church. We can always drive around and look at Christmas lights if we're early. Go on," I shooed, "get ready."

In a state of surprise the kids followed my orders, for once not questioning or protesting. Maybe they were glad for something to do. Bob gave me his "are-you-sure-about-this" look, but he too went to get ready.

A two-legged fleece-covered sheep scooted past as we entered the church, the outside bells chiming the start of the service. Katie Jeffries stood near the entry, clipboard in hand.

"Oh, Hiiii!" Her eyes caught mine. If she noticed me flinch at her extended, familiar-sounding greeting, she didn't let on. "You're just in time." Katie's eyes roamed the full church looking for four empty spots. "Here, follow me."

Without a backward glance she marched down the center of the aisle, leaving us no choice but to fall in behind her. Stopping at the second pew from the front, Katie motioned for the family of five already occupying the pew to scoot over. Almost as an afterthought, Katie pushed four small candles into my hand and then hurried off.

I led the way, already second-guessing my decision to come. What were we doing here? My shoulders were scrunched between a stranger's on my left and Brian's on my right. The church felt too crowded and I wondered how we could walk out without attracting attention.

Emily leaned around Brian and whispered, "Mom, look."

Just then a half-dozen glittering angels scurried onto the stage, the older of the girls climbing onto a platform that had been made to look like a pile of large stones tucked neatly against the base of one of Katie Jeffries' carpet-roll palm trees. The trees looked surprisingly real surrounding the facade of a run-down inn and a cardboard stable filled with real hay bales. A hush settled over the crowd, and at a nod from the sidelines, the obviously well-coached angel announced, "Behold, I bring you great tidings!"

The organist took her cue and began playing with all her might. To the tune of "Angels We Have Heard on High," four bathrobe wrapped shepherds tried to hurry into place, poking and prodding a herd of loud and giggly sheep who crawled slowly from the choir area, milking every moment of their time in the spotlight.

The congregation chuckled as one after another the sheep stood and said their parts. Some were budding actors, others sought out parents before uttering a single word, some waved to grandparents as they spoke, and others forgot their lines altogether. Only after a loud whisper from Katie Jeffries, squatted on the floor near the stage, did they utter their rhyming lines.

Emily watched wide-eyed as the children of the cast acted out their parts. Mary and Joseph made their way slowly down the aisle, no older than Emily but seemingly the wiser as they found no room in the inn and shook their heads in dismay. What were they going to do? Mary was going to have a baby this night!

Apparently, the five-year-old visitor sitting in front of me wondered the same thing, for he whispered loudly to his mother, "Should we invite them to Grandma's?"

Before the child's mother could reassure him, the crabby innkeeper had a change of heart and rushed after Mary and Joseph, offering them space in his barn. Sheep and shepherds scurried around the young couple, humming the tune of "Away in the Manger."

By now, even I was caught up in the ancient story, forgetting the man scrunched next to me until I heard him humming along with the children on stage. When the spotlight suddenly illuminated Baby Jesus, held tenderly by a smiling Mary and watched over by an adoring Joseph, the congregation collectively sighed.

Three miniature kings, heads wrapped in gleaming satin, walked regally down the aisle, not seeming young at all. They were kings, bowing deep and presenting precious gifts of gold, frankincense, and myrrh.

The program was almost over. I could see Katie Jeffries shifting onto her knees, ready to stand as soon as the children had said their last lines. It was obvious they had a big finale planned. The stage buzzed with excitement as the sheep curled at the foot of the manger, the shepherds kneeling nearby. Mary and Joseph formed a still life, the Baby Jesus between them. The kings were poised with their heads tilted, gazing at the bright Christmas light star that had been illuminated high over the manger. Only the angels moved.

Taking their places on boxes and stools that had been cleverly tucked into the scenery, the angels stood like sentinels surrounding the stable. The older angel stood alone, her back to us, facing the manger.

All was quiet as the scene went dark. Even the guiding star had been unplugged.

Into the darkness Katie's amplified voice spoke, "He was born this day."

The star over the stable was lit, casting its soft glow over the stable.

"A Savior."

Suddenly, all the angels were holding small, flickering lights, their tinsel halos and wings glittering as if made of star dust.

"Christ the King."

The tall center angel now turned, a thick white candle glowing in her hands.

"Remember," the angel said so clearly her words were almost glass, "He came to save..." she shifted the candle to her right hand and pointed the other into the crowd, "...you!"

"Me?" shouted the little boy sitting directly in front of me.

But I knew better.

The angel was pointing directly at me. It was me He had come to save.

Me. The woman with the heart of stone.

Tears began to form at the edges of my eyes.

Seemingly out of nowhere, the church youth group had surrounded the congregation, each holding a tall white taper candle. The organist began playing "Silent Night," soft as a wispy cloud. My vision was so blurred I could barely see the youth lighting the first candle from the flame the angel held. One by one the youth passed the light to each other, encircling the church with the symbol of God's encompassing love. When the light had completed its circle, the organist held the final note, giving us the cue to sing along.

"Si-i-lent night. Ho-o-ly night. All is calm. All is bright..." Voices blended around me; Brian's tenuous tenor, Emily's airy soprano, and Bob's solid bass joined with the congregation.

I tried.

I really did.

But no sound would come from my mouth. Only tears that began to flow from my eyes in a neverending stream. At the end of the row, one of the youth group members lit Bob's candle. Bob turned to Emily, carefully guiding her candle to his; Emily turned to Brian, then Brian to me. I held my dark candle into the glow of Brian's, watching my wick flicker as if to go out, then catch, burning with an intensity I hadn't expected.

A memory of something Anne had told me shortly before she died floated into my mind. *I know I'm going to heaven; I want others to have that chance, too.* I knew now she had meant me. Me. The woman with the heart of stone. The woman who didn't want this heavy heart any longer.

Oh, God...

It was a prayer, straight from the depths of my heavy hurting heart.

In that instant, like the cool wash of a wave on a beach, I could feel my heart of stone crumbling into tiny grains of sand that were whisked away as if by a breath. In its place was left a new heart, just as the minister at Anne's funeral had said.

My very own new heart.

Made up of faith.

And hope.

And love.

Three things I could never seem to find on my own were given to me in an instant.

Tears continued to wash my face as the minister stepped forward to close the service, asking us to bow our heads. I didn't hear the prayer he said. Instead, I repeated the prayer the minister at Anne's funeral had said to pray, asking God to love me as He'd loved Anne.

I may not have been the first person to accept Christ as a personal Savior at a Christmas program, but it certainly felt like it.

I looked around. Other people were wiping their eyes, too. Their faces were filled with other emotions—longing, nostalgia. I didn't have to see my face to know that it was filled with joy. Just like my heart.

"Joy to the world" sang the angels, Mary, Joseph, the kings and the shepherds. The little sheep fairly danced as they chimed in loudly, singing whatever words they knew. My tuneless voice joined in as well, not caring one iota if I was on key or not. It felt wonderful to give voice to my joy.

I tried to temper the grin on my lips as we were ushered out of church, not wanting people to label me as "that strange, grinning woman." I felt as if I were sharing a huge, grand secret with Anne. I'm saved!

Katie Jeffries stood at the back of the church handing out candy-filled bags to all the children, members or not.

"No one's too old for candy," she said, winking at Brian as she handed him a bag.

Emily didn't hesitate. "Thank you," she said before she'd even been handed hers. "That was a good program."

My heart swelled with something I could only describe as pure love. The conflicting emotions of the day filled me. Grief for the friend I had buried. Joy for the One I had found. It had taken a funeral and a Christmas program to give me, Olivia— *Libby* Marsden a new heart.

Oh, Anne would have liked that.

I couldn't stop crying. Tears continued to gather in my eyes, spilling over as I reached Katie.

"I know," Katie said, putting her arm around my shoulder, "it's just a little kids' program but it gets me every year, too." Her eyes glistened. "I tell you what, as soon as all this holiday stuff settles down, I'll call you for coffee, okay?"

In a voice that was thick with emotion I replied, "I'd like that."

So would Anne.

Epilogue

A New Beginning

Surprisingly, life went on after Anne was gone.

I didn't go crazy.

I didn't die of loneliness.

At times it did seem as if there should be easier options than slogging through one more lonely day. I don't know how many times I reached for the phone, ready to tell Anne the latest news.

"John Erickstad resigned! The bank board asked Bob to be the new president!"

"Brian's got a girlfriend!"

"Can you believe it? Jan's getting married to Dan Jordan!"

Anne was the only person who would have been as excited or as astounded as I was. It was incredible how much I didn't have to say when there was no one to tell it to. No one who really cared. Sharing something with Anne had been like reliving the great events all over again and halving the upset of the bad times.

For a while I was actually mad at Anne for dying. After all, she went to heaven, I got left without a best friend. My anger didn't last long. I never could stay mad at Anne.

I missed her.

Every day.

But life did go on.

Katie Jeffries called me for coffee shortly after the new year. Since we live in different towns we don't get to see each other all that often, but Katie did invite me to join a book club she's belonged to for years. I drive over to Carlton once a month to meet Katie for an early supper. We try to get some eating done between our gabbing, often going out for coffee after book club to continue our conversations. She's become a good friend.

Kevin moved less than a year after Anne died, taking Janey with him, of course.

He got a new job. One of those high-tech computer jobs that he's explained to me a dozen times. I still don't know what he really does. The important thing is that he's home with Janey every single night.

Anne's cancer changed Kevin. He used to be a workaholic, now he's got all the time in the world for his family. Kevin remarried two years ago. Stephanie. They're expecting a baby within the month and Janey is wild to be a big sister. Steph welcomes us into their home with open arms, offering us seats on their red couch, allowing us all the time we want to fuss over Janey, thanking Brian again and again for the cards he sends Janey for every holiday. Me too. It could be my imagination, or just my middle-aged eyes, but I think Janey is the spitting image of her mom.

I know Janey doesn't have a clue who I am, other than a nice lady who used to live in the same town her daddy did. But I'm hoping someday I'll have the chance to tell Janey about the wonderful woman her other mother was. Steph's a great mom to Janey, but she's not Anne.

Shortly after the funeral, Kevin stopped by our house with a small box.

"Here," he said, thrusting the box into my arms before I had a chance to ask him into the house.

The box held Anne's Christmas gifts to me. Gifts Anne and I had planned to exchange on the day she died. Gifts I had no interest in opening.

"Thank you," I croaked, not caring any longer who saw my tears.

I sat the wrapped gifts on the shelf above my computer—the same shelf where the silver pen Anne had given me for my birthday had sat for so long, wrapped, while I gathered courage to open it. This time, however, the gifts didn't mock me as before; instead they lay like puzzles. Waiting for me to open them, waiting for me to put together the last remaining pieces I had of Anne.

I didn't want to finish the puzzle, to complete the picture. Not then. It was better to imagine Anne was still somewhere near, anticipating my joy. Opening the presents would be an admission of sorts that Anne was finally gone.

It was easier to leave them on the shelf.

At first, Emily almost drove me batty, asking daily, "Aren't you going to open your presents?"

"Not yet," I'd answer calmly.

Later I just said, "No."

Finally, Emily forgot about them.

But I didn't.

Emily's finishing her junior year of high school this spring. She went through a sassy, push-everything-to-the-limit stage a couple years ago. Lately she's dropped the attitude, not needing it to let us know she's growing up.

"Do you need any help, Mom?" she'll ask when I start making supper, and she'll actually pitch in without complaining if I say yes.

"I'm going to Jessica's; I'll be home by ten," she'll answer our unasked question, without acting as if we're violating her First Amendment rights by wanting to know.

Emily has continued her piano lessons all these years without prodding, whining, or coercion. She's an excellent pianist, her slender fingers gliding over the keys with a confidence that has never wavered through all her other teenage angst. She accompanies the school choir and volunteers Sunday mornings to back up the Children's Choir at church. Even though Emily can play the advanced version of most every type of music, every now and then I hear her softly playing the simple "Jesus Loves Me" Anne taught her so long ago.

Brian. Where do I begin with Brian? So many changes. He's a junior in college now. Six-foot-two, broad shouldered, and so handsome his high school classmates didn't even have to consult me to vote him "Best Looking Guy" in their senior class. I was more proud however to find out he'd been voted "Nicest Guy" as well.

Brian started college with plans of majoring in business, but after a year of boring economics classes he switched to elementary education, a major much better suited to his personality. For a while after Janey moved, Brian walked around like a lost puppy, seemingly uninterested in the things his friends were doing—cruising Main, playing video games. I have Coach Rollins to thank for asking Brian to help referee the fifth grade basketball games on Saturdays. Working with those kids opened up a new world for Brian. Other people in town noticed his knack with kids, too. That summer he was asked to help coach the peewee baseball league. Brian looked like the Pied Piper, a trail of little kids following him wherever he went, asking a million questions that Brian always had time to answer. Lately he's been mentioning that after he graduates he may go on to get a counseling degree.

Then there's Bob. After a stress-filled day at work Bob often remarks, "This being president isn't all it's cracked up to be." He works as hard as ever, but his attitude about work has changed. No longer would he dream of spending the evening at work if Emily is playing for a school concert. And hopping in the car for the three-hour drive it takes to visit Brian is a suggestion Bob welcomes with a glad, "Let's do it."

Something about losing Anne brought a new understanding to our marriage. Finally I understood why I'd kept Bob at arms length all those years, holding back my affection and my emotions, never allowing myself to truly love him. It was the same relationship I'd had with my father. I've since come to realize you can't have a close relationship with someone unless you spend time with them. I see now that I was the one who pushed Bob away, pushed him to immerse himself in his work—something that would make him feel needed. I realize how lucky I am that it was only from his work he sought comfort.

More than once I've asked Bob's forgiveness for the years I blamed him and took him for granted. Once I got started, the words came surprisingly easy. There was something freeing about admitting my mistakes and asking to be forgiven. Bob was more than willing to accept my apology. Frankly, I think he'd been so used to my closed emotional state that he hadn't even noticed it after a while. To think of that makes me sad.

Bob and I have both made an effort to be better partners. I often meet Bob for a quick lunch downtown, and he calls to tell me if he's going to be late getting home. We make a point of sitting together each night to share the events of our day. Emily rolls her eyes and refers to these talks as our "dates." But she smiles when she says it and usually ends up curled into the corner of the couch, listening intently.

And me? I wish I could say I turned into a whole new person after my prayer the day of Anne's funeral. I found out that Anne made forgiving and loving look much easier than it actually is. But I keep trying.

For so long I had thought that if I could just learn how to forgive, all my problems would be solved. If I could forgive my father for his emotional absence from my life. If I could be forgiven by Bob and my kids. Then I would be free. But it wasn't them I needed to ask so much as it was God. Once I did that the other part came easier.

Loving.

Simply loving those around me. Anne taught me that. Not by preaching at me. Not by lecturing. Simply by her example of living. And loving.

I now make a point of telling Emily, "I love you," every day—whether she wants to hear it or not. It's not always easy, especially when she's in one of her "Whatever!" moods. Some days I have to force the words out. But I do it, if for no other reason than to remind myself of all the times I didn't say the words and should have.

Telling Brian is easy. It's always easier over the phone. But I have to admit that when we do see him I get a lump in my throat every time he throws an arm over my shoulder and says, "Love you too, Mom."

Bob laps up my words and returns them to me twofold.

Who knew loving could feel so good?

Obviously Anne did.

A couple of years after Anne died I got up the nerve to talk to a counselor. I was beginning to sound as though I was a broken record talking to Bob, trying to work through years of emotions on my own. And talking to Anne in my mind wasn't the same as talking to her in person. We used to joke that our long conversations were cheap therapy. I found out it wasn't a joke. Counseling was expensive.

I should have purchased Kleenex stock before my first appointment. Either that or flood insurance. The minute I sat in that chair it was as if a dam had broken.

I sobbed and sobbed.

When I finally managed to choke out my story, the therapist got one of those fake sympathetic looks on her face that people do when they're trying to wheedle for information. "I suppose it's been hard for you to make new friends since your good friend Anne died?"

I'd read enough psychology books to know what she was getting at. She thought that I didn't want to ever again get that close to another human being. She imagined I'd built a high, impenetrable wall around myself so no one could get through. She imagined I was afraid to love, because I'd lost.

Actually, she was wrong. I had turned into Little Miss Social Butterfly. If I heard there was someone new in our neighborhood, I'd be the first one on their doorstep, cookies in hand. If I stood by somebody new at exercise class, I'd ask them if they wanted to go for coffee afterward. People weren't even safe from me in the grocery store. I'd strike up a conversation with any woman who happened to glance at my cart.

No, it wasn't hard for me to make new friends.

"So then, you're looking for Anne." The counselor stated it so matter-of-factly, but it was as if a gong had sounded in my head.

Of course—that was why I'd been running myself ragged. I'd been looking for Anne in everyone I met.

That one simple statement was worth the price of the appointment.

I stopped charging from one activity to another, realizing that I had been trying to fill my time in an effort to keep from thinking about Anne. In an effort to find her in someone else. That wasn't going to happen.

I needed to stay home for a time and work through my emotions instead of looking for ways to avoid them. I could see I wasn't ready for new friends. I spent all my time comparing them to Anne.

I forced myself to have a quiet time each morning, thinking over moments with Anne, praying for guidance to make something meaningful out of the friendship she had shared with me.

It was after one of those mornings, when I felt as if my prayers were stuck under my living room ceiling, that I raised my eyes and saw the specks of dust layering the shelves next to my computer. Actually, they were more than specks—more like a good start on topsoil.

I grabbed a rag and started dusting. The physical activity felt good after watching my unanswered prayers hover around my head. I moved a stack of books and polished the wood beneath them, then the top of my computer. I squirted polish on my rag and reached for the shelf above. My hand stopped as my eyes landed on the snow globe I'd intended to give Anne almost four Christmases ago. There was the ragged little girl enclosed in glass, her face looking skyward, hopeful as ever. I dusted the top, then shook the globe, bits of glitter twinkling like stars before my eyes. I was watching the sparkling scene when my hand absently came to rest on the Christmas gifts Anne had intended for me. My body froze. These were the gifts I'd placed on my shelf and dusted around for years, purposely not thinking about what could be in them.

Today however, I found myself taking the gifts off the shelf, sitting on my couch, holding them in my lap. I ran my fingers over the two packages. Anne had purchased these gifts for me, wrapped them in shiny paper and tied the gold ribbon. For me.

I took a steadying breath. Today I would open them.

My fingers hesitated. I felt scared.

Don't be silly, open them. What scary thing could possibly be in them?

Tentatively, I tugged at the ribbon on the smaller package. It fell away. Carefully I slid my nail along the paper, slitting the tape on the wrapping. Pulling it aside, I opened the box and lifted the tissue paper. There lay a beautiful royal-blue silk scarf. Bits of silver thread were woven here and there in a delicate design. I knew immediately what Anne had intended. The scarf was to match the royal blue suit I'd worn to Janey's baptism, the royal blue suit I'd donated to Goodwill last year.

Suddenly, I missed Anne so much it was a physical pain. I bent over as a sob wrenched from my throat. Tears streamed down my cheeks as I recalled our shopping trips and coffee times, doctor appointments and Anne's silly, "What If…" game. I missed them all. I missed her.

I don't know how long I cried; I just know that when I was through I felt cleansed in some odd way. Almost as if I'd spent a moment with Anne.

I went to the kitchen and splashed cold water on my face, then walked back to the couch, ready to open Anne's last gift to me. Again, I sat and held it for a time, remembering my friend. Finally, curiosity got the better of me. I shook it. No rattling. The rectangular package felt heavy for its size. Now that I examined it, it had to be a book.

Go on, open it.

I untied the ribbon, removed the wrapping paper and held Anne's last gift to me. *Writing Your First Novel*, the title read.

Put it in the book.

Immediately, Anne's charge came back to me, settling on my shoulders, a burden and a blessing.

No longer did I have to wonder what to write about. I knew. I was to tell Anne's story.

I picked up the silver pen Anne had given me, scribbling a few times to get the ink flowing. It wasn't long though, until I put down my pen and turned on my computer, the words coming too fast to write by hand.

After Anne died I thought I had two options:

One. Go crazy.
Two. Die of loneliness.
Turns out there was a third option I hadn't known to imagine.

So here it is, Anne's story, which in the end turned out to be as much my story as Anne's. Maybe she knew it would be all along.

How many times have I heard the old adage, "Be careful what you wish for—you might get it?"

All my life I'd dreamed of writing a novel. I just never imagined I'd have to lose my best friend in order to write it. A high price for a dream, I'd say.

Would I wish Anne back?

In a heartbeat.

But then again, if I wouldn't have lost Anne I might never have found God. And I could hardly wish that either. After all, discovering faith turned out to be my third option—the one I hadn't known to imagine. The one option I couldn't imagine living without.

But then Anne knew that all along.

A Note from
Roxanne Sayler Henke

I hope you enjoyed reading *After Anne*. It was a deeply personal book for me to write. While the story is fiction, unique to Anne and Libby, the essence of the friendship portrayed in the book is real. I wrote *After Anne* to honor the power of all friendships.

The questions on the following pages are intended to help you examine and discuss the book on a more personal level. They may also be used as discussion starters for book groups who have chosen *After Anne* to read. Hopefully you will find that the questions lead you to a deeper understanding of the role Christian friendship can have in your relationships.

I would love to hear about your experiences with this book. You can contact me by email me at:

roxannehenke@yahoo.com

or contact me through my website at:

www.roxannehenke.com

After Anne
Conversation Questions

1. Why did Olivia dislike Anne when she first saw her? Have you ever taken an instant dislike to someone? Did you later change your mind? Why or why not?

2. Like Anne, have you ever taken an instant liking to someone even though they didn't seem to notice you? What do you feel attracts us to certain people?

3. Have you ever had to depend on a friend? How did it make you feel?

4. Have you ever been in a position to offer help to a friend? Did you ever tire of helping? Are you more comfortable giving help or receiving it? Why?

5 Do you think Olivia purposely overlooked Brian's behavior because she didn't want to know the cause? Are there areas besides drug use where a parent may choose to ignore their child's behavior?

6   Has a friend ever told you something you didn't want to hear? How did you react? Have you ever had to tell a friend something they may not have wanted to hear? Why did you feel compelled to tell them? How did they react?

7.   Olivia is not afraid to ask questions of Anne's doctors. Is this appropriate? Why couldn't Anne ask the questions?

8.   Talk about Anne's mother. Is her way of coping—denial—acceptable in certain circumstances? Why or why not? What about Kevin's matter-of-fact reaction to Anne's illness? Is his reaction appropriate?

9.   Discuss Olivia's feelings at the baby shower. Have you ever felt defensive without basis? Why did Olivia get upset?

10.   Why didn't Olivia let herself cry when her father died?

11.   Sometimes people build walls around themselves for protection. Discuss how this can help a person cope, yet ultimately harm them.

12. *After Anne* is based on Proverbs 18:24: "There is a friend who sticks closer than a brother." Discuss how Anne was this kind of friend. How Olivia was. Have you ever had, or been, a friend like this?

13. How did you feel when you read Anne had died? Do you think the way she died had any special significance in the story?

14. How did Anne's illness change the people around her? Olivia? Kevin? Evelyn (Anne's mother)? Bob? Emily? Brian?

15. Why was it so hard for Olivia to acknowledge God? Discuss the times you see God working in Olivia's life. Do you think Olivia would have come to faith without her friendship with Anne?

16. Who in the story do you identify with the most, Anne or Libby? Why?

Becoming Olivia

ISBN13: 978-0-7369-1149-8
ISBN10: 0-7369-1149-9

In this third novel, Roxanne returns to the life of Olivia "Libby" Marsden, the main character in After Anne.

Libby has the perfect life...good kids, a wonderful husband, and a strong Christian faith. Why then is she increasingly depressed?

Libby discovers that sometimes God works through the most unexpected circumstances to help us become who we're meant to be, as readers will discover in this touching novel.

Always Jan

ISBN13: 978-0-7369-1150-4
ISBN10: 0-7369-1150-2

Jan Jordan is having a birthday—a birthday she's been dreading since she learned to count...surely life can be nothing but downhill from here.

Kenny Pearson is old enough to know better, but he doesn't care. As long as he can still knock a softball out of the park and brag about it over a beer with the guys afterward, life is good.

Ida Bauer is old and doesn't mind saying so. Her husband is gone and so are most of her friends—and she has to face it—soon she will be too. Does she have anything left to offer in the time she has left?

God has a plan for all these people...if only they will listen.

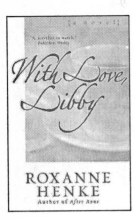

With Love, Libby

ISBN13: 978-0-7369-1197-9
ISBN10: 0-7369-1197-9

The concluding book in the popular Coming Home to Brewster series follows the faith journey of Libby Marsden, who faces the question, "What happens when a dream comes true?" After she accomplishes her goal of writing a book Libby must figure out if her desire to write has clouded her understanding of purpose.

Vicki Johnson has big dreams for her daughter, Angie, who is about to graduate from high school. Only after Angie is in college will Vicki explore her personal passions and plans. But when Angie reveals ambitions of her own, Vicki must readjust her vision of the future.

Fans of this series or those just introduced to Henke's writing will be captivated by this character–rich, compelling story.

Now available...Roxanne Henke's
new "stand-alone" novel, *The Secret of Us*

Housewife, Laura Dunn, and her husband, advertising executive, Donnie Dunn, have been married for twenty three years. Donnie has spent these years building his agency into the premiere ad business in the state of North Dakota. He has high hopes of branching his business into the competitive Minneapolis market.

Laura has stood by as her workaholic husband has provided a *more-than-nice* life for them and their twenty-one year old daughter, Stasha. In addition to raising their daughter almost single-handedly, (and putting aside her dreams of being an artist), Laura has immersed herself in community activities, building a life as full and busy as Donnie's.

The only thing either of them have neglected is each other.

As *The Secret of Us* opens, Stasha, is getting ready for her wedding to Josh MacKay, a recent college graduate hoping to teach junior high math, preferably in North Dakota. Stasha has bigger dreams. She'd love a career like her dad but without the constant pressure she's seen over the years, and she certainly doesn't want to stick around "home."

A series of business opportunities keeps Donnie on his toes...and away from home...as usual. The fact that his mother suffers a mild stroke in the midst of a high level deal doesn't derail his intentions a bit. After all, Laura is there when he can't be.

But, with Stasha married and starting a life of her own, Laura suddenly realizes she faces an empty marriage. When she repeated her wedding vows twenty-three years ago, she meant them with all her heart...but back then she had no idea that young love could fade into middle-aged indifference. Is a promise enough to carry her through the remaining years? Or is there a new life waiting for her on the other side of marriage?

Roxanne Sayler Henke lives in rural North Dakota with her husband, Lorren, and their dog, Gunner. They have two very cool young adult daughters, Rachael and Tegan. As a family they enjoy spending time at their lake cabin in northern Minnesota. Roxanne has a degree in behavioral and social science from the University of Mary and for many years was a newspaper humor columnist. She has also written and recorded radio commercials, written for and performed in a comedy duo, and cowritten school lyceums. *After Anne* is her first novel.

Acknowledgments

There are many people to thank for the existence of this book:

First and foremost are my parents, Walter R. and Jean Sayler. My dad has been gone for many years, but he was the person who taught me that stories could grow inside your mind. My mother spent many a night tickling my arm while she told me tales of her adventurous youth growing up on a farm during the depression. I want to thank you both for the gift of imagination and a love of words.

My sisters, Kim Anderson and Ann Jensen, for never laughing at my dream. Or at least doing it where I couldn't hear you!

Debbie Turner, book club partner and (as I like to call her) writing therapist. Without your constant question, "When can I read more?" who knows where these words would be?

My sister-of-the-heart, Yvonne Engelhart. You are an encourager extraordinaire.

Jenel Looney, e-pal from Saudi Arabia (via Wisconsin). You provided me with more encouragement than you can possibly know. (Maybe someday we'll actually get a chance to meet.)

Oprah Winfrey. Though you don't know me, your Millennium Challenge was just what I needed to kick-start (and finish) this book. Thank you for helping me complete a dream!

Dave Talbott and the staff at Mt. Hermon Christian Writers Conference. Or as I like to call it, Mt. Hermon Writers *College*. You'd think a writer could think of better words than thank you. Unfortunately, I can't. My heartfelt "Thank you" will have to do.

My editor, Nick Harrison, Carolyn McCready, and the wonderful people at Harvest House who took my dream and turned it into reality. There are no words for that.

And, as the Bible states, "The last shall be first." Last on this page but first in my heart, thanks, appreciation, and love to my husband, Lorren. You are one of the few who truly know what a long journey this has been. And to my daughters, Rachael and Tegan, my constant cheerleaders in writing and in life.